MARQUE AND REPRISAL

By Elizabeth Moon

The Deed of Paksenarrion
SHEEPFARMER'S DAUGHTER
DIVIDED ALLEGIANCE
OATH OF GOLD

The Legacy of Gird
SURRENDER NONE
LIAR'S OATH

Planet Pirates *(with Anne McCaffrey)*
SASSINAK
GENERATION WARRIORS

REMNANT POPULATION*

The Serrano Legacy
HUNTING PARTY
SPORTING CHANCE
WINNING COLORS
REMNANT POPULATION
ONCE A HERO
RULES OF ENGAGEMENT
CHANGE OF COMMAND
AGAINST THE ODDS

THE SPEED OF DARK*

Vatta's War
TRADING IN DANGER*
MARQUE AND REPRISAL*

Short fiction collections
LUNAR ACTIVITY
PHASES

**Published by Ballantine Books*

MARQUE AND REPRISAL

ELIZABETH MOON

BALLANTINE BOOKS • NEW YORK

Marquee and Reprisal is a work of fiction. Names, places, and incidents are products of the author's imagination or are used fictitiously.

2005 Del Rey Books Mass Market Edition

Published in the United States by Del Rey Books, an imprint of The Random House Publishing Group, a division of Random House, Inc., New York.

Del Rey is a registered trademark and the Del Rey colophon is a trademark of Random House, Inc.

Originally published in hardcover in the United States by Del Rey Books, an imprint of The Random House Publishing Group, a division of Random House, Inc., in 2004.

This book contains an excerpt from the forthcoming edition of *Engaging the Enemy* by Elizabeth Moon. This excerpt has been set for this edition only and may not reflect the final content of the forthcoming edition.

ISBN 0-345-44759-X

Printed in the United States of America

www.delreybooks.com

OPM 9 8 7 6 5 4 3 2 1

For all who serve in the armed forces, or in any other capacity in which they discover and must learn to cope with the darkness within, with gratitude for the service, and understanding of the dilemmas. And for Jen, for a rescue.

ACKNOWLEDGMENTS

The Usual Suspects outdid themselves again, from the fencing group to the family. Thanks are also due to the Camp Allen staff, for letting Michael come another year (during which week I got a lot done), and to his special-ed teachers at the high school. The helpers who pitched in with Fox Pavilion (Scott Hawes, Leslie D'Allesandro Hawes, Ruta and Ferris Duhon) saved me a lot of work and worry with that project, and freed more writing time. Beth Sikes is due thanks for insightful comments on some of the characters. The terriers in the Leading Rein, in Austin, instructed me on the character traits of Jack Russell terriers. L. D. offered technical expertise on certain aspects of military procedure. S. and G. shared technical expertise in the areas of communications, corporate organization, finance, and related matters. My agent and editor cheered me on when I felt stuck (which, in this book, happened more than once), and Jennifer Davis helped me unstick from a bad musical situation and get into a good one. Several used-book and antiquities shops in London contributed their ambience to a seedy space station. As always, mistakes are mine.

CHAPTER ONE

Kylara Vatta looked at the mass of paperwork from Belinta's Economic Development Bureau and sighed. The real life of a tradeship captain: paperwork and more paperwork, negotiation with shippers, customers, Customs officials. The life she hadn't wanted, when she chose to enter the Slotter Key Spaceforce Academy, and the life she had fallen back into when she was expelled. Boring. Mundane.

Not that her recent experiences in Sabine had been boring or mundane—terrifying was more like it—and no one would want another trip like that.

Except that she did. She remembered very clearly the rush of excitement, the soaring glee of the fight itself, the guilty delight when she'd killed Paison and Kristoffson. So either she wasn't sane or...or nothing. She thought of the diamonds tucked into her underwear drawer. Not enough to restore her old tub of a ship completely, but enough to take her to somewhere else, somewhere she could make the kind of life she really wanted. Perhaps the mercenaries would accept her violent tendencies; they'd offered a chance. Perhaps someone else. It would annoy her family, but not as much as the truth would hurt them.

No. She had to finish one job at least. Crew depended on her. The ship belonged to her family, as well, and she could not possibly earn enough to buy it away by the next stop or the next. She sighed again, signed another sheet, and stared at the next. All right, then. Take this old tub to Leonora, deliver that cargo, then to Lastway. If she couldn't finance a refit by then, return to the original plan and go home by commercial passenger ship. If she made enough profit, enough to do the refit, she could get that done and bring the ship back to Slotter Key, and then resign. Or—she stared into a distance far beyond her cabin bulkhead. She could send the ship back with someone else. Quincy, for instance, knew enough to run the ship herself.

In the long run, her family would be better off without her. If her father knew how she'd felt when she killed . . . no. She had had those nightmares, trying to explain to that gentle man, hoping for his understanding but seeing the horror in his face. Better the smothering, overprotective love that had annoyed her in their last conversation than that horror, that disgust, that rejection. If she went home, he would sense something; he would try to probe, try to get her to confide in him, and eventually he would wear her down. It would be worse than anything else that had happened, to have her father sorry she was ever born.

She should just go away. Years later, maybe, she might be able to explain it to him, and he might be able to accept it. Years might put a safe skin on the raw truth of what she was.

She worked her way through the rest of the forms, then decided to take them to the local postal drop herself. Belinta Station had few amenities, but a walk would be refreshing in itself.

"Quincy—I'm going to drop the paperwork off," she said into the ship's intercom.

"Find anything to load, or do you want us to start transferring what we left in storage?"

"I haven't found anything yet," Ky said. "I may have to go downside for that. Go on and load . . . see if you can get some of the station dockworkers to help with that. Usual rates and all."

She glanced at herself in the mirror and decided she was presentable enough. She needed a new uniform—the one she had left after Sabine no longer had the crisp, perfect tailoring her mother had paid for—but only if she was staying with

Vatta. If she joined a mercenary company, she would wear its uniform; if she stayed independent, she'd have to find one of her own design. But to drop off forms to be transmitted to a bureaucracy, gray tunic and slacks should be sufficient. She clipped on the Belinta Station access pass.

Outside the ship, Belinta Station hardly bustled with activity. Only three ships were in dock, and the other two were in-system haulers servicing Belinta's meager satellite mining operations. On their own dockside, Quincy was talking to a burly man in the ubiquitous green tunic of Belinta dockworkers. Beeah, beside her, held a compad ready to record employee data if Quincy's negotiations were successful. Ky walked briskly past two men chatting on a bench, a woman standing by a lift entrance, barely restraining a bouncing toddler, the faded ads for Belinta's few and unenticing tourist resorts, and turned left into the wide main corridor. Here were the currency exchanges, banks, communications services—local and ansible—Belinta Port Authority, the hiring hall, and, finally, the postal service. Midshift, few others were in sight. Someone with a briefcase just going into Belinta Savings & Loan, two women chatting as they emerged from Allsystems Exchange.

Beyond were rows of blanked openings to spaces that would someday, if Belinta proved prosperous, house more services, more stores, more people. No traffic at all moved down there.

Ky turned into the postal service's entrance and walked up to the counter where a display read NOW SERVING NUMBER SIX EIGHTY-TWO. The only clerk in sight did not look up, but said, "Take a number." *Typical Belintan courtesy,* Ky thought, and looked around for the number generator. By the entrance. She pulled the tab; the counter display changed to NOW SERVING SIX EIGHTY-THREE and the clerk said, "Number six eighty-three!" in an annoyed tone, as if she'd kept him waiting.

"This is all for the Economic Development Bureau," Ky said.

"To whose attention?" asked the clerk.

"It doesn't matter. Just the EDB."

"It has to be directed to an individual," the clerk said. "You can't send mail to the whole bureau."

"It says on the form," Ky said, pointing to the block under RETURN TO. "No name, just the bureau."

"It has to have a name," the clerk said. "It's the rules. All mail to government agencies must be directed to an individual."

Ky was tempted to make up a name. Instead, she said, "Do you have a directory?"

"Customers are not allowed to use our confidential directories or communications devices," the clerk intoned. "This is a security issue. Customers are advised to identify the correct recipient prior to arriving in the postal service office. Next, please."

Ky glanced behind her. No one stood in line. "It wouldn't take a moment to look it up."

"Next, please." The clerk still wasn't looking at her. Ky wanted to reach across the counter and wring his skinny neck, but that was the impulse of a moment. This was part of being a tradeship captain; this was the kind of senseless, ridiculous, annoying nonsense she could expect.

"Fine," she said instead. "I'll deliver it myself." After all, she had to go downside anyway, to find out if there was any cargo worth carrying from this wretched planet.

"Glad to be of service have a nice day," the clerk said all in one breath.

Ky went back the way she'd come, past the corridor that led to the docking area, past Goodtime Eats and Jerry's Real Food and Quick-snack, where the two women she'd seen earlier were head to head over a small table, to the ticket office for the shuttle service. She could not remember just when the daily service left—

"Two and a half hours," the clerk said. "Be at the boarding area a half hour before departure."

That gave time to go back to her ship and change. She turned to go but a screech from the PA system stopped her. "What's that?"

"I don't know," the clerk said.

"Stay wherever you are," a bone-shaking voice said. *"All personnel stay wherever you are. Emergency crews one and two, to dockside on the double. All personnel . . ."*

"My ship!" Ky said. "I have to get back—"

But the ticket office entrance was closed, the metal grate locking with a final *chung* even as she moved toward it.

"You heard 'em," the clerk said. "We're all supposed to stay put."

"Well, I can't," Ky said. "Open that thing."

"Can't," the clerk said. "It's automatic, like section seals. Station Security controls it. Unless you've got the override code like one of the emergency crews . . ."

The PA announcement had stopped. Fifteen minutes later, the grate slid back into its slot, squeaking a little. *"Return to normal activity,"* the PA said. *"All personnel return to normal activity."* Still no announcement of what had prompted the lockdown. Ky hurried back to the docking area. She saw nothing unusual except a Station Security officer standing near *Gary Tobai*'s open hold bay talking to Quincy.

"What was that about?" she asked, coming up to them.

"Nothing to concern you, madam," said the officer. "Please stand away."

"It's the captain," Quincy said, just as Ky said, "It's my ship; it concerns me."

"Oh." The man looked confused. "You're not in uniform."

"It needs cleaning," Ky said. "Here's my tag." She held it out, and he scanned it. "What happened?"

"We believe an attempt was made to rob your ship," the man said. "Individuals known to us as of dubious character were hired to move cargo, and this individual"—he nodded at Quincy—"noticed something untoward with one of the containers and challenged the individual transporting it, suspecting that a substitution had been made. Two individuals ran away; this individual called the alarm."

Theft by casual dockside labor was a constant threat, Ky knew. "Did you catch them?"

"They have not been apprehended yet," the officer said. "They made it to the unoccupied spaces. We are confiscating this container, which they tried to put aboard, and we are searching for the legitimate container your crewmember reports missing."

"I'm sure you'll take care of things," Ky said.

"We will find you here?" the man asked.

"No," Ky said. "I must go downside to deliver reports to your government. My shuttle leaves—" She checked the time. "Sorry, I must hurry. Quincy will serve as my agent for the duration of my visit down. All right, Quincy?"

The old woman nodded. "I can do that. Will you be buying cargo?"

"Quite possibly. I expect to be downside a few days. I'll keep in touch." Ky hurried into the ship. She put on her remaining uniform with the formal captain's cape and made two quick calls to arrange lodging at the Captains' Guild and an escort to meet her at the downside shuttle terminal. She hesitated, then put several of the diamonds in her pocket. She didn't expect anything to cut off her access to Vatta resources, but just in case, it couldn't hurt to have hard currency.

She made her shuttle connection with a few minutes to spare, and rode downside with a mixed lot of Belinta station workers going home for the weekend break. She cataloged them automatically—*clerical, clerical, equipment operator, service worker*—and wondered why she bothered. It was the same mix she could find anywhere across the galaxy, no duller here than elsewhere. She spotted her escort at the passenger exit and they exchanged the passwords and ID checks, another familiar routine. The ride into the city passed fields striped with a more vivid green than Belintans ever wore. She recognized the machine working its way across one of the fields as one she'd delivered from Sabine, and felt a surge of satisfaction. If she could learn to appreciate the good done by the cargoes she transported, if she could see things from that angle, maybe.

Airlines
Name
WEAVER/GWENDOLYN
Mileage:
1,208 Miles
Flight
CO 1859
Gate
14
Seat:
Depart
Arrive
Board Time
PM
PM

This portion of the boarding pass should be retained as evidence of your journey.

Esta porción del pase de abordar debe guardarse como prueba de su viaje.

* * *

Gerard Avondetta Vatta watched as his pilot loaded his small case in the light plane. They would be back in the city by nightfall; he and Stavros would have a working dinner, and tomorrow he would tackle the delicate political tangle still left by his daughter's abrupt departure from the Academy. Now that she was out of danger, now that he had seen her face, had spoken to her, his attention had returned to the reasons behind the obvious reasons.

Why had a Miznarii complained about religious discrimination in the Academy? Miznarii were a difficult sect, to be sure, but they'd served in the Slotter Key Spaceforce for the past thirty years or so without any problems he knew of. And why had Ky been chosen as the vehicle? Her habit of helping lame dogs made her gullible, of course, and yet it did not quite satisfy him. She was a naturally generous person, yes, but he had noticed a streak of hardness in her that boded well for her survival in the cutthroat world of interstellar shipping. When she came back, it might be time to tell her a few things not in the basic Vatta database her implant contained.

The Miznarii . . . were they part of the resurgence of anti-humod feeling some of the Vatta captains had reported? They were certainly foundational purists who refused even the most common enhancements and modifications, such as cranial implants, but he hadn't heard they bothered with off-planet politics. Besides, Ky had little exposure to humods; she could hardly be a target for anti-humod bias.

Then there was InterStellar Communications. Vatta had supported ISC all along, and he fully appreciated what ISC had done for Ky at Sabine, but he wondered if its judgment matched its power. He'd tried to say something about that to Lew Parminer, the last time Lew visited, but Lew had shrugged off his concerns. "We pay our researchers enough to keep them quiet," he'd said. "No muzzling the ox that treads the grain, you know."

Still . . . there were other sources of wealth in the galaxy. Some who would be willing to pay almost any price for the secrets of ISC's labs. Some already funding research, he was sure, trying to duplicate the secrets of ISC's technology, or trying to advance it. The attack on the ansible platforms at Sabine had been crude, but to Gerard's mind clearly a test. How strong was ISC, and how fast could it respond?

The pirates, too . . . the information from Sabine was disturbing. An alliance of pirates? Of their agents in legitimate firms? And how did that work? Vatta had thousands of employees on dozens of ships, more dozens of support offices. Was one of them a traitor, feeding information to pirates? So far, the pirates had concentrated on smaller shippers, driving several out of business. According to the Captains' Guild figures—if they were accurate—the largest shippers hadn't been hit. But that wouldn't last, he was sure. They would run out of easy targets, and move on to take other prey. The great merchant companies, Vatta among them, had never persuaded the planetary governments that their trade served to combine and create a true interstellar space force capable of policing the spaceways. ISC had the resources, but refused to use them for anything but maintaining its own assets.

Gerard pinged his implant to remind him to call Gracie Lane when he got to the city. Vatta's spy service, Stavros called her, though her title on the books was special assistant to the chairman.

"Expecting company?" the pilot asked suddenly.

"What?" Gerard turned; his pilot was staring into the limpid afternoon sky.

"My implant says the airfield's scans have picked up two unidentified aircraft. Coming in from the east."

From the great ocean? That made no sense. The regular inter-island passenger plane for the mainland had already been and gone, and anyway they didn't overfly this end of the island. East of Corleigh, the next inhabited island chain was the Merrill Archipelago, and its air traffic avoided the fifteen-hundred-kilometer gap, flying south to the Rim Reef, then back west along it. Between Merrill and here were only a few uninhabited chunks of rock, recently emerged and sometimes temporary volcanic peaks.

His implant, not linked to the private airfield's minimal scans, fought its way through the safety lockouts, but by the time he had access to the airfield scans, he could see the two tiny dots rapidly growing larger and hear their thin whine.

"Gaspard, do you have any idea—" he began; then his implant squealed a warning relayed from the airfield scans. Weapons. Those little flying things had weapons—he whirled, started to run toward the office building beyond the airfield.

"No! Sir, get down!" Gerard paid no attention, but his pilot, younger and faster, tackled him just short of the grass verge. He hit the ground hard, furious . . . the snarling whine overhead much louder now, coming at him. Fear soured his mouth; he covered his head with his hands, realizing how useless that was.

His implant threw up visuals of the things—windowless, short-winged, unmanned—just before the flash of light, the noise, the blow of rushing air and debris that rolled him over and over on the tarmac, then the second flash, the second boom and roar much fainter.

He blinked, rolled to his knees. Gaspard gripped his shoulders; the pilot, already on his feet, was pale as cheese curds. Ahead, the office building was a mass of flames and roiling black smoke. And beyond, to the right, where the house, the comfortable home had stood—a column of flame and smoke.

"Myris!" he said. "San!" He wrenched free of Gaspard and ran to the office first because it was closer. He was aware of Gaspard running beside him, though he could not hear his footsteps through the roaring in his ears and the clamor of the flames.

Someone staggered out, ahead of him, and Gerard slowed to look. One of the clerks, white-rimmed eyes staring out of a smoke-blackened face. "What—?"

"Take care of her," Gerard said to his pilot. "Call—" But emergency services for this end of the island were housed in the other end of the building. If they had survived they'd already be at work. "Call back to the town. Medical. Call the city—warn Stav—" Two more figures staggered out, one half carrying the other; Gerard moved toward them.

"You have the skullphone," Gaspard yelled to him.

He blinked against the stinging smoke. Yes. He did. Mental fingers fumbling with the shock, he called his brother.

"Gerry?" Stavros answered. "What's wrong—aren't you coming in this afternoon?"

"Evacuate the building," Gerard said.

"What?"

"Someone's just dropped bombs on us here on Corleigh," Gerard said. "Some kind of drone plane thing. Clear headquarters—they'll hit there next."

"I just got an ansible call about some trouble on Allway," Stavros said. "Connections?"

A burning cinder landed on Gerard's hand; he flicked it off. "Certainly. Clear the building, damn it."

"I've already hit the alarm, Gerry. They're going. It takes time, you know."

They didn't have time. He knew that, even as he closed on the fiery maelstrom and tried to steel himself to go in and help survivors.

"Put out an allsystems warning. Let our people know . . ."

"Right. On it. Are you all right?"

"I'm alive. I've got to get in there and see if San—"

"Gerry—don't. Let the rescue squad—"

"It's gone," Gerard said. As the afternoon breeze pushed the column of smoke to one side, he could see that the bomb had hit on that end of the office building.

"Myris?"

"The house was hit. I don't know. She was going out to swim after lunch; I pray she did." If even the pool would be enough protection. And that still meant the household staff, cleaning up after lunch. He squeezed his eyes shut a moment, and said a short, fervent prayer. "Stav—I heard what you said. *They're* leaving. You leave, too. Get in the bunker."

"I will," Stavros said. "When I'm through. I'm sending out the allsystems warning now . . . all right. I'm leaving it to a volunteer, I'm moving."

It was too hot, the flames burning his face meters from the fire itself. He had just remembered the fuel storage tanks for the emergency vehicles when the next explosion threw him off his feet, onto something sharp and hard, and the next three tossed more of the building his way, debris as effective as any other form of shrapnel.

He was just waking up when Gaspard and old George dug him out of the pile. His left side hurt with every breath. A rib, he suspected, or two. He coughed, and the pain stabbed deep. Smoke still billowed from the wreckage, but most of the flames had blown out . . . stubs of walls, spikes of unidentifiable framing members. With the survivors—pitifully few—he stared at the ruin. Somewhere in there was San, his only son onplanet. Surely dead . . . he turned away, unwilling to look anymore.

Gaspard stayed with him as he staggered toward the house. Here nothing was left but a hole in the ground; the gardens were covered with debris; a single flowering spray of luchis orchids curled up from beneath a window frame, still unwilted. They made their way around to the back, where parts of the roof had breached the garden wall. A mat of debris floated on the water of the big pool . . . shards of wood, sheets of paper, bits of cloth, fronds of jabla still pink with bloom, and wide leaves of the haricond like rafts, each with its own burden of grit and unidentifiable pieces. Some sank as he watched, as the wind ruffled the surface.

He was on his knees on the edge of the pool, mouth stuffed with fear and anguish, unable to call her name, unable to see. Someone was crying, someone was saying her name, someone's hands were wet, the water stinging the burns. Someone was pulling at her shoulder, struggling to get her face out of the water, ignoring the red streaks turning pink in the dirty water.

And then he was lying back against someone, someone talking to him, and he could see her lying in the sun as it dimmed and brightened with the whirls of smoke blowing past. Water pooled under her, water stained red, and she did not turn her head to him, did not cry out, did not ask what happened.

Someone put a flask to his lips. He smelled the sharp edge of whiskey he didn't want, but he sipped because his throat was dry and then nearly choked because it was raw, pain almost as sharp as that in his heart. He smelled clean earth and onions, and saw that the hands of the person he lay against were crusted with earth and a shred of green. A gardener. His mind seemed to float, slowly noticing, slowly combining what it noticed.

Then it all came together. Attacks. Explosions. The house and his wife gone. The office and his son gone. He had warned Stavros. He had to—he tried to sit up, and his ribs stabbed him again. The hands behind him helped, lifted.

"They're dead," he heard himself say. His ears still rang; his voice sounded tinny. "They're all—who's alive?"

Gaspard had the list. Soler, Tina, Vindy from the clerk's section. Bonas, who had been in the toilets on the end not directly hit. Gaspard. Old George. All three gardeners. Little Ric, who had been sweeping the front porch and drive, and been blown into the ornamental grove of palms and jablas that the drive circled.

Everyone was watching the sky; he had to do something, start sorting things out.

"Water," he heard old George say. "Gotta get some water first."

"I'll check the tanks," said the gardener who'd been supporting him. "If you can stand, sir?"

He could stand; he had to stand; he still had people depending on him. "Go on," he said. "Check the tanks. Thank you."

Water. Shelter. Food. Protection from whoever had done this. Transportation. Medical care. He prodded his sluggish mind. Decisions to be made. Make them.

By the time the island's town-based emergency evacuation system arrived, one of the survivors had already died. Gerard struggled to talk to the officials who arrived with the rescue squad. His ears still rang; he could barely stand, and they were asking him why the attack came, as if he knew. As if it were his fault. Why didn't the fire/rescue service respond? Why were they housed in the office building anyway? Why had they put the reserve fuel storage underneath? Why, why, why?

His implant offered no answers, either. Who had done this? How had they done it? More aircraft arrived, full of law enforcement investigators, some he knew and some he'd never seen before. Someone brought a scorched chair, blown from the office, for him to sit in. Aircraft departed, taking away his injured employees. The afternoon passed; the hill's shadow stretched across the airfield. Someone looked him over, advised hospitalization; he refused. His mind felt numb, smoke-blurred, but he could not leave, not yet.

Then the parrot-squawk of a voice he knew penetrated the blur. "Get him out of here, you idiots. He's a target." The voice came nearer. "Gerry—Gerry look at me. Focus."

She looked no less dotty than she had looked for the past twenty—thirty—years, her graying hair unruly in the late-afternoon breeze, her print silk dress, her strings of beads and jangling bracelets, but her eyes were bright.

"Gracie," he mumbled.

"You look horrible," she said. "Gerry, get up."

"I don't know if I—" But he was on his feet, supported again by someone's shoulder under his arm, following the quick clatter of Gracie's incongruous high heels across the tarmac. Pain stabbed his side with every step. "I can't leave," he said to her back. "Myris—San—the others—"

"They're dead," she said over her shoulder. "You're alive. You need to stay that way. We need you, Gerry."

A cold chill ran down his spine that had nothing to do with his injuries. "Stavros?"

"Later." And to his helpers: "Get him in, get that oxygen hooked up."

He felt himself heaved up into the plane; pain so great he almost passed out turned his whole left side to white heat. He panted in his seat, let his eyes sag shut as he felt the cool flow of oxygen under his nose.

"Breathe," he heard Gracie say. "And keep breathing, damn it." He felt the craft vibrate under him, engines starting, the bumping of taxiing for takeoff sending knifelike flashes of pain through his side, his shoulder, and then the lurch as they took off.

"Where?" he asked, that one word exhausting him.

"Someplace safe, I hope," Gracie said. He heard her sigh, a little grunt as she shifted in her own seat. "If there is such a place. We thought the headquarters bunker level . . ."

"Not?" he asked.

"Just lie still, Gerry. Nothing to do now but live till we land."

"Don't let them . . . ," he managed. Then some salty fluid filled his mouth; he choked, swallowed, and nearly heaved it up.

"Damn," Gracie said again, more quietly. He felt the oxygen mask pulled aside, and something soft wiped the corner of his mouth.

"Get the implant," he said. His mind cleared briefly. Oxygen would do that. His implant, Stavros' implant. Whoever had done this must not get the master database. "Gracie . . . take implant. Command database."

"I know, dear," she said. Dear? Gracie had called him dear? The same Grace who had once told him, when they were both much younger, that he would be on his deathbed before she would praise him?

"'M hurt," he said, loathing the weakness and confusion in his voice.

"You are," Gracie said. "We'll try to get a doctor to you, once we're safe. Not a hospital, so don't exhaust yourself explaining." She sighed again. "Gerry, Stavros is dead. Headquarters was hit; the bunkers didn't hold. Someone knew enough about them." He heard a high-pitched noise, something like metal on metal. "Someone wants to destroy Vatta, Gerry. You have to hang on."

No doubt in her voice. He could do what she said, until she doubted. He breathed in spite of the pain, in spite of the weakness that crept up from his legs, the dark cloud that tried to cover him.

Questions remained. Who? Why? How?

Gracie Lane Vatta forced herself to ignore the medical team working on Gerard, forced herself to concentrate instead on the attack, on the methods and the meanings. Unmanned drones; the airfield's security system had produced identifiable visual and internal data scans. Military weapons, and not a type used by Slotter Key's own planetary forces, or so they insisted. Satellite scans had revealed the origin: Bone Island, an uninhabited, barren, rocky volcanic spur 430 kilometers east of Corleigh. Someone was—or had been—on Bone Island long enough to launch the drones. One of her contacts in the government was even now going back through scans from the previous days, to see when and how they had arrived. And—though she doubted this was possible—to find out who they were.

At corporate headquarters, the attack had been different, but equally devastating. Up from the utility tunnels below the city... boreholes to the foundations of Vatta headquarters, boreholes around the outside of the bunkers, bunkers reinforced to withstand earthquake, storm, even attack from atop and collapse of the building atop them.

But not explosives applied directly to the bunkers, to the sides, to the floors. It would have taken, at shortest estimate, weeks to bore those holes, place those charges.

Until this, she'd thought the worst threats to Vatta were the growing menace of pirates on the tradeways and possibly an assassination attempt against Gerard's daughter Ky in retaliation for her actions in the Sabine conflict. She had just completed a report on piracy, which she'd planned to present to

Gerard and Stavros sometime in the coming week. She had, weeks ago, alerted all senior staff to the increased possibility of assassination attempts. An attack of this magnitude had not even occurred to her, and she was furious with herself for not seeing it coming.

The aircraft they were in, escorted by Slotter Key military aircraft that did not make her feel as safe as she would wish, flew not to the capital but to her private residence near Corleigh Town. She had balanced the greater protection the government already provided to the capital with the vulnerability of several hours over open water . . . with the ease of tracking aircraft from space . . . with Gerard's condition.

Who had done this? Why? And why do it this way, an open declaration of war not only against Vatta, but also against Slotter Key? What was the message here? Would there be more attacks, and when, and where?

Her implant, customized for her work, laid out for her the information so far obtained, in the usual matrix. What resources were implied by the choice of weapons, the choice of launch site. What conditions were necessary for the attack to succeed, what were the pinch points in the execution where it might have been frustrated. Which known enemies of Vatta or Slotter Key had such resources.

Working through the usual routine of analysis held off, for the time being, the shock she knew was hovering just overhead. It wasn't supposed to be like this. These things didn't happen in real life, to ordinary people. She knew better. She had seen war before; she knew its terrible thirst for death, for the destruction of beauty.

By the time the plane landed, she knew this attack could not have occurred without help from somewhere in the Slotter Key government. Her anger spread from herself and the attackers to that as-yet-unnamed traitor. Someone had kept Spaceforce from reporting a shuttle dropping from a ship in orbit, or someone had deep-sixed the report. Someone had kept the satellite surveillance from reporting that installation on Bone Island. Someone—someone here, within her reach—

had connived at the attack, had wanted to destroy her family, her life.

Gracie Lane Vatta smiled to herself, a smile that old enemies, now long dead, would have remembered. The enemy had won the initiative. The enemy had caused great damage. No doubt the enemy was dancing or laughing or in some other way enjoying the triumph. But Gracie Lane Vatta would wipe that smile off the enemy's face, stop that dance in its tracks, stuff the laugh back down the enemy's throat. She could not do it all by herself, and her resources at present were limited. But at least the traitor or traitors on Slotter Key . . . those she could reach and those she would take care of, whatever else happened.

CHAPTER TWO

The voice in Gammis Turek's earbug said what he expected to hear: "—unexpected attack on our citizens. Outrageous. Can't be tolerated—"

But they would tolerate it. They would do nothing effective, while pouring out torrents of words, because they knew what he knew, that they could do nothing. Their fancy Spaceforce, so shiny and proud, could do nothing because they had no way to operate outside their own system. Their privateers, so hated and feared, could do nothing because they had no command structure. Slotter Key had dealt with the rest of the sector in its own way: arrogantly. A combination of cheese-paring caution—using privateers for outsystem operations cost less than funding a real space navy—and exuberant flouting of the rules, such as they were, that governed such uses. No other planetary system would come to their aid just because one of their richest corporations had suffered a terrorist attack.

Time for turnabout. Time for reversals. Time for Slotter Key to realize that, just like Vatta Transport, it didn't have any recourse. It might be only a side issue in a greater war, but it was a side issue that gave considerable satisfaction to some of its allies. He didn't doubt that in five or six years, the Slotter Key Spaceforce could be a force to reckon with, but it wasn't now, and now was all that mattered.

"You listen to me," he growled at the voice; it stopped in midword. "You will do nothing. The time has changed, and Vatta serves us well as a warning to others. Stay away from them. Give them nothing. Anyone near Vatta will fall in the same catastrophe."

"But they're our—"

"They've supported you and your party, of course we know that. They think you owe them something. Well, it won't be the first promise you've ever broken." Gammis had a list, in case it should become useful.

"But—"

"If you move against us," Gammis said, "we will destroy not just Vatta, but Slotter Key, as well. We have the ships. We have the weapons. Ask your Spaceforce—go ahead. They'll tell you. We have many allies who would enjoy seeing your presidential palace a smoking hole just like Vatta headquarters, who would be delighted if your people died of plagues or starvation." He paused; the jittering voice in his ear said nothing. He let his voice soften. "And there is, of course, something positive to be gained by freeing yourself of Vatta's trade domination. If Vatta takes the fall, trade will not be interdicted . . . it's just that someone else will profit from their tik plantations . . ."

Silence continued. Gammis counted seconds. They would take the bait, but how long would they think about it?

"Vatta," the voice said, this time calmly, "has done nothing to deserve this. If you had attacked privateers—"

"Hitting the innocent is a more effective warning," Gammis said. Not that Vatta was entirely innocent. They had stupidly supported InterStellar Communications all these years; they had reported suspicious ships and persons . . . and besides, it was one of their own who betrayed them, who urged that they be made an example. In the longer plan, in the greater scheme of things, that one would surely fall since he could not be trusted, but in the meantime he was useful, worth doing a favor for. "You will do nothing," Gammis said again. "If you want your government to stand."

"I don't know how we're going to explain . . . ," the voice said.

"You'll figure something out." Gammis cut off the connection.

"Will they behave?" his second in command asked. "Or will they leak?"

"They'll leak in time," Gammis said. "Vatta's got supporters on their own world. But they have no way to spread the word. They don't realize it yet . . ." He chuckled, and his second in command grinned back at him. This was the way they should have done it from the first. The Sabine mess had been a big mistake; Gammis conveniently ignored the fact that he had voted to blow the ansible platforms. This time . . . this time they had a better plan. He knew the coalition wouldn't last forever, but for now, for the length of time it would take to bring down InterStellar Communications and consolidate the power they needed, it would hold.

They didn't have to kill all the Vattas, whatever that idiot said. They only had to kill enough, at once or within a short interval, enough to shock and terrify the rest: Vatta and non-Vatta shippers, Slotter Key and other planetary governments. No more little bangs, no more sporadic raids. One big paralyzing, terrifying, enigmatic explosion . . . He grinned wider. He could just imagine the frantic scrambling, the panic spreading through Captains' Guildhalls, government offices, corporate headquarters, all across this sector. Everyone trying to figure out who, and why, and what would happen next. He and his allies were the only ones who knew the answer.

By the time they figured it out, if they ever did, it would be too late. He knew all about Slotter Key's President; the President didn't even know his name. Someday everyone would know it.

Ky checked in at the Captains' Guild and took her duffel up to her room while her escort waited. It took only a few minutes to unpack and freshen up. She would take the paperwork to the Economic Development Bureau first, and then pay her courtesy visit to the Slotter Key legation. With any luck, she could have the afternoon free to start looking for cargo. She'd downloaded a list of recent shipments, but Belinta's exports didn't match well with her understanding of what would sell at Leonora. Lastway was a mystery; from the records, its markets went up and down dramatically, depending on what preceding ships had delivered.

At the Economic Development Bureau, she handed the paperwork to a bored clerk and received the confirmation of the final funds deposit in the Vatta account. She was almost back to the legation when her escort turned to her.

"Captain, there's an urgent message from the Captains' Guild. Your ship wants to contact you, and you have no implant."

"Call the legation and tell them I may be delayed," Ky said. "We'll go to the Captains' Guild."

Only a few minutes later, she was in a secure communications booth in the Captains' Guild lobby, talking to Quincy aboard *Gary Tobai*. "Slow down," she said finally. "I thought it was cargo thieves and now you're telling me it's sabotage?"

"The station police say it is. Was going to be. They found our cargo—the original, part of the consignment to Leonora—in a utility closet. They're sure it's the same; it's got the consignment IDs on the tape. But what was in the container that fellow loaded was a time-delayed explosive. They said it could have blown up the ship. And part of the station if we'd still been docked. If I hadn't noticed—and I almost didn't, he was just a dockworker, I thought—Captain, we could have been killed—!"

"But you did spot him, and we weren't," Ky said. Her mind whirled. Sabotage was not unknown, and Paison's allies might consider that they had a motive. They knew—anyone who followed the news stories would know—where she was going when she left Sabine system. But Belinta was an unlikely place for an ambush, she'd have thought. Well out of the way, small, little traffic, an insular, suspicious culture. It would have been more cheaply and easily done somewhere else.

"They want us to leave," Quincy went on. "For our own safety, they're saying, but I can tell they're scared."

So was Quincy, by her face and voice, and no wonder. "A good idea," Ky said. "How close were we to finishing loading?"

"Another six to eight hours."

"It will take me that long to get back up to the station," Ky said. "Unless I charter a flight." Would that be reimbursable as a legitimate expense, under the circumstances? "I'll let the consul know something's come up, and forget looking for cargo."

"Don't forget to report this to headquarters," Quincy said.

"Headquarters?"

"All material threats against Vatta ships—you'll need to give them an ansible call right away. So if it's more than local, they can warn other ships."

"That seems a bit extreme," Ky said. "I think it's probably something to do with Sabine; it shouldn't affect anyone else."

"If you had the Vatta implant, it would be in emergency procedures, Captain. Piracy, sabotage, anything like that. Call headquarters immediately—I would have, if I hadn't been able to raise you within the hour."

"You still could—" Ky began.

"No, it's captain's responsibility; they'll want to hear from you."

"I should wait until I'm up there and have the report from the police," Ky said. "They'll ask questions I can't answer—"

"Immediate notification is the priority," Quincy said. "It's in the implants."

If she did what she planned, she'd never have the Vatta implant. Wrong time to think about that, though. "All right. I'll call right away, then see how soon I can get back up there. Once you've got the ship loaded, button us up. Will the police put a guard on our dock space?"

"Yes. There's one out there now."

That was a help. She hoped that was a help.

"I'll be there as soon as I can," she said, and signed off. Now for the ansible call home. Belinta's ansible-access procedures worked normally, the status lights blinking appropriately through their sequences. She had no idea what time it would be at Vatta corporate headquarters, but it didn't matter. They had someone on duty in the communications suite at all hours. The green lights blinked three times, and the screen lit, but showed no image.

"Vatta Headquarters," a voice said. "This call originated on Belinta. You are Captain Kylara Vatta, is that correct?"

"Yes," Ky said. This didn't sound like standard procedure. "Are you transmitting visual? This screen is blank."

"Link your implant for urgent download," the voice said without answering her question.

"I don't have an implant," Ky said. "What is it? I was going to report a threat—"

"Uh... go ahead. Report the threat." She heard voices behind the voice she was listening to, as if the sound shielding weren't on. She couldn't quite hear what they were saying.

"Unknown persons posing as dockworkers attempted to load an explosive device onto my ship," Ky said. "The ship is safe and undamaged, but they got away."

"Understood," the voice said. "We have a situation here, too, Captain. We are sending a warning to all ships; there appears to be the possibility of multiple threats to Vatta personnel."

"What kind of threats?" Ky asked.

"I... am not at liberty to say," the voice said.

"Could you connect me to my father, please?" Ky said. She would find out more from him than from some communications tech. "Gerard Vatta? Or my uncle?"

"Uh... I'm afraid that's not possible at this time," the voice said.

"Why?" Ky asked. "He's got his skullphone."

"He is..." A pause. "He is temporarily unavailable. Your message will be forwarded immediately and I'm sure he will want to speak with you."

Cold swept over her. "What's wrong?" she asked. "You said a threat—what's happened?"

"Captain—" Another pause. "It is not for me to say. There is a Situation."

"Are the senior officers all right?" Ky asked.

"I believe so, yes." Something in the voice conveyed doubt, not assurance.

"But you aren't sure—"

"It's the—" The screen blanked, and the status light went to yellow, blinking. SIGNAL LOST. DO YOU WANT TO RECONNECT? Y/N appeared instead. Ky sat back; she could feel her pulse racing. Whatever had happened had happened—instantaneous communication or no, whatever it had been was over. She could do nothing about it. She would try a direct call to her father—much more expensive, but at the moment money didn't matter.

She cracked open the booth door to let her security escort know that she would be making more calls, but before the door was fully open she saw a trio of masked figures push through the inner door of the lobby, weapons out. Her escort, standing at the desk chatting with the assistant manager, whirled, but too late: he was dead and so was the assistant manager before either of them could push a panic button. Ky ducked back into the booth, but did not latch the door; that would turn on the ENGAGED light. Instead, she held very still.

"What room?" she heard one of the intruders ask. A mumble, then the same voice said, "Upstairs." An instant of relief. She eased around to peek out the door. One of the figures was crouched over the bodyguard, going through his pockets. No chance then to run out the door and get help. She could almost feel the blow in her back if she tried it. But once they found she wasn't in her room they'd search the place, including this booth.

The booth held nothing she could use as a weapon. The booth could not be used for local calls—and would not function anyway without the door being latched, at which the telltale light would come on. All this ran through her mind, a cascade of logic that came down to one conclusion—and she was already in motion when she became aware of it.

The masked figure frisking the dead guard had his back to her at the moment—five strides took her across the lobby. Three before he noticed anything and whirled, but she was already moving so fast that his hasty shot missed, and she was on him. Primary disarm—the weapon flew out of his hand and skidded across the floor. Her chop at his throat met a hard surface; he wore armor under his clothes. He uncoiled a vicious kick; Ky evaded it, whirling and noticing the movement of his left hand toward his side. The next weapon—instead of trying to intercept that movement, she dove toward the dead guard, snatching his weapon as part of a sideways roll, and shot her attacker square through his mask before he had his weapon all the way out. She recognized the stab of emotion that passed through her, sharp and sweet; a wave of guilt followed: *Not again.* She shook it away.

Seconds had passed. They would be at her floor now. They would be opening the door. And how many were left outside, in case she managed to escape and try to flee? If she'd had an implant, she could have called for help by now. Ky reached over to the reception desk's outside line. It hummed, and she punched in the local emergency code. A faint rhythmic buzz . . . three, four, five. Behind the reception desk was the office—she hadn't been in it, but brief glimpses when the clerk came in and out suggested the usual work space, which might or might not have another exit. The corridor to the left led to the dining room, and from there to the kitchens and presumably another exit, which might also be covered by the assassins. But offices, dining rooms, and kitchens had lots of hiding places. Which . . . ?

The lift hummed suddenly, then clanked into motion. The assassins? Or some innocent bystander? For the first time she thought about the other possible captains in residence. Two—but they might or might not be in their rooms. Around the desk, a glance at the assistant manager, a crumpled heap on the floor, at the monitor. The lift stopped, but now she heard footsteps on the stairs. No time to make it to the corridor. She ducked into the office with its desks, cabinets, shelves stocked with office supplies. Another door led into a smaller room that seemed to function as a storeroom for linens and cleaning supplies. She moved into it, checked that nothing had a reflective surface to reveal her to someone outside, and flattened against a stack of toilet paper cartons.

Voices outside. "Piet's dead... somebody's given the alarm."

"Stupid bitch wasn't in her room—could be her?"

"Doesn't matter. No time—we go now."

"Piet?"

"Leave him. Come on."

Footsteps across the lobby floor, the squeak of the inner door opening, then hissing shut, a clear invitation to someone in hiding to emerge. Ky stayed where she was, counting to herself. Five, ten, fifteen, twenty. Something scraped, thumped faintly. The hair on her arms stood up; she held her breath. She hadn't felt nausea this time when she killed, but now her stomach clenched. The outer door of the office swung suddenly, banged against the wall.

"Hey! Anybody home? What's going on here?"

It was not the officials. A different voice, but not the officials because she would have heard the front door.

"I seeeee youuu...," the voice mocked. "Better come out, sweetheart..."

Ky held still. She could not be seen; she knew she could not be seen. She heard a breath drawn in, let out.

"If you're here, bitch, we'll get you later," the voice said, now quietly serious. "But I don't think she is," it went on, this time clearly a comment-to-self. "And here come the puds." The footsteps retreated. She dared not peek out to see where the man went, but a moment later she heard a cry from the direction of the kitchen.

Now the wheeze of the front doors, banging, stomping, clattering, several loud voices. Ky slid out of the storage room, her knees shaking with reaction, and looked out of the office to see a startled man in uniform staring at her.

"Freeze!" he yelled, bringing his weapon to bear. Ky stopped. *"Drop the weapon!"*

"But I'm the one—"

"Drop the weapon!"

Now there were five of them, their own weapons leveled at her. She dropped the guard's weapon.

"Get on the ground!"

"But I'm the one who called—"

"Now! Facedown! On the ground!"

"I'm the one who called you!" Ky said. "They were trying to kill me—!"

"Get. On. The. Ground."

It was infuriating. How could they think she'd done it? Though she had killed the one. With a sigh, Ky got down on the ground. Feet came closer. It occurred to her, just as the feet came into her range of vision, that maybe these weren't the police.

"Who are you?" Ky asked. "I hope you're official."

"We're official all right," a voice said overhead. "Just don't give me any trouble now."

"There were three of them that I saw," Ky said. "All with masks—"

"Hands behind your back," the voice said.

Ky complied, in the hope they would finally listen to her when they had her trussed up. Instead, she was rolled over, propped against the wall, and told to stay put. The hand she'd whacked against the assassin's armor throbbed unpleasantly. At least now she could see... men in dark green uniforms with markings she didn't recognize on cuffs and collars. They were hunched over the dead clerk, with more beyond the desk.

One of them came to her again. "Is this your weapon?" he asked, holding out the one she'd taken from her bodyguard.

"No—it belonged to my security escort."

"Yours—he was working for you? Then why did you take his gun?"

"He was dead at the time," Ky said. "And the other one was trying to kill me."

The man looked at her sourly. "So you say—" A voice from down the corridor interrupted him.

"Shem! Here's another one!"

The man left. Ky fretted. No one ever seemed to consider that the person being restrained might be innocent. Her instructors had commented on that fact when telling cadets how to behave if they were ever stopped by law enforcement. She'd already violated rules one and two: don't be where trouble happens, and never be caught with a weapon in your hand.

And here she sat, immobilized. What if the assassins came back? Her muscles twitched; she took a long breath, trying to calm herself.

The man reappeared. "You say you're the one who called us?"

"Yes," Ky said.

"When? Why?"

"Because of the attack," Ky said. "I had seen them kill my bodyguard and the clerk, and then—"

"Them? How many?"

"Three on the inside," Ky said. "I was over there in the combooth—" She gestured with her chin. "—when they came in. My bodyguard and the clerk were at the reception desk, chatting. The assassins shot them both, then two went upstairs. Looking for me, probably. The other was searching the guard's body." She stopped for a moment to get her thoughts in order.

"Go on."

"I couldn't use the combooth because the light would come on and they'd know where I was."

"Why do you think they were after you? You, particularly?"

"I don't know," Ky said. "My engineer had just called to let me know that the fake cargo container put on my ship was explosive. Your colleagues up on the station can tell you more about that." Should she even mention the call to Vatta headquarters, the lost connection? Yes. "I had called my company headquarters," Ky said. "Apparently some group is targeting Vatta Transport. They were about to put out a warning. Then the connection failed, so I don't know any more than that. Anyway, I couldn't use the combooth, and I couldn't see how to get out without him seeing me."

"Why didn't you use your implant?" the man asked.

"I don't have one," Ky said. "Head injury—they had to take it out and it can't be replaced for six standard months."

"Ah. So . . . you tried to escape and—you're asking me to believe a trained assassin couldn't hit you?"

"No. I thought if I rushed him I could knock him out, maybe." The policeman looked at her with obvious disbelief. "It could work," Ky said. "And I didn't have a weapon."

"Did it work?"

"No. I surprised him, but he was wearing body armor under his mask. He threw me off, I landed near the guard's weapon, and snatched it—and got off a shot before he did."

"Hmmm." He looked thoughtful.

"Shem, these wounds were made by different weapons," said one of the others. "The guard and the clerk were both hit with Staysil rounds, and so were the cook and the helper in back; the masked one with a Conroy."

"Staysil rounds. Sounds like the Edmunds crew," the policeman said. He looked at Ky and shook his head. "Someone wants you dead very badly, if they're after you. Edmunds and company are not just trouble, but expensive trouble." He sighed heavily, and reached over to release Ky's arms. "Don't try to run. We did not need this. Diplomatic mess, too. You'll want to see the Slotter Key consul, no doubt. And I don't suppose you know why anyone would be after Vatta captains?"

"No," Ky said, rubbing her wrists. She glanced at the painful hand. Swollen and darkening. She hoped she hadn't broken a bone. "I don't. I need to get back to my ship—"

"Not yet," he said. "You did, after all, kill that man." He cocked his head toward the outer door. "He may be a criminal, and he may have tried to kill you, but we have to determine whether, under our laws, this excuses your killing him. You can count on at least overnight, Captain Vatta. You may inform your crew, but we will monitor the conversation. You may have access to the Slotter Key legation, of course, but with an escort we provide. Since—if it is the Edmunds crew—your life is in danger, we will provide protective custody."

Ky tried not to glare. "You're going to put me in jail because I was attacked?"

"Not exactly. Because you killed someone *and* you were attacked. And not exactly jail, but someplace safer than the Captains' Guild."

"Let's go see what they did to my room," Ky suggested. "My luggage—"

"Fine. But I'll go with you. Do not try to touch anything. It would be against your best interest." Nodding to the others, he let her lead the way upstairs.

"They used the stairs," Ky said. "And I think also the lift." She was carefully not touching the stair rail.

"They will have worn gloves," the man said. He sounded glum.

In her room, the bedcover was missing, and her empty duffel lay open in a corner. The closet was open; her clothes were gone; all the drawers were empty. In the bathroom, all the toiletries were gone as well.

The policeman grunted. "Typical," he said after a moment's look around. "They want everything to check for DNA and anything else that might be useful. I hope you didn't leave them something juicy."

Ky's stomach churned again. Being physically attacked was one thing, but having her things taken—all of them—was in some ways more upsetting. "The—valuables—are in the safe downstairs. If they didn't break into that."

"No," he said. He had pulled on gloves; he opened the drawers all the way, looking into them for anything left behind, opening the cabinets in the bathroom. "So you're a prudent traveler... I suppose one expects that from spaceship captains."

"I wasn't prudent enough to put a set of underwear in the safe," Ky said ruefully. "I hope you have a good 'fresher in the jail."

"I'm sure someone can obtain the necessary items for you," he said.

"It doesn't make sense," Ky said. "Surely someone would notice men in masks carrying a bundle that looks like a bedspread..."

"I doubt they carried it far," the man said. "Or they had something else to put things in and just used the spread to make it easy to collect them."

"I almost came up here to make the call," Ky said. Her knees felt shaky again. "I thought, walking back, My feet hurt and I'll just go upstairs and kick my shoes off. But the combooth in the lobby was closer. If I had come up here I'd have had no warning..."

"Sit down, Captain Vatta," the man said. "You're looking pale." Ky sat on the bed, which was nearer than the chair. She told herself to get a grip, but tremors shook her. "A natural reaction... though it took you rather longer to get to it than most."

"I... thought I was all right," Ky said. Her hand still hurt where she'd hit the man's armor.

"I think I will call your legation, if you permit, on your behalf," he said. He sounded almost friendly now. Ky tried to focus, tried to grasp why, but she couldn't.

"Thank you," she said. The tremors eased, but she still felt cold and sick.

The consul appeared only minutes later. "Captain Vatta, the captain has explained what he understands happened. How can we be of service?"

She could not imagine asking the consul to go buy her some underwear, and at the moment the lack of underwear loomed larger in her mind than anything else.

"I'll be all right," she said, aware that the statement made incomplete sense at best. "The ship needs to know."

"I think she's in shock," she heard the policeman say. "I thought at first . . . but then she went pale and started shaking."

"Reaction," said the consul. "You're a bit pale yourself, you know." Ky could not think of the consul's name. His face seemed to leap nearer. "Captain—do you know my name?"

"I'm sorry," Ky said. "But no." She should remember it, she knew that much. She had called him from Belinta Station when she arrived; they'd discussed the Sabine situation. She had arranged to meet him at the legation this very morning. But everything had gone fuzzy at the edges and all she had the energy to do was sit there.

Then the policeman canted slowly to one side and collapsed. People shouted, ran to and fro, and Ky watched it all with a detachment that she knew was unnatural, until someone picked her up and put her on a litter and she slid into sleep.

CHAPTER THREE

The room smelled of familiar tropical flowers, lush and spicy. A floral print on the bed, on the dressing table with its low bench, on the lamp shade. Walls of soft peach, with a faint cream stripe. Ky lay back against the piled pillows, wondering where she was. The last she remembered was the Captains' Guild...men with masks and guns...police... then it came back, all a rush of memory. She blinked. This wasn't a jail, she was sure of that. She'd never seen this room before, but the fragrance, familiar since childhood, suggested the legation and its garden of Slotter Key natives.

Before she thought to reach for the comunit on the bedside table, someone shouldered the door open and entered with a tray, a stout woman in a flowered tunic. She brought the tray to the bedside and began offloading dishes onto the bedside table.

"Ah, good, you're awake. You'll be wondering where you are and what happened," the woman said. "Slotter Key legation. The doctor wants to talk to you and so does the consul and the Belinta police. I'm Carla, by the way, and you're supposed to take your time eating as much as you want before anyone tries to talk to you. Doctor's orders." She poured out a cup of tea; Ky hitched herself more upright in the bed, took it, and sipped.

"Tell me what happened at the Captains' Guild," Ky said. "Upstairs, I mean."

"My feet hurt," Carla said, ignoring the question. She plumped down in the upholstered chair and kicked her shoes off. "I'm not supposed to talk to you about what happened; I'm supposed to be sure you're really awake and have had something to eat." She laid her head back and sighed. Ky stared a moment then picked up one of the pastries and started to bite into it. Then she stopped. Whatever had happened after the part she remembered, someone had tried to kill her—not once, but twice, counting the attempt to smuggle explosives onto her ship. And she was supposed to eat and drink whatever she was brought?

She put the cup down; it chinked on the saucer, and the woman—Carla—opened her eyes. "Sorry—can I get you anything?"

"How do I know you're who you say you are?"

"Excuse me?"

Ky realized, as she sat up and threw the covers back, that she was wearing someone else's nightshirt. She'd never owned one in lavender and green, and besides it was hugely too big. Her head spun for a moment, then cleared.

"You say this is the Slotter Key legation—"

"Yes, of course. Where else would it be?"

"And you're—a legation employee?"

The woman drew herself up, red patches coming up on her cheeks, and gave Ky a hostile glance. "I am the consul's wife," she said. "Carla Maria Inosyeh."

Ky felt her face heating up. "I'm so sorry," she said. "You weren't—I didn't meet you before, at the dinner."

"I was indisposed." An impatient movement in the chair, then the woman fished for her shoes and put them back on. "And before you ask, yes, this is my bedroom you're in, and my nightdress you're wearing. I was told your things had been stolen."

"I'm sorry," Ky said again. "I didn't know—I am confused—they tried to kill me, and I was afraid—"

The woman's expression softened. "I suppose it's understandable. It's been a very strange day, I hear. But perhaps you should see Parin—my husband the consul—now. I will have to tell him later that I managed to frighten the redoubtable Captain Vatta." She actually smiled as she went to the door.

The tea must be doing its work; Ky felt more solidly there than she had a few minutes before. "Wait," she said. "I believe you. Please—stay, sit down, and I'll eat—" She picked up the pastry again and bit into it. It was delicious.

"If you insist," Carla said, this time with a genuine smile. "My husband has been telling me about your trip to Sabine. The news reports of the attacks there were terrifying. I can't imagine someone blowing up ansible platforms." She glanced up as if she could see through the roof to Belinta's ansible station.

"It was scary," Ky said, through another pastry, this one meat-filled. She felt better with every bite.

"I can't understand why anyone would attack ansible platforms," Carla said. "It only makes ISC angry, and Parin always says they're the glue that holds the galaxy together."

Ky, her mouth full, nodded but said nothing.

"And you were captured by mercenaries, the news report said."

"Yes," Ky said, wiping her mouth. "But they were polite mercenaries." When they weren't almost killing her, but that had been an accident.

"Did you really kill the ringleaders?" Carla asked.

"Yes," Ky said. "And I suspect that's why someone's trying to kill me, in retaliation." She decided that one more pastry wouldn't hurt and picked one up.

"I can tell you're feeling better," Carla said. "More color in your cheeks. The clothes you had on have been freshened, if you feel able to get up now."

"Yes," Ky said. "I do . . . but I'd still like to know what happened. Did I just . . . faint?"

"A contact poison," Carla said, with the satisfied tone of someone who knows something unusual. "That policeman with you fell over like a cut tree while the consul was in the room; you were pale and turning gray, Parin said."

"A contact poison! On top of the shooting?"

"Yes. They didn't leave much to chance, is the way the consul put it. It penetrated ordinary gloves as if they weren't there." Ky remembered, now, the policeman pulling open drawers, lifting the sheets of the bed, touching this surface and that. "Then they found the bedspread bundled into a trash container, and the poison was all over that. Three of them are down with it. You only sat on the bed—the poison didn't penetrate your clothes that well. The antidote worked quickly; you were only unconscious a couple of hours. The doctor's off working on the others."

"So . . . did they catch the assassins?"

"No. They're searching, of course, but except for the one you shot, the gang's all disappeared."

"Is my ship all right? My crew? Has anything else happened up there?"

"They're fine," Carla said. "No attacks up there at all, and shuttle travel's been suspended, so no assassination teams can get there from here. There's a com console in my sitting room, just outside here. Then there's a policeman who would like to speak to you; he has assured the consul that they have no more interest in arresting you. When their people went down from the contact poison, they decided that your having shot one of the assassins wasn't so bad after all."

"I need to check with the ship. Can you hold the policeman off that long?"

"Of course," Carla said. "This is Slotter Key territory, after all." She winked. "Take your time getting dressed—through that door there."

Quincy, predictably, was appalled at what had happened, and worried, and wanted Ky to come back immediately.

"I'm safe here," Ky said. "I'm not going out, I promise. They've suspended shuttle flights, you know."

"Yes, but for you—can't you get a charter?"

"Probably not, not until tomorrow anyway. Are you satisfied with the police guard on our dockside?"

"They've doubled it," Quincy said. "I think we're secure. But you—"

"I'm fine," Ky said again. "I got hold of Vatta headquarters before this happened…" Should she tell Quincy everything, or would it just make it worse? "There does appear to be a general threat; I'll give you the details when I'm back on the ship. And if I'm stuck down here for days, I might as well see what I can do about cargo."

"Cargo! There's your life to consider! Don't you dare go out!"

"I won't go out. I can do business from here; the consul's helping me arrange things. I won't say don't worry, but don't lose sleep."

Quincy sniffed and signed off.

The policeman who interviewed Ky had the same dour expression as the others she'd met. "We are convinced that you were the innocent victim of an attack, and that your killing the assassin was self-defense," he said. "Under our laws, this is legal, and anyway the dead man was someone we wanted to arrest on other charges. Saved us the cost of a trial. Even so, we cannot recommend that you resume unrestricted travel in the city, or your residence at the Captains' Guild."

"I can't stay cooped up here forever," Ky said. "My ship is already under threat—"

"We think you could be escorted safely to the orbital station," the policeman said. "But an extended stay…we understand you were seeking outbound cargo…"

"Not after the attempt to sabotage my ship and kill me. I want to leave as soon as possible. If for some reason I had been detained here, then I'd ask the consul to help me make some contacts to seek cargo. But if I can leave now—"

"Are you well enough to travel?"

"Yes," Ky said. "The doctor advises twenty-four hours of observation, but surely overnight is enough."

"Perhaps a chartered shuttle flight—we would of course validate the crew—"

"Sounds good to me," Ky said. The only goods she'd seen explained why Belinta had a deplorable trade balance.

When the policeman excused himself, she considered going out to find the consul, but decided to rest just a few minutes; her head felt strange again. She lay down on top of the covers. When she woke, some unknown time later, someone had covered her with a knitted shawl and set another tray on the bedside table; steam rose in curls from the teapot.

Ky wasn't very hungry; she was struggling with her reaction to the day's events. Her annoyance with the postal clerk seemed far away now, almost as if it had been someone else. Someone had tried to blow up her ship. Someone had tried to kill her. Something had happened during her call to Vatta headquarters. She had to think those were related, and the only thing she could think of was whatever criminal group Paison and Kristoffson had been part of, taking vengeance for killing them.

She started when she heard the sound of the door handle turning, but relaxed when she saw the consul. He came in, shutting the door behind him. "How are you feeling?" he asked.

"Much better," Ky said.

"That's good," he said, and sighed. His expression did not lighten; her stomach clenched.

"What's wrong?" she asked.

"We've lost contact with Slotter Key," Consul Inosyeh said. He sat heavily in the other chair.

She remembered suddenly that she had intended to call her father directly, only to be interrupted by the assassins. "Completely?" she asked. Her mouth went dry.

"Yes. It appears that something's wrong with the ansibles there. I don't know if it's anything like what happened at Sabine . . ." His voice trailed away.

Ky watched his face; he stared at his hands. "What else?" she asked finally when he didn't look up.

"There's . . . another problem. Before we lost contact. I had reported the attack on you—purely routine, something I'd do if a Slotter Key citizen had been involved in a barroom brawl—and I was told something that shocked me." He paused; Ky waited it out. "Vatta's always been in good odor with the government. I am sure you know that. There's the contributions, of course, but beyond that, it's an enterprise that has a long and honorable history in interstellar trading. Due all assistance, favored status, whatever you want to call it. And I liked you personally, when I met you on your first visit. I was looking forward to having lunch with you."

"And?" Ky prompted, when he stopped again. He looked up, his expression grim.

"And for reasons I do not understand, that has been reversed. At the highest level. Vatta is, in the words of my superior, not to be accorded any status whatever. *Get her out of there,* he said. *Have nothing to do with Vatta.*"

Ky stared at him, shocked. "What—"

He shook his head. "I don't know, Captain. I demanded answers, and got nothing except that the situation had changed and I was to follow orders. I pointed out that you were sick, incapacitated, in danger, and was told to get you a room in a hotel. Whatever happened, it's got the government scared. Some threat, I'd guess, to them as well as to Vatta." He sighed, then went on. "I tried calling some other people I knew; one of them told me there were rumors of attacks on Vatta holdings, but had no details. It was on the third call that we were cut off. I asked the police to check the combooth records from the Captains' Guild; that was about six hours after you lost the signal to your headquarters."

Six hours. Much could happen in six hours... or in six minutes, or six seconds.

"I'm guessing that ISC's enemies are behind the ansible failure, but whether that has anything to do with this change in policy about Vatta, I don't know."

"It must," Ky said. "The ansible attacks on Sabine were certainly aimed at ISC, or so ISC thought. And I can understand the people who did it blaming me. I did kill two of them. Maybe it's a two-pronged attack."

Consul Inosyeh shook his head. "Wrong scale. A criminal organization wanting to punish you might send an assassination team, yes—though it's more likely they'd have some local thug beat you up in a bar somewhere—but not take out ansible service to your home planet." He paused, and Ky nodded. He went on. "The thing is, I'm under orders to dump you on the street, effectively. I'm not going to." The look he gave her was brimming with mischief.

Ky stared at him.

"Instead, I'm going to commit time travel and have a conversation with you that actually occurred prior to that ansible call. In fact, we're already having that conversation. If anyone asks later, this conversation occurred in the morning. Is that clear?"

Nothing was clear at the moment, but the intensity of his gaze suggested that she needed to answer. "Yes . . . I guess."

"Good." Consul Inosyeh leaned back in his chair, hooked a heel around the leg of a hassock, and pulled it nearer before stretching his legs onto it. "I'm going to share with you what I might have shared if not instructed otherwise—because from my point of view, I haven't yet been instructed otherwise. And if you think that merely proves the moral elasticity of diplomats, please keep it to yourself." He ran his hands through his hair, leaving it in rumples.

"Er . . . yes, of course." How had she ever thought this North Coaster stuffy and arrogant?

"How much do you know of Slotter Key's foreign policy, especially as regards maintaining the safety of the spaceways?" That last might have been set in inverted quotes, so marked was his emphasis.

"That's what we have a space navy for," Ky said promptly. "Our strong Spaceforce deters . . ." Her voice trailed away at his expression. "Doesn't it?"

"I always wondered what they taught cadets," Consul Inosyeh said. He sighed. "You know, the universe would work much better if people just told the simple truth, and you may think that's the stupidest thing ever to come out of a diplomat's mouth, but really!"

"My father always said honesty in trade was better than trickery," Ky said. "If you wanted repeat customers."

"And let's hope that honesty didn't get him killed," Consul Inosyeh said. "All right. Here's the truth of it. Slotter Key, our mutual home, is widely disliked for its way of handling interstellar security. Our Spaceforce, for all the resources dedicated to it, defends only the home system. One star system, three inhabited planets, some colonized satellites, and so on. We have pickets at several nearby jump points, as an early warning system. We don't take our ships into other people's systems without elaborate preparation—if we just waltz in, they call it invasion. They have called it invasion."

"But I thought—" Ky stopped again. Nothing she'd been taught actually contradicted what Consul Inosyeh was saying, though this was a strange interpretation. "But then what keeps pirates from raiding our tradeships?"

"That, Captain Vatta, is the reason Slotter Key has a shady reputation. Slotter Key runs privateers, private armed vessels authorized by the Slotter Key government to pursue and take action against the enemies of Slotter Key. Which, broadly defined, means anyone who messes with our trade in ways we don't like. We're not the only ones to do what we do, but we do it fairly aggressively."

Shock like an ice-water bath stopped Ky's breath for a moment. "Privateers! They're—they're nothing but pirates with a piece of paper!"

"That's exactly what some other systems call them, yes. It's what we call foreign privateers, too, if they interfere with our ships. But, Captain Vatta, every government finds itself in need of force—clandestine, unofficial, deniable force—in some situations. Vigilantes, privateers, bounty hunters, mercenaries, someone who would do the dirty work but whose dirty work could be disavowed if things went sour."

"But—but it's wrong." Even as she said that, she knew how naïve, how immature, that sounded. Consul Inosyeh did not laugh at her, or even smile.

"It's certainly not ideal," he said. "At best, the use of such methods should be reserved for a few rare difficult situations. But for economic reasons, Slotter Key and several other planetary systems have come up with this way to fund police in space. I'm sure you can imagine the diplomatic problems that arise. Innocent ships seized, disputes over the proof of guilt, that sort of thing. The Merchant Council agreed, in the Commercial Code, to recognize privateers as separate from pirates, and privateers—including ours—are bound to adhere to the code for the treatment of prisoners, for instance, just as mercenaries do. Privateers have provided the only space police for many decades now, and on the whole the merchants are happier with them than with the real pirates."

"There should be a real space police," Ky said. "Surely the various systems could get together—"

"So far they've refused," Consul Inosyeh said. "The closest thing is ISC's enforcement branch, but they don't do anything about piracy that doesn't affect them directly, and they aren't enthusiastic when systems do try to combine forces. But here's the thing: merchant firms, including some you know, have participated in the privateer program, committing a small percentage of their fleet. What's lost in cargo capacity to the armament they carry is made up for in prize money. Spaceforce usually assigns an officer—always on the larger ships, or if they're working in a group—to keep an eye on things. We in the diplomatic service are provided a list of privateers operating in our area, in case we need to contact them or vice versa."

Despite her initial disgust at the thought of privateers, Ky imagined herself on such a ship—almost as good as a real warship—protecting Slotter Key's merchant fleet from pirates. Maybe it wasn't *that* bad.

"So you see, I can think of reasons why Slotter Key might be attacked, even without an attack on ISC. We've annoyed a lot of people, not just our intended targets."

"Are . . . uh . . . Vatta ships among the privateers?"

"Not on any list I've ever had," Consul Inosyeh said. "I believe it was the policy, when privateering was first authorized, that at least one carrier should not be invited to participate, so that its sterling reputation could cover the others." Sarcasm soured his voice. "I don't know the whole history, but Vatta appears to have been chosen as the unspotted lamb of an otherwise motley flock." He looked at her closely. "You didn't know any of this, I gather."

"No," Ky said. Some of the reactions she'd gotten here and on Sabine now made sense, though. So did that model kit with stray electronic bits Master Sergeant MacRobert had sent her back before she left Slotter Key. *If you need help,* his letter had said, and he was Spaceforce. He must have known about the privateers; he must have been trying to give her a way to contact them. But why hadn't her father told her? Surely he'd known.

"Well . . . you need to know it now. You're going to be facing hostility and suspicion in many quarters, and whatever is presently going on, with Vatta and Slotter Key's government at odds, can only make things worse. I don't suppose you have any seasoned veterans among your crew?"

"No," Ky said. "My father thought he was sending me off on a quiet run; he chose crew for their experience with the ship."

"You need force you can trust, Captain. The best thing you could do is hire some good toughs. The kind of person you can depend on, so you don't have to hire guards at every stop."

And where would she find someone like that? How could she be sure they weren't part of a plot to kill her? He must have seen that in her expression.

"There's one of our legation guards very close to retiring," he said. "He's a bit rough at the edges, but very experienced and strong as an ox. I could speak to him, if you'd like."

The memory of what had happened the last time she took on a diplomat's problem was clear in her mind. Caleb Skeldon had nearly gotten her killed. Would this be another rash idiot?

"The thing about ex-military is they have discipline as well as training," Consul Inosyeh said, as if he could read her mind.

"What I really need is a cargomaster," Ky said. "Someone who's good at inventory as well as handling cargo loading."

"He is," Consul Inosyeh said. "That's if—given what I've told you about the government's position—you trust me."

She had already made a fool of herself with the consul's wife. She had to trust someone, and Inosyeh had missed better chances to do her harm.

"Ask him, then," she said. "But I'll want to talk to him first, if he agrees."

"Of course. Now, remember—this conversation took place in the morning, when you arrived here and before I contacted my government."

"Yes," Ky said. She felt numb, even more battered than before. What could she do with one small, slow, unarmed tradeship? How could she find out what was going on? "Um . . . do you want me to leave now?"

"Now? No, of course not. It's night and you're still not fully recovered. Get a good night's sleep and by morning I expect the Belinta authorities will have found a way to return you to your ship." He pushed the hassock away, stood, and stretched. "I have to attend a terminally boring dinner during which I shall pretend that nothing whatever is going on, and you are the hero everyone here thinks you are. I'll talk to our man when I get back and he's on duty, and you can meet him in the morning."

Ky was sure she would not sleep, and for some time her thoughts ran in giddy circles, but exhaustion took her finally. On her breakfast tray the next morning was a note from Consul Inosyeh advising her that Staff Sergeant Martin would like to speak with her before she left, and she had reservations on a shuttle leaving at 1015 local time.

Staff Sergeant Gordon Martin was a tall, blocky individual with graying blond hair and gray eyes like frozen pebbles. Though he was out of uniform, no one could have mistaken him for anything but a military man, not with his stance, expression, and attitude. Ky glanced at the information he handed her—he was younger than she'd expected, he had experience in both supply and security, and the summary of his fitness reports suggested why he was retiring that young. No hint of dishonesty or substance abuse, but a pattern of "borderline insubordination." One commanding officer's comment, "This individual does not know where initiative ends and rocket-propelled idiocy begins," stuck in her mind. She looked back up at him.

"Not going to be promoted, Captain," he said. "Too independent."

"I don't need a loose cannon," she said. "I've already had one of those, and he almost got me killed."

"Ma'am, I'm not a loose cannon. I know what statement you're referring to, and that officer was willing to let the depot be robbed blind rather than admit he'd trusted the wrong civ. What I did was go over his head, when he wouldn't do anything about it." A tight grin split the man's face. "I couldn't go over your head, ma'am—you're the top of your command chain."

Despite herself, Ky grinned back. "Did the consul explain that I've been attacked and so has my ship? It's not a safe berth I'm offering."

"Yes, ma'am, Captain. It'll be my pleasure to keep you alive and the ship safe. And I understand you need someone with expertise in inventory control?"

"Yes. My cargomaster was killed last voyage; his second is excellent but not experienced with inventory, since Gary did all that."

"I've handled inventory control for this post and others."

"The shuttle leaves in an hour and a half," Ky said. "I don't know about transport out—"

"I can take care of that, ma'am. If you're willing."

It was crazy. But something about him, about that solid, obviously experienced man, gave her the first real confidence she'd felt since losing contact with Vatta headquarters. He was certainly not the type to need saving, either—for once she couldn't be accused of playing rescue. "Let's not miss the shuttle," she said. "Glad to have you along."

The trip back to Belinta Station aboard a governmental supply shuttle was as boring and uneventful as she hoped. Flanked by a police escort, with Martin beside her, she made it unscathed through the station corridors to her own dockside and aboard.

There she found not the calm she expected, but chaos and dissension, a knot of obviously scared and angry people yelling in the rec area.

"I'm not staying," Riel Amat, her senior pilot, was saying. "You can't make me. It's too dangerous."

"You can't leave!" Quincy's voice was hoarse, as if she'd been talking a long time.

"What's going on?" Ky asked. Her crew whirled to face her. Martin, she noticed, had placed himself along the bulkhead in a position to shield her from Riel.

"Captain—" Riel reddened, then plunged on. "I just can't do it. It was bad enough before, and now that someone almost blew up the ship—I just can't. The station board says there's a Pavrati ship headed insystem; I want to transfer."

Quincy was glaring at Martin now. "Who's this?"

"Our new cargomaster and security chief," Ky said. "We need someone in charge of ship security—meet Gordon Martin. Ex-Spaceforce, just retired. Also experienced in supply." She turned to Riel. "I don't know if you realize it, but there's a break in communications between here and Slotter Key—something's going on, and there's no guarantee there'll be another ship home anytime soon."

"I don't care. I do not want to stay on this ship and you can't make me."

"I can take care of the piloting, Captain," said Lee. She hadn't noticed him before; unlike the others in the compartment, he was sitting relaxed on the bench. "I'm staying."

"Who else wants to leave?" Ky said.

"If there was a ship," Sheryl Donster, her navigator, began, "I'd want to take it. But there's not. And I don't want to stay on this station; we've already been attacked here. So I guess I'll stay . . ."

"Crew briefing in an hour," Ky said. "I'll tell you what I know then. Meanwhile, start preparing for departure. Riel, I'll see you in my cabin now."

"Ma'am?" That was Martin, still by the bulkhead.

"We have police security outside for now. Alene, if you'll show him how to access the cargo records—and by the way, Quincy, did the police give us back our missing cargo?"

"No. They say they need it."

"Not as bad as we do. I'll speak to them, after I've talked to Riel. I'll want a time to departure as soon as you know, Quincy."

Riel followed her to her cabin, silent but radiating stubborn resistance.

"Sit down," Ky said, when she had seated herself in her desk chair. He perched on the edge of the other chair. "Look, Riel—I know you're scared and I understand. You have every reason to think I'm a dangerous person to be around, and you may well be right. But before you decide to jump ship, you need to know what I know about the situation out there."

"It doesn't matter," he said.

"It may not matter, but I will feel better if you know, so hear me out, please." He relaxed a little, and Ky went on. "I was talking to Vatta headquarters about that sabotage attempt when the connection went. The assassins came into the Captains' Guild before I could try calling my father directly. Later—about six hours, we think—the consul was on the horn to Slotter Key when the entire Slotter Key ansible connection went down. It's still down. He doesn't know if it's an attack like that at Sabine, or something else entirely. From the little he was able to get before he lost the connection, it appears that either someone has a multiple grievance with ISC, Slotter Key, and Vatta, or by some chance different someones with different grievances have hit at the same time. I think the first is more likely. You were in Spaceforce, right?"

"Yes, but—but nothing like this ever happened. I never saw combat."

"But do you still have any ties to Spaceforce? Some kind of duty to get back to them?"

"No," Riel said, with emphasis. "I just—I just want to do my job, without any of this excitement."

"I hope you have that chance," Ky said. "I'll authorize payment to date, and you can go."

"Now?" He stared at her.

"Now. If you're not coming, then you don't need to attend the crew briefing, and we're going to be busy getting ready to leave. I'll contact the bank right away; they'll have your severance ready. Under the circumstances, I believe you aren't really entitled to anything but salary to date... but on the other hand there is a crisis, so I'm going to authorize a month's extra. My father can scold me later."

"That's—that's very generous. I don't know if I should—"

"Riel, don't argue. It's my decision. Now get your gear while I call the bank."

It took only moments to authorize a draft for him. Ky went to the bridge, where Lee and Sheryl were working on the departure sequence. "Destination still Leonora, Captain?"

"I'm not sure. Set us up for that, Sheryl; it's days to the jump point anyway, if I change my mind. Lee, what have you got on departure clearance?"

"Anytime, basically. They like a half hour's notice, is all. It's not exactly a busy station."

"Riel should be offship by then." The sooner they were out in space, the better. She called down to Quincy. "What's our status?"

"We've been on standby since yesterday, Captain. We're ready to go, and, yes, before you ask, fully provisioned."

"Good. I'll contact the station authorities. Have Beeah check to be sure when Riel has cleared the ship, would you?"

"He shouldn't be leaving," Quincy said. "Your father trusted him—"

"At this point, I don't," Ky said. "I don't need an unwilling pilot." Quincy sniffed audibly. "Just have Beeah make sure he's gone."

"All right."

Getting departure clearance from the stationmaster was as quick as Ky had hoped; clearly the local authorities would be glad to see the last of *Gary Tobai*. Ky instructed Crown & Spears to forward her balance to her account at Lastway. Leonora was only a stopover; she shouldn't need much money there. She tried again to reach her father from the ship's secured com desk. CONTACT UNAVAILABLE was all she could get, using any of his numbers.

Then *Gary Tobai* uncoupled from dockside; the station seals closed and vented the little airspace remaining around the ship. Lee backed them out smoothly; the insystem drive spun up normally, and she was once more in command of her own ship in space.

CHAPTER FOUR

"Now that we're safely back in space," Ky said to the assembled crew, "you need to know the latest information. You know about the attempted sabotage of this ship, and the attack on me personally."

"Is it because of the Sabine affair?" Quincy asked.

"I don't think so," Ky said. "Not now. Too much is happening. The Slotter Key ansible isn't functioning—that happened sometime yesterday. I was in contact with Vatta headquarters, and that signal was also cut off, but hours earlier, before the assassins attacked. I don't know why Vatta would be a target, but apparently we are."

"What can we do?" asked Mitt.

"The first thing we need to do is figure out what the situation is," Ky said. "Right now we don't know if Slotter Key's ansible platforms were blown, or if there's another reason their ansible's offline. We don't know enough to make a plan. But we do know there's danger, and being a moving target will make it harder for our enemies to hit us."

"Move fast, stay alert," Martin said. The others looked at him. "Makes sense, Captain," he said.

"Our stated itinerary is Belinta to Leonora to Lastway," Ky said. "But we have supplies enough to go straight to Lastway—"

"Why go to Lastway at all?" Quincy asked. "Why not head back to Slotter Key, find out what's really going on?"

"I'd rather stay out of systems with no working ansibles," Ky said. "We've been in that situation before. Not good.

Lastway's remote enough, out on the fringe...I'm betting that it'll have ansible function even if others are shut down. It's also a high-volume system, plenty of traffic. That could bring us trouble, but it can also bring us news and allies. From there we can hop back to Leonora with their cargo if things settle down."

"What kind of internal security scans does this ship have?" Martin asked.

"Just the usual for civilian tradeships," Ky said. "Some of it's down, too, thanks to the mutiny at Sabine. Video and audio to each compartment, mostly for communication. Why?"

"Someone tried to put explosives aboard—I'd like to be sure nothing else came aboard. No offense intended to your crew, but just in case."

"Good idea," Ky said. "You mean check out compartments personally?"

"That, and with some of the kit I brought along." He patted his tunic.

Ky thought of asking where he'd gotten whatever it was, and decided now was not the time. "Go ahead, then," she said. "Cargo's secure; I'll take the other sections' reports while you learn where things are."

"Yes, ma'am," he said; his arm twitched in what would, Ky knew, have been a salute.

Mitt was halfway through giving his report when muffled thumps made them all look up. The intercom clicked, and Martin's voice said, "Intruder, cargo hold two. In custody. Request orders."

"I'm on my way," Ky said. "Mitt, Beeah, come with me."

Just inside the open hatch of cargo hold 2, Martin stood guard over a prone figure in rumpled green tunic and kilt whose ankles and wrists had been trussed up with elastic cargo binders. "If you can take charge of him," Martin said, "I'll keep looking for any others."

"Mitt, you stay with him; Beeah, be ready in case Martin needs you."

It took several hours for Martin to be confident that no

other stowaways were hidden away. "And I'm still not one hundred percent sure," he said. "Just mostly sure."

By this time, Ky had looked over their prisoner, an unprepossessing youngish man with straggly hair and at least a day's growth of beard. He had a darkening bruise on one cheekbone. From his clothes, he was a Belinta native, but that was all she could tell.

Martin yanked the man up and propped him against one of the shipping containers. "Give me one good reason why I shouldn't space you!"

The prisoner's eyes shifted to Ky's face. "Please! I didn't do anything! Don't let 'im kill me."

"Didn't do anything?" Ky said. "You stowed away on my ship. What were you up to? Planting more explosives?"

"No! I swear! Nothing like that."

"What's your name, boy?" Martin asked.

"Jim. Jim Hakusar. And I'm not a boy—"

"Really." In that one word, Ky heard a tone that had turned many a raw recruit into a soldier. Martin turned to her. "Captain, this stowaway claims to be an adult, which means he's legally yours; it's up to you. I'll be glad to get rid of him for you."

"No! No, please! I—I can do things. I'll—I can work for you. That's all I wanted, was a chance—"

"You mean you wanted to be crew?"

"Yes . . . anything to get off Belinta. I can do a lot of things, really I can."

"Like what?" Martin asked.

"Well, I . . . I can build things. You know, like sheds and fences and that." Mitt gave a choked laugh; Ky fought down her own laughter. "And I can take care of critters, y'know. Carry feed and clean up . . ." His voice trailed away as he looked around the cargo hold and its obvious lack of wooden sheds, fences, or livestock. "I thought . . . I heard . . . ships grow their own food, right, and that means crops and things and I know how to plant and hoe and—"

"Large ships," Mitt said. "Large ships grow some of their

food in hydroponic gardens. We grow algae in tanks. We don't use hoes."

"But this ship is big . . . I saw it on the vidscreen. It's . . . it's lots bigger than our house back home; it had room in it for all those tractors and things." He looked around at the cargo hold. "I mean, look at it. It's huge."

"I'm afraid—" Ky began, but he interrupted.

"Please, lady! Please let me work. I'll work hard, I promise."

"That's the captain," Martin said, with emphasis. "You say *ma'am* to her."

"Please . . . ma'am . . ."

Why did it always happen to her? She could just hear what Quincy would say. But Martin's gaze was direct, steadying.

"If there's no evidence he was trying to sabotage the ship, I have no reason to space him," Ky said. "That'll be your responsibility, Martin—find out. Meanwhile, we'll confine him—" And where would they confine him? And could he do anything at all useful, or would he be just another mouth to feed?

"I'll take care of him, ma'am," Martin said. "Find out what he's done, what he can do, give him something useful to do." He reached over and unhooked the cargo ties, then pulled the prisoner to his feet. "Now you listen to me, boy. The captain's said you live—for now. But you're under my orders, understand?"

"I—" The prisoner looked at Ky. "Don't let him hurt me! I'll do anything you say."

"What I say is, do what he tells you. And Martin—the ship comes first."

"Yes, ma'am." Ky turned away, prepared to ignore whatever Martin did, but his stentorian roar almost made her jump. *"Stand up straight, you!"* She clamped her jaw on a giggle. She *had* jumped when MacRobert first roared at their cadet class. She knew within a centimeter what that young man was going to be feeling in the next few hours, and for the first time since she had left, memory of the Academy lightened her heart instead of saddening her.

* * *

By third shift, Ky felt that the ship was running smoothly. With the help of the rest of the crew, Martin had finished searching the ship to his satisfaction and was sure that no more stowaways were aboard; nor was there any explosive device. The young man had spent hours scrubbing the decks and finally, after a modest meal, had been locked into a closet with a mattress, pillow, and blanket.

"He'll be a challenge," Martin reported, with the satisfied tone of someone for whom a challenge was welcome. "Not born on Belinta, but his family moved there when he was a toddler. Poor colonists, out on the frontier. I know the type, ma'am. Brogglers, we call 'em back home, the kind that live off trapping and frog sticking and the like. Thing is, they can make passable workers if you polish 'em up. He can shoot, he tells me. We'll see about that later."

"If it saves me scrubbing things," Alene said, propping her elbows on the table, "I'm all for him."

"Oh, he'll scrub," Martin said. "It's about all he can do, at this point. Little enough education, and I doubt he paid much attention to the schooling available."

"We'll do something about that," Ky said. "If he's going to be in my crew, he's got to be certified." She looked around at the others who'd gathered in the rec area. "I know—there's all kinds of trouble going on. But precisely because of that, we need qualified people aboard, not just pot scrubbers. I want him educated at least to basic space-crew level."

"We can try," Quincy said.

"With all the expertise on this ship, we can do more than try," Ky said.

The passage out began smoothly enough. Gordon Martin kept their intruder busy two shifts of the day, with four hours of schooling worked in. Martin seemed to get along well with the rest of the crew, too. The other men joined him for physical training; Ky, who maintained her own training program, found that the women were joining her—not all of them at each session, but even Sheryl, who had claimed to hate exercise, was now using the machines every other day. Ky shared piloting watch-and-watch with Lee. She worried about every blip on the scans, half convinced that marauders were lurking, ready to take out the ship. Each one turned out to be harmless: the Pavrati ship edging in toward Belinta Station, the Belinta ore haulers and service vehicles.

At closest approach, four days out, *Gary Tobai* and the Pavrati ship passed each other. Ky made a courtesy call to the other ship.

"You might as well skip Leonora," the Pavrati captain told her. "They're not letting anyone in. We were coming in from Darttin, headed this way, and they chased us right back out as soon as we'd cleared jump."

"What—why?"

"Some kind of communications problem, and they're convinced something like Sabine will happen to them if they let outsiders into the system."

"They didn't say what?"

"They didn't say anything but *Go away and tell everyone else to leave us alone.* System closed indefinitely, they said. That was three weeks back; we were set up wrong for a direct vector here and had to use an intermediate jump point. They have some hot defensive ships, let me tell you, and acted like they'd just as soon blow us as let us go. But go if you want to—I'm just giving a friendly warning."

"Thanks," Ky said. "I appreciate it. Belinta's still open, as far as I know, but if you're headed for Slotter Key you may run into trouble. Ansibles down, apparently."

The Pavrati captain muttered something Ky was just as glad she couldn't hear. "Damn pirates," he said then. "Or whoever's doing this. It'll be the ruin of trade. We need supplies; I was going to restock at Leonora, but I guess we'll be satisfied with Belinta cabbage."

When she'd signed off, Ky said, "Sheryl—make our course for Lastway. Let me know how fast we can make it, too."

* * *

"This is a fine mess," Gerard Avondetta Vatta said. He hurt all over and he looked as bad as he felt—he could see that in the faces around him, and he had no time to deal with his pain or his grief at the many losses. Or to worry about his youngest child, who had just survived a nearly disastrous first voyage. He had to think of the future, what could be salvaged from the bleak reality of loss.

"It is a disgrace." Gracie Lane Vatta, inimitable and invincible, sat bolt upright in her seat. "I cannot imagine what the government is thinking of, to let such things happen."

A question Gerard didn't want to consider yet was just how much the government had been involved. Or part of the government. Or what the disasters still falling on Vatta heads meant to the part of the government he had thought he influenced.

"How's the roll call going?" he asked his brother's widow, Helen Stamarkos Vatta. He liked Helen; he respected her abilities, but he could still hardly believe that Stavros was gone, that he would never have that steadying hand on his arm again.

"Two hundred nineteen responses," Helen said. The dark rings around her eyes were the only sign of grief; those, and the mourning band she wore around her hair. She had lost her husband, her elder daughter, a son. "We know of thirty-seven deaths."

But there would be more deaths, of that he was sure. The ones he knew were bad enough. His wife, his son, the household staff, the men and women in the office building.

He pushed the memories away. Myris was dead, drowned in the midst of a fireball, her skull crushed by some piece of debris. San was dead, with all but two in the office building. And he still had responsibilities, work to do that could not wait for him to recover either physically—from the burns and broken bones—or emotionally.

The remaining Vatta family members on Slotter Key were

all present, crammed into the storm bunker under a tik warehouse now a pile of twisted blackened steel overhead. It was the safest place he could think of, but his skin crawled at the thought that someone else might know of it, and even now might be about to blow them all away.

"What about communications?" he asked.

"The ansible message bins are stuffed," Helen said. "Timmis Hollander"—the local ISC manager; Gerard knew him well—"doesn't know why, he claims. I suspect whatever the cause, it's affecting more than Slotter Key. This list is just the ones who got through before—" She looked at her list. "—before 1453 Capital Standard Time yesterday."

"All right." Gerard took a deep breath. It hurt; he struggled not to cough. The family physician wanted him in a hospital, but he wasn't about to sit still in so obvious a target. "We still have local communications with our remaining people on the mainland. *Perry Adair* is positioned in this system, not docked at the Slotter Key main station, and nothing has attacked the ship." He didn't have to add *yet*. "We have one remaining shuttle, now docked at the station, under local guard. We have been advised that permission to transit planetside will not be granted at this time."

"So we're stuck here," said Gracie Lane.

"Not . . . completely. Commercial carriers have agreed to transport less . . . er . . . prominent family members to the station for a hefty surcharge." They would not transport him, or Helen, or any other officer of the company.

"Does anyone know *why* we were attacked?" Gracie asked. "Other than our being rich and powerful and making a move on Pavrati last year?"

"No," Gerard said. "No definite indication has come. I suspect that it is not unconnected to the problems ISC is having, since we have long been public in our support of ISC's monopoly, and opposition to it has been growing for the past few decades."

"Is it because Kylara got involved with those pirates in the

Sabine mess?" she asked, with an unerring instinct for the one thing he did not want to think or talk about.

"She did not *get involved,* as you put it," he said. "She had no choice—"

Gracie sniffed. "She doesn't see choices, that girl. She sees openings." Then she grinned. "Not a bad way to fight a war, actually."

Gerard blinked. He remembered suddenly that the scrawny, pestiferous old woman, the bane of the family in some ways, creator of the least edible but most valuable fruitcakes in the universe, was enough older that she had been in the last war. He wasn't sure as what, but he remembered his father saying something . . . he queried his implant and there it was, her military file. Gracie? Behind the lines? Somehow he had not connected her expertise in surveillance and information collecting—suitable civilian activities for a nosy old lady—with their military equivalents.

"Well, don't stare like that," she said, misreading the cause of that stare. "It is a war, isn't it? We have an enemy, whether we knew it or not. They killed our people, attacked our business and our homes, broke our line of communication. Did it fairly well, you have to give them that . . . we certainly weren't prepared. But now—it's a war, and we'd better win it. I do not intend to spend the rest of my days sitting in some smelly, stuffy bunker under the wreck of a tik processing plant."

"I . . . hadn't thought of it as war, Gracie," Gerard said. "I mean . . . of course it was an attack—is an attack—but wars are for . . . for governments."

"War is war," Gracie said. "And our government is doing damn-all about it. Just as well young Ky had those years in the Academy, and just as well she didn't graduate. She couldn't help us then."

"She can't help us now," Gerard said. "If she's even still alive." He wanted to pray that she was, but he had no prayers to speak, not after losing Myris, San, Stavros, the others . . .

"We'll see," Gracie said. "I will say, she's not an idiot."

That was a concession, considering how she'd spoken of

Ky before. Gerard cleared his throat with difficulty, and went on with what he thought the agenda should be.

"The point is, what we have left of Vatta Enterprises is now in serious trouble. Vatta Transport in space is out of communication, except for *Perry Adair*. Insurance reimbursements on our Slotter Key planetary assets—land, improvements, movable property—will have to be used to cover contractual obligations. If we're lucky, if they actually pay out in a reasonable amount of time, it won't exceed contractual obligations. Out of system—as of our last incoming data burst—we have lost insurance coverage on our ships, and as a result we have lost contracts. And as you know, we had purchased fifteen new hulls in the last four years . . . well, now those loans are being called in. Ordinarily, we would be able to cover that. Now . . . we can't."

"So . . . you're talking bankruptcy?" Gracie asked.

"I'm talking ruin," Gerard said. "You talk about war, and winning . . . Gracie, we have nothing to fight with. We have no money. We have no credit. We have no capital assets with which to make money."

"Nonsense! We have Vatta ingenuity, Vatta drive—"

"We don't even know if we have Vattas, other than ourselves," Gerard said. He pinched the bridge of his nose. "My best estimate, prior to this, is that we've lost eighteen percent of our interstellar tonnage—but if we can't get insurance, and no one trusts us with cargo, that's eighty-two percent useless and expensive junk. Can we sell the ships? Certainly, at a loss, to our competitors . . . but only if we regain communications with their captains. We don't have any procedures whereby captains can sell Vatta-owned ships on their own responsibility. And more—the Slotter Key government is distancing itself from our problems, just when we need it. There have been mutters in the Circle that we brought trouble here by being so obvious a target. We have been informed that protecting Vatta interests is a drain on taxpayer resources."

"We aren't nearly as conspicuous as some I could name," Gracie said. "President Varthos—"

"Yes, I agree," Gerard said, cutting off what he was sure was her usual rant about the President and his family. He himself thought the pink shellstone presidential palace was a bit overdone, but quite attractive in detail. "But the point is that we were attacked and they weren't, and they don't want to give us the kind of protection we want—and need—for fear of becoming targets themselves. I've tried pointing out that we are also taxpayers, but right now we aren't likely to be major contributors to anyone's campaign budget."

"He's been got at," Gracie said.

"Possibly, but it will do no good to say so." Gerard pinched his nose again. Gracie was so talented at giving headaches—he wished he could sic her on whoever their enemy was. "Here's what we have to decide. Our private funds are still intact, so far as I know. Banks on Slotter Key haven't failed, and though there may be problems related to the failure of the financial ansibles, I'm assured that my own accounts, for instance, are available. We here can choose to put our own money back into the company and try to keep Vatta afloat, at least here, or we can take our money and . . . and run, not to put too fine a point on it."

"How much would we need?" Helen asked.

"I—I'm not entirely sure," Gerard said. He hated saying that; as CFO, he should be able to give precise figures. But his office, like his home, was a smoking hole in the ground, and he was finding it increasingly hard to think clearly. "More than I have myself, I know that. But I wanted to determine if you were willing, first—"

"I am," came a voice from the corner. Gerard had almost forgotten Stella Vatta Constantin, Helen and Stavros' younger daughter. The others turned toward her. "Don't stare like that," she said. "I screwed up once . . . just once . . . and you all thought of me as that idiot Stella from then on, right?"

"It's not that—" Gerard began. Stella interrupted.

"Yes, Uncle Ger, it is. Just as you all thought of Ky as the gullible one. The thing is, I care about this family as much as anyone else. More than some. And I think Ky has more sense than you realize. I'm willing to bet my last credit on Vatta. How about the rest of you?"

"Some of us have families . . ." That was Vasil Turolev, whose Vatta wife and children had survived.

"Some of you are lucky," Stella said, before Gerard could get his jaw unlocked. "So are you going to kick your luck in the teeth and run away?"

"I have to think about them," Vasil said. "What will they live on if I do, and it fails?" Vasil's wife shook his arm and muttered in his ear. When he looked away, she spoke up.

"I'll put in mine," she said. "Celia Vatta."

"Mine, of course," said Gracie. "Vatta will survive."

"I certainly hope so," Gerard said. He did not feel confident at all, and the pain clouded his vision; the stimulant dose he'd talked the doctor into was wearing off. "And we need to decide how to distribute the database we have . . ." His head rolled sideways; he couldn't point to his implant without moving an arm, which took too much effort. "Stav's was destroyed; I think mine should be duplicated . . . find Ky . . . tell her . . ." He could not keep his eyes open; the post-stim crash rolled over him, sucked him into darkness.

"Stella, dear, I need to talk to you . . ." Gracie's voice stabbed his ears even as he drifted off. By the time she lifted his cranial flap and removed his implant, slipping it into the protective case with its nutrient bath, he was unconscious. He did not hear the family disperse, the low-voiced decision to bring a medical team here rather than move him. He did not regain consciousness before the emergency surgery, before his death.

Gracie Lane Vatta moved about the kitchen, mixing dried and candied fruits, nuts, flour, sugar in a large bowl, while the kitchen's owner greased and floured deep pans.

"I can't believe you're making fruitcake now!" Stella Vatta Constantin said. The other woman, who had been introduced to her as Louise, glanced up and then continued her work. "People have died, others are dying, and—"

"Stella, I appreciate your sentiments, but if you make me forget the recipe these will be even viler than usual. Put that"—she nodded at the sealed implant case that held Gerard Vatta's implant—"in one of those insulated bags."

"You are not going to put it in a fruitcake and bake it! It'll destroy it!"

"No, it won't. I've done this before. There's dual protection; the implant case itself is insulated, and the bag will give it another thirty minutes at baking temperatures." Gracie looked blank, then began dumping spices into the batter. "The thing about fruitcake, Stella, is that no one thinks it's anything but fruitcake. An aunt's fruitcake is one of the most innocuous substances in the universe. It fairly reeks of family duty, stuffy traditions. You know about cover. How else could someone carry a highly valuable implant—"

"You're taking it somewhere?"

"No, my dear. You are." She glanced at the other woman. "Louise, could I trouble you to fetch the bottle of rum that's in the guest room, the one I sent Pauli out for earlier?"

"Of course, ma'am." Louise left the kitchen. Gracie moved closer to Stella.

"Stella, we can't have just one copy of the command database. I've got one now; I'm not giving you one in case . . . in case someone tries to pry into yours. This is for Ky. I'm sure you can find her. She was going to Lastway as a final destination after Belinta. She'll end up there sometime. But you won't go directly there. I've got a courier drop for you to get to ISC headquarters. You'll leave tomorrow morning, and you'll travel as you have before. Legal representative, not family."

"Right," Stella said. "With a fruitcake."

"With several fruitcakes. All reeking of rum." Gracie finished stirring the batter. "I know I forgot something . . ."

"Vanilla?" Stella asked.

"Vanilla . . . no . . . not in the recipe. Something Gerry said, back at the house. Too much too fast . . . I should've been recording . . ." She shook her head. "I hate age. Wisdom—assuming you gain any—is not enough to trade for the youthful ability to stay up two days running and still remember things. Here, put the implant case into this pan; balance it on these little pins. And this little packet in the other. And for goodness' sake, remember which is which." The batter slumped into the circular pan, then the rectangular one, filling them, hiding the contents as Gracie nudged it around with a spatula. "Now—into the oven with them."

Stella put the cake pans into the oven just as Louise returned with the bottle of rum. The three of them sat around the table until the cakes were done and cooling on racks.

"Better get to bed, Stella," Gracie said. She fought off her own exhaustion. She had things to say to Louise, things to do, secrets still to keep, even from Stella. The girl—woman now—had come a long way. She had proved herself before now. And she was the only one who might—*might*—be able to do what Gracie considered essential.

In the predawn dark, Stella came back into the kitchen, dressed in the sober business suit that fit her cover story, her golden hair dulled with a rinse and slicked back into an unbecoming knot. Nothing could obscure her cheekbones, but makeup subtly denied the obvious beauty, masking the flawless skin with vague blotchiness. Gracie looked her over carefully. "Good job, my dear," she said at last.

"Will you be all right, Aunt Grace?" Stella asked.

"Me?" Grace said. She allowed her smile to convey her intent. "Oh, yes, Stella, I will be all right. Very much so."

Stella's expression shifted, but she had been well trained; she did not even look at Louise as she said, "Do take care, Aunt Grace; I'll miss you."

"And here are your fruitcakes, Stella."

"Aunt Grace, I don't really need—"

"Of course you do." Grace handed her the sack. "And there's a little something in there for you, too, Stella." A packet of diamonds, that most useful portable currency.

Stella already carried some, in the pocketed camisole under her blouse, but it was impossible to have too many diamonds. "Lunch for your journey."

"Thank you, Aunt Grace," Stella said, and hugged her lightly. Then she was gone, and Grace, already packed, left the house by another entrance, to meet another driver. En route to her next destination, she stopped briefly to make a call from a shielded site. Just before dawn was a fine time to wake a traitor, to whisper into his ear, "You will regret this . . ."

Gammis Turek read the reports with satisfaction. They had calculated correctly: they had beheaded Vatta Enterprises, and chopped off more than enough limbs. The Slotter Key government had been cooperative in rendering no more aid. What was left of Vatta would be harmless, the disconnected twitching limbs of what had been a formidable creature. They had missed the daughter, but she was a minor target anyway, and she was on a small, slow, unarmed ship. If he wanted her later, he could take her.

He placed the call to the Slotter Key presidential palace, aware that the very existence of the call would puzzle and alarm them.

"You were wise to take my advice," he said without preamble. "You see how fortunately it turned out."

"What I see is a big mess," the voice replied. It did not sound nearly so cowed and compliant as he expected. Gammis scowled.

"It is not your mess," he said. "It is Vatta's mess, and they are now helpless to cause us—me or you—any problems."

"I'm not so sure of that," the voice said.

Cowards. Timid sheep. Gammis chuckled indulgently. "Their senior officers are all dead. Their headquarters is destroyed. Some of their largest and most profitable ships. They cannot get insurance; their accounts are frozen. What is the problem, then?"

"You missed one."

"Missed one? I don't think so. My intelligence reports that their CEO and CFO are both dead, and the entire second level of vice presidents—"

"You missed the old lady. She knows someone got to the government—"

Gammis laughed aloud this time. "Everyone knows someone got to the government. What of it? And what old lady? We have no profiles on old ladies—they can complain all they like."

"She called me."

"Oh, for—grow a spine, man. An old lady, some old dowager Vatta, without strength of arms or resources . . . she can whine all she wants. She is toothless." Gammis closed the connection, shaking his head at the timidity of grounder politicians.

CHAPTER FIVE

During the passage to Lastway, the crew seemed to adjust to the new situation and crewmembers, though not without some friction.

"He's so . . . so military," Quincy said to Ky some three days into the passage. "Everything spit and polish, all the time." Ky didn't have to ask for a name: Gordon Martin, of course. "I think he's too hard on that boy," Quincy continued. *That boy* being Jim Hakusar, who claimed to be twenty-three. "Yesterday he had him down on his hands and knees for hours, scrubbing, just because he had forgotten to shower."

"It won't hurt him," Ky said. "Are you getting soft on Jim?"

"Not soft, no. I agree he needs training. But Martin—"

"He is military, Quincy, just out. It's been his career. You can't expect him to change overnight, and frankly I'm more comfortable having him in charge of Jim than if I had to supervise him." Ky stretched. "Is he bothering you any other way? Martin, I mean?"

Quincy shook her head. "Not really. He doesn't want us to use his given name—that's kind of odd, we're all used to first names—but he's not ordering the rest of us around or anything."

"Do you think Jim will ever make a spacer? Is he doing well in his studies?"

"Maybe, and not really. Martin thinks he's not applying himself; I'm beginning to wonder if he has one of those learning things. I was asking him about his schooling and it didn't sound like the Belinta primaries had any of the corrective software we use."

"Do we have any of that kind of thing aboard?" The crew had a library for continuing education.

"I'll look," Quincy said. "Sorry—I hadn't thought to check that out."

"If we do, see if it'll help him," Ky said. "I saw those original test scores—he's about as far down the scale as you can go. If he's going to be with us, he needs to be more than a drudge."

Alene had accepted Martin as the new cargomaster—she'd already told Ky she didn't really want the job herself—but she, too, found him rigid at times. "He wants a full inspection every day," she said. "Gary never did that, and he had years of experience."

"He might do it now, under these circumstances," Ky said. "Martin's got the background in security as well as supply; he wants to keep us safe."

"I'm all for safe," Alene said. "And I don't mind the extra work, really. With Jim doing most of the scut work, there's little enough for a cargo second to do en route. It's just . . . his manner, I guess."

"Is he rude?"

"No. But I can see him stopping himself from ordering me around the way he does Jim."

"Give him time," Ky said. "At least he's trying to stop himself."

As for the stowaway, Ky had little to do with him. She noticed that his shaggy hair had changed to a short bristle, and his face was always smooth, his slouching posture more upright, his expression less foolish and more alert. He always seemed to be busy; the galley and toilets gleamed, the decks were always swept. Every five days, she asked Martin for a progress report, and learned that "the recruit" was making progress, albeit slowly.

"It'd go faster in a real basic training course," Martin said. He sat upright, as always, and Ky found herself resisting the urge to sit at attention herself. "Here on the ship, with no other recruits to measure himself against, he can fool himself, think he's working as hard as he can. You remember that yourself, I expect, from your Academy days."

"Indeed yes," Ky said. Competition, as well as the staff, had fueled much of her hard work.

"And I do realize we're civilians, not military. It's just that boys like this need the discipline, or they'll never give up their evasions. They always have excuses; they always have tricks to avoid the work. They're not bad, exactly, but they're thick-skinned as well as thickheaded. That learning software your chief engineer found is helping, though."

"If you can make a decent, competent spacer out of him, that will satisfy me," Ky said. "Just don't break anything we need later."

Martin laughed. "I'll take care of him. Without breakage, I promise you. Another thing, though." No laughter now; his expression hardened again. "We need to consider security issues for when we dock somewhere. I've been through the procedures manual you've got, and it's totally inadequate. We're lucky we didn't have an entire crew of stowaways and a kiloton of weaponry aboard. This thing of trusting local police—"

"I'm sure you already have ideas on that," Ky said. "Do you have them ready to present?"

"As a matter of fact—" He brought out several large sheets of hardcopy. "I could put this on a cube, if you want, but sometimes it's easier to see in this format. We can cobble together some of our existing equipment for part of it, but we're going to need better sensors, and many more of them."

Ky looked at the diagrams. "You're talking military-grade coverage, aren't you?"

He nodded. "From the little we know, things are coming unstuck in several places, and we may come out of FTL in a war zone. Civvie stuff to ward off the casual sneak thief just won't do. Now, I've looked into the cargo manifests—that stuff we can't deliver to Leonora includes components we could turn into the basic net I'm talking about."

"We can't breach cargo seals," Ky said. "It's against policy, not to mention law."

He grimaced. "Policy . . . is for the last war but one, ma'am. Leonora won't let us deliver, didn't you say? So their cargo's forfeit, isn't it?"

"Not exactly," Ky said. "In something like this, it would go before a magistrate to determine whether we could sell the cargo and put the money in escrow for the original consignors, or whether we could sell the cargo and keep the profit. Nothing in the law as I understand it allows us to break the seals and use the cargo for our own purposes."

"We're not going to be hauled away to jail if we're in pieces because someone got to the ship," Martin said.

"True, but—how much can you do without using the Leonora cargo?"

"Depends on what resources you authorize from engineering stores."

"Let's look at this again," Ky said, leaning over the diagram. "Hm. Motion sensors, infrared—"

"Ma'am, I know you have some military training, but how much was specific to security concerns?"

"Not much," Ky said. "I couldn't help noticing how different it was, when we were taken to training venues, but we didn't have it in class. That was coming later, once we were commissioned, they said."

"Well, here's the short and dirty. To keep a ship like this, and a crew this size, reasonably safe in the kind of situation we're talking about, you need three things. Hardware—the sensors deployed in appropriate locations. Software set up to interpret input correctly. And procedures that everyone follows. I don't mean any insult by it, but this is not a military crew. Your people aren't used to discipline, other than doing their jobs, isn't that right?"

"Right," Ky said.

"I've been paying attention, listening to them talk about how they spend their time when a ship's in dock. They walk in and out, go visit a station bar or café, go run errands, do some shopping—"

"Yes, that's normal," Ky agreed. "And?"

"Well, ma'am, seems to me normal just went out the door and didn't look back. Somebody's trying to kill you and destroy your ship. That means we—you—can't be having any of that casual strolling around. I can make up some of the deficiencies with hardware and software—if I get enough of it—but you also need to set up procedures for how people behave on the next place we dock."

"Procedures restricting their movements, you mean."

"Movement, communications, everything. It's not going to be easy; they'll think they're being careful when they're leaving holes in your security I could walk a whole platoon through."

"If that's the hardest job, I think we should start with that part," Ky said.

"What weapons do you have aboard?"

"Mehar's two pistol bows and some knives," Ky said. "And whatever that is you carry."

"This?" He opened his tunic and pulled out a matte-black handgun, laying it on the table without, Ky noted, ever allowing the muzzle to point toward her. "Eleven millimeter, Standard Arms; manufactured on Slotter Key under license from Bascome. Same as our utility issue, but this one's custom." He cocked his head at her. "You don't have a weapon? I expected you would."

"I was rushed off Slotter Key in a hurry," Ky said. "At the time, a weapon was the last thing in my mind. After Sabine, though—"

"I heard you killed two of them," Martin said. "Mind telling me how you did it without a gun?"

"Crossbow," Ky said. "Mehar's pistol bow, in fact. The

mutineers had knives, no firearms; the mercs had made sure of that."

"Ah. Not a bad ship weapon, a bow. Not enough penetrance to damage a hull or even a bulkhead. But I would recommend, ma'am, that you arm yourself as soon as you can."

"Lastway's bound to have weapons shops," Ky said.

"I could pick up something for you," he offered. "Safer for you."

"No, thanks. If I'm going to shoot it, I want to choose it," Ky said. His brows went up, and she went on. "I did learn to shoot, you know. As a girl back home, as well as Academy training. Now, if you'll draft some procedures for me, we can go over them and start training the crew."

"Right away, ma'am. And given the lack of arms, I think I'll add some basics in unarmed fighting techniques. Some of them might get it." He nodded and left the compartment.

Down transition at Lastway went smoothly enough; Sheryl had dropped them in farther from the planet than usual, with as little relative vee as possible. Scan cleared in a few minutes, and Ky checked the Lastway ansibles, querying for "current sectorwide commercial news." She didn't expect much, but a large download came into the bin a half hour later.

COMMUNICATIONS BLOCKAGE STILL THREATENS COMMERCE was one headline. According to that article, ansibles had gone down in a number of systems within a few hours, disrupting not only communications but also trade. Several planets—Leonora was listed—had closed their systems to outside traffic. ISC had begun repairs at both the hub and periphery of its systems simultaneously, and Lastway now had unimpeded communications with two other systems. ISC wasn't saying what it had found, just that "work is in progress to restore clear, reliable communication as quickly as possible." Slotter Key was one of the systems listed as "still not open," as were Belinta and Leonora.

Ky flicked through the list, and the next headline stopped

her breath in her chest. VATTA EMPIRE FALLS. She scrolled down.

The quadrant's second largest interstellar shipper, based on Slotter Key, has suffered a series of devastating attacks on its ships and personnel. Disaster has followed even onto their home planet, with explosions in warehouses and tik processing plants, as well as the deaths of many family members in explosions at the family compound on Corleigh. Bankruptcy seems imminent, as customers flee the ill-fated line...

Ky stared at that a long moment. Corleigh bombed? The house she'd grown up in... that garden, that pool, the cool tiled terraces, the comfortable rooms... gone? Her family... her busy, bustling mother? Her brothers, her cousins, her *father*?

It couldn't be. They couldn't be dead. It had to be a mistake. It made no sense anyway. Why would anyone attack Vatta like that? They had no enemies—commercial rivals, but not enemies. Her breath came short. She tried to find out more, but the writer preferred to speculate on the effect of Vatta's disintegration on the price of shipping and the fortunes of rival firms.

Two others stories mentioned attacks on Vatta Transport, one from Highdare, a system near the sector hub, and one from ISC sources. More ships had been attacked onstation, and two Vatta ships were overdue at their next port. Insurance carriers had dropped Vatta as too risky; shippers were avoiding Vatta because of the lack of insurance. ISC issued a statement disclaiming responsibility for the attacks on Vatta:

We are quite sure that the involvement of a Vatta ship in the situation of Sabine System is not related to these attacks... ISC's relationship with Vatta Enterprises, Vatta Transport, and individuals of the Vatta family has been strictly business and no closer than our relationship with other customers.

Ky stared at that. So someone else had thought this might result from her actions in the Sabine System? And then had discarded that idea? Were they right, or were her fears right? Was it her fault? For a moment, the invented mental images of destruction she hadn't seen swamped her mind... the house burning, the office exploding, the warehouses and processing plants aflame... family members whose faces she would never see again...

No. That wasn't going to help her get her cargo sold, her crew and ship safely in and out of Lastway space. They might be alive, some of them at least. She had to think that way; imagining the worst would paralyze her.

She scanned the rest of the download, concentrating on the here and now. She shunted prices to Martin and Alene in Cargo and Quincy in Engineering.

Two hours later, Lastway Traffic Control inquired if they were in transit or on approach.

"Approach," Ky said.

"Be advised, Vatta ships are under special advisory concern," Traffic Control said.

"Explain," Ky said.

"How long have you been in transit?" came the answer.

Ky gave the date in universal.

"Ah. So you aren't aware of the situation?"

"What situation?" Ky asked. What would they say? What would they do?

"Vatta Transport, Ltd., has been subject of some form of attack, and we have been informed that upon docking, all prior insurance coverage for Vatta hulls is canceled. Vatta personnel are considered to be at risk, and Vatta family members at special risk. Lastway Militia Services disclaims responsibility for their safety, and recommends extreme caution and additional private security—"

"Any Vatta hulls presently docked?" Ky asked.

"No. Yours is the first into our space since all this blew up." Traffic Control heaved an audible sigh. "Whatever did you people do, and who did you annoy?"

"I don't know," Ky said. "I've been in transit. What have you heard?"

"Two dozen rumors, nothing solid," Traffic Control said. "But here—if you dock here, you may have problems getting out, and you will have to pay cash—Vatta credit's down the tubes."

"If I don't dock here, I may run out of air," Ky said. "So bring me in."

"Your choice," Traffic Control said. "There's an eight-hundred-credit cash deposit on docking; Immigration Control will be there to collect it."

"Thank you," Ky said through clenched teeth. Then she called the crew together.

"What I know is all bad, but I'm sure we don't know everything," she said, then went on to describe the news. "It may be that all the other Vattas are dead. It may be that the news is all wrong and they're all alive. But for our own safety, we have to assume that there is someone—apparently a lot of someones with plenty of resources—after Vatta."

"You aren't setting foot off this ship," Quincy said.

"On the contrary, I must, to do what needs doing," Ky said. "At any rate, it would do me no good to sit here and have my crew picked off one or two at a time. I can't run this thing alone.

"But we are going to be careful. Those procedures that Martin developed, that we've been practicing—we are all going to adhere to them. No casual wandering around the station, no letting people wander into our dock space. We're going to carry taggers; we're going to put up extra security screening, the whole bit."

"What do you think you have to do that requires you to go offship?" Quincy asked.

Ky looked at her, but Quincy didn't back down. Not surprising. "To start with, I have to pay docking fees in advance, in cash. Vatta credit's been frozen. I should have a private account here, but since we don't know when the Belinta ansibles went out, I don't know if the transfer I set up before we left actually went through. I need to exchange hard goods for cash, open an account, get us back into business. None of you can do that. In addition, I need a way to defend myself," she said.

"You . . . are you talking about weapons? About arming the ship?"

"I'm not telling any of you all my thoughts," Ky said. "Not even you, Quincy. Not because I don't trust you—" Though she did not entirely trust the new crewmembers. "—but at this point the fewer people who know my plans, the fewer people can be forced to share them."

Their expressions showed that none of them had considered that possibility yet.

"You think someone might—might grab one of us? Shake us down?" Mitt asked.

"It's possible," Ky said. "We have to think of things like that, Mitt. If they'll attack corporate headquarters on Slotter Key, and kill family and crew on other stations, then a snatch isn't the least likely thing to happen, if we're unprepared. That's why we'll take precautions. Those of you with implants, make sure you keep your communications channels alive. Talk to the ship anytime you're out . . . anything, everything."

"You don't have an implant," Quincy said. "Isn't it time to use that implant your father sent you?"

"It hasn't been six months," Ky said. "In the meantime, the first trip out is going to buy me the best nonimplant personal communicator on this station. I'll wear it from then on, and when I go out I'll have both crew and—depending on what I find out in the next couple of hours—hired security as well."

"Captain, if Vatta Transport is really gone—really defunct—are you going to try to start it up again, or go independent?" Beeah asked.

"Beeah, I can't answer that one now. I don't know enough. We just fell into a war with these attacks. I don't know who the enemy is, or why the attacks happened, or how strong the enemy is, or which of our forces are left. The main thing now is to survive, gather data, get someplace from which we can move, if a move is possible."

"You ought to go back to Slotter Key," Quincy said. "Your family needs you."

"If I have a family," Ky said. Images of horror flickered through her mind, and she shoved them away. "Attacks on headquarters, warehouses, processing plants, the private terminal, the family compound... where else would my family be? And it will do no good to go to Slotter Key and be cut off from ansible communication. What they need—if they live, if the whole corporation hasn't been bankrupted—is someone out here doing trade and showing that Vatta ships still carry cargo safely."

"But if we have no insurance, no one will ship with us."

"Not the big shippers, no. But there are always people desperate to get cargo from here to there, and willing to assume the risk themselves."

Quincy pursed her lips. "Vatta has never carried that kind of cargo."

"Oh, yes, we have. Long ago, admittedly, but it's in the family histories. Vatta wasn't always completely pure and aboveboard—no one was, in the early days after the Rift. So what we're going to do is trade and profit, along with skulking and hiding and being extremely careful."

"I don't see how we can carry the Vatta colors and be careful both," Mitt said. "I'm with Beeah—why not go independent now, change the ship's registry?"

"We can't—we're already widely known as Vatta," Ky said. "If it comes to that, we'll have to do it somewhere else, some port that is even less law-abiding than Lastway."

They stared at her in silence.

Ky spent the next two hours looking at the threat assessment she and Martin had made on the approach when she had nothing else to do. Too many question marks, too many things she could not know. The lessons from the Academy came back to her. No commander ever knew everything; the ones who thought they did were often in the worst trouble. Good commanders took what they did know and made good plans—and contingency plans—anyway.

She doodled on a blank page of her log. MISSION: what was her mission, anyway? She had no higher command, at the moment . . . surely the original mission, to sell the ship for scrap, was irrelevant at this point. Stay alive. Keep her crew alive. Keep her ship whole and functioning. Find out who was behind this. What were victory conditions?

As cadets, they'd been introduced to the concepts of tactics, strategy, grand strategy . . . but most of their time had gone into the things a junior officer might need to know. Strategy was for older, more senior, and hopefully wiser heads. Juniors succeeded insofar as they figured out ways to carry out the designs of their seniors.

Ky shook her head at that moment of nostalgia. Prepared or not, she was the person on the spot. She was senior now. It was all up to her. No use to whine that she wasn't ready or didn't know enough. Nobody was around to advise her.

Victory conditions: start with alive and free, all of them. Alive, free, with the ship. Alive, free, with the ship and crew and some prospect of making a living. And then doing something to save her remaining family members and if possible the family business. Revenge on whoever had done this would have to come later, much later, but survival itself depended on figuring out who it could be.

Paison's allies were the obvious choice . . . and if true, that meant it was her fault. If she hadn't killed Paison, they would not have attacked her family. But that made no sense. Why would pirates waste all that money and effort to attack her family when they had to know where she was? Why not just kill her?

Now was the time to find out who, and then how and why and the rest, while keeping herself and her crew alive and out of enemy hands. She looked at the locker in which she'd stowed the Vatta implant her father had sent her. It was still too soon, according to the Mackensee surgeon, to have an implant installed, but at this moment she would have liked access to the proprietary Vatta information. More important, though, was keeping it out of enemy hands—a security issue that hadn't occurred to her until this moment.

When the crew reassembled, she asked for their ideas, their threat assessments. It occurred to her, as they ran down their lists, that they were doing much better than they would have before the Sabine mess. Still, Jim seemed to have a talent for thinking up ways someone might do them damage... his list was longer than anyone else's.

Ky looked at him, when they'd all finished. "Where did you get those ideas?" she asked. He looked worried. "I'm not angry. I just wonder what else you were doing besides fixing ship engines."

"I'm not doin' it here," he muttered. "Wouldn't do anything to this ship, Captain."

"I'm glad to know it—and glad you're on our side." She looked at Alene. "First, I'm going to see if the legal firm I contacted has any final word on that Leonora cargo, then we'll list our cargo on the Exchange boards. Martin will concentrate on security issues, so you'll have to run Cargo on your own."

"Prices are volatile, Captain," Alene said. "How long d'you think it'll be before we get clearance?"

"Less than an hour after we dock, I'm hoping. Certainly by end of shift. As soon as we start selling, we start resupply. Environmental, insystem fuel, general supplies. Now: can we offload to the secure dock area without outside help?"

Alene shook her head. "I don't think so. The Leonora cargo's all palleted, too heavy to shift without a loader. We could rent a loader, I suppose... I've handled one. But who else?"

"I can," Jim said. "At least... I've used one once." With Jim, Ky thought, that could mean he'd seen someone else use one once, or he'd driven one off a dock into the water, or—possibly—he had actually driven one without incident.

"How long will it take with one loader, to clear the holds?"

"If some of the others will help with shifting and positioning, we can have the Leonora pallets off in a shift. The rest . . . you know our difficulties, Captain. Several days."

"Here's what we'll do, then. First Martin will supervise setting up our security net. Meanwhile I'll arrange loader rental, and as soon as we're cleared for it, we'll start unloading those pallets. I'd like to minimize exposure of personnel to possible . . . problems. The fewer outsiders who come aboard, and the less time anyone spends onstation, the safer we'll be."

On final approach, Lastway Station looked like what it was: a vast and complicated construction that had grown far beyond its original design to accommodate the needs of its local and transient populations. Below it, the planet's cloud-wrapped surface was invisible. Two centuries earlier, terraforming had begun on a moderately appropriate base; the information packet supplied by the station to all incoming ships described in detail the processes that continued, but Ky was far less interested in the details of biogeochemical processes than in the price of refreshment cultures for the environmental system and what she could hope to get for the cargo originally consigned to Leonora.

As Lee eased the ship nearer and nearer to the docking booms, Ky reviewed the current list of ships docked, their origins and destinations. Another had been waved off from Leonora, and she learned that the onstation legal services had already certified its cargo as undeliverable, available for resale. At least she didn't have to fight that battle on her own. She called Martin and told him that he could scavenge freely in the Leonora cargo.

"Thanks, ma'am," he said. "As it happens, those containers were right handy . . . won't take much time at all . . ." The suspicion crossed her mind that he had already taken what he wanted from them, but there was no reason to push the issue. None of the ships onstation now seemed like a pirate ready to blow her ship away, but she hadn't spotted Paison as a problem until too late. She had to assume that danger lurked here, everywhere.

Her own ship's needs ranged as usual from must-haves like refreshment cultures for the environmental tanks; to very desirable, like better longscan; to wishful thinking, like an insystem drive that would move them faster than a snail on a hot rock. At least she hadn't spent all her money on Belinta.

Lee docked neatly, and the station crew hooked up the support umbilicals. Ky found several small chores to do until she realized she was anxious about opening the hatch, then made herself go down to cargo hold 1 and do it. Martin materialized from one of the cargo hatches, and stood in front of her as the hatch opened.

Lastway Immigration Control—one unarmed and six armed—were waiting at dockside, by their expressions none too patiently. The one without weapons had two forearms on one arm, and a wrist tentacle on the back of the other wrist. Ky managed not to blink in surprise; that was a humod form she hadn't seen before. "Eight hundred, cash or trade goods to be valued by an independent assessor," said the humod. The tentacle uncurled elegantly, and the input connectors glinted.

"Trade goods," Ky said. She handed the tentacle one of Aunt Gracie's diamonds.

"Submitted for assessment," the humod said. The tentacle transferred the diamond to that hand, then removed a sealable pouch from a pocket, plucked up the diamond again, and inserted it, then sealed the pouch. "You will want a receipt."

"I will want an assessor here, at dockside," Ky said.

"You think Lastway Immigration Control is dishonest?" That with a ferocious scowl.

"I think diamonds are too easy to misplace or confuse with other diamonds," Ky said.

"I will call." Silent moments, as the humod communicated by interface; then it nodded sharply. "Yes. One expert in assessing crystals comes."

"Are you from here?" Ky asked.

Again the humod scowled. "Why ask that?"

"No insult intended, but your accent is not the same as what I heard from Traffic Control—I merely wished to know which accent is native here, to adjust my interpretation to that norm."

Its face cleared. "Ah. You have old tech implant, yes? Mine adjust by self." On input maybe, but the output wasn't. "From Vastig, I am, eight years agone taking ship away from sad family. You know Vastig?"

"No," Ky admitted.

"But such ships come there, Vatta Transport. Many ships Vatta has—or had. Someone likes Vatta not."

"True enough," Ky said. "And I don't know why—do you?"

"Not I. Others make guesses, only guesses. On Vastig we do not make guesses. We say the truth. But here comes one to assess . . ."

Ky looked around to see a man in a dressy business suit; as he came closer, she began to wonder if he, too, were a humod. One eye appeared to have a magnifier built into it, the rim sunken into the skin. When he opened his mouth to speak, his tongue was dark and heavily furred.

"Licensed assessor Grill, at your service," he said clearly enough, bowing to both the Immigration Control officer and Ky. "A crystal for assessment, yes?"

The Immigration Control officer transferred it to Grill's hand—a hand that appeared to be normal, to Ky's fascinated gaze—and Grill put it into his mouth for a long moment, then spat it back to his hand. "Carbon," he announced. "Impurities negligible to value." Now the magnifier extended, lenses telescoping from his eye. "Cut . . . Melique-cut diamond, crystalline structure excellent, flaws . . . minimal. Value for official purposes 2,443 credits." He handed it back to the Immigration Control officer, who tucked it into the sealed pouch again. "Good day," Grill said to the space between them, turned on his heel, and walked away.

"Your receipt for a credit balance of 1,643 to be set against docking and service fees," said the Immigration Control officer, handing Ky a hardcopy strip that had just extruded from his lower forearm. "Welcome to Lastway and enjoy your stay." Then he and his escort marched off.

Ky shook her head and spoke to the ship's intercom. "All clear now. I don't see the loader that should be here; I'll contact them and the security company again."

"The captain should reenter the ship," Martin said. "I'll want to get the net set out. I'll need Jim, Beeah, and Mehar."

CHAPTER SIX

Before Ky could contact the rental agency, Martin reported that the loader had arrived. He and his crew had already installed the first of the visual scans, so Ky could watch the loader grind across the dock toward the ship and listen in on the conversation with her crew.

"Sorry," the operator said. "Had to get clearance from Immigration and check your financials." The operator had a gray uniform with RENTALL EQUIPMENT in red on the front and back.

Martin held up a hand. "We will need to scan your machine."

"Fine. I get paid by the hour; don't hurry." The operator lounged in his seat.

Martin used a long-handled mirror and various other tools to check over, under, and around the loader. "Now you," he said. "Get down."

"Me? You're only renting the loader; you don't need to scan me."

"Oh, I think we do," Martin said. The man shrugged, started to climb down, and suddenly launched himself at Mehar, whipping a knife from his boot. She sidestepped neatly and thrust a short baton into his gut. He folded around it, dropping the knife. Mehar stepped back; Martin moved in, swung the man around, and clipped him smartly on the jaw. "Good job, Mehar," he said. "You're a natural at this."

"I would rather not be," Mehar said, hooking the baton back on her belt.

"Beeah, Jim—perimeter." Martin's reminder focused the

other two on the dock access. Ky watched, fascinated, as Martin secured the man's knife by scooping it into a plastic bag, then fastened his wrists and ankles with cargo cords, as he had done with Jim at first.

"Captain—"

"Yes," Ky said. "I saw that."

"You said station police didn't want to give us protection. Think they'd be interested in taking in a perp?"

"I suppose we'd better ask," Ky said. "And I'd better talk to the rental company, too."

"Threaten them," Martin advised. "They sent you a ringer or they were bent to start with."

Ky looked up the emergency numbers and called the station police, here called the Garda. "You did *what*?" was the response of the desk clerk. "You can't just hit people and tie them up."

"My crew was attacked with a knife," Ky said.

"Witnesses? Other than your own crew?"

"Recorded in video," Ky said.

"Oh. Well. We'll send someone over."

Who to call next? Getting more security on their dockside seemed more important than wrangling with the rental company. Lastway's business directory listed five security services, but only three were bonded and insured: Baritom, Maxx, and Padilla Protection. She had no clue which to pick. The stationmaster, she knew, would not be allowed to give an opinion—who else could?

ISC. They had their own security, but they must use onsite firms for personal protection sometimes, and they would surely know who to contact for dockside surveillance. Ky contacted their Lastway office and asked for the station director.

"Who's calling, please?"

To ISC, the Vatta name should still be gold-plated, Ky thought. "Captain Kylara Vatta," she began, "of the—"

"Vatta!" Then, "Just a minute . . ."

Less than a minute, and a gruff male voice barked at her.

"Who do you think you are, queen of the spaceways? Don't you realize we have better things to do than babysit some rich trader's brat?"

"I beg your pardon!"

"You Vattas are spoiled rotten," the voice went on. "Can't wait your turn like everyone else! Think you're special. Well, out here, *Captain* Vatta, we're all citizens and we don't try to cut in line. You'll take your place in the outgoing queue just like everyone else and that's final." The connection blanked.

Ky stared at the console as if it had grown actual teeth, and then called again.

"What?" said the angry voice she'd just heard.

"I wasn't trying to cut in line," Ky said. "I had a question."

"I'm not a damned information desk," he said, and cut the connection again.

Ky told herself that everyone at ISC must be under tremendous strain. She still found it hard to believe that the station manager of an obscure office like Lastway could have reason to be that angry with Vatta Transport, or any particular Vatta, but he was, and that was a fact to cope with.

Who else? She scanned the business directory, looking for familiar names. Somewhat to her surprise, Lastway Station had three branches of Hark!, the sectorwide pastry franchise: "The original Hark!, in business at this location for seventeen years..."; "Hark! #2, convenient to the financial district"; and "Hark! Light: same flavor, less filling." She doubted that they'd have much knowledge of security companies. The Captains' Guild? She contacted them.

"I'm sorry but we consider the Vatta account closed at this time," said the reception clerk as soon as she gave her name. "Any services would be on a cash basis only."

"I'm not planning to stay there," Ky said. "I just had a question."

"A question?" He sounded as if he'd never heard of asking a question. "What about, then?"

"What private security companies onstation would you recommend?"

"The station business directory has a list."

"I know that, but only three are bonded. What services have other captains found reliable?"

"I'm afraid, under the circumstances, that I can't take the liability risk of recommending anything in that line. Now if you wanted a recommendation for a good restaurant—"

"Oh, fine," Ky said. The clerk went on, completely missing her tone.

"Julian's is very nice—they grow their own fresh vegetables, and they have a cultivar of synthibeef that's extremely good. Or, if you prefer seafood, there's Fish Heaven. All local produce—"

"Thank you," Ky said. "That's very nice. I don't suppose you have any idea where I can purchase ordnance?"

"Ordnance?" The clerk's voice squeaked. "You mean like . . . er . . . weapons?"

"Exactly," Ky said. It was a forlorn hope, but scaring him looked like the only fun she was going to have.

"Well . . . there's always the MilMartExchange, over on Hub Four."

"Thank you," Ky said again. "Are they in the business directory?"

"Yes, Captain. Under HEAVY EQUIPMENT NEW AND USED."

"You've been most helpful," Ky said, her good humor restored. Heavy equipment new and used, huh? Was this why the Sabines had been so suspicious of her "farm equipment" on the manifest?

She looked at the directory again, shrugged, and called Baritom Security Services because it came first on the list. Baritom Security Services put her on hold long enough to be annoying; then a senior sales representative came on. "You can understand that we have concerns about any assignment with a Vatta family member at this time—with Vatta accounts frozen—"

"Hard goods," Ky said. "Acceptable to Immigration Control."

"Oh. Well . . . the liability risk—"

"I am willing to waive liability where no misconduct by your employees is involved," Ky said. "We need dockside security as well as personal escort."

"I'm afraid we would have to add a surcharge for the additional hazard."

"If you add the surcharge, I'm less willing to waive liability," Ky said.

"Surcharge. Dockside... that's a minimum of six personnel, two on each shift. Escort charges vary with shift. When would you want them?"

"As soon as possible," Ky said. "I'm uncertain of the duration at this point."

"That's all right. We can have a team at your dockside in... fifteen minutes. An escort will be dispatched when you request—were you needing one this shift?"

Ky looked at the chronometer, set now to Lastway Station's standard time. The shift would end in a half hour, and the next shift was mainday or business. She wouldn't get out of here before then. "No, not this shift," she said. "I'll let you know."

The police still hadn't arrived. Ky looked up MilMartExchange, and found that it occupied almost half of Hub Four's extensive storage holds. "Surplus new and used military heavy equipment: no credit" was its subhead. No more details available without a personal visit, but she could apply for a customer ID that would, the site said, "facilitate entry to the facility for first-time customers. Confidentiality assured. Recommended procedure." Ky hesitated, then decided to apply: anyone interested already knew she was docked here; the public-access ship listing would tell them that. To her surprise, the "application" consisted of asking for a number; she did not even have to give a name.

She took down the number she was given—fifteen digits—then looked up WEAPONS, where she found six gun shops listed, ranging from Bernie's Knives and Guns, "cheap, reliable personal protection," to Blade, Bullet, and Bow—"blades, firearms, and archery tackle for the discriminating." She looked for ORDNANCE and found "see heavy equipment," plus a small boxed notice that Lastway was not responsible for the legal status of ships mounting heavy equipment—captains should check with their relevant political units.

Sabine's concern now seemed more reasonable. And Lastway Station's regulations on personal weaponry were clearly less stringent than those on many other stations. Ky looked at the available live shots of station activity and noticed that a number of the people walking past were obviously armed. Probably others carried concealed weapons.

The directory listed a number of sources for surveillance and security systems, including most of the weapons sources already shown. Vic's Precision Protection Supply was closest, on the same sector of the same hub. She had Martin's wish list of gadgets and software. No, the first thing was to arrange handling of funds.

All the major quadrant banks had branches here; Ky picked Crown & Spears. Their representative regretted any inconvenience that it might cause, but they had put a lock on Vatta corporate accounts until matters had been adjudicated. Ky had expected that. "Did you receive a transfer from Belinta a few weeks ago? It was in my personal account, not a company account."

"I regret, madam, that I find no record of such a transfer. The last value we have for madam's personal account, based on ansible data, is indeed healthy, but those funds are not presently available because of the ansible failure. In the present crisis, we cannot advance monies based on remote accounts."

"Very well, then. I want to open a new account," she said. "We're selling cargo here and I'll be making purchases."

"It would have to be cash or hard goods," the bank's representative said.

"Of course," Ky said. "I'll courier over about four thousand credits' worth—using as a rough guide the official appraisal from Immigration—"

The face in the screen smiled more naturally now. "That will be fine, Captain. Their assessments are often . . . less than we might give, shall we say. And you say you have cargo as well?"

"Yes. We're unloading now; my cargomaster will be dealing shortly."

"Excellent. Now—is this to be a Vatta Transport account, or a personal account?"

"Personal," Ky said.

"Very well. We will await your courier and make funds available as soon as the valuation has cleared."

Ky had just closed the connection when Martin called to her. "The Garda are here," he said. "Their officer would like to speak with you."

"I'll be right out. Baritom Security is sending a couple of personnel to help guard dockside, and I'm going to need a courier to Crown & Spears to open an account. Would you say another Baritom agent, or a courier service?"

"Neither," Martin said. "When Baritom takes over dockside coverage here, I'll escort you or a crewmember."

The Garda who met Ky held out a legal notification pad. "Make your mark here, madam. You're being notified of your legal status on this station, your legal rights and obligations . . ." Ky read the notification and signed her name. She handed him a data cube with the recording of the man's attack, and he nodded. "We'll be in touch," he said. One of his fellows took the cargo cords off the operator and put on their own restraints; then they hauled the man away.

"I've got a list of what we need to complete our own perimeter security," Martin said.

"There's a supplier on this hub, not that far away," Ky said. "When I get the bank account set up—and by the way, I haven't contacted the rental company yet. In the meantime, can we start unloading?"

"Yes, ma'am. Jim here has convinced me that he does indeed know how to handle one of these things—I had him move it around while we were waiting for the Garda to show up." He paused, then said, "And here's Baritom."

Ky glanced toward the dockside entrance and saw two uniformed men waiting by the entrance. She started forward, but Martin stopped her.

"It's my job," he said. "If you'll just get whatever you need for the bank run... and I'd recommend Mitt for your courier. He has an implant and he looks nothing like you."

By the time Ky came back, Martin had assigned the two Baritom guards to the dockside entrance and told Alene to open up the nearside cargo hold. Beeah and Mehar were pacing around the dockside; Jim was backing away from the cargo hold with the first stack of containers. Mitt, his face sober, took the packet with two diamonds from Ky and put it in an inner pocket in his tunic.

Shortly thereafter, she had an account with a balance of 5,876 credits and a Crown & Spears credit chip, with authorization code. With that, Vic's Precision Protection Supply was willing to send over 648 credits' worth of surveillance gear. It arrived just as Martin and Mitt returned from the bank; Martin took charge of it and began installation at once.

Unloading proceeded; Ky looked at the tradehall listings and saw that the Leonoran pharmaceutical components should do very well, bringing much more than they would have on Leonora. Now that she had a bank account, she could list the cargo on the boards, and bids began to come in. She shunted those to Alene's attention. Her own attention focused on what she needed most to make her ship and her crew safer while in port. Any port. The attack on Belinta had involved both firearms and contact poison; they would need their own weapons, personal armor, and antidotes to such poisons—if any existed.

The tricky part would be getting to the small-arms dealers before someone got to her. Martin would come with her, but would that be enough? If she didn't wear Vatta colors, and carried her own weapons after she got them... who else in the crew knew how to use any? She paused to ask Martin.

Mehar, of course, was an expert with the pistol bow. It

turned out that she had also handled needlers before. Jim, as Ky now began to expect, rather shamefacedly admitted to having handled a variety of weapons.

"There were sorta like pirates hanging out in the estuaries near where we farmed. So I kind of picked up some of it—and my father, he always hunted even though the landlords didn't like it."

"So what do you know enough about to be useful?"

"Slug throwers. We didn't have stunners and needlers and all those spacer things. Make a big enough hole in it, my dad always said, and you're sure it's dead. There was this thing that lived out in the woods, big as a cow, and had these scales on it—"

"Slug throwers . . . handguns or long barrels?"

"Both, Captain. Now what I really liked, but only got to use once and he was really mad about it, was the mayor's Schneider-Watson .44 automatic. Made a lot of noise, it did, but you could put holes in those bitty little pirate speedboats with it. Or give me a rifle like my dad had . . ."

"How about accuracy?" Ky said.

"I'm pretty good," Jim said with unusual modesty for him. "My dad, now, he was a dead shot at any distance, but I qualified top in the marksmanship class for the local militia."

"Militia? You were in the militia?"

He turned red. "Well . . . actually . . . not that long. See, they didn't like my family that much, and when they found I'd shot a swamphog—well, three actually—with one of the militia weapons, they used that as an excuse to kick me out. I don't see what's so wrong about that. I was going to replace the ammunition, and I cleaned up the rifle before I put it back."

Ky bit her lip. It would not do to laugh, but she was beginning to have a good idea what kind of family Jim had come from. They had a few like that on Corleigh—old George was one of them—who had not, as her father put it, ever moved into the city from the frontier, even after the frontier was settled. You want them on your side, her father had told her.

Their virtues weren't needed most of the time, but when they were, nothing else would do. So now she had what her father called a "bush rat" of her very own, and she'd better make proper use of him.

She called Martin in to look at the catalogs from the various shops. Martin's face was eloquent; she didn't need his verbal comments to second her opinion that Bernie's Knives and Guns was out of the running, along with Arms4U. He thought the gun club might have serviceable weapons for the crew, but Ky noticed that the list of available weapons hadn't been updated for several weeks. Blade, Bullet, and Bow had top-quality weapons and prices to match, like Terrifield, back home on Slotter Key.

Her father's personal weapons were all from Terrifield; she had gone there with him once, and remembered the quiet shop with its slightly faded green carpet and old-fashioned display cases where the weapons on display were all antiques, and customers and staff spoke to each other in strings of cryptic numbers. "I'm looking for a P1400 with the 21–37 adapter," she'd heard one customer say. And the clerk had retired behind a curtain—a bulletproof curtain, her father mentioned later—and returned a moment later with something in a flat gray case. Her father tapped her shoulder—rude to stare, that meant—and made his own numerical request, which appeared on the counter in a few moments in a dull green case. It had been years before she understood what the numbers meant, and the difference in quality between the weapons there and the ones at Connery's Sporting Goods in Corleigh Town, which all had names as well as numbers: Hotshot 2100, Blastem—which came in attractive colors—Matchmaker. She shook herself out of that memory, and the surge of fear that her father was dead. She had to hope he wasn't.

Crash, as the obvious favorite shop for law enforcement and military, would have a wide selection and no trashy stuff, but Martin objected. "It's got ties to law enforcement; they'll have someone in there who talks to them. Until we know more about how things work here, that's not a good idea. Blade's a good choice for your weapons, if you can afford it. I've heard of them from people who've been here before."

From their docking slot at Hub Two, Hub Four with its multitude of arms merchants could be reached by external shuttle or internal tram, with transfers. Blade, Bullet, and Bow, though in Hub Three, was reasonably close by tram, and on the way to Hub Four, where she planned to visit MilMartExchange. One trip would be safer than several. Martin recommended she take Jim along as well as himself and Beeah.

"The boy's an obvious gawking tourist," Martin said. "He'll be a distraction to others, and anyway he's got to get better shore clothes."

Lastway Station was as bustling and colorful as Belinta had been quiet and dull. Despite the danger, Ky's heart lifted at the sight of hurrying pedestrians, bright shop entrances, exotic smells, the dock entrances of other ships, familiar and unfamiliar logos. She wanted to take off and explore, like any giddy apprentice on a first visit to other worlds, but she schooled her pace to a steady walk and managed not to gawk and point the way Jim was.

They reached the interhub tram stop without incident. Martin pointed out to Jim the kind of shore suit he should buy as soon as possible: plain, dark, suitable for any of several occupations. Ky wondered if Jim was paying attention; his eyes were wide. The tram itself was much like those on any station; they bought five-day passes and boarded one of the pressurized cars. Only one other passenger was in their car, a young girl with an obvious schoolbag. She was slumped in a corner, staring at her hand reader.

The tram slid away from its stop, moving smoothly through the translucent transport tube between hubs. Ky craned her neck, trying to orient herself to the whole station, but it was impossible. Hubs two and three and their arms blocked most of her view. The planet below was beneath the car's opaque floor. Her stomach lurched as the tram spanned between the artificial gravity of Hub Two and Hub Three, then they were pulling into the Hub Three tram stop as the usual voice synthesizer announced "Approaching Hub Three station. All Hub Three passengers transfer here to Hub Three radial trams. Approaching Hub Three station. All Hub Three passengers . . ." The schoolgirl didn't look up as Ky and her crewmembers rose.

Hub Three, where passenger liners docked, had a fancier tram station. Sound-reducing tiles covered the floor and walls in an attractive blue, green, and beige pattern. Instead of ticket machines, there was an information booth with a live clerk behind the window. Ky had already looked up the location of the shop—less than a hundred meters from the tram station—so she turned right and found herself in a passage with obviously expensive shops on either side.

Past a haberdashery, a jeweler's, a window display of fine china and crystal, a window with two lengths of velvet on which rested three silver salvers, she came to the windows of Blade, Bullet, and Bow: on the right, a pair of swords like something out of legend leaned against tall black boots and a cocked hat with a plume; on the left, a fan-shaped array of arrows around a recurved bow. The door had no handle, just a button. Ky pushed it.

The door opened; she faced a slender middle-aged man, clean-shaven, in a gray suit as plain as her own and as well tailored. Behind him, at a discreet distance, was another man whom Ky knew would be armed. "May I help you?" the man said. As he spoke, his gaze slid past her to Martin, Beeah, and Jim, then back to her face.

"I want to buy a personal weapon," Ky said.

"Meaning no disrespect, madam, but if you are a stranger to this station, there are less expensive shops . . ."

"But not, I suppose, those carrying better quality," Ky said, smiling.

"No, madam. Would madam care to step in? I am Andrew Barris." He said that as if she should know the name.

"Thank you," Ky said. "May my escort attend?"

He looked past her again. "Perhaps madam would feel secure with only one?"

"Of course," Ky said. She turned. "Martin, two of you can wait outside."

"Beeah, Jim, stay close to the shop," Martin said.

Ky smiled again at the salesman. "You will of course wish to ensure that he is not armed."

Now the smile widened. "Madam is perceptive. Ardin: you may proceed."

Martin quirked an eyebrow. "Standard Arms eleven millimeter, shoulder holster. I presume you'd rather I didn't reach for it?"

"Is that all?"

"The only firearm, yes."

"Would you remove the holster harness?"

"Be glad to." Martin removed his tunic and shrugged out of the harness. The store employee took it carefully, without touching Martin's weapon, and placed it on the counter before running a hand scanner over Martin.

Then he nodded at his employer, who nodded at Ky.

"How may we serve you?" was the next question.

"I'm thinking a ten- or eleven-millimeter Rossi-Smith, with whatever ammunition is legal for everyday carry on this station. Frangibles? Spudders?"

The man's eyes widened just slightly. "Is this for yourself, madam, or your . . . um . . . escort?"

"This would be for me," Ky said, smiling. "When I shoot someone, I expect them to stay down awhile."

He looked at her as if he wanted to say more, but didn't immediately speak. When he did, his voice was even softer. "We have a number of weapons of that caliber. We have three ten-millimeter Rossi-Smiths in the shop at present. Two are customized, one with rose-gold inlay and floral carving on the grip. I'm sure madam would like to see the one with rose-designed—"

"The plain one, please," Ky said. For just an instant he stared.

"Wait one moment, please," he said. "And if I could just have madam's credit references?"

"Cash," Ky said. She did not want some spy at the bank to know exactly what her weapons were. His eyebrows went up and his lips tensed. Ky went on. "Perhaps you would be good enough to switch on the excellent site security I'm sure you have. I would then be glad to explain." His mouth was still tight, but he nodded, pressed a button, then brought out from beneath the desk one of the squat cylinders Ky recognized.

"The outer perimeter is now shielded to most scanners," he said. "This completes the acoustic shielding, and the windows behind the display cases are one-way. Is madam satisfied?"

"Thank you," Ky said. "My name is Kylara Vatta." His lips twitched; she nodded. "Yes, that Vatta family. As you clearly are aware, my family is under attack. I was in transit when the trouble started and know no more than what's in the newsfeeds. I have been informed that the local station considers Vatta corporate accounts unreliable and is demanding cash; I assumed that you would follow suit. If I have insulted your honor, please accept my apologies."

His face softened. "My dear... madam... I understand completely. If the local financial institutions have frozen Vatta accounts, then you are right. I'm sorry to say that because of our location, so far from the center of humanspace, we are unable to offer credit if local accounts are frozen. However, we would be pleased to accept barter, if you do not, perhaps, have access to local supplies of cash."

"My cargo's selling," Ky said. "And I've opened a separate account; I expect to have access to cash shortly. However, in addition to purchasing a weapon from you, I wanted to ask your advice on two things. First, I have some... er... family valuables that I could sell, but I have no idea who would give me an honest price. I have had to rely, so far, on assessors attached to Immigration."

"I understand your concern, madam. As for the valuables... it depends on the type. Items of historical value, or precious materials?"

"Materials," Ky said.

He glanced at her case. "With you, perhaps?"

"A portion," Ky said. She slipped her fingers into the pouch and removed one diamond. "This, for instance."

He nodded, showing no emotion. "Quite nice," he said, as if customers laid diamonds on the counter every day. Perhaps they did. "We can arrange immediate appraisal; the firm we use is certified by interstellar convention and bonded. Is that satisfactory? I am already persuaded that your items are of sufficient value to cover any likely purchases."

"Quite," Ky said.

He opened a drawer and laid the Rossi-Smith on the pad in front of her. She picked up the weapon. Perfectly plain, the grip of some dark . . . "Wood?" she asked. It felt organic, but not quite like wood.

"No, madam. That's bloodbeast tusk, from Xerion. It shares with Old Earth ivory the characteristic of remaining grippy even if one's hands should sweat, but it has much better impact resistance. Madam will note that the action is the classic 1701 model, rather than the newer 1900—"

"Which tends to develop a stick with repeated rapid fire," Ky said.

"Exactly," he said, smiling. "Perhaps madam would like to try it out on our range?"

"Indeed yes," Ky said. She followed him through a curtain, down a narrow passage, and then into a two-person gallery. Here he offered ear protectors, goggles, and discreet assistance; the rounds he gave her were clearly marked target rounds. She loaded, lined up, and fired; the trigger pull had just enough resistance, and the recoil, with the target round, was negligible. Her first three shots were in a line, left to right, across the middle of the target. "Drat," she said mildly. "It's been too long."

"Not bad," he said. "But you were rushing."

She tried again, this time remembering all the tricks her father had taught her, and produced a tight cluster.

"Better," he said, as if he were her instructor. He probably was. "You are aware, madam, of the difficulty of hitting targets in variable g?"

It was something they'd studied in the Academy; Ky remembered the frustration, on that trip to the Academy's own orbiting training station. "Oh yes," she said, perhaps a bit too fervently. "Luckily, I'm not going to be shooting at anyone who's not shooting at me . . ." She took another clip of target rounds, loaded, and placed the group in half the area of the last one.

"Very nice, madam. Now, station regulations limit the permissible ammunition loads to frangibles and chemical immobilizers, no . . . er . . . spudders. Rounds with total delivery force small enough to avoid structural damage to the station, of course. For this model, we recommend the Rossi-approved PF for a frangible round, and the CPF, which encapsulates the latest legal release of an immobilizer–marker combination. Dispersal is limited by droplet size to within a meter of the impact point, so there is minimal collateral involvement."

"Does the station management have a preference?"

"Some criminals do wear protective gear, which of course limits the utility of the frangible rounds—"

"Personal armor," Ky said. "I meant to ask about that, too."

"We carry protective gear, of course, in a range of sizes and price points."

"I'd better take a look," Ky said. "And yes, I'll take this one." How much trouble did she expect to have? "I'll take another two clips to sight in with, and then five each of PF and CPF."

"And perhaps a holster and concealed carry permit? The background check is, I assure madam, brief and discreet. If madam's escort does not already have one, it would be advisable to obtain one for him, as well."

She had not carried a weapon on her person except for forays into the woods back home, where a very obvious holster on the hip was fine. "I'm thinking," she said with a smile, reaching for the next clip.

Her bill mounted up. Weapon, ammunition, carrying case, cleaning kit—"Alas, madam, no one has ever been able to make a firearm perfectly self-cleaning..."—permit to carry openly or concealed, and finally the wearable protection. Here the top-grade torso armor was so thin and flexible that she found it hard to believe it would do any good. Barris put it over a human form whose base wobbled when he nudged it, stood it up in one of the lanes, and fired at it. The torso model on its pole barely moved; the armor stiffened, changed color, and the light towel he hung down the back appeared scorched brown when he lifted it to show her.

"One-way heat radiation, madam. Substantially reduces impact effect, as well as protecting against penetration. Only recently licensed for civilian use, though supposedly it's been available in the black market for several years. Not that I would trust my life to that version." His expression reminded Ky of a cat that had accidentally stepped in something abhorrent.

She tried on one of the vests in her size. Not much heavier than a wool vest, and surprisingly comfortable. It fit invisibly under her business suit. "Serious assassins go for the head, of course," Barris said apologetically. "We can't armor that without being obvious, which I gather is not madam's desire."

"I would prefer to be inconspicuous, yes," Ky said.

"We can offer basic torso protection to your security personnel at competitive prices." *After all, the profit on what you're getting for yourself covers our cost of stocking it* went unsaid. Merchant to merchant, Ky looked at him. He smiled. She smiled back. Well, if someone took a shot at her people while she was getting from here to Hub Four she would feel guilty for leaving them unprotected.

"Economy is a factor," she said.

"Of course, madam. I shall be glad to call up the current price points from the other onstation dealers..."

"Quite all right," Ky said. No need to say she had already. He would assume she had.

Somewhat to her surprise, just one of Aunt Gracie's diamonds covered the entire cost with credit left over.

Fitting Martin with a conventional vest took only a few minutes, but when Ky went to call Jim and Beeah inside, they were no longer near the door. Instead, Jim was crouched near the display window of the china shop with Beeah standing over him.

"What's wrong?" Ky asked. "Are you all right?"

"I am, but look at this . . ." He turned and stood, cradling in his arms a small black-and-white animal with stiff, spiky fur. "Someone's been messing it about—I found it in the rubbish bin, trying to get out."

"What *is* that?" Ky asked. Bright black eyes, little black nose, and the moist pink tongue that suggested Old Earth origin. Hairy, so a mammal of some kind. She glanced around and saw that Jim had indeed dismantled a rubbish bin to get it out, leaving trash strewn about. "And you'd better clean up the mess you made before someone fines us for littering."

Jim stared at her as if she'd said she didn't know what two plus two was. "It's a *puppy,*" he said. "A terrier puppy. Here—you can hold him while I pick this up." He shoved the wriggling little animal into her arms and turned; the puppy promptly fastened onto Ky's hand with sharp little teeth.

"Ow!" she said. Beeah came up beside her. "Here—I expect we're now in trouble for harboring an unlicensed animal onstation, but at least we can contain it. And it bites," Ky added, as the puppy fastened its teeth on Beeah's thumb.

"I noticed," Beeah said, but he was grinning, prying open the puppy's jaws to retrieve his thumb. He offered the puppy the cuff of his suit, and the puppy worried it, growling.

"I hope it doesn't piddle on you," Ky said. Jim stuffed the last of the trash back into the container and set the lid on. "Come on," she said to him. "Let's get you fitted."

"Some guard you are," Martin muttered to Beeah, as Ky led Jim back to the shop. He had retrieved his weapon and followed her out. "What did you think you were doing?"

When she came back, trailed by Jim, Beeah had the puppy

cradled along one arm, upside down, and was stroking its belly. He handed it to Jim, reluctantly it seemed, while Martin rolled his eyes. Fitting Beeah also took only a short time; Ky accepted her change in local currency, and excused herself. She arrived outside just in time to see an obvious station guard staring at the sight with disgust. The guard moved across the passage toward them.

"You there!" he said. "Do you have a license for that animal?"

CHAPTER SEVEN

This had not been part of her plan. “It’s not our—” Ky said, but Jim blurted, “Not yet.” She glared at him.

“You’ll have to come along now,” the guard said, flicking open what Ky was sure was a combination comunit and data entry. “Exposing the station to an unlicensed animal... where are you people from, anyway?” His gaze roved over Jim’s unattractive rumpled Belinta tunic, which, Ky noticed, failed to completely conceal his brand-new armor. The guard’s gaze sharpened. “Wearing armor, eh? And you, you’re carrying a weapon...” Now he was glaring at Ky.

She tilted her head back to the doorway of Blade, Bullet, and Bow. “We’ve just come out—”

“And put the animal in the waste can while you were in there? Do you have any idea—?”

“I didn’t put it there,” Jim said. “It was in there, whimpering and scratching, poor thing, and I couldn’t leave it—”

“Is that true?” the guard asked Ky.

“I was inside,” Ky said. “I didn’t hear it. When I came out, he was holding it...”

“Uh-huh. Well, it’s in your possession now, and if this is your employee, you’re responsible for it, and for not having a proper license and health papers for it... and how about a license for that weapon?”

Ky fished her new license out of her pocket. “Here.”

He glanced at it. “All right then. Come along to the office and take care of this...” He glared at the puppy.

Never argue with law enforcement in the street, her father

had told her. Go pleasantly along to the office, cooperate, and you'll be done much faster. So probably it was only seeming to take an hour, Ky thought, to follow the guard along the passage, past stores that changed gradually from the upper margin of the upper crust to the solid commercial filling of any major space station that saw a lot of traffic. And there was the guard office for this arm of Hub Three, with its hull-quality door standing wide open.

"What's this, Mally?" asked the man behind the desk.

"Unlicensed animal. Claim they found it in a trash bin, but it seems to know *him*." The guard jerked a thumb at Jim, who still cradled the puppy along his forearm; it looked asleep.

"Fine's two hundred credits a day, crate license fifty credits, out-of-crate license one hundred credits, both require health certificate available from any onstation veterinarian and you can look them up in the business directory using a public-access com line or if it's not your animal or you wish it destroyed that will be two hundred credits fine, ten credits disposal fee, payable immediately by cash or approved credit line only . . ." The desk clerk rattled this off in a rapid monotone, then looked up. "Name, ship name, names of all persons who have contacted this . . . whatever it is . . . ?"

"Jim Hakusar, from *Gary Tobai*—I'm the one who found it in the trash container. He was crying and trying to get out—"

"And you are . . . ?" The clerk looked at Beeah.

"Beeah Chok, same ship."

"Gordon Martin, same ship."

"Captain Vatta, *Gary Tobai,*" Ky said.

"Ah—you're armed, Mally says. Your permit number?" Ky handed the permit over. "Um. Not in the database—what's the date on this? Oh, today. I guess you won't have any trouble paying the fines for your pet, then, will you, shopping at Blades? Though if it's really not yours, you'd be smart to let us get rid of it."

"No," Jim said. Ky looked at him. "You can't let them kill a *puppy,*" he said.

"What do we need with a puppy?" Ky asked. Jim gave her a stricken look.

"Dogs can be useful," Martin said. "Dockside, I mean. This one's very small—"

"He's a puppy," Jim said. "He'll grow. I'll bet he'll be fierce."

"He won't be much trouble," Beeah murmured. Ky looked at him in surprise. She hadn't known Beeah had any interest in animals.

"Up to you," the clerk said. "There's also the mandatory decontamination and observation period for personnel in contact with an unlicensed animal lacking health papers. You can locate the nearest clinic in the business directory using any public-access comlink . . ."

The puppy opened one limpid eye, squirmed, and piddled down Jim's front.

An astonishing amount of money later, Ky looked at her protectors with less than favor. "You two made enough commotion that any enemy we might have now knows where we are, what we're wearing, and that I'm armed. Next time just smash a window and start screaming obscenities, why don't you?"

"All right . . . ," Jim said, looking worried. "But how do I know when?"

Ky appealed to deities she'd heard of and didn't believe in. The puppy, now listed as "Puddles" in the vet's database, was being inspected, disinfected, and would be delivered the next day. The vet had informed her that it was almost certainly a purebred, a Jack Russell terrier. She privately thought of it as another kind of jack-something-terrier, but didn't mention that. She and the others had been through a standard decontamination procedure, which had turned the damp patch on Jim's tunic bright blue, though the technician insisted it would return to normal color later.

"It's coming out of your salary," she reminded Jim. He and Beeah had agreed to split the cost of the fines and vet care.

"He'll be a help," Jim said. "He can guard the dockside, like Martin said."

"Not until it's grown," Ky said. "And puppies that size don't grow into guard dogs." She plugged into another link and called the ship on a secure line. Quincy answered. "We're fine, Quincy. Just had to see a man about a dog—no, really. Jim found a stray puppy and had to rescue it."

"I thought that was your strategy," Quincy said, with a bite that Ky recognized as relief.

"Not this time," Ky said. "We're just now leaving Hub Three for Hub Four. I'll check in when we get there."

"Wait—you've messages. A sealed hardcopy from someone named MacRobert, originating at Slotter Key, and a call from that security firm, Baritom. They said call them back."

MacRobert again? What did Master Sergeant MacRobert of the Slotter Key Spaceforce Academy want with her? "How big is the package?" Ky asked.

"Small. Not too heavy. You think it's a trap or something?"

"No. Just put it in my cabin; I'll get to it later."

"Well, Baritom really wanted you to call back."

Ky muttered, but took down the number and called them.

"Captain Vatta," said the voice on the phone. "Our dockside staff reported that you left the secured area . . . did you not wish an escort?"

She was about to refuse, when she thought to ask Martin.

"You can send Jim back—tell him to buy some clothes on the way—and have the escort meet us," he said. "I'd like a chance to assess their personnel."

"Fine." Ky turned back to the combooth. "I'm presently at Hub Three, second ring, green sector. I'm on my way to Hub Four. If your agent meets me at the tram station—"

"We prefer to have the operative meet the subject at a secure location."

She was already behind schedule. She did not want to return to the Garda station to meet an escort. But surely Mil-Mart counted as a secure location.

"MilMartExchange," she said. "How's that? Otherwise, it'll be after I get back to the ship, some hours from now."

"That will be adequate," the voice said. "We supply our operatives with the usual identification kits. You are not at a secured com outlet now—"

"No," Ky said. "I'm sure MilMart has one."

"All right. We will provide you with the operative's code there."

Ky shook her head as she turned away.

"What?" Beeah asked.

"Just the day. Jim, you head back to the ship—you have your tram pass, right? I know Martin suggested you buy clothes on the way, but I'd rather have you safe on the ship. In fact—Martin, should Jim go back alone? Shouldn't I send Beeah with him?"

"No, he should be fine for now," Martin said. "You're more likely to be attacked than he is; I'd rather have backup with us."

Ky turned to Jim again. "Remember what Martin told you. Be careful, go straight back. No more puppies, kittens, lost children, or whatever else comes into your path. Martin, their agent will meet me at MilMart."

"I'll bet it's a trick," Jim said. Ky eyed him with disfavor.

"Nothing like your trick of getting us in trouble with the law," she said. "Go on, now. I want you back on the ship by the time I call Quincy from Hub Four."

The tram to the next hub was much the same, though this time their car held two women chatting, both with small children in tow, and a man in a shipsuit with a *Navarre* ship patch. With them in line was another woman with a small child, who greeted the first two cheerfully and sat down in the next row. From their greetings, Ky learned that they met every ten days, taking their children to a play area on Hub Five. She watched one of the children wipe a sticky red hand along the seat, leaving a smear.

"Now, Donal . . . what do you think wipes are for?" said

one woman, cleaning up the smear and handing the child the wipe. He tried to stuff it into his mouth, and she took it away.

At Hub Four, Ky stepped out and spotted the next mother of the bunch, with a baby in arms and a pair of twins clinging to her legs. Behind her, the Hub Four station was even plainer than that in Station 2: gray industrial flooring, cream tile walls. When they came out into the passage, it had none of the amenities of Hub Three. Signs advertised ship stores—none, Ky was sure, with gold-eye raspberries or fancy sliced meats—hand and power tools, parts and fittings, navigation software, navigation hardware, tech modules for cranial implants, shipsuits and patches. Ky paused to call and let Quincy know they'd arrived, checked the directory display to be sure she was oriented correctly, and led the way down the passage. Here were the front offices of the yards that performed major repairs and replaced spacecraft engines or entire environmental systems.

Ky had checked the locations she wanted before she left her own ship, and knew they had to work their way inward two rings and then left. Just behind the shops to their left were the warehouses of MilMart, but the access was somewhere else. She assumed it gave the MilMart surveillance ample time to collect good clear images before someone arrived on their doorstep, or whatever they had instead.

They had passed the first ring crossing and were almost to the next when Ky's eye was caught by a familiar symbol. Here? She looked again. A narrow storefront bore the neat legend MACKENSEE MILITARY ASSISTANCE CORPORATION: YOUR PROBLEMS—OUR SOLUTION. She slowed. It was one of a row of storefronts, all of which appeared to be mercenary offices, between Barkley's Best—GOT WAR? GET THE BEST! BARKLEYS!—and Answenia Military Advisers, EXPERIENCE COUNTS.

"Now that's interesting," Beeah said.

"What?" Martin said. He followed their gaze. "Oh . . . mercenaries. Which group was it you ran into, ma'am?"

"Mackensee," Ky said. Martin nodded and said nothing

more. She wondered if these Mackensees had heard about Sabine—about her. Surely they had. Surely if . . . if Vatta was completely destroyed, she could always join them, as they'd offered before. She pushed that thought away. Vatta would survive; she would ensure that Vatta survived. The nagging question of how, she ignored for the moment.

Around the corner to the left, large red letters announced the entrance to MilMartExchange in three languages. Armed guards—not the station Garda—stood outside. A steady stream of customers went in and out.

"There it is," said Beeah. "What are you going to get, Captain?"

"What we can afford," Ky said. "Which certainly won't be all I want or all we need."

The guards at the door seemed to pay no attention to her, but just inside the entrance to MilMart was a check station where Ky gave her customer ID number. She and her entourage then put on ID wristbands, and a door opened that led into a room of vidscreens. "You can look at the catalog here, and if there's something you want, ring for assistance to go into the back and look at it. There are secured comlinks if you need to check with your financial institution."

Ky called back to Baritom and exchanged recognition codes with the office, then told a MilMart employee that if anyone asked for "Ambergris," it was for her. The employee nodded with such complete boredom that Ky realized a lot of people probably made contact here in this well-lighted, well-guarded place.

Then she turned to the catalog. Her first look almost made her gasp. Here were no circumlocutions: the main divisions were ORDNANCE, DEFENSIVE; ORDNANCE, OFFENSIVE; ORDNANCE CONTROL SYSTEMS; DEFENSIVE HARDWARE AND SOFTWARE; SMALL ARMS; and IFF SYSTEMS. Each was divided into ship-based, space–non-ship-based, and ground-based. She was partway down ORDNANCE, DEFENSIVE, SHIP-BASED, SELF-POWERED when she spotted familiar names and numbers. She blinked. The Slotter Key Spaceforce would choke if they knew their supposedly first-run ship weapons were being sold to anyone with the money out here. Thornbat missiles? She scrolled through to DEFENSIVE HARDWARE AND SOFTWARE. DeepPilot stealthing systems? This couldn't be surplus; scuttlebutt at the Academy had been that funding was too short for DeepPilot to be installed on all the cruisers, let alone the smaller ships. She glanced at Martin, at an adjoining station. His face looked grimmer than usual; she wondered what he thought, finding his world's advanced weaponry for sale to anyone with enough credits.

The catalog seemed to have something from everyone's arsenal, in fact. Items coded as FmPr in the catalog turned out to be manufactured by FarmPower on Sabine Prime... ground-based armored vehicles and heavy equipment for preparing landing sites and fortifications. Nothing from Belinta—she had scrolled to the list of source manufacturers—but dozens of other systems had contributed their bit. She wondered if it was all stolen... but the important thing was, enough money and you could outfit a space fleet from here. Considering those mercenaries' offices, quite possibly someone—several someones—did.

Not that everyone could afford it... she blinked again at the prices, mentally calculating what she had to spend. Not enough, not nearly enough. She'd been taught that war was expensive; she'd memorized the estimated costs given in class—the Reandi Incursion 2.3 times as costly as the Belaconti Uprising—but she'd never considered what it might take to convert one small ship from an old, slow, unarmed trader to a fast, powerful raider. All Aunt Gracie's diamonds wouldn't put a dent in her wish list.

Raider? She paused, not really seeing the page of display in front of her. She had come here looking for ways to protect the ship from Vatta's enemies. When had her intentions slipped sideways into something like... *raider*? Dangerously close to *pirate,* that was. *Privateer,* came a whisper in her mind, if she had authorization from the government.

But what else was there, for one captain and one small vessel? Nothing she could put on the ship—even if she could afford the stealth package, the point defense missile system and its software, and a faster insystem drive—would really protect them against the kind of enemies she seemed to face. She couldn't trade effectively while evading pursuit—good cargo ships were predictable, reliable; that's what customers paid for. On-time delivery. Guarantees of complete cargo.

"Captain?" Beeah spoke suddenly.

"Yes, Beeah," she said, not looking at him, seeing instead the narrowing funnel of choices facing her, none of them good. If she could not use her ship as Vatta had always used their ships, what could she do with it? With her crew? With that idiot puppy? Could she really become a raider—her mind shied away from *pirate*—and attack other ships? And if she could, mentally, take that on, what would it take in resources?

"If you can give me a budget, I can prioritize upgrades on the basic functions," Beeah said.

"That's what I'm thinking about," Ky said. "Maybe we should have waited until we'd sold our cargo, so we'd know what our resources are. I can estimate, but—this is not a place where I want to come up short."

"I see that. The cargo's selling, though, isn't it?"

"I certainly hope so. Let me just check with the ship and see how it's going..." She signed on to the secure com again, and called her crew.

"More offers are coming in," Alene said. "The only other tradeship in the past two weeks had a totally different cargo mix, so the market's on our side."

"Good," Ky said. "You've got the account number for deposits."

"Excuse me, Captain Vatta?" That was a MilMart employee. "There's a person wishing to speak to you. He says he's from Baritom Security Services, and he gave the correct countersign."

"Thanks," Ky said. "I'll come out. Beeah, you wait here; I

won't be long." Then to Alene, "Go on and make the best deals you can. We want to move the Leonora consignments first. I'll be back in a few hours."

Back through the door, into the anteroom, with Martin at her heels. Baritom Security Services outfitted its agents in brown with green facings. Willem Turnish was a little taller than Ky, appeared to be middle-aged but fit, with warm brown eyes. "Captain Vatta?" He held out a datapak.

"Yes," Ky said. "Your code, please?"

He rattled it off, word and number both; Ky replied with hers, and then inspected the datapak. Name, height, weight, thumbscan—she held it out and he pressed his thumb to the plate, which flashed green. So he was what he claimed to be.

She handed the datapak back and glanced at Martin. His face conveyed no message at all.

"I'll probably be another hour here," she said. "You can wait out here, or—if there's a café nearby—"

"I'll wait here," Turnish said, gesturing to a bench along one wall.

"Fine," Ky said.

When she came back to the terminals, she turned to Martin. "Well?"

He shook his head. "He's a professional; he's armed; he has the right codes. I can't tell how competent he is, from that brief an encounter, but he has the look of someone with experience. I can tell more after we've been on the street with him."

Ky turned to Beeah. "Beeah, if you went back to the ship, now you've seen the catalog, you could discuss with Quincy what they've got, and how it might fit our hull. And you could get Alene's best guess on what our cargo might bring."

"If you're sure, Captain," Beeah said.

"Martin's with me," Ky said. "With the escort, that's two—two should be enough. Besides, I'm wearing armor now, and I've got my new toy." She patted the holster.

"More dangerous than you look," Beeah said, grinning. "I'll be off, then."

Ky turned back to the catalog. If she bought the defensive suite, item number 34-5000-89357, then she could just—maybe—afford the single launcher installation, item number 68-4322-7639. But the only reason to have a launcher was . . . to attack other ships. Other defenseless ships: a single launcher was too puny to go against real warships or better-armed pirates.

She could not do it. To become a pirate, a thief . . . that would end Vatta, even if she herself lived, became wealthy, tried to reconstitute the organization. If Slotter Key had turned on her family—a mystery that she could not solve here and now—they would certainly not authorize her to be a privateer. Nor did she have the resources to make a living on the run without raiding. She would have to . . . to what? Admit they were all doomed? Not that, either. Run? Run where? To another sector, far across the spaces where Vatta had traded, back to the old worlds her family had once fled? Out to the unknown worlds beyond the Rift?

She leaned her head on her hand, refusing all those choices, and unable to think of any others. No, she had to think and she could not think. The self she had been in the crisis at Sabine—the self who had taken quick, decisive action—seemed to have vanished, leaving a sour confusion behind.

Sighing, she stretched and exited the catalog to look at the information on purchase agreements. She could put items on hold with no deposit for twenty-four hours, or with a deposit for up to five days. In hard, cold, rational analysis, they needed that defensive suite in any case. In fact, they needed a better one. Item 35-4571-983324 would be ideal, but the catalog listed only one in stock. She put a hold on it, no deposit. That at least would give her time to think. Could Quincy install it? Would they have to find someone else who could?

Back to the list. If offensive ordnance was too expensive and only good for preying on others, what about defensive? ORDNANCE, DEFENSIVE, SHIP. Ky looked down the list. If they had Slotter Key ordnance, maybe they'd have . . . yes.

Mines, self-powered, autostabilizing, Model 87-TR-5003. Top of the line, as far as senior students at the Academy knew. Compared to the other ordnance, mines were economical, even cheap. Nor did they take up much space. If you understood how to use them—and she had written a paper on the use of passive and active defensive systems, including mines—they could be very effective. Of course, there were a lot of complications, including the inherent instability of anything in space: mines drifted with gravitational forces, and eventually their "self-powered" ability to correct their drift wore out, leaving lethal hazards scattered in unknowable locations.

But Ky was willing to make the universe more hazardous for others, if it would save her own ship. She put a hold on the mines, too. If she took that defensive suite, she could just barely afford fifteen mines. You can't ever have too much ammunition, one of her instructors had said. Maybe some of their cargo would bring premium prices.

She collected Martin, checked out of the catalog viewing area, and picked up her escort. He preceded her to the exit, and certainly seemed to be competent in his check of the passage outside. Unlike the hapless Jim, he would not be plucking puppies from waste cans. That thought reminded her of another errand.

"Do you know a shop near here, or on our way back to the interhub tram, that carries pet supplies?" she asked.

"Pet supplies?"

It was an unusual question, but he didn't have to sound *that* amused.

"Pet supplies," she said again. "We have acquired a . . . mmm . . . puppy. It'll be released from quarantine tomorrow."

"Let me check . . ." He looked momentarily blank, accessing his implant, then he nodded. "BioExotics, down this way," he said, gesturing to a cross-passage ahead of them. Above the official numbered designation, someone had added a pink-and-green sign with WILLOW LANE in curly letters.

"It's lunchtime," Martin said quietly. "How about a stop for something to eat?" Ky glanced at him; he'd mentioned before the security risks of public eating places. Was this part of his assessment of their escort? Ky started to refuse, but her own stomach growled.

"There's a café on the corner," her escort said.

"Fine. A quick lunch, then." Martin didn't say anything, and when she looked at him, his face was impassive.

The café was not crowded, in the postlunch period, but the smells from the kitchen were all good. Mindful of Martin's earlier lecture, she went to a table against a wall and placed herself with the wall at her back. Martin sat on her right, facing the door squarely; Turnish flanked her, sitting across from Martin—which put his back to the door, but facing the kitchen hatch. She offered Turnish a meal; he said he'd eaten before he came on duty. Even though she was paying for his time, Ky felt subtly pressured by his stolid demeanor, as if she were eating in front of an instructor. An escort shouldn't involve himself in chitchat, true, but Turnish radiated patience at a level that felt impatient. Ky worked her way through a delicious soup and fresh-baked bread that made it clear how this café stayed in business. Martin, she noticed, had inhaled a thick sandwich while hardly taking his gaze off the door.

Out in Willow Lane, late first-shift meant almost no traffic. Turnish led the way past open shop doors in which no one appeared... a succession of small businesses: laundry and cleaners, bakery, used-clothing stores, hand-tool repair, sign studio. It could have been afternoon in a small town. Ky relaxed. Yes, it would be easy for an assassin to set up on a quiet street, but who knew she'd be coming down this way? Any rational assassin would assume she'd head straight back to her ship.

"Look out!" Turnish said suddenly and started to turn toward her.

Ky dove for the deck, shoving Turnish aside; he fell beside her. The first two shots missed all of them by a meter. Ky glanced back at Martin; he had his weapon out and squeezed off a shot as she watched. She braced herself on her elbows and looked for her target. There . . . peeking out of the doorway of Andy's Tailor Shop ahead of them. She squeezed off one round of CPF; she saw the assailant's body jerk, withdraw, then topple slowly out into the passage. The weapon fell with a clatter. A familiar surge of satisfaction pulsed through her. No time for that . . . Ky looked for cover, and the backup. There would be another; whoever was doing this would not have hired a single shooter. Nothing. No one came to the door of the shop—of any shop—to look. She could feel the hairs standing up on the back of her neck. A doorway to the right gaped empty only a meter or so away. She tapped Turnish's leg with one hand, looking past him for more trouble.

"Move to cover," she said. "Four o'clock. I'll cover you."

"I don't think so," Turnish said, rolling over. Her breath stopped as she stared down the bore of his weapon . . . *That's really big* ran through her head in a soprano squeak. The man grinned. "Checkmate, Vatta. Game over."

She could not move fast enough; her weapon was offline, aimed at where trouble had been, not where it was. She knew she could not move fast enough, and that knowledge made it impossible to move at all. He kept smiling, clearly aware of her thoughts, of her fear, of her weapon's position. Her throat was dry; icy sweat trickled down her spine. Martin couldn't possibly—but then noise blasted her ears, and the man's head exploded in a spray of blood and brains before she even saw what it was Martin was doing.

Breath rushed back into her lungs in a gasp. Ky swiped at the mess on her face. "You—"

"I wasn't sure until he turned on you," Martin said. "Sorry. He could've been just careless, about the café. Get on into that doorway." Still no alarm—the passage might have been empty. Perhaps it was. Perhaps everyone had been paid to go have a midshift snack or something.

The dead man's weapon lay farther away than Ky expected... with his hand still on it. Martin must have fired two shots, then—that fast?

Not that it mattered now. What mattered now was getting some official help. Cautiously, she eased into the doorway she'd spotted and looked for a com port. The one in the red booth three shops down was far too exposed, but most stations had them in more discreet locations as well.

Before she located one, she heard the shrill whistle of approaching law enforcement.

CHAPTER EIGHT

"Too bad," Martin murmured. "I suppose we're in for the traditional bad quarter hour."

"I hope it's only that," Ky said. "We've already been a problem twice today."

"Yes, you'll have quite a reputation when we're done here," he said. It wasn't quite a chuckle. "You're . . . remarkably calm for someone who just killed someone and was nearly killed herself. Is it calm, or are you in shock?"

"I'm supposed to know?" Ky said. "I don't feel panicky, if that's what you mean. A little worried about the men with the uniforms."

"I presume you've been told how to behave when arrested?"

"Oh, yes. But I'd just as soon not spend another hour facedown on the floor, like I did on Belinta."

"On Belinta—but you were nearly killed on Belinta."

"And one of the men who tried to kill me was thoroughly killed."

"By—?"

"Me," Ky said. "I thought you knew."

"No; I heard about the mutineers on your ship. I knew this wasn't your first."

"The first for this weapon," Ky said, tucking it back into its holster as the first guard came into view. Martin had already holstered his.

The Garda—another two had entered from the far end—were fully armored, weapons out. Someone out of sight had a loud-hailer. "Anyone in this area, come out with your hands up!"

"That's us," Ky said. "Here we go." She put her hands up, and stepped out of the doorway, Martin beside her, hoping that no other sniper remained. Her skin tightened, but no one shot her.

"Any more of you?" asked the loud-hailer. Whoever had it must also have a view of the passage.

"No," Ky said. "Not on our side."

The armed guards moved in. "Armed?" one of them asked.

"Yes," Ky said. "Automatic in waist holster; three rounds fired. Safety's on."

One of the guards plucked it out gingerly and put it in a safe hanging from his shoulder.

"Yes," Martin said, with a glance at her. "Shoulder holster, Standard Arms eleven millimeter, and the safety is on." The guard removed this weapon and dropped it into the safe as well.

He turned back to Ky. "ID?"

"Kylara Vatta, of *Gary Tobai,*" Ky said. "This is my crewman Gordon Martin."

After a moment, the guard said, "You've had contact with the law twice already today: an altercation at your dockside, and possession of an unlicensed animal."

"We *found* that unlicensed animal," Ky said.

"And I suppose you just *found* some dead bodies?"

"No. We were coming along this passage when someone started shooting at us. We hit the deck; I got that one—" Ky nodded to the body in the street some thirty meters away. "—and this one, who was assigned to me by Baritom Security, supposedly a fully licensed escort guard. He turned on me, close range."

"Excuse me?"

The back of Ky's neck prickled, a signal she was in no mood to ignore. "Could we go to the station, please? Two people tried to kill me today. I'd like to get off the street and into cover."

"You're scared with all of us here?" The sneer was palpable.

"Yes," Ky said. "And with some reason, I believe. I am willing—no, eager—to give a full report, but I'd rather not be shot in the head while standing out here in easy range of anyone in any of these shops."

The man made no response at first. Ky assumed he was getting instructions through an implant or his helmet com. In a few moments, he said, "All right. We're taking you in. Hands on your head."

The Garda station was around the curve from where they'd been, in the direction they'd been walking. No one else appeared until they were out of sight of the carnage behind. There, a curious crowd had gathered behind a taped perimeter. The guards answered no questions, but hurried Ky and Martin on until they were inside the station. There, since nothing had shown on the autoscanner as they came in, they were allowed to lower their hands.

"You're getting quite a reputation, Captain Vatta," said the person behind the desk. "Illegal biologicals, assaults, murder—"

"Self-defense," Ky said. "Attempted murder, on their part. And what I hope is impersonation, for which Baritom is legally responsible."

"So you say," the man said. "An investigating officer will be here shortly to take your statements. You can wait in there—" He jerked his head toward a doorway.

"I need to inform my ship," Ky said. "They're expecting us to return."

He scowled at her. "You're under suspicion—"

"Of course," Ky said. "But there's no reason to panic my crew, is there? After all, I'm still responsible for them; I'm sure you'd rather not have them involved in any other incidents."

"You can use the public com outlet, there," he said.

"Go on, Martin; I'll be with you shortly," Ky said. Martin nodded and preceded one of the Garda down a hall. Ky gave the ship's code.

"*Gary Tobai,* Cargo Specialist Barikal speaking." Cele

looked calm, so Ky hoped that meant nothing had happened while she was gone. "Oh—Captain! Sorry—the screen didn't show your ID at first."

"That's all right. Is Quincy there? Has Beeah come back?"

"No, Captain. Quincy's gone out to one of the chandlers to select rations. She took Jim with her; she's not alone. Beeah called in to say he was having lunch on Hub Three. Do you want Mehar? She's in Engineering—"

"No. That's all right. But I've run into some problems. We were attacked on the way back from out here; I want all ship personnel to return to the ship at once and stay there. Who else is out?"

"Besides you and Martin, just Jim, Beeah, and Quincy, Captain. Are you all right?"

"I'm fine. But I'd like you to contact Quincy and Beeah—get Mehar to do it by implant—and have them return immediately. I'll be tied up here in the Hub Four Garda station awhile—probably some hours—but she can try to contact me here. I don't know if they'll put calls through. Just sit tight."

"Yes, Captain. I do have some good news on the cargo side. Alene got quite a profit on one part of the Leonora cargo."

"That's fine," Ky said. "But I'd rather not discuss that on this line. I'm using the public com at the guard station. I'll call again when I can."

"Yes, Captain."

Ky signed off, smiled at the still-scowling man behind the desk, and went into the waiting room, furnished with a bench, narrow table, and two chairs. Martin sat on the bench with his usual composure, radiating calm patience despite the smears of blood and dirt on his clothes. He gave her a pleasant smile. Ky was sure she looked worse than he did; the stench of blood and brains on her face was nauseating. One of the armed guards followed them and stood by the door.

"Is there a toilet?" Ky asked.

"You'll have to wait until forensics has tested your clothes," the guard said.

They didn't have long to wait. The man who came through the door introduced himself as Inspector Grant. "We'll need to do some forensic tests on your clothes," he said. "If you'll follow my assistant here into the changing area, this won't take long, and then I can take your statements."

He had two assistants, one male and one female, both humods with low-pressure adaptations. Ky disrobed under the eye of the female and handed her suit over, changing into the simple gray coverall provided. "Now we'll need to test your hands," the woman said. She took the sack with Ky's clothes and led her to another room, where a technician sat behind a machine with a slot in the front. Ky put her hands in the slot as directed, and, after a minute or two, the technician nodded. The technician wiped her face with a cloth and took a blood sample. Then the woman led her back to the waiting room, having handed over the sack to the technician.

"If you need the toilet, you can use it now," the woman said.

"I'd like to wash my face," Ky said. "Is that all right?"

"Yes," the woman said.

In the washroom, Ky scrubbed all the visible bits off her face and wished she could wash her hair. Even as she brushed it with the packet of dry wash, it didn't feel clean. What she really needed was a long, hot shower. She used the facilities, then scrubbed her hands again. When she emerged, she went back to the waiting room and sat down across from Inspector Grant.

"You've had a bad day, I gather," he said, pleasantly enough. "So, Captain Vatta—suppose you tell me what happened. Starting with . . . let's start with when you left the Garda station on Hub Three after arranging for that animal to go into quarantine."

Ky related her travels as best she could. Grant asked for descriptions of the people on the various trams.

"Why did you elect to walk back that way?" he asked,

when she told about turning down the passage where they were attacked. "Didn't it occur to you that staying in the main thoroughfare might be safer?"

"My escort, Willem Turnish. I had asked if he knew of a place that carried pet supplies. If we were going to be stuck with that puppy, we'd need some. He said there was a shop called BioExotics on Willow Lane. In fact," Ky continued, "he recommended the café—Murphy's—where we ate lunch."

"Murphy's has a good reputation," Grant said. "Do you think they'll remember you?"

"I'd think so. It wasn't very busy when we were there. I remember which table. Anyway, we started down Willow Lane, and the passage cleared out after a while; we were walking along fairly quickly and I was looking at storefronts, reading the names and numbers. Then Turnish said look out, and I was diving for cover when the first two shots came. We were all on the ground when the next shot came, then I had my weapon out. I got the one up ahead, and told Turnish to take cover in the nearest doorway while I covered him."

"And?"

"He rolled over and had a weapon aimed at my head. I was so stunned I couldn't move—he was too close, and I was stretched out, my weapon pointing away from him . . ."

"You're sure it was Turnish?"

"Absolutely," Ky said. "He'd been with me the whole time, never more than an arm's length away."

"So what happened then?"

"Next thing I knew, Martin bobbed up and shot him. I don't suppose Turnish knew he was armed, or could move that fast. Then we got into that doorway and waited until the guards showed up."

"You have a license for your weapon," Grant said. "They checked that at the other guard station. But your crewman—do you know if he has a concealed carry permit?"

"Yes," Ky said. "I arranged for that when I purchased mine, along with my weapon, at Blades on Hub Three."

"Um. And you were both wearing torso armor?"

"Yes," Ky said. "Also purchased today at Blades. We had some reason to expect trouble, as I'm sure you know. But my real concern," Ky said, "is that someone I hired from a bonded protection company tried to kill me. He had all the right recognition codes, the ones the company provided to me. Does this mean the company is bent, or are they missing a legitimate agent?"

"I assure you we will investigate that aspect," Grant said. "They say they did dispatch an escort named Willem Turnish, but we do not yet know if the dead man really was Turnish." He shook his head. "Do you know why he warned you? If he was part of the plan to kill you, that doesn't make sense."

Ky had not thought of that. "I don't know," she said.

"Unless," Grant said, "he set it up so it could look like someone else shot you. Though that seems complicated. Tell me how he came to you. Had you arranged for an escort with Baritom?"

"They contacted my ship; a message was relayed to me and I called the number provided. They said their dockside personnel had noticed I went out and asked if I wanted an escort. It was something I'd mentioned to them before. Why?"

He sighed. "I don't know yet. I'm just trying to understand what exactly happened. Preliminary forensics confirms that the individual in the doorway of Andy's fired the three rounds we found onsite, and that those rounds were fired before the ones that killed him."

How else, Ky wondered, but didn't say.

"Forensics cannot confirm that the individual known to you as Willem Turnish was in fact menacing you with his weapon before your crewman shot him. We are experiencing difficulty in obtaining uncorrupted vid surveillance data from that area. It looks as if someone intended to insert a very different scenario, but we tapped into the system too quickly." His smile now was predatory. "We are not happy to find that someone is attempting to corrupt our surveillance."

"That would be . . . very bad," Ky said.

"Yes. At any rate, the evidence at this point does not support holding you in custody, even though you might be safer here than out on the streets. Though it's clear from both your stories that your crewman Martin shot and killed this Turnish fellow, the previous threats against your family suggest that it's not that unlikely he was trying to kill you. Therefore I am willing to release him, as well, into your custody. Excuse me a moment." He left the room.

Ky leaned back. The gray jumpsuit smelled of harsh institutional soap, but she could still smell *something* in her hair. She would have to get in touch with Baritom . . . would they blame her for the death of their operative, or would they accept that he had turned on her? She ached all over. She did not want to hike over to the station to take the tram back to Hub Two.

Grant came back. "Since it's clear you're the target of malicious intent, I'm authorizing the use of a patrol scooter to get you back to your docking area. We can't provide around-the-clock protection—we don't have the personnel—but that much we can do."

"Thank you," Ky said, feeling absurdly grateful.

"Your clothes and weapons will be returned to you at dockside," he went on.

Everyone was back at Vatta dockside when Ky and Martin returned. Ky brushed off the concerned questions. "We both need to clean up," she said. "And I need some sleep. I'm hoping the ship unit will restore this suit." She didn't think it would, but it was worth trying.

After she put her filthy, stained clothes in the 'fresher, she took a long, hot shower and fell into bed. She lay still, breathed deeply, and didn't go to sleep. She tried meditation, attempted to visualize the rainbow . . . but all she could see was the blank black circle of the gun muzzle pointing at her face, and the red blood, all she could feel was the shock of fear and despair, the elation of killing, side by side and overlapping. Again and again, she tried to work her way through the color sequence, the calming words, and each time the black circle and red splatters dominated her thoughts. Finally she emerged from her cabin, still tired, aching, sore where her elbows and knees had hit the pavement . . . but too alert, too tense. It would almost be better if her father was dead, because then he would never know that his daughter, his precious little girl, got a charge out of killing people.

True, they had been trying to kill her—all the ones she had killed—but they were still people, and Sapphic Cyclans considered killing people as primal dissonance. Her failure to visualize the Cycle proved they were right, at least as far as the use of that guided meditation went.

"Jim's sleeping," Quincy said, when she asked about him. "And we've got these for him." Standard spacer shore rig for those not fashion-conscious, blue trousers and a belted tunic in shades of tan with brown trim on sleeves and neck that would pass unnoticed on every station in the quadrant. "Kind of dull, but we thought just not wearing dull green would be a shock." She grinned.

"Good idea," Ky said.

"Are you all right, Captain?"

"I'm fine. Well, I have bruised elbows, but it's not serious." With a wave, Ky headed upship.

On the bridge, Sheryl sat watch. "I won't have to go out for anything, will I?" she asked. She looked as tense as Ky felt.

"No, of course not."

"Good. Lee half wants to, I think. He thinks all this is exciting." Her tone said she thought Lee was crazy.

"You don't," Ky said.

"No. I—I know I'm the only navigator you've got, Captain, and I like you, but if I weren't scared to set foot off the ship, I'd ask to separate. I just want a nice safe berth on a nice safe ship."

Some people just were not cut out for adventure, Ky thought, and then wondered why she herself was. "Sheryl, if there's another ship in that needs a navigator—or whose navigator wants some excitement—I'd say take the chance. But I'm not sure there are going to be many nice safe ships for a while now. Sure, Vatta's being attacked at the moment. But there are other wealthy cargo lines out there, and unless we find out who's doing this and stop them, everyone's at risk."

"I suppose," Sheryl said. She sighed. "I just . . . my stomach gets all knotted up and I can't sleep."

"I know the feeling," Ky said.

"Yes, but you are actually doing things; people have tried to kill you. I haven't been hurt at all yet, and I'm this scared. I'm just sitting here . . ." Her voice trailed away.

That could be fixed. "Sheryl, sitting here alone will just make it worse. So I'm relieving you of bridge duty, starting now. Just a second—" She called the other sections, and found that Alene could indeed use more help with cargo shifting. "You're now a cargo handler. Not dockside—just shifting things inside the ship. No more risk than up here, and you'll be busy and with others."

For an instant Sheryl looked annoyed—a navigator doing physical work?—then she smiled. "Maybe that'll keep my mind off it," she said.

"Hope so," Ky said. "Now scat. I need to make some calls." What she'd told Sheryl was perfectly true. Once the attackers finished mopping up Vatta resources, they would turn on others. If she could get some support from other traders—or even information—she would no longer be fighting this war alone.

Sixteen interstellar ships besides her own were docked at Lastway at the moment. Three were corporate: Pavrati's *Emerald Sky*—she wasn't going to try to talk with *them*. Mellin & Company's *Sunburst*. She didn't know much about Mellin & Company, except that they traded into the next quadrant. Outbound's *Ringwalker*. Outbound typically hauled supplies for start-ups, the basics for terraforming and initial colony construction. The rest were listed as independents, from a huge bulk carrier *Orlando's Song* to little *Lacewing*, with even less cubage (but better engines) than *Gary Tobai*. Ky started at the head of the list, excluding Pavrati, and worked her way down in the order given.

"This is Captain Vatta," she began, when *Sunburst* answered and her call had been transferred to Captain Sunder. "I'm wondering if you have any information about these attacks on trading vessels—"

"On Vatta vessels," he corrected. Onscreen he was clearly a humod, though she didn't recognize the function of some of his physical characteristics. Why the sagittal ridge, for instance? The large bulge on his left forearm? And were those functional gills on his neck? "I have heard nothing about attacks on other registrations."

"That's reassuring for now," Ky said. "But I presume that when whoever it is finishes with Vatta they will start on someone else. Do you have any concerns about that?"

"If I did, I would not share them with you," he said. "Your luck is down; I do not want to be contaminated." And he shut off communication.

"Well, thank you very much," Ky snarled to the blank screen.

With minor variations, this was the response she got from all of them. They all worried; they all recognized that whoever was attacking Vatta might shift to another target. None of them thought allying with Vatta would improve their chances. Nor were they making any effort to cooperate with each other—at least none they would admit to a pariah like her.

"Shortsighted idiots," Ky muttered to herself. "They'll end up in my fix soon enough if they don't start thinking ahead."

"Talking to yourself?" Lee, yawning, came onto the bridge. "Where's Sheryl?"

"I sent her down to work cargo; she was getting twitchy up here by herself."

"If you want privacy, I can go fix us something to eat," Lee said. "It's my turn for galley duty anyway."

"Good idea," Ky said. "Though I don't know what I need privacy for, since none of the other captains will talk to me about the situation. Some offer sympathy, at least, but they're afraid we'll infect them with our bad luck."

"You could try telling them that you are the very embodiment of good luck," Lee said. "Look how many attempts on your life you've survived."

Ky laughed. "I don't think that's the sort of good luck they'd appreciate," she said. "But yes, I'm hungry."

When he brought in a tray for her, he said, "Quincy said to remind you about that package, the one that came while you were out. She put it in your cabin; did you see it?"

"No," Ky said. Hunger beat curiosity for the moment. "I'll look at it after I eat." She worked her way through a bowl of Lee's spicy meat-and-vegetable concoction, then went down the passage and retrieved the package. She recognized MacRobert's handwriting. Probably another spaceship model, and what would this one have as a little surprise? She took a bite of the custard Lee had brought for dessert before she put her thumb on the integral scanner. The top layer of wrapping opened along a flat seam and rolled back. Underneath was another layer of wrapping.

She opened that and found a thick padded folder with the seal of the Slotter Key Diplomatic Service embossed on it instead of the box of model spaceship parts she expected.

"What's that?" Lee asked.

"I have no idea," Ky said, running her fingers over the seal. She opened it. Behind a clear plastic protective cover lay a document with the State Seal at the top, and blocks of dense printing. She started reading. What—? It couldn't be what it looked like. She put it down and rummaged in the depths of the package. An envelope, with a letter from MacRobert.

"No, this isn't another spaceship model," the letter began:

Your family said you'd show up at Lastway eventually, so this was sent by hand to a trusted local agent. Trouble's brewing. Don't know how bad it is, but there are things you need to know. First off, Spaceforce is only a small part of Slotter Key's space defense. The other part is contracted out to private concerns—what you'd call privateers. Your actions at Sabine show that you have, as I always thought, the right mix of attitude and ability.

So, fine, MacRobert suspected she was a killer at heart... then her mind really registered *privateer*. "Pirates in traders' clothing," as one of her instructors had called them... Was MacRobert trolling through the cadets at Spaceforce Academy, looking for potential pirates?

"You always were a bit too independent for Spaceforce," the letter continued:

That fancy folder from the diplomatic service is a letter of marque, authorizing you to act on behalf of Slotter Key to do harm to our enemies, to attack and seize ships and cargo. At your discretion, and using your own best judgment. You're supposed to keep the letter handy to show when called for. You'll notice that it could be mounted on your bulkhead with the handy bracket on the back of the frame. It's not worth the antique materials it's written on when it comes to stopping return fire and it's recognized as a legitimate charter or commission only in the jurisdictions listed at the bottom. Be sure to read that, or you could get interned in a very boring jail somewhere. You won't be able to do much in that little tub, so I suggest you get yourself a better ship as soon as you can.

In the meantime, be sure you order galley supplies from Buchert Brothers and specify the following under "odor barriers": MASKEM *315–2337, six units. Someone will call and ask if that is the correct code, and you'll say yes. When the delivery arrives, be sure to open that container in a secure location. You'll recognize the contents. Right now that's all the help we can give you.*

You'll want to know who Slotter Key's enemies are... I can't tell you that right now. We know something's wrong at ISC, more than what happened at Sabine, and there are other indications that something big is coming. Use your best judgment. The Commandant sends his respects.

Ky looked back at the letter. In archaic and complicated language, it authorized her, Kylara Evangeline Dominique Vatta, to seek out and impede, harrass, annoy, frustrate, confiscate, attack, and destroy any and all enemies of Slotter Key wheresoever she might find them, in space or in dock, by any means whatsoever that lay within her power, and further instructed officers of Slotter Key, diplomatic, military, and "affiliated," whatever that was, to assist her in these endeavors.

Along with stunned astonishment, she was aware of feelings she could not entirely approve. Excitement. Anticipation. Glee.

"It's . . . interesting," she said to Lee, after a long breath. Should she tell him? Why not, after all. In the unlikely event she ever used it, she'd need a pilot. "Our government wants me to turn pirate."

"What?"

"Privateer, actually. This—" She tapped the padded folder. "—is a letter of marque. We studied this kind of thing in school; I had no idea anyone actually did this. Now, not centuries ago somewhere else. It's . . . license to do just about anything."

"To anyone . . . ?"

"No, to the enemies of Slotter Key, which this other letter states they can't identify at the moment. It must've been sent—" She looked again at the letter and its date. "Yes. Before the attacks on Vatta started, and before we became *persona non grata* to the Slotter Key government. Which may make this null and void, though I don't know . . ."

"Only if they formally rescind it, I'd think," Lee said. "Not that I'm an expert, either, but surely they'd have to give you notice."

"And they can't," Ky said. "Because their ansible's blocked."

To her surprise, Lee looked more excited than afraid. "We aren't exactly privateer material, though, are we? Did they send you money for a better ship?"

"Not unless it's hidden in the deodorant I'm supposed to order from a grocer. Why—do you like the idea?"

He didn't answer that directly, but asked, "So . . . are you going to do it?"

Her earlier objections to turning pirate came to mind, but—what choice did she have now?

"I'm going to see what's in the deodorant, anyway," Ky said. "For the rest, I don't know."

"If we had the right ship, it could be fun," Lee said. Then, at her look, he pulled his face into a frown. "Difficult and dangerous, I know. Not fun in the usual sense, but—more fun than just driving a tradeship back and forth."

"You were wasted in commercial shipping," Ky said.

"You, too, Captain."

"I don't know . . . not being shot at for weeks at a time is beginning to look better and better."

Lee shook his head. "You'd get tired of it."

"Maybe. Sheryl and Alene and Ted wouldn't. They hate the excitement, as you call it."

"Maybe they'll find another ship. If any ship is safe."

She looked up Buchert Brothers in the directory. "Restaurant and ship supply, variety and quality at a reasonable price." That's what they all said. The list of products looked normal: bulk and packaged staples, brand-name and "private-label" goods, everything from cleaning supplies to "fresh tank-grown fish, alive until harvested." She compared prices with two other suppliers—about the same. A quick look at their supply situation . . . she entered an order for cleaning supplies, protein powder in five-kilogram containers, a dozen sets of assorted processor flavors, a set of oven trays, and the specified "odor barriers."

A few hours later, uncrating the order in the cargo hold, Ky found herself staring at a shape she knew very well. Here was the other—and more expensive—version of the mines she had put a hold on. Smaller, a little lighter, these contained the most sophisticated electronic attack available.

Properly set and delivered, they could disable an entire ship's systems without causing significant structural damage. An excellent choice for piracy—privateering—and she now had six of them.

"My, my, my," Martin said. "Someone likes you."

"They did, but I think they don't now," Ky said.

"Care to explain?"

"A letter of marque," Ky said. "The package came while we were otherwise occupied, though at the moment I can't recall if it was the puppy or the assassins. Anyway, it was signed and authorized well before the attacks on Vatta, and before the government chose to ignore us."

"Very handy," Martin said.

Ky closed the crate again. "Put this where we can get at it quickly," she told Alene. "We're going to need it once we're back out there."

"What is it?" Alene asked.

"Something I'll tell you all about once we're in a secure location," Ky said. Six mines. And she had fifteen with conventional explosives on hold at MilMart. As soon as she had enough money in the account, she'd put a deposit on them.

CHAPTER NINE

Toby Randolph Lee Vatta slouched on the hard bunk in the cell. He hadn't done anything wrong, but here he was in jail. Without any way to communicate to the family, and no explanation why he couldn't call them.

"Here you are," one of the guards said. "Lunchtime." This was the nicest one, Toby thought. He looked like he'd be a good older brother or father or something. For someone who wasn't a prisoner.

"Thanks," Toby said, as the guard put the tray on the table.

The guard cocked his head. "You aren't hungry again?"

"Not really . . ."

"Thinking about your family?"

"Yes." How could he not? *Ellis Fabery,* blown up in dock, with casualties in the thousands because it had taken out a whole sector. Half the crew was Vatta-born, from captain to cargomaster. And Toby hadn't been aboard to be killed, because he had been rewarded for his spit-clean record the first six months of his apprentice voyage. His cousin Dex, the captain, had let him off the ship to run a simple errand. *Take this message over to the bank, bring back the return message, don't dawdle on the way, act like a grown-up.* So he'd been four sectors away, cooling his heels in the bank manager's waiting room, when the ship blew and the chair shuddered beneath him, and all the intersection seals locked down. When his implant had stabbed him with the burst of static. Sole survivor, so far as they knew. Underaged. Potential target of assassins.

"Nobody likes jail," the guard said. He sat down on the other end of Toby's bunk. "But it's for your own safety."

They had explained that before, as if he was too stupid to understand the first time. He understood. He just could not figure out a way to deal with it. In all his life he had never been alone among strangers, completely separated from his family or friends.

"I know you're doing your best," Toby said. Always be polite to strangers; always be polite to law enforcement. "I just . . . I just don't get hungry." He smiled. "I'm not exercising enough, I guess."

"You're losing weight," the guard said. "We don't want you to fade away by the time some family show up."

"They're coming?" Toby asked. Hope surged; his heart pounded.

"I'm sure they will," the guard said.

"But you don't know . . ."

"No." The guard sighed. "Look, son. Communications are down everywhere. We sent word; we don't know if it got through before the ansibles quit working. ISC will fix them eventually, and then someone will come. We just don't know when. Allray's a little off the main lines."

Allray had seemed exotic once. Allray Station had a live display of its indigenous life-forms, the smaller ones. Toby had seen the online pictures; he wanted to see a hextan and a hexbear in real life. Dex had promised him a free afternoon, if all went well, and Anders, in Engineering, had promised to take him to Allray's open market as well as the life-forms display.

Now all he saw of Allray was this cell and the rooms visible from it. He had a vid setup, and the guards brought him entertainment cubes, but they wouldn't give him a live outside data line. There were only so many hours of the day he could stand to watch episodes of *Lang's Gang, Beyond the Law, Ghost Ships* . . . He'd never noticed before, but now every explosion, battle, and fight reminded him of his loss. He didn't complain. What else was there to do? He'd asked about student programs, hoping to bury himself in math homework problems, but it turned out that he was several levels beyond the highest they kept onstation. His big sister Erin had always told him he was too smart for his own good, but he hadn't imagined the result of racing through his schoolwork would be boredom in a jail cell when he'd done nothing wrong.

"Forensic's through with their... with the... uh... remains," the guard said. "Do you have... do you know... what they'd want?"

He hadn't ever thought, in his darkest adolescent humors, that he'd have to arrange the funerals of his family and other shipmates. The lump in his throat was too big; he couldn't speak. He shook his head.

"You don't have any religion or anything?"

The family altar, back home, and the deities he'd been taught to name, now seemed as meaningless as a plastic cube. What good had it done Cousin Dex to adhere to the standards of ethics? What good had it done Hallie and Prin and Veeah to observe the Days of Silence? They were dead, dead for no reason but malice, and no god they prayed to had kept them safe. He could not explain this to the guard, however friendly. He shrugged, instead, blinking back tears.

"I guess we can keep 'em in the freezer awhile longer," the man said. He sighed, heavily, and stood up. "Son, you're going to have to talk sometime, to someone. Are you sure there's nothing more we can do to help? We're not your enemies, you know."

"I know," Toby said. His voice rasped; it wanted to shake, and only by sounding angry could he control it at all.

The guard left. The smell of food permeated the cell; it made him sick, yet his hunger gnawed at him. Could he eat any of it? Two bites of bread, and he wanted to throw up. He lay back on the bunk, covering his face with his arm. When the guard came back to remove the tray, Toby had curled to face the wall, with the blanket pulled over his head.

* * *

Stella Maria Celeste Vatta Constantin looked around Allray with wary interest. Thanks to the mess that had made her the laughingstock of the family and the bad example held up to youngsters, she had never taken the usual apprentice voyage offplanet. She had traveled, of course, but when she was older, and always with a mission in view. Allray might have looked exotic when she was fourteen, but not now she was thirty. It looked scuffed and tawdry instead; she was too old to mistake scuffed and tawdry for exotic. Traveling under her married name, as she was, she raised no comment in the Customs line. It was one of the things she enjoyed about traveling: no one associated the given name *Stella* with *idiot stupid enough to give family access codes to her first lover.*

The captain of the ISC courier had given her the bad news about *Ellis Fabery* as soon as they downjumped into Allray space, but he had no details. Stella's own implant did not have a complete crew list; the *Ellis* had changed out crew at the beginning of the standard year, and the old list would not be accurate.

She made her way to the station police. They would surely know who had been killed on the ship.

"You're a relative?" the desk clerk said. Stella smiled.

"I need to speak to the officer in charge," she said. "I carry credentials from the family, permission to arrange for disposition of remains."

"But what about the boy?"

"Boy?"

"The kid—someone needs to take him."

"I was not informed of any boy," Stella said, rummaging rapidly through her implant's file of Vatta younglings. Apprentice age . . . Keth? Preston? Toby? Gio? "How old is he?"

"He's fourteen. The only one left. Toby, he says his name is. I guess, if you're the family's representative, you'll have to take him."

All she needed was a fourteen-year-old boy tagging along on this mission. She couldn't say that, though, not to a desk clerk.

"Your officer in charge?" she said again.

"Ah. Right. I'll get him."

The shape under the blanket looked too small to be a fourteen-year-old.

"He hasn't been eating well," the guard said. Stella glanced at the tray, which looked untouched, cold, and unappetizing.

"I can see that."

"We've tried—I've tried myself—but he won't open up at all."

And no wonder, Stella thought. "Toby," she said softly. "Toby, wake up."

The blanket twitched, then stilled. "Toby," Stella said again. "Time to go . . ."

The blanket twitched, then he poked out a thin face, eyes dangerously intense. "Who . . . who are you?"

"Stella Constantin. I've come to settle things here. You can come with me."

Suspicion hardened his expression. "How'd I know you're not one of them?"

"She's not, lad. We checked," the guard said. But Toby's eyes never left hers.

Stella sighed. "Toby, did you ever hear of Stavros' idiot daughter Stella, the idiot who gave the family codes to her lover?"

His brows went up. "You're—?"

"That Stella, yes. But even I didn't stay an idiot forever. Let's get you out of here, shall we?"

He unrolled the blanket and sat up unsteadily. "I—I don't feel well."

"You haven't eaten enough to keep a mouse alive, is what I hear—and what that tray looks like. Don't faint on me, Toby; we don't have time for that."

"Ma'am," the guard said, in a worried voice.

"You can eat the roll," Stella said, ignoring the guard. "Here—" She broke it in half, spread jam on it, and handed it to Toby. "Eat it."

He stared at her for a moment, then took the roll and bit into it.

"Toby, I want to get you off this station before someone finds both of us. I have taken care of everything else—" She saw his jaw stop moving as he took that in, and then resume chewing. "I have your personal belongings, and I brought you something to wear other than jail garb or Vatta uniform. You'll travel as my son."

"I—you aren't old enough!"

"I will look old enough, don't worry. Finish that roll, and another." She turned to the guard. "Can you get us a couple of hot sandwiches, maybe?"

"Of course," he said.

When he was gone, Toby said, "Where are we going?"

Stella raised her brows. He had not said *Where are you taking me*... he was starting to engage. Promising. "I don't want to tell you here," she said. "These people have done a good thing in protecting you, but I'm not sure their records are as secure as they think."

He had wolfed down another roll already and was looking at the rest of the tray, despite the layer of congealed fat on the blob that might be meat.

"Don't," Stella said. "If you haven't been eating, let your stomach get used to the rolls first."

"But you asked for hot sandwiches."

"I asked for time alone, but in different words," Stella said.

He looked at her curiously. "You're—not like... like the captain."

"No. I'm not. I'm not a spacer. I'm administration—" When she was anything. When she was not just "that idiot Stella," the permanent example of what could go wrong. The petty little position she'd held until her pregnancy was only "administration" to someone aboard a ship. What she'd done since, no one knew about.

"But to lie..."

"Misdirect," Stella said. "Similar, but different."

"I don't think it's right to lie," he said.

"I don't think it's right to end up dead just because it's convenient for someone else," Stella said. "Now—can you stand up yet?"

He could, just, though he wavered a bit. Stella handed him the sack. "Put those on. I'll turn my back."

"You're not going to leave?"

That terrified modesty—she remembered that, from her own adolescence. "No," she said, turning her back. "I'm not. I'm also not interested in your skinny little body, except in keeping it alive. Change."

Behind her, the indignant rustles of an annoyed teen. Good. It would keep him from fainting, if he was angry enough with her. She focused her attention outward. The guard should be back by now. Why wasn't he? Why wasn't anyone coming? Why wasn't she hearing the routine noises that she had hardly noticed coming in? She queried her implant just as it pinged her, warning of chemical contamination. She held her breath, reached into her pocket, slapped a full-face membrane onto herself, then pulled out another and whirled to see Toby opening his mouth to gasp.

"No!" she said, and tossed the mask. Thank all the gods, the boy had been properly trained—he knew what it was, didn't breathe until he had it on. His new outfit—the one-piece gray suit—was half fastened. He fumbled at the closure, and then picked up the jacket, eyes wide.

"Can you use a weapon?" Stella asked. He shook his head. "Stay behind me then," she said. She drew her own. For all the good that would do if their enemies had the weapons she suspected.

Out in the corridor, nothing stirred. She saw, just at the corner, the guard who should have brought sandwiches—and there were the sandwiches, on the floor beside his outstretched hand. The other way . . . deeper into the jail . . . she paused a moment to slip a highly illegal dataprobe into the 'port on the wall, at the guard's duty station, and suck out the plans for the police station. Every space on a station had at least two exits. This one had four: the main one to the passage, two rear entrances, and one to the side, through a smaller office.

No time to ponder; she led Toby to the right, toward the cellblock rear exit. If the enemies trusted their gas, they might not have someone outside, or he might be careless.

The outer door was locked, of course. She had expected that. Toby's eyes widened farther when she pulled her tools from her pocket. Picking locks both mechanical and electronic wasn't the usual skill set of a Vatta daughter, but Stella had seen no reason not to learn from later acquaintances—or to tell her father all she'd learned.

Outside, the passage appeared to be a service corridor, set with trash containers neatly labeled with the type of trash each should contain. To the right, she saw the open back door of what, by the smell, was a café of some kind, its BIOLOGICALS trash bin overflowing. She remembered that Huntari Café had been next to the police station . . . probably a favorite hangout of the police, and thus not a good back door to enter. Farther down, a bakery and a greengrocer . . . she hurried Toby that way.

"Can we take off—?" he began.

"No," Stella said over her shoulder. "We may not have any warning next time."

She turned back in time to see someone glance down the passage and quickly turn away. Not good. They were opposite Murchison Books and Antiquities, whose bin contained packing materials. The door seemed ajar. Stella yanked; it came open. She pushed Toby in, slid in herself, pulled it closed, and leaned on the locking bar until it caught firmly.

They were in a cluttered back room with more packing materials and open containers piled on a cluttered desk and on the floor. A closed door in front of them suggested that the actual shop lay beyond. To the right, a narrow staircase rose toward the ceiling where another door was labeled PRIVATE. Stella heard nothing from any direction; she boosted her implant's sensitivity and heard something from outside—footsteps, probably—and the rise and fall of voices from the other side of the closed door. Two voices? Three? She could not make out what they were saying.

From outside another set of footsteps, this time coming closer. She looked around again. No place to hide, really, but up the stairs. She motioned to Toby, finger to lips. If the owner had the private office on an alarm system, they were out of luck, but otherwise . . .

They were almost to the door when the pounding began on the back door. Stella tried the door of the private office—open, and no alarm sounded when she opened it and she and Toby went in. She closed it behind them as her enhanced hearing picked up the sound of the shop door opening and footsteps coming through.

"What is it?" asked the shopkeeper.

"Open up," a voice outside said.

"The shop entrance is 3214 Scurry Lane. This entrance is secured," the shopkeeper said.

"Open up, damn it! We think fugitives got in!"

"Not through this door. Who are you, anyway? You don't sound like—" A scuffling noise. "You aren't the police!" Another noise Stella couldn't identify, a sort of metallic grumble, then a loud clang. A mutter, clear enough with the augmented hearing: "What kind of idiot do they think I am, anyway?" Then, more clearly, "Sam, it's Rafe. Something's happening over here; you'd better check the substation on Fourth Blue East. Some yobbos are trying to get in the back door of my shop claiming to be after fugitives but they aren't any of yours." Click and another click, then, "Hardy—this is Rafe. Block trouble behind me now, probably coming around front. Police not responding. Could be the bunch we're looking for."

Stella blinked. *Yobbos?* The last time she'd heard that word in a very similar voice had been two years back somewhere very far from here. Rafe? *That* Rafe?

"Ahh . . . no answer, eh? Well, I've got to close up shop before they come in the front. Ta." Brisk footsteps, fading into the distance; no sound of the door closing between shop and office.

Stella looked around the office. Neater than that below, a desk with ordinary data hookups and displays, a bunk covered with a striped blanket, a small synthesizer and meal prep center, a curtain across—she glanced in—a tiny but very clean toilet–shower combo. Cabinets above and below the desk, along the walls. A secondary screen, on which movement caught her eye—the display of a security system, now showing the back of someone she assumed was the proprietor, as he pulled down louvered screens across the shop displays. The door, she noticed, was already closed and barred. The man looked to be of medium height, slender, with thinning gray hair pulled back to a braid tied with a ribbon. He had the second display covered now, and turned.

Stella caught her breath. That Rafe, indeed. He glanced up into the security system's scan, and smiled. Winked. Well, that cinched it. He knew. Naturally he would. Naturally he would have video pickups in his inner office, as well as downstairs, and naturally he would have checked them. He walked back to the store's service desk without looking up again. That, too, was Rafe; he had made his point. Now he would wait around for whatever help he'd called in. Stella glanced at Toby, wishing she could spirit him away somehow. He was too young for this, and she couldn't explain; Rafe would have audio pickups everywhere.

If he knew they were there, if he knew who they were—who she was—then she might as well use his systems. Stella found the security system controls for the interior scan and re-aimed the pickup so that she could watch Rafe. He was just standing there, entering something in the computer—a list of books, she saw when she zoomed in, from the stack of books on the counter. Old books, antiques, real paper. She couldn't quite focus on the titles, but she could, from up here, link into the computer he was using.

She did that, first returning the surveillance vid to a scan that included the shop's front door. Under the day's date, a list of titles sufficiently odd that Stella paused, scrolling down, and tried to think what scam he was up to now. Some historical society's volumes thirty-two through forty-seven? Estate rolls of places she'd never heard of? Three cookbooks? A book of instructions for butlers? Surely no one actually bought these things to read . . .

Toby tapped her arm and pointed at the toilet cubicle. Stella shook her head. It would make a sound anyone could hear—though she suspected that Rafe had the upstairs soundproofed and scanproofed as well as he could, gurgling and whooshing in pipes was one sound that no soundproofing really damped.

Something moved on the surveillance vid, catching her peripheral vision. She glanced up. Rafe was moving toward the door, holding a weapon she didn't recognize. She turned up the sound. A loud clang, followed by a whistle . . . Rafe swept an arm down, to a pocket, then to his face. Stella checked the chemscan sidebar: nothing yet, he was just being cautious. Light blossomed in the middle of the door; the attackers were trying to burn through. Then a confusion of noises from outside: voices, thumps, crackles, small explosive cracks, and the cloth-ripping sound of rapid-fire small arms loaded with station-safe frangibles. Silence.

Rafe, standing alert beside the door, said, "Block party?"

"Got 'em, Rafe," came a voice from outside. "Ten of 'em. Pollies aren't here yet—wait . . . there they come."

"Any chem stain, Hardy?"

"No. You can open up, if your door's not too damaged. Security screen has a hole as big as I am melted through."

"Right." Rafe tucked his weapon behind a display and hit the door controls. The outer louvered screen slid aside slowly, then stopped halfway, and he opened the inner door. Stella touched the controls, aiming the vidscan at the outer door. Now she could see the melted section—another sidebar gave its probable temperature on the basis of thermal radiation—and beyond it a scatter of bodies and some men holding weapons, already walking away. Others appeared in uniform: the arriving police, she presumed.

"Looks like you had a problem," the first of these said.

"We all do," Rafe said. "Did you find out why station Fourth Blue East didn't respond?"

"Chemstunned," the man said. "We think the attackers were after the Vatta kid. Must've got him, too, because he's not there. Why were they after you, Rafe?"

"They said, escaping fugitives. Tried to get in my back door, claimed they were pollies. Luckily I keep it locked. So I'm guessing that somehow the kid got away. After all, you'd had us all warned off to shelter him—somebody must've taken him in."

"Not you?"

"Not that I know of," Rafe said. "Like I said, my back door's locked except when I'm putting out stuff to recycle or going over to Huntari for lunch—and then I lock it behind me. Nobody's reported them?"

"Not yet." The policeman shrugged. "Could be anywhere if the attackers didn't get him. We'd better find him, in case there's more bad guys. By the way . . . you do know that vigilante action is illegal?"

"I was inside the whole time, Fred."

"Right. Your close friends and neighbors just showed up fully armed and chem-protected by chance . . ."

"The whole station's jumpy, Fred. If they choose to help me out when the police have been immobilized . . . I'd say that's a good thing."

"I'm not complaining," the policeman said. "Just pointing out the law, which is my duty. If the violation of ordinance has ceased, then . . . that's all I have to do."

"Thank you," Rafe said, in a tone that Stella recognized. Rafe had always had a gift for irony.

"Want us to check out the store?"

"If you wish, but as I said I was locked in back when they came, and you can see they didn't get through the front. Almost, though."

"If you're sure—we do have other things to do. I'll have a new roster in that substation within the hour—our people there are all headed for hospital—and we'll add patrols.

Forensics have to check out these bods and see if they can identify them. If you see any sign of the Vatta kid, let me know. Oh, and there's a Vatta family representative around somewhere—was supposed to be headed for the police station, but we don't know if she got there."

"She?"

"Yeah, a woman. I'll flash you the picture. Not a Vatta herself, apparently, but a family retainer. S. M. Constantin. Probably a lawyer. Came in on an ISC courier."

"I should report her, too?"

"If you see her. Let's hope these scum didn't get her."

"Let's hope," Rafe said. "Look—I've got to call Maintenance to get a repair crew over here. Talk later?"

"Right." The policeman turned away.

Rafe shut the inner door, picked up the weapon behind the display, and came back to the shop counter, with another grin for the camera. At the counter he made what seemed to be a perfectly straightforward call to Station Maintenance, requesting repair or replacement of the security grille and inner door of the shop on an urgent priority basis. "And I may be up in my back office—just give me a call before you arrive." Then with a final glance at the camera, he headed toward the back of the store.

Stella turned down the sound augmentation on her implant and turned to Toby. "We're about to have company, it looks like. Remember—we're trespassing, and we have no rights."

"Yes..." Toby looked pale again. Stella slid her own weapon back into its holster. She heard the footsteps come into the stockroom, pause, and then come up the stairs. The door opened.

Rafe stood there, lips pursed, and shook his head. "Stella, Stella, Stella... do you have to be so dramatic?"

"Me?" It was all she could say; as always, he took her breath away, and memories crowded her mind.

"My dear, if you just wanted to see me again, all you had to do was give me a call... though I suppose with the ansibles down that might have been difficult." He glanced aside at Toby. "Vatta kid, I suppose? Escaped from custody? You'd better go use the toilet, boy; you look ready to puke on my floor, and I wouldn't like that."

Toby gave Stella a desperate look; she nodded and he fled to the toilet cubicle.

"Nice work, Stella," Rafe said, ignoring the sounds from that direction. "Spurn my invitation, ignore me for years, then break into my shop and bring down gods only know what on my head... I suppose you'd rather I didn't tell the pollies where you were?"

"When and if the personnel from that station wake up, they'll explain," Stella said. "I went there to authorize handling the remains of the others, and they told me about Toby, wanted me to take him. Then it got very quiet, and when I looked out... they were down. I took him out the back—"

"Which you just happened to know about, and how to open the door," Rafe said, nodding.

"I still have the picklocks," Stella said.

"And the dataprobe, I'll bet," Rafe said, this time with approval. "I always said you were more like me than you wanted to admit."

"And *your* door was ajar," Stella said.

"Luckily for you," Rafe said. "Since your picklocks would have set off a stunblast. I heard the front bell just as I came back in and didn't make sure it closed all the way. Foolish of me. Could've been fatal if the others had made it here first. I suppose you think I should thank you for that?"

"No," Stella said. "But I'll take thanks if you're offering them."

Rafe laughed. The same laugh. Warm tingles ran over her. Damn the man. Legend said it was your first love that always held some power over you, but in her case the first love was an unpleasant memory—how could she have fallen for that toad?—and Rafe a constant temptation.

Toby came out of the toilet cubicle looking pale, but less strained. "Sorry," he muttered.

"Fear does that," Rafe said. His grin at the boy was entirely comradely, with none of the rakehell glint he gave Stella. "You look half starved, boy; didn't they feed you over at the station?"

"Couldn't eat," Toby muttered. "Now—"

"Now you could eat a whole rationpak in one bite, eh? Stella, it's up to you—I can feed you here, or we can play lost-and-found and let the police know where you are, then take the lad to Huntari for a good meal."

"I want to get him to safety—which I suspect means on a ship with no Vatta connections, out into space—as soon as possible. What do you think—are there still assassins out there?"

"Mmm. Could be. Finding a ship's not going to be easy, either. Most of 'em won't take anyone with Vatta connections, or anyone from Slotter Key, just in case. You'll need other ID, if that's your plan. Where'd you want to go? Back to Slotter Key?"

"No. Lastway, I'm thinking. Nobody'd expect us to go there, and it's right out on the fringes."

He tilted his head. "Lastway. But Vatta trades there, don't they?"

Stella cursed silently. Of course he would know that. Rafe had an information network galaxywide.

"Sometimes," she said. "No regular schedule that I know of, though I'm not in on all the family business."

"Your checkered past," Rafe said, feigning sympathy. Stella wanted to hit him.

"My checkered past," she said instead. "So . . . I suppose you could arrange alternative IDs?"

"Easier if the pollies don't know you're around," he said. "They have such . . . traditional attitudes toward identity."

"That's a yes," Stella said to Toby, who was wide-eyed. At least he wasn't interrupting.

"We'd better feed the boy something here, then," Rafe said.

CHAPTER TEN

While Toby spooned down a bowl of flavored mush larded with restorative additives, Rafe sat at his desk manipulating his security scanners. Stella lounged on the cot, uncomfortably aware of its other use.

"Station's in an uproar," Rafe said over his shoulder. "Casual muggings dockside, nothing unusual. Vendettas, brawls, even wholesale gang fights in dockside bars—we're used to that, same as any station is. But blowing a docked ship—that shook everyone. Killed not just the crew, but about half the people in that sector, including the emergency response team there. Half the ships here pulled out, right then, and no one blamed 'em, though it meant we're short of some supplies. Nothing critical, but a nuisance. Pollies're overstretched; you know how station militia are . . ."

"Yes," Stella said. She did not want his lecture on police and militia organization; she'd had it before.

"So stationers organized block defenses. Everyone knew the perps were still here, most likely, on the hunt for the boy, or for any more Vatta ships that showed up. Or ships that might be friendly to Vatta. Technically, it's illegal, but practically speaking the pollies were glad of our help and so was station management. Longtime stationers were even able to access police armories. I'm not in that group."

He couldn't be, since five years before he had been somewhere else. With her, one way and another. Stella said nothing, and he went on.

"You came in on an ISC courier, I hear. You know anything about the ansible problem?"

"Only that they're down almost everywhere, and ISC is trying to get them back up. Apparently some are fried, and others just trashed."

"Mmm. Frying suggests sabotage to me, someone internal. What do they think?"

"I was encouraged not to ask," Stella said. "Condition of transport. But they'd take Toby and me, if we got to them and wanted to go where they're going next."

"Which is?"

"I don't know. Another thing I was encouraged not to ask. Eventually, I have a message for their headquarters, but I have no idea how many transfers that would be."

"I see." Rafe turned his chair around. "I don't see you having any advantage to me, at the moment. What do you have to trade?"

"Sufficient hard goods," Stella said. Of course he wouldn't help them for nothing; this was Rafe, after all.

"I'm moderately concerned for the welfare of this station," Rafe said. "It has been a profitable connection. However, additional security measures and lower levels of trade may cut into my profits. Seeing as how Vatta seems to be involved in causing me inconvenience, perhaps I should find another source of income."

"Such as?"

"Perhaps we should consider a partnership," Rafe said, studying his fingernails. "Your family is in disarray; you must need allies. I have... certain... expertise, and certain connections. You have, as you said, hard goods, and your family's legendary expertise in trade and profit... and a trade network second to none, I understand."

"But if we are in disarray, how can that help you?" Stella asked. "I fear you suggest a partnership in which we cannot provide a fair balance of advantage—"

"Disarray, perhaps, but I've no doubt—however they've kept you sequestered—that you have access where a..."

where someone like me might not. And vice versa. As I said before, Stella, we would make good partners."

"Possibly, for a limited time. But you know, Rafe, I have other loyalties."

"I know. So you said." He glanced at Toby, who was now staring into an empty bowl, studiously ignoring them both. "And I can see that the survival and welfare of this boy must be a priority. What is he to you, anyway?"

"A cousin," Stella said.

"Ah." Rafe stretched out his legs. "Well, let's start with keeping him safe. Does he have living family anywhere, or is this a lifelong commitment?"

"I have ears," Toby said, not looking up. Stella grinned at this proof of Vatta spirit.

"Sorry, boy," Rafe said. "But you were so quiet—"

"I don't know!" Toby burst out. His eyes glittered dangerously. "I know my uncle's dead, and everyone on the ship, but I don't know about others—my parents—" He looked at Stella. "Do you?"

"No," Stella said. "I know Vatta ships and holdings have been attacked in many places, but with the ansible shut down, I don't know about your parents specifically. Still, you're alive."

"And we want to keep you that way," Rafe said. The smile he turned on the boy was full of his rakish charm. "If that sat well enough with you, dial another bowl of it. We need you strong and fit for whatever comes next."

"How do you know Stella?" Toby asked instead.

Rafe's grin widened. "Let me count the ways... no, that's not nice. At least you have enough blood to blush. Stella and I met some years back, and nothing more, is the truth of it. I asked her to partner me, and she refused. She wanted to get back to her family."

"Are you the one—er, sorry..." Toby's blush deepened with the swift embarrassment of the adolescent who has just put his foot in it.

"No," Stella said firmly. "No, he's not. He was after . . . after that." Her heart thundered and she took a deep breath. Damn Rafe! This wasn't anything she wanted to discuss with a youngster, even if they'd had time to explain it all. "He's right, though. You should eat a little more, if you can."

"And you, Stella," Rafe said. Stella shook her head. "Suit yourself, but you need a clear head, and hunger isn't."

"I'm fine," Stella said. "Good breakfast and all that."

"So . . . partners?"

"You'd just close up your shop and leave?"

"Not much market for antiquities and books without a certain number of travelers coming through," Rafe said. "Hard to get new stock, too, and the stationers have bought all they're going to until trade picks up."

"Rafe—what were you *really* selling?"

His face hardened. "My business, isn't it?"

"Not if we're going to partner. I have enough wolves on my tail already; I want to know what other hazards you're bringing into this."

He spread his hands. "None I know of. Some of the packages may have contained . . . additions . . . to the objects on the manifest, but you saw how friendly the pollies were." He glanced again at Toby. "Perhaps this discussion could take place another time?"

"Perhaps," Stella said. She felt exhausted; after-action letdown. "I will have something to eat, I think."

"Good," Rafe said. "I don't want you to regret a decision made by low blood sugar."

"You're so thoughtful," Stella murmured, and smiled when he glared at her.

"What do you need from your base?" he asked. "And are you still based on the courier or do you have a rental?"

"Everything I actually need is with me," Stella said. "I have a duffel aboard ship, though. And I'd have to let them know, if I take another route out."

"They have room for three?"

"Probably not." Her cabin had been cramped for one; she suspected the life support on couriers was less flexible than on tradeships.

"We'll need to find out. Do you trust them?"

"Of course," Stella said. He said nothing, just looked at her. She remembered what he'd said about the implications of the ansible problems. "Oh. You mean do I trust this particular courier crew?" He nodded. She thought about it. Scrupulously polite, uninquisitive just as they had been uninformative. "If they'd wanted to kill me, it would've been easy."

"Yes..." That in a long drawl. "But you're not traveling as Vatta, are you? Vatta representative, the police said."

"They surely know," Stella said.

"Um. Probably. And probably safe enough. But you'll need a secure way to communicate. Something better than station lines, which are...possible to compromise."

"Meaning you have," Stella said. She was not surprised.

"I could," Rafe corrected gently. "And so could anyone else with my expertise. For the boy's sake I suggest extreme caution. And—forgive my suspicions—I would like some assurance that you actually do have those items of value you spoke of."

Stella slipped her weapon out; Rafe did not move, but she felt his attention sharpen. She handed it to Toby, who hastily put down his second bowl of food. "Toby, this is a model you may not be familiar with. Safety's that red knob. Pull it out now. It's off safety now. Keep it pointed at Rafe, whom I trust absolutely to be Rafe..."

Rafe smiled, this time with what looked like genuine appreciation.

"And do not hesitate to shoot if he makes a move, or if I suddenly fall over."

"Yes...," Toby said. His hand, she noticed, did not shake.

"Now," Stella said. She reached into her bodice and fished into the top pocket of the safe, pulling out the little suede container. She shook the stones out on her hand; they flashed brilliance around the room. Rafe caught his breath. "Yes," Stella said. "Genuine. Natural." She rolled them back into the suede pouch, and tucked it away again.

"I gather there are more?" Rafe said. His pulse had quickened, visible in his neck.

"Oh, yes," Stella said. "But not all in the same place."

"Of course," he said. "I am satisfied, then, that you have sufficient stock of value to enter into an equal partnership. I suppose I should show you mine—" He turned the chair.

"Toby," Stella said. Rafe froze. "I suppose you should sit perfectly still," she said, "until our agreement is finalized."

"You don't want to see my accounts?" Rafe said, too lightly.

"I don't want to see the business end of any of the weapons you have in your desk or on your person," Stella said.

"My, you *have* learned," Rafe said. He spread his hands. "All right. Terms?"

"Recording," Stella said. She indicated her implant with one finger. "I know your scans are on, at least in here, so you'll have your own record as well." She took a deep breath and went on. "Partnership, limited, sixty days to start with, renewable by agreement of both parties. Can be unaffiliated by either party, with due notice of not less than twenty-four hours onstation, or twenty-four hours after arrival if on shipboard. Absolute for personal protection from physical, chemical, or biological attack by the partner or partner's agent for the duration of the partnership and for a minimum of three standard days following its ending. Usual for sharing of information: all information relevant to the partnership shared, other information optional. Do you agree to these terms, Rafael Stoner Madestan?"

His expression was rueful. "I should never have taught you so well, Stella. Yes, I, Rafael Stoner Madestan, agree to these terms as offered by Stella Maria Celeste Vatta—sorry, I don't know your married name. I swear to abide faithfully by my partner in . . . in this enterprise, and to consider paramount the welfare of all partners. Does the boy enter into this?"

Stella carefully did not look at Toby. "He is of age, just.

Toby, do you agree to these terms as full partner, or do you wish the protection of a minor?"

"You're asking me?" His voice squeaked, then firmed. "As a member of Vatta family... Yes, I agree to these terms as a partner, accepting both Stella Maria Celeste Vatta Constantin and Rafael Stoner Madestan as partners for this enterprise."

"Good," Stella said. "And I, Stella Maria Celeste Vatta Constantin, accept you, Toby Lee Vatta, and Rafael Stoner Madestan as my partners in this enterprise, according to the terms as recorded in my implant and in Ser Madestan's office security recorders."

"Fine," Rafe said. "Now can the boy—sorry, Toby—quit threatening me with a live weapon?"

"Of course," Stella said. "Toby, point that weapon at the floor and push in the red knob."

"You're sure we can trust him?" Toby said.

"At this point, we have to find out," Stella said. "But yes, Rafe has his own code of honor and I believe we can trust him."

Toby nodded and complied; Rafe sat very still until the weapon was back in Stella's hands and hidden away once more in her holster. Then he heaved a sigh.

"Stella, dearest, you nearly made me create a mess. I do believe Toby would have shot me."

"Indeed he would," Stella said. "But he didn't, so you have no complaints now, right?"

"Right," Rafe said. "To work, then. When I realized trade was going right out the air locks, after the explosion, I began converting some of my assets to the same kind of portable hard goods you have. Of course, it was difficult because others on the station were trying to do the same thing, and antiquities are not necessities."

"And you always have your run money," Stella said. Rafe shook his head.

"I am well reproved for earlier misdeeds," he said. "Yes, of a sufficiency. What I propose to do now is put my stock in storage, explain to the authorities that without trade there's not sufficient profit, and depart. If you are known to have employed me, perhaps as a bodyguard, that would explain—"

"That an antiquities dealer has bodyguard capabilities?"

"No, simply my departure. Perhaps you engaged me as the best you could find, all the regular bodyguards being unwilling?"

"Would they be unwilling?" Stella asked.

"They could be . . . dissuaded," Rafe said.

She could not stop the chuckle that emerged. "I see. So you have far more deals going on this station than selling books and things and . . . whatever comes in the parcels."

He spread his hands. "You know me too well, Stella."

Alas, she did. But after the first appalling realization that she had put herself and her emotions in danger, she had also realized that Rafe was the one person who might, just might, help her get to Lastway and find Ky. Especially since she had Toby along.

"So my thought is first to tell ISC that we need more berths, if they've got 'em . . ."

"A secure line. You need a secure line. Do you have the courier's contact number?"

"Yes. What do you have, optical spider hooks all over the place?"

"Not exactly all over." Rafe pulled out a number of thin, stiff fibers from beneath a book and ran them into a standard-configuration plug, which he then plugged into the side of his desk unit. "Berth number . . . got that. All right. Since I'm sure you don't trust me, you enter the contact code with your own lily-white hands."

Stella came over to the desk and entered the code. Of course his system would capture it, but it wasn't the hidden one. When the linkage icon went green she looked at Rafe. "Do you want me to stick to text?"

"Better," he said.

"Fine." Stella keyed in the pertinent data, as she saw things, and waited until the answer came back, demanding a visual. Rafe shrugged and moved over to take the blanket off the bunk while Stella sat at the desk.

"Vid hookup's on your left, third row," Rafe said. Stella found it and plugged in.

The courier's com officer stared out of Rafe's desk monitor, in the crisp brilliant color she'd have expected from one of Rafe's hookups. "Are you all right?" he asked. "Something's got the station police stirred up—captain wants to leave as soon as we can."

"I'm fine. Jos, what they didn't tell us is that there was a survivor of the Vatta attack—an apprentice who was offship at the time. They've had him in protective custody. I was signing him out when there was . . . a bit of trouble. Thing is, I need to get him offstation and somewhere safe, but I'm betting you don't have room."

"Er . . . I can ask the captain. How big is he?"

"And a third party," Stella said without answering that. "I'm bringing an escort, from here—I can't take care of the kid alone."

"I'm sure we can't do that," the com officer said. "I'll ask the captain, but—we're only a courier."

"I know. And I'm very grateful, but that's how it is."

"Understood. But you still have gear aboard, and you had urgent messages for the Chair . . . and where are you calling from, anyway?"

"Secure line," Stella said. "I know; I'm hoping you can offload my gear and take a burst message."

"That we can do, but if you're in danger—"

"I'll be all right," Stella said, "if I keep the boy and myself out of sight for a bit."

Toby did not want to stay alone in the upper office, but Rafe insisted that Stella not go to the dock alone. "Chances are they're all dead, but if they're not, Stella needs an escort, and I can't guard both of you at once."

"What if someone comes here?" Toby asked. "I'm not

even supposed to be here." He looked better; the enriched mush had made a big difference, Stella noticed.

"I just asked Maintenance when they might get around to repairs, and they said a minimum of two days—they're still coping with the blast damage on the docks. And I've told the block protection group that I'm closed until I get the repairs done. No one should come, and if they do, you ignore them. Just in case—" Rafe opened one of the file drawers in the cabinet: whatever was inside wasn't files in the usual sense, and he came out with a bell-barreled weapon. "—this is a crowd control weapon, Toby. It will take out a substantial number with each shot, because it's loaded with shrapnel—and no, Stella, it's not legal, but it's dead easy to use. What you do, Toby, is point this at the bad guys and pull this lever. It kicks like ding-dong, so brace it on your hip or a desk or something. It will make a horrible mess, including of the wall behind your target, so be sure it's necessary. Otherwise, don't hesitate. For chem protection, I can do better than those membrane masks Stella had—good for out and around and being inconspicuous, but this—" He hauled out a standard Pittsdon protective suit. "—is your best bet. Ever worn one?"

"We did drill in them aboard the ship," Toby said.

"Good. Now. I've set all the external systems on full alarm. You have an implant—let's see—you should have channel fourteen open, right?"

"Right," Toby said, looking more enthusiastic.

"I'll program the alarms to ping your implant. First ping—anything, no matter how minor—suit up. Second ping, get the weapon and back into the toilet space. You have a clear line of fire, and they have to find you. Don't, please, shoot us when we come back."

"I won't," Toby said.

"And dial yourself some high protein now, about a hundred grams. We'll be back in a couple of hours, I expect."

Toby looked at Stella, and she made herself smile at him. "Don't fret, Toby, we'll be back for you."

Not surprisingly, Rafe had covert exits from his shop, and he and Stella finally emerged two passages over. They looked, she thought, like any young businesswoman and her older male escort—his gray hair and conservative clothes were, she knew, a disguise—but she was too aware of the potential danger. The attackers would certainly have vidscan of her from dockside, and possibly a line into Customs and Immigration.

"We need to stop by here," Rafe said, as they neared a small café.

"We do?" Stella said, but followed his lead. She was certain he wasn't after a quick snack, but he sat down in an empty booth, facing the door. Stella sat opposite him, and her back itched. Facing the door was her choice.

"Rafe—heard you had some problems over at your place." That was a brisk-looking man with a long apron and a pot of something in his hand.

"Idiots tried to burn in my front door," Rafe said. "I tell you, Lars, this about does me in. Trade's been down, and I've foisted off all the old books and prints and statuettes you longtime stationers can absorb—"

The man laughed. "You're right there. We still haven't finished *The Longway Saga,* and *Myths of Ancient Rome* may never make it off the shelf."

"They don't know when they'll get to my security grille, let alone the door, and I don't know if I can afford it anyway. Can't do business until it's fixed, not without going out with a box and obstructing the common walkway."

"Which is against the fire code. Right. Coffee?"

"No . . . I was wondering if you'd seen Joey."

"Ah, Joey. Well, I heard he was assisting the police with their inquiries . . . I told you, Rafe, Joey could get you into trouble."

"He's not bad," Rafe said. "Want you to meet my friend Sally here."

"Sally," the man said. "Any friend of Rafe's . . ." His voice trailed away; he looked past them, his gaze sharpening.

"Be right with you," he said; then, to Rafe, "Strangers. Trouble?"

"Maybe," Rafe said. "I'd hate to cause a problem—"

"No problem." The man moved in the direction of his gaze; Stella fought the urge to turn around.

"We might have to leave," Rafe said to her. "I'm sorry—I thought a snack would do you good."

Stella kept her own voice low. "Very interesting girl, Sally."

"Oh yes. Known her a long time, I have. Once had a thing for her. She teaches primary."

"Teaches?"

"Quite firm with the little lads, I understand. A bit of a softy with the girls, especially the pretty ones."

Stella felt her face heating. "You are a wicked man, you know that?"

"Oh, darlin', I know that very well. You look pretty when you're mad, Sally dear."

"You do realize I don't have to be mad to move fast?"

"That's good because—come on!" He was out of the booth, walking toward the back entrance, as someone behind her let out a yowl of pain. Stella slid out of the booth and followed, not looking around. She could hear the proprietor's apologies, profuse and urgent, and the angry voices of at least two men, and then they were through the swinging door in a cramped kitchen, where a gray-haired woman kneaded a pile of dough on a counter and a skinny girl had her head in an oven, an array of tools spread on its open door.

"Oh, Rafe," the older woman said. "I've been meaning to tell you—I'm really enjoying *The Longway Saga*."

"I'm glad, Tulie. Catch you later, maybe?"

"Sure. Ginny, get your head out of that oven and say hello to Rafe and—"

"Sally," Rafe said firmly. "Never mind, Ginny, we're just passing through."

"Some idiot put a number six cone in here instead of a number eight." The girl's voice sounded strange, coming from inside the oven. "Hi Rafe, 'bye Rafe."

The back door let them out into a passage much like that behind Rafe's shop. "So all the bad guys aren't gone," Stella said.

"Apparently not. We'll have to go to Tommy's. I was hoping to avoid that. Joey's a leetle more reliable, for this kind of thing."

"Picking up my gear at the dock?" Stella said.

He looked at her. This time her insides did nothing. "No," he said, after that long look. "And we have to go to Tommy's first."

Tommy's appeared to be a home furnishings store, complete with new and used items and an instore fabricator for custom orders. DESIGN YOUR OWN BED, the poster read. The illustration was nothing Stella would want to sleep in, but she supposed there were people of certain persuasions who would find it... useful. Certainly not restful. As she looked around, more and more of the items seemed suitable for a particular clientele.

"Don't worry," Rafe said. "Tommy's staked out a market niche, but it's not the one he lives in."

Before Stella could ask, Tommy himself appeared. He dressed to appeal to the market niche, Stella assumed, and since it wasn't the one she lived in, either, she felt uncomfortable.

Rafe wasted no time in pleasantries. "Alternate IDs, Tommy. How much, how fast?"

Tommy's full red lips pursed. "You have a problem, Rafe? I don't want trouble with the police. In my line of business, you know, I can't afford—"

"To have them know that you're playing with the stationmaster's daughter? I suppose not."

Tommy paled. "How'd you—what makes you think I—"

"She told me," Rafe said. "I'm her father confessor or something like that... you really shouldn't, Tommy. Young girls are not reliable about keeping secrets. You know that."

"I know you're a pain in the—" Tommy looked at Stella. "And who's this, some female agent?"

"A friend," Rafe said. "To return to my first question: how fast, how much?"

"Two hours each. Five thousand each. Hard goods."

"Fine. We need three. Me, her, and a fourteen-year-old kid, male, shorter than her, dark hair, dark eyes—"

"I need the data."

"Tommy . . . these are alternate IDs. You make the data up. And you don't screw around. We'll be back in two hours, with the goods. Squeal, and the deal's off."

"But I—I said two hours each."

"And I said we'd be back in two hours. Get busy."

"But if I—"

"If you don't," Rafe said, rounding on him, "then the stationmaster's daughter will have a very unpleasant discussion with her mother, and her mother will have an even more unpleasant discussion with you. You did know the father's one of Bruno's men?"

Tommy's skin paled even more and acquired a green undercast.

"So you will have them ready, and we will pick them up, and you will have some trade goods and all will be calm and bright . . . won't it?"

"Y—yes, Rafe. Ma'am."

"Come on, Sal. Time to make tracks and drive a train on them."

From Tommy's, they traveled a fast, direct route to the docks, and Rafe stayed back as Stella walked up to the ISC dock warden, who waved to her. "Glad you're here, Sera, because the captain is ready to break loose. Your duffel's here; they said something about a burst message?"

"No recording where I was. Can I use your set?"

"Of course, Sera. I hear one of the crew lived?"

"A boy. Apprentice. I've got to take him somewhere. Nobody's going to Slotter Key, I know that . . . I've hired a guard."

"Yeah. I see him. Looks kinda old."

"Age and treachery over youth and beauty, Pete," Stella

said. She put on the headpiece, tapping the connection to be sure it was seated against her implant's external pickup, and closed her eyes. Composing a burst message required total concentration. She had thought through what she needed to send, and was almost finished when her concentration broke at the sound of weapons fire.

CHAPTER ELEVEN

Pete hunched behind the service counter, weapons in hand. An alarm whooped. Stella couldn't see what was going on without unhooking the burst message headset; she reviewed what she'd recorded already, decided it was enough, coded it "interrupted/trouble," and detached herself. The recording booth would already have transmitted the message to the courier's shielded com center. At the ship's access, two armored ISC security personnel were firing at something in the middle distance—near the dockside entrance, she guessed. Prudence suggested that down on the deck would be a good idea; the recording booth wasn't armored. Stella slid down and eeled her way to Pete's side.

He turned and tapped his implant; Stella nodded.

"That guard of yours . . . told us he spotted . . . some trouble." Pete's transmission was punctuated with little bursts of white sound when he fired. "He was right . . . dunno if . . . it was you or us . . . they were after."

"I'm armed," Stella said into her skullphone.

"Figured," Pete said. "Just stay down."

Always listen to the professionals, Stella had been told often enough. She pulled out her weapon anyway, and waited. Return fire ceased; the alarms silenced. Stella stayed down, not needing Pete's reminder.

"Police are arriving," he said, relaying information from the ISC guards at the ship access. This time he spoke into the air, and Stella answered the same way.

"Good. Safe to get up?"

"Probably, but I'd stay down another tick or so if I were you. Just in case. Oh—here comes your guard..."

Rafe came around the end of the counter. "You have interesting friends," he said. "Persistent, too, if not very bright."

"Good job you spotted them," Pete said.

"Thank you," Rafe said, with demureness alien to his nature. "I was lucky—they didn't see me, and they were talking openly."

"Ah. I'll be glad to get off this place, and I wish you were coming with us," Pete said to Stella.

"I'll be all right," Stella said, with confidence she didn't feel.

"Hope so," Pete said, with another glance at Rafe, this one slightly edged.

"I'll take care of her," Rafe said. His smile appeared entirely genuine, even to Stella.

"We'll get your burst to HQ soonest," Pete said to Stella.

"Anyone hurt?" came a hail from the other side of dock space.

"Not here," Pete called back. "Just being careful."

On the way back to Fourth Blue, Rafe took every opportunity to check for followers. They dodged through restaurants, clothing stores, even a weapons shop—Rafe seemed to know everyone. Finally they took a drop tube to Second, and worked their way back up through Blue Sector, stopping at Third to pick up the new ID from Tommy.

"Don't be surprised," Rafe said before they entered. "Tommy's been a bad boy and I have to do a little cleanup."

Cleanup, where Rafe was concerned, had many variant meanings, including sudden death. Stella shrugged. If Tommy had set pursuers on them, she didn't care what Rafe did to him. Inside, Tommy was talking to two—no, three—people who seemed to share the dominant decorating style of the place. He didn't notice them until Rafe picked up the bald man and deposited him on an odd-shaped couch. The skinny one whirled, but Stella had her weapon out.

"Don't," she suggested mildly. He backed away, almost

falling over a low table. That left the woman with the low-cut silver snugsuit, who walked over and sat on the bald man.

"Tommy," Rafe said. Tommy shook his head, eyes wide, even before Rafe said, "Have you been a bad boy, Tommy?"

"Not me!" Tommy said. "I didn't—it was—"

"I think you have, Tommy," Rafe said. "I think you've been a very bad boy..."

Stella realized, with a lurch of disgust, that Tommy's former customers were watching this avidly, and that Rafe was playing to them as well as to Tommy.

"I asked you to do one simple thing," Rafe said. "One simple thing, and you couldn't even get that right... went whining off to somebody for sympathy, didn't you, Tommy?"

"I—I told you it'd take longer... I couldn't..."

"Excuses, Tommy. Excuses are worth... nothing. You know there will be consequences..."

"No..."

"Oh, yes," Rafe said. He glanced at the erstwhile customers, who were sitting in a row now, flushed and excited, and then watched Tommy as he ticked off points on his fingers. "First, disobedience... then disloyalty, in running off to someone else... and then... I don't suppose you have completed the assignment?"

"I... I did... it's ready, but..."

"Well, that's something," Rafe said, as if sorry to hear it. "But the fact remains, Tommy, that you've been a bad boy and bad boys must be punished. Sally, check in Tommy's office and see if he's telling the truth about the assignment, or if he lied..."

Stella, in the persona she'd been assigned, wove her way quickly through the furniture and into Tommy's office. A folder on his desk with RAFE on the cover... she looked inside. Three sets of alternate ID that looked reasonably good to her less practiced eye. A stack of credits, which probably came from betraying them, with a call number, lay beside the folder. She scooped it all up, stuffed it in another folder, and went back to the front, where Rafe's rather disgusting banter had Tommy trembling and the watchers bright-eyed.

"The assignment was complete," Stella said. "But he had a stack of money and a call number with it."

"Tsk, tsk," Rafe said. "Naughty Tommy . . . and what shall we do with a naughty boy, mmm?" He glanced again at his audience. "Should I tell them who else you've been playing with, perhaps?"

"No!" Tommy jumped as if he'd been touched with a live wire.

"He has very special tastes," Rafe said to the audience. "You would be surprised." Then to Tommy, "But I think there's a punishment to fit this crime. One particularly suitable to someone of your . . . type. Over here . . ."

Stella pretended disdain, while Rafe attached Tommy to some of his merchandise, explaining to the audience that of course Tommy would forfeit the reward he'd been promised for doing a tedious chore, but that he, Rafe, had matters awaiting and perhaps they would like to amuse themselves in the store until Tommy managed to get himself loose. If he could.

"And don't pay any attention to his protests, of course. When Tommy's been bad he likes to pretend he's better than all this." They nodded. "I'll just shut the door on my way out, and turn the sign . . . everybody knows Tommy's hours are irregular . . . along with other parts of his life . . . I am in your debt." He put his hands together and bowed.

"We'll . . . we'll be glad to help . . . we . . . haven't seen you before."

"Few see me," Rafe said. "But all remember me."

Stella nearly choked on that one, but maintained her calm until they were outside and Tommy's store had a big CLOSED sign facing the passage. "What were you doing in there?"

"Having fun," Rafe said. "Surely you've noticed how easy it is to get people to join the right party . . . all you have to do is make whatever's going on the right party. I'm assuming you got the cash and the number."

"Of course," Stella said.

"Then it's back home in a hurry, and hope that our boy Toby hasn't had to use that blunderbuss I left him with, or there won't be much left of the shop."

But Scurry Lane was peaceful and normally busy. Stella called Toby by implant, and he said nothing had happened.

"We're coming in the back, Toby. Rafe's going to pick up some food—" And some gossip, she was sure.

Ten minutes later, they were all in the upper office. Rafe peered at the new ID. "Functional, not perfect. But it should do. Stella, you'll want to dull your hair a bit, maybe use a cheek pad. Toby will do as he is. Now to find transport . . ."

"There is one ship leaving today and two tomorrow," Toby offered. "I checked while you were out. Thought you'd need to know."

"Did I tell you to open a com line?" Rafe said.

"Good thinking, Toby," Stella said, with a glare at Rafe. "What ID did you use?"

"None," Toby said. "Straight open inquiry, by implant, ID hidden." He did not quite stick out his tongue at Rafe, but his tone was sufficient. Rafe rolled his eyes.

"Two of a kind, I see. All right, Toby, who's off today and what capacity?"

"*Rose of Bannoth,* Roselines Limited. Dex said Roselines were small but pretty good, just not as fancy as the Empress Lines. Mostly passenger, light cargo. She has ten berths available to Placer B, then eight to Golwaugh, and then she's going to Lastway."

"That's handy," Stella said. "Rafe?"

"We need to leave," he said, "and this ship is leaving. I wouldn't care if she was going to Slotter Key or Sabine. All right—I'll book us passage. Stella, if you'll keep an eye on the external scans . . . and Toby, make a list of anything you need. A little ship like that won't have much commissary capacity."

He opened up his secure line and got to work. Toby, after a look at the back of Rafe's head, put on the thoughtful look that Stella knew went with accessing an implant database. Stella hoped his apprentice voyage had borne in on him the need for extra underwear, but she wasn't going to embarrass him by mentioning it.

"I've got the berths, but they're not taking credit," Rafe said, after a few minutes. "They'll accept hard goods, with a current appraisal, and they're undocking in five hours, sixteen minutes. We have to be aboard in four and a half."

"You know an appraiser, of course," Stella said.

"Several," Rafe said. "Let me just check with one of them—" He went back to work.

Toby glanced at Stella.

"I have a list—I don't know if it's too much."

"'Port it over and let's see . . ." He had remembered underwear, she saw. Three additional shipsuits, another pair of ship boots, underwear, toiletry items.

"That's fine," Stella said. "I think you could use more than that, though. You need your own pressure suit . . . a fleece jacket . . ."

"We've no time for custom-fitting," Rafe said. "I've got our appraisal lined up. A couple of those rocks you had will cover your ticket and Toby's . . ."

"And yours?"

"I pay my own way," Rafe said. "Partnership."

"Fine," Stella said. She fished out the top pouch and shook out two of the largest. "I'll get Toby's kit while you're doing that. Want me to pack for you?"

"No. I can do that in fifteen minutes. Will you have to take him out?"

"No. I was going to work through a chandler's and order it delivered to the ship. I can draw on the existing Vatta accounts here to cover it. I'd already talked to the bank manager."

"Good. I'll be back shortly. I'll call before I come in."

Left alone, Stella measured Toby, contacted a chandler's nearest *Rose of Bannoth*'s dock, and ordered his clothes, pressure suit, and the duffel to carry them charged to the Vatta account number and delivered to the *Rose*'s dockside. Then she contacted the *Rose*'s purser to find out if passengers could, or were expected to, contribute to the mess supplies. Optional, she was told, but the *Rose* carried standard-plus rations, not superior. Stella ordered in four sets of ration upgrades. When Toby's appetite came back he would probably eat twice as much as she did. In Rafe's bathroom, she found supplies to dull her hair to a more maternal shade, and tried the cheek pads, which blurred her prominent cheekbones.

Rafe returned without incident, with jewels and a current appraisal. He packed almost as swiftly as he'd said, then called the police to report his departure "until business improves" and put a large deposit with station management to reserve his space.

In less than two hours, they were on their way to Third Green, where the *Rose* was docked. Stella felt itchy all over, but nothing happened. No assassins leapt out of doorways, no shots were fired, no one accosted them for being who they were or anyone else. At the docking bay, Toby's duffel was being inspected by the ship's sergeant at arms; when they identified themselves by their new ID, he nodded. "Just step over there, please, and see Anson about your ticket; your berths are on hold. If you'll leave your duffel here, I'll check it for you."

"Restrictions on weapons?" Stella asked.

"Ship-safe ammunition only," he said. "No chemstun, no bios. We allow small arms only after inspection."

"Here's mine," Stella said, pulling out her weapon and handing it over. Rafe said nothing, but handed over three to her one. The sergeant looked at Toby, who shook his head.

Then they lined up at the ticketing booth, where the agent approved the appraisal, put the diamonds in a lockbox, gave them a receipt, and issued boarding chips and shipboard ID tags with locators on them. "Wear these at all times," the agent said. "That way we can find you in an emergency, and you'll be recognized by the ship security systems. You still have a little time before mandatory boarding, if you need to purchase any last-minute items from dockside, or you can go aboard now."

"We'll board," Stella said.

"Is all your duffel wanted on the voyage, or do you wish some in deep storage?"

"All wanted," Rafe said, before Stella could get it out.

"Fine. It will be delivered to your cabins before undock. Probably a half hour, not more. If you decide to leave the ship for any reason before undock, you must inform the purser and check with me, here, where you will exchange your shipboard ID tag for a dockside locator/call button."

Stella clipped the shipboard ID tag to her lapel.

The gangway into the *Rose* had a thin strip of industrial-grade carpet, with a bright yellow reflective strip on either side and the warning STAY ON CARPET. Once inside, the ship's decor carried out the Roselines theme with soft roses, creams, and touches of red and green. They were met by a steward who checked them off a list, and led them to their cabins down a passage carpeted in rose with a burgundy geometric border. The cabins connected to form a small suite, complete with a small common room. Stella, recently off the courier with its cramped, bare-bones passenger space, was delighted with them.

"You're welcome to visit the main passenger lounge and the dining salon," the steward said. "You'll find a layout in hardcopy in the desk, or onscreen—just follow the menu directions. Or you can wait here until your duffel arrives. However, when the undock warning sounds, all passengers must return to their cabins, and the sector seals will come down."

"Thank you," Stella said.

When they were alone, she and Rafe examined the safety features of the cabins and that end of the corridor. Their ship ID tags each opened one of the three cabins; these could be rekeyed, the desk brochure explained, for members of one party traveling together.

"Or by members of a party that has the right members," Rafe said.

Each cabin had its own vacuum seals, and each connecting suite had an additional seal in the passage. Clearly Roselines took safety seriously. So did Rafe. When their luggage arrived a few minutes later, Rafe insisted that they unpack everything and put it away in the cabins. "If we have an emergency, we want our suits out. Toby, did you have suit drill aboard ship?"

"Yes, of course. I told you already."

"Good. We'll have them here, whether the captain orders them or not."

The voyage to Placer B and then Golwaugh was uneventful except that Toby's appetite returned and he seemed to hit a growth spurt as well. Toby seemed fascinated by Rafe's chameleon kit and begged to try it; Rafe taught him the rudiments of disguise. The shipsuits that fit Toby at Allway were almost too small by the time they got to Golwaugh. Stella and Toby stayed aboard at these intermediate stops—each of only a couple days' duration—but Rafe bought Toby some larger clothes at Golwaugh. After Golwaugh they were the only passengers on the way to Lastway. The news was not reassuring; only 20 percent of the ansible platforms were up, so that most systems had a several-week communications lag. Both passenger and cargo shipments were down; investment market reports were all out of date, but expected to worsen. Golwaugh was one of the lucky systems with a functioning ansible, so Stella was able to contact ISC HQ and discover that her report had made it there safely.

In Lastway's system, the ship's crew reported that the Lastway ansibles were also functioning. Stella checked the list of ships docked at Lastway . . . a K. Vatta, with the ship *Gary Tobai,* was listed. That would be Ky, of course. The local news channel, piped to passengers' quarters, mentioned sporadic gang attacks on travelers and warned any tourists to keep alert and stay out of danger zones.

Through the purser, Stella booked onstation quarters for the three of them at a moderately priced hostelry. She could only hope that whoever was after Vattas didn't have a face-recognition program that included hers and Toby's. Rafe, she knew, would take care of himself. The purser arranged transport of their duffel, and the three of them made it to the hotel without incident.

The next job was contacting Ky. Stella considered, and rejected, the onstation communications lines. Too dangerous. She and Rafe and Toby, posing as tourists, climbed on the tram and headed for *Gary Tobai*.

Baritom had withdrawn its dockside security personnel after what it continued to call "this unfortunate incident," but Martin felt that the automated security he had put in place was adequate. Ky was unwilling to hire replacements even if other firms were willing to take a contract with her. How could she trust them? She had ordered some basic torso protection in standard sizes for those of her crew who were outside the ship for any reason, though only Martin and Jim carried firearms. Small deposits kept a hold on the items she most wanted from MilMart, but she had still not figured out what to do next. The three apparent tourists who tripped the perimeter alarms were standing in a row, with Martin and Beeah looming over them, when Ky made it down to the cargo entrance.

"Hello, Ky," said the curvaceous but faded blonde in the taupe suit. "I'm your cousin Stella. Remember me?"

Ky could not believe it. Stella? Here? With a teenaged boy and a man? Surely that wasn't her son . . . She struggled to remember how old Stella's child might be. Stella did look older and plainer than she remembered. That Stella had a man, she could believe: he was medium tall, handsome as a vid star in spite of his graying hair, and very aware of it.

"What are you doing here?" came out of her mouth before she could stop it, and the tone was almost accusatory.

"Running away," Stella said. "Or running to you, depending on how you look at it. How much do you know?"

"Vatta's been attacked; I don't know how bad it is."

"Not a very big ship, is it?" the man commented, in a tone that made her angry.

"Big enough," Ky said shortly.

"Have there been any attacks on you?" Stella asked.

"A few," Ky said. "Unsuccessful, obviously."

"Oh, my heavens," the man said, rolling his eyes. "She's a total innocent. What are you thinking, Stella? She can't possibly—"

"I don't know what you think is innocent," Ky said. "I've killed—" She had to stop and count... appalling that she didn't know immediately. "—four men."

"We heard about one at Sabine," the man said. "You did it yourself, really?" He looked completely unimpressed.

"Yes," Ky said through gritted teeth. "And it was two, there."

"My, aren't we the rough girl," the man said. He turned again to Stella. "So she can kill. But can she—"

"Stop it," Stella said. To Ky's surprise, the man stopped, arching a brow at Stella, who turned to Ky and went on. "Ky, this is Rafe. We're partners for the present. He's under partner bond. He has many talents."

"That's nice," Ky said, thinking that *many talents* didn't equate to much manners.

"And this is Toby Vatta. He survived the blowout on Allray Two—have you heard about that?—and he's also a partner for the present."

Ky looked at Toby and had an immediate flashback to her own apprentice voyage. She'd thought having Captain Furman on her tail was bad, but she hadn't been through what he had. "Welcome aboard, Toby," she said. "I'm sorry for your loss." She looked back at Stella. "I assume Rafe has a last name?"

"Yes. Which we will give you when we come aboard, not

standing here on a cold dockside. Ky, we had trouble on Allray. Serious trouble."

"I can imagine. We've had some, too. Come on aboard then." She stepped aside and let them pass; Stella gave her a look she could not interpret, and Rafe a look she could interpret all too well. If he thought she was like Stella, he would soon learn different, and he could keep those eyes to himself. She nodded at Martin when they had cleared the locks. "Come on, Martin. If anyone comes looking for cargo, let Alene handle it. It's close of trade anyway."

"Yes, Captain."

The others had stopped in the rec area; Ky nodded to a table. "Have a seat. Let's find out what's up."

"It's a long story," Stella said.

"It's a long shift," Ky said. "Go ahead."

"You know about the attacks back home, on Slotter Key?"

"Some, not much. They hit corporate headquarters and the family compound both, one report said. I—I expect there were injuries. And for some reason the government is down on us."

Stella nodded. "Ky, I'm sorry . . . I have bad news for you. Your parents—your mother died in the attack on the house; your father died of injuries received trying to save her and others."

Ky felt her face stiffen. Now that tiny sliver of light, that window of hope, slammed shut. She had been so sure—she had hoped so much—that they had not died, or at least one of them survived—she thought she'd anticipated this, but . . . it was too much.

"And your brother San. I'm sorry, Ky. My father was killed, too, in the bombing of corporate headquarters. My sister Jo died in a separate attack."

Ky felt each name as a separate weight falling on her, pushing her deeper into darkness. Her father, her mother, her brother, her uncle. "Aunt Helen?" she managed to ask.

"Mother was alive when I left Slotter Key," Stella said. "So was Aunt Gracie Lane."

Gracie Lane and her fruitcakes-with-diamonds were a poor substitute for the rest of the family. The memory of her father's face, in that last call, the look in his eyes, came to her vividly. She squeezed her eyes shut, trying not to think, not to see.

"Aunt Gracie sent me to find you," Stella said.

"To find *me*!" Surprise almost melted the numbness; she opened her eyes. "She thinks I'm an idiot."

"She thinks everyone our age is an idiot," Stella said. "But she thinks you're the one person who can sort this out, and she thinks I'm capable of helping you. She knew you needed more data and some help."

Ky's mind grabbed for this distraction from the news that her whole family was dead. "Aunt Gracie is—"

"Pretty smart, actually. Did you know she'd been in the war?"

"Aunt Gracie?" That seemed as likely as that Aunt Gracie had wings or gills.

"Yes. I didn't know, either, until she told me. And showed me. At any rate, she told me to come find you and bring you the Vatta command database, to download into your implant."

Ky's hand went to her head. "I don't have an implant. It was destroyed."

"But I know your father sent you another one—"

"I haven't put it in," Ky said. "I'm not supposed to put one in for six months..." When she counted up the weeks in transit to Belinta, from Belinta to here, it was a lot closer to six months than she'd thought.

"Brain damage?" Stella asked.

"Possible neural instability," Ky said. She didn't even want to think about whether that constituted brain damage. "And how did you get hold of the command database? I mean, if my—your—our fathers were killed in the attacks..."

Stella looked away, and swallowed. "Your father lived a few days, Ky... and Aunt Gracie... took charge of the implant."

Ky stared at her. Her stomach roiled; she did not want to consider what that meant, or how it had been done.

"At any rate, if you're going to take over as the offplanet Vatta representative, you'd better find a way to use the implant information."

"You could—" Ky began, but Stella shook her head vigorously.

"You have military training, Ky; I don't. My expertise is all in another direction."

Ky hadn't heard that Stella had any expertise, but then she hadn't seen Stella for years, what with school, the Academy, and all. "And that is?" she asked, trying to keep her tone light.

Stella grimaced. "If you access the database you'll know. I'm not sure I should tell you here." She glanced aside at Rafe and Toby. Ky felt a cold prickle run up her spine.

"As if you hadn't learned half or more of it from me," Rafe said. "But I suppose we must protect innocent young ears." Toby turned to glare at him. Ky felt the same way, but didn't let herself show it.

"Later, then," she said. "If I'm the designated whatever, though, I'll need to know."

"Understood," Stella said.

The others could be another distraction. Ky turned to the boy. "Toby, how far along in your apprenticeship were you? What kind of ship duties did you learn?"

The boy flushed, but met her eyes and answered steadily. "I was over half through, and had completed the training modules in all the specialties, so I was working full shifts under supervision. I'd done environmental and engineering, and was working on navigation and piloting. In port, of course, we all worked cargo."

"Excellent," Ky said. "I know you don't have any of your scores, and unfortunately I need documentation of your training, but we have new crew who are working on their certification exams. Lastway has a complete roster of spacer certification courses, and the sooner you begin the better. What's your strongest field?"

"Probably drives, ma'am. I did well in all the engineering

subspecialties, but piers—uh, Chief Barklin—said I had a good feel for space drives."

"Good. I could definitely use a good backup drives specialist." Any Vatta, however young and inexperienced, who had ship service would be better than Jim. "I'm going to assign you to that area; you'll be informally assessed, and then start formal classes in a couple of days. That suit?"

"Yes, ma'am," Toby said.

"I don't know when we can get you back to a place where you can have regular formal schooling," Ky said. "What were you planning on, or had you decided?"

"I was supposed to go to Terqua—the main engineering prep school on my home planet, ma'am—and then I hoped to get into Davisi Tech for advanced work, and then back to the fleet."

"Um. I'll download additional course work for you, for when we're en route. No sense in having you lose more educational time than necessary." Ky turned to Rafe, who was watching this with a condescending expression. "Now you, sir. Your last name, if I may be so bold..."

"Of course, Captain," he said, leaning forward, meeting her eye, and putting on what Ky assessed as a pseudo-honest expression. "Though you may as well know that I have several last names, by which I'm known on different worlds. I was born with Dunbarger, but haven't used it for years. Stella first met me as Rafael Stoner Madestan."

"Dunbarger!" Stella said.

"I said I haven't used it for a long time," Rafe said. "It's not... euphonious. It is, however, my birth name if anyone were to track it down."

"Dunbarger...," Ky said. Where had she heard that name before? Somewhere that had meaning to this whole situation?

"*That* Dunbarger," Rafe said. "The one you're so obviously trying to remember. ISC senior officer. Very senior, at the moment."

Into Ky's mind popped the memory of ISC's command structure: Dunbarger stood right at the top.

"You might consider me a remittance man," Rafe said. "If you know what that is."

"You're Garston Dunbarger's son?" Stella said. "You?"

"I had to learn company manners somewhere," Rafe said. "The knowledge of which fork to use and how to tie a cravat is easiest learned in the kind of home my . . . parents . . . kept." He kept his gaze on Ky, nonetheless.

"Very interesting, if true," Ky said.

"Oh, it's true. I can even prove it, though I would prefer not to call down the kind of trouble *that* would bring on Lastway. At any rate, I was sent away, for cause I might add—no bad feelings on my side—and strongly encouraged to choose another name, or fifty. And later—here's another new tidbit for you, Stella—later I was hired back, as it were, after a bit of good behavior, which somewhat softened my father's attitude."

"Hired back how?" Ky asked.

Rafe's gaze dropped to his fingernails, which he appeared to study with great interest. "There are things that a supposedly disaffected, disinherited former member of a powerful family can find out—can elicit—that almost no one else can. If you know where both ends of the string are, as it were, untangling the mess someone's made of it is far easier. By birth I know one end . . . by experience I discover the other."

"You're a company spy," Ky said.

He gave her a straight look and shrugged. "That's a bald word for a very . . . fluffy . . . concept. Let's just say that I have been put in the way of finding out things ISC needs to know and have been well paid to transfer that knowledge to ISC. I'm still not welcome at home, but relations are, as it were, softening with time. None of my sisters has produced an heir, and Father would like a grandchild—well, actually it's Mother who wants one worst, I suspect, but Father is putty in her hands."

"You—you!" Stella sputtered, clearly outraged about something. Ky looked at her. "You contemptible toad!"

"Now, Stella, sweetling, no need to blow a jet."

"Don't sweetling me, you—you—" She turned to Ky. "This... this miserable excuse spent two whole days lecturing me on the evils of my past, my luxurious and pampered past, convincing me that I was to blame for the inequalities of the universe because I'd never questioned where Vatta money came from, and all that time—"

"How do you suppose I knew what leverage would work, my dear?" Rafe asked coolly. "It takes one to know one; I knew what would sting me, and thus that it would sting you. And besides, you are so sweet when you feel guilty. As opposed to the way you are when you don't." He held up a finger. "And don't say you'll hate me forever, because you know you won't."

Toby, Ky noticed, was watching this with eyes wide.

"I still don't have a last name," she said to Rafe. "Not the one on your current ID, at least."

"Oh. Yes." For an instant, a patch of color appeared on his cheeks. He fished out the ID packet and handed it over. "It's fake, of course, and only of moderate quality. I had it done in a rush before we left, to throw off pursuit, we hoped. Stella's is fake, too, at the moment. It seems to have worked."

"Ralph San Volan," Ky said, reading it off.

Rafe shrugged. "I was using Murchison back on Allray, and running a shop selling antiquities and books."

"And other things," Stella put in. Ky could tell that she was still furious.

"And other things as necessary to keep my lines of contact open with the kinds of people ordinary ISC personnel cannot know," Rafe said, glancing at Stella and then back to Ky. "You must realize that those people do not trust straight arrows."

"I know that," Ky said.

"Good. Because if I'm to be any use to you, I need to establish my lines of communication here."

Ky ignored the presumption in that for the moment. She wasn't sure she wanted him to try to be of use to her. "You've been here before?"

"Oh, yes. Some years back."

"Just as a matter of curiosity, when does your partnership contract with Stella and Toby expire?"

"Um . . . not too long now, I think," Rafe said.

Ky let her teeth show. "I suspect you know to the minute, Rafe. Let's not play games."

"But games are such fun. All right, in about twenty-three hours. Why? Are you going to ask me to extend?"

"I'm thinking about it. It seems to me that Vatta and ISC interests run together lately."

"They may do. But my interests intersect ISC's only in particular areas. Perhaps we should both think about it."

"And discuss it in, say, four hours?" Ky said.

"As the captain wishes," he said, all courtliness. Whoever he really was, someone had taught him manners, and more than one kind. Ky looked again at his gray hair. "How old are you really?"

"You want all my realities revealed?" he asked. "Very well—" And he scrubbed at his face with his hands. When he brought them down, a much younger man grinned at her, his face subtly reshaped, his eyes sparkling with mischief. "The hair's not this gray or this thin, either, but I'd prefer to deal with that in a proper bathroom, if this ship has a proper bathroom. I'm only a year older than Stella in true biological time, but I'm much, much older in experience."

Ky caught a movement of Stella's hands, and glanced over to find the perfect cheekbones restored to the breathtaking beauty she remembered. Stella opened her hand. "Cheek pads," she said. "And my hair's not really this color. Rafe's got black hair, if you want to know."

Ky looked at Toby, who shook his head. "Rafe wouldn't let me," he said. "He says as fast as I'm growing, I'm not the same two days in a row anyway."

"That's a relief," Ky said.

CHAPTER TWELVE

"Wait here," Ky said, "while I get Toby settled, and see about finding you berths—I presume you'd rather stay aboard than onstation?"

"I would," Stella said.

"Even though a Vatta ship was blown up in dock at Allray?" Rafe said.

"Even though," Stella said.

"I will do as the captain prefers," Rafe said, tilting his head at Ky, and leaving *for now* hanging between them, unsaid.

"Fine, then," Ky said. "I'll be back shortly. Come on, Toby."

Toby followed her out of the rec area to Engineering; Martin trailed along. "I need to get back to dockside, Captain, if that's all right."

"That's fine, Martin, go ahead." He nodded and turned away. Ky walked on, wondering what she could say to comfort a boy who had lost his family and shipmates. Damned little comfort in the universe, but that wasn't what he needed to hear. On the other hand, maybe he didn't need comfort as much as something to do. Ky said, "Stella says you're also in this partnership?"

"Yes, ma'am—Captain."

"What do you think of Rafe?"

"Me? I'm just—"

"Old enough to be a partner, Toby. That's old enough to assess the character of a partner, by law. What do you think of him?"

"I don't exactly know. He's—he knows a lot of things I think are probably bad things, but he's been a good partner so far."

"Does Stella trust him?"

"In partnership yes, but not before. She had me hold a weapon on him, before they—we—formed the partnership, when she was showing him what she carried."

Ky turned and looked at him. "Trusts *you,* doesn't she? Could you have shot him?"

"I—I think so." He looked tense and worried, which was, Ky thought, exactly how he should look when he contemplated the possibility of killing someone.

"Good," Ky said. "We'll try to keep you out of such situations in the future, but just in case, I'm glad to know you're that reliable."

He said nothing, and she led him on into Engineering, where Quincy was leaning over Jim at one of the work spaces; Puddles lay at his feet, chewing vigorously on his leash. Quincy looked up. "Who's this, then?"

"Toby Vatta," Ky said. "Survivor of the attack on *Ellis Fabery* at Allray. News was wrong—they weren't all killed."

"How'd he—"

"My cousin Stella brought him," Ky said, and cut off further questions with a warning glance. "Toby, this is Quincy Robins, one of the most senior engineers in Vatta, and from this point on your tutor. Quince, Toby was more than halfway through his apprentice voyage, and he says his instructors thought he had an aptitude for drives. Since I have no idea when we can get him home, we need to set up a complete educational course for him, find him bunk space, and get him fitted out with whatever he needs. Can you see to that? Order in whatever you need. I have some other urgent business."

"Of course," Quincy said. "Toby, is it? You're in a growing stage, aren't you? I recognize the signs."

Toby nodded. "Is that a . . . a dog?"

"It's a nuisance," Quincy said. "Jim's idea." She glared at Ky.

"It's a puppy," Ky said. "Do you know anything about dogs?"

"I had a dog back home," Toby said. "Before I left for ship duty. She was a mazehound. She didn't look anything like that, even when she was born." Ky had no idea what a mazehound was, but for the first time thought there might be a purpose in having a puppy aboard.

"This one's supposed to be a Jack Russell terrier," Ky said. "Whatever that is. His name's Puddles."

"We'll need to stock extra rations, Captain," Quincy said. "Boys this age eat like a regiment."

"I'll put it on the list," Ky said. Quincy seemed to glow with a sudden burst of grandmotherliness, which was just what the boy needed, Ky felt sure. "Jim, come along with me." Jim's face took on a worried expression, but he got up quickly and followed her back to the rec room.

She heard the low murmur of voices, but not what they were saying; Stella and Rafe were both silent when she came in.

"Toby's getting settled," she said. "This is Jim, one of my crew, late of Belinta."

"Belinta!" Rafe said in the tone of *that mudball.*

"What's wrong with Belinta?" asked Jim, scowling.

"You wanted to leave," Ky pointed out. Then she shook her head at Rafe. "Don't tease him."

Rafe grinned. "Happens to everyone, one time or another. And you got out of Belinta. So, what else are you bringing to the party?"

"It's not a party," Ky said. "I need to talk to my cousin alone, and I don't want you wandering the ship by yourself. Jim, you'll stay with Rafe until I come back. And I mean stay with, not just in the same half of the ship."

"Oh." Jim looked at Rafe with sudden suspicion.

"I am *so* misunderstood," Rafe murmured.

"The misunderstanding, if any, is mutual," Ky said, trying not to grin. It would not do to let this rascal know he was amusing her.

"Is it?" he said, but then sobered, and nodded with what might be respect. "Perhaps it is, Captain Vatta. I will be good."

"Excellent," Ky said. "Jim will show you around; if you decide to ship out with us, you'll know what you're getting into. Now you'll excuse us—Stella, come with me, please." With a final nod she left them, and Stella trailed after her.

In her own cabin, she gestured Stella to the bunk and sat at the desk herself.

"You've changed," Stella said.

"The last time we met I was what, seventeen?"

"There's that," Stella admitted. "But I was worried for you, when I heard about that mess at the Academy. You had always been such a straight arrow."

"I've wanted to thank you for your note," Ky said. "It did help, especially since I'd just had a stinker of a letter from Hal—from a man I'd known there."

"Men," Stella said. "And while we're on that subject, a word of warning about Rafe—"

"You think I need one?"

"Every woman needs one with him. I'm sure you feel the magnetism—I certainly do—but he's not a safe ride."

"I could tell," Ky said. "But let's get to business, Stella. You say Auntie Grace sent you—"

Stella sat up straighter. "Yes. Your father tried to call a meeting of the adult Vattas on Slotter Key, after he was hurt—but he collapsed, and Auntie Grace took over. It surprised everyone when she picked me to be her messenger. She knew—well, she'd kind of pushed me into it—that I acted sometimes as a special courier for Vatta. You didn't know that, I think—"

"No," Ky said. "I thought—"

"You thought I was flighty Stella, still in disgrace. So did a lot of people, which made my other role more effective. When I traveled, people assumed it was just that idiot Stella wandering around being a tourist." Stella cocked her head to one side and her expression shifted; she looked the picture of an inexperienced pretty girl.

"Mmm..."

"My father knew, of course. Your father didn't. That made it awkward sometimes." Stella had lost the innocent-waif look, and Ky admired the technique. She didn't seem to move, and yet she changed.

"I can imagine." Her own father bragging about his practical, sensible, obedient daughter, while her uncle had to pretend that Stella was still a bubblehead.

"Anyway. Auntie Grace downloaded the Vatta command dataset to her own implant. She doesn't think any of the surviving Vattas offplanet have it, and she wanted you to have it because of your military training." Stella paused, and when Ky said nothing went on. "Ky, how bad was your head injury? If you're going to be in command out here, we need to know if you're capable—"

"I'm capable," Ky said, and hoped it was true. "Stella, the things that I've done after that indicate that I'm functioning just fine. It was bad . . . they had to do a memory dump off my implant."

Stella paled. "A memory dump—who did that?"

"Mackensee—a mercenary company. Quite respectable; they're in the green book. Vatta's transported them or their cargo more than once. It was an accident, really." Quickly, Ky gave Stella the bare-bones account of the incident, ending with "And then I woke up, in their sick bay, and all the interesting stuff happened later. So if I could cope with mutinous prisoners and an uncontrollable ship and near starvation, I think that means my brain is working. Right?"

Stella was still pale. "Right," she said. "I don't quite understand why you can't install another implant, though."

"Their surgeons said I should wait six months to be sure the memory dump and the structural repairs were consolidated and stable. I don't know the details, but I'd had those years of training without an implant at the Academy, aimed at preparing for just such an emergency. It doesn't bother me to be without one."

"I don't know if the Vatta situation can wait another—what is it, three months more?"

"Less than that by now, I think. But I don't see why that matters. Unless the command dataset explains who our enemy is and what's going on, and if it does, our fathers would have been prepared. I don't need an implant to fight a war."

Stella shivered. "A war...that's what Aunt Gracie said. It's war now, she said, and we need someone with military training to take over. Meaning you." She shook her head. "I still think you need an implant... wait a minute. You already thought of it as a war? And yourself as fighting it? Without any resources but what you have here?"

Ky shrugged. "Not many options, are there? What was I going to do, run away and hide somewhere? I was sure other Vattas had survived somewhere; we'd need to get together somehow."

"I suppose...I just didn't expect you to have worked all that out. Well, then, general—or admiral, or whatever you are—what do we do now?"

Ky was ready for this one. "I find out what you've brought besides the dataset, and I see if the dataset can be accessed without an implant. I doubt it has anything really useful to me at this point, but it might. I find out what Rafe's up to—because I'm sure it's more than he's said—and decide whether to take him with us, let him go, or kill him."

"You'd kill *Rafe*?"

"If I judged him a danger to the family, of course," Ky said. She enjoyed the shock on Stella's face. "It is a war, Stella. We're already in trouble, already losing, if you look at the numbers. We can't afford to let anyone, however charming, cause us more damage."

"Now that's sensible." Rafe was at the cabin door, with Jim behind him looking worried. "Captain, you were right—I did underestimate you."

"And I clearly underestimated you, thinking that Jim could keep you away from my cabin—" She kicked herself mentally for not having closed and locked it.

"We were on our way to the bridge. I merely overheard one sentence of extremely good sense, nothing more, I assure you." Rafe gave them both a smile of blinding goodwill. "Stella, you are a genius in your way, but your cousin Ky has won my fickle heart..."

"The reverse, however, is not true," Ky said.

"Of course," Rafe said. "I would not expect it. I look forward, Captain, to our discussion of partnerships when the time comes." He turned to Jim. "The bridge, perhaps? And perhaps we should close the hatch, to allow the captain more privacy?"

"Thank you," Ky said. On the bridge he would find Lee less malleable than Jim. When they were alone again, she said to Stella, "So tell me about Rafe...everything you know."

"Everything I thought I knew," Stella said. "I certainly did not know he was Dunbarger's son. If he is. Though that explains a lot."

Stella took a deep breath. "It was after that disastrous mess with Jamar, the one I gave the codes to. I'd been stuck at home for months, of course, lectured at by everyone over the age of ten. Stupid Stella, idiot Stella, how could you Stella, didn't we tell you Stella, and so on and so on. Of course, I was telling myself the same thing. Then Aunt Gracie showed up, shooed everyone away, told me to quit moping and get a hold on myself, and sent me to an old friend of hers over on Cassagar. Find out what you're good at, Gracie said, because you are a Vatta and therefore you have talents besides looking pretty and attracting bad men."

"Sounds like Aunt Gracie," Ky said, hoping Stella would quit telling her story and get back to Rafe.

"Yes, well, her old friend Halma turned out to be a fellow veteran—that's when I found out about Aunt Gracie's own checkered past. I got a fast course in courier protocols and she sent me off to another friend, halfway around the planet. Apparently I did all right, because that one sent me back with a good report. I thought it was all great fun—you had to follow the rules to the letter, of course, but it was the kind of challenge I like, blending in and being someone else, or at least being the foolish, stupid Stella on the outside while being a competent Stella on the inside. If you can follow that."

"Yes," Ky said, "I can." Especially after seeing those lightning changes of expression and character.

"Well, I was on another job for Aunt Gracie's old friend, at an embassy party on Cassagar, when I met Rafe. He recognized that I was trolling for information just as I recognized he was the same, and he called me on it. I didn't know what to do—it was my first political assignment—so I fell back on girlish giggles and sex appeal, and he wasn't having it. I'm still not sure exactly how it happened, but the next thing I knew he was teaching me to use his picklocks—which is a very useful skill, and I still use the set he gave me—and not too long after that I realized he was the sexiest man I'd ever met. Jamar wasn't within six orders of magnitude." Stella grinned and shook her head. Ky thought of Hal, but shied away from that memory.

Stella went on. "Also the most dangerous. Also someone with contacts I'd never even imagined existed . . . he seemed to have a finger in every clandestine organization on Cassagar. His story then was that he'd worked his way up from a state orphanage to a private investigator's license, learning formal etiquette from training tapes, but we both understood that considerable dubious actions were involved. We worked together briefly, then I went back home to Slotter Key to be debriefed by Aunt Gracie. After which she and my father employed my skills at intervals."

"I see. So . . . do you consider Rafe trustworthy?"

"Before the latest revelations, I would have said that Rafe stays bought if you pay his asking price, and that he's reliable in partnership agreements. After all, I turned my back on him this time. But I'm not sure now . . . if he's really Dunbarger's son, and really a permanent ISC agent, then he'll be with us—or anyone he contracts with—only so long as it doesn't cross ISC."

"I'm not planning to cross ISC," Ky said. "And they should be pleased with me, after the Sabine thing. So with those circumstances, what about partnering or hiring Rafe? And which would be better?"

"Partnering," Stella said. "And yes, I think he'd be a good asset, though . . . though I'm still peeved that he never told me . . ." She cocked her head at Ky. "But what use am I, Ky? What can you do with me?"

"I don't know yet. We may have use for an agent of our own, when we come to someplace where you aren't known and won't be an instant assassin magnet. Meantime, you were home more than I was, the last few years. You may know a lot about recent developments in the company that I didn't know."

"And I can scramble eggs," Stella said, grinning. "I'm not trained for ship's crew, but some of my skills will transfer."

"That's good. Besides, you're family. And there's little enough left." That black weight bore down on her shoulders again; Ky struggled not to break down.

"True," Stella said. She looked sad. "I don't—there's not been time to grieve, really. It all happened so fast. Though at least I had the time on the courier to myself. It must be worse for you, being out of touch when it happened."

"I don't know," Ky said. "It still seems unreal. They've always been there . . . parents, aunts, uncles, corporate headquarters, the house. I can almost pretend they're still there, but you can't." And neither could she, for more than moments. She could not make the right decisions if she clung to the wrong data.

"Reality bites," Stella said. She stretched. "Well. You've got Toby settled; that's a good thing."

"Unless someone blows this ship," Ky said soberly. "I do think about that. We should find him a safer place; he's our future. Stella, do you—does Aunt Grace—have any idea why the government turned on us?"

"She wasn't sure if someone had outbid us, or scared them silly. When I left she was planning to find out and see if she could correct their thinking, as she put it. I would not like to be the President, with Aunt Grace after him." Stella drew her finger across her throat.

Ky debated for a moment and took the plunge. "Stella, there's a very odd thing. Before this happened, someone had sent me a message here to be held for my arrival. I have a letter of marque from Slotter Key—"

"But nobody does that anymore!" Stella said, eyes wide.

"That's what I thought, but they do, and I have one. Here—" Ky handed Stella the padded folder.

"This is incredible... when did you get it? You're sure it's official?"

"It came via... someone I knew at the Academy. I'm sure of the provenance, but I'm not sure it's still valid." Ky took the folder when Stella had finished reading and put it away. "Still, it gives me justifications other than family to go after whoever's doing this."

"I never knew Slotter Key ran privateers," Stella said, shaking her head. "I thought I knew a lot about local politics... how did they keep this secret, I wonder."

"I heard rumors," Ky said. "I just thought it was vicious slander, but clearly it wasn't."

"Privateer," Stella said. She grinned suddenly. "Valid or not, with the Slotter Key ansibles down, who's to know?"

"Not Rafe," Ky said. "I'm not ready to tell him all my secrets. Besides, can you really see this ship attacking and capturing anything? Thing is, even if I were a military genius, I can't see how to fight a war with one old tub like this one. She's slow, she's vulnerable, and she has no teeth."

"Would money help?" Stella asked. "I've got some in the usual hard goods, from Aunt Gracie and my own resources."

"Money always helps. Enough to buy a real warship would certainly help, but I doubt you've brought that much. Upgrading this one—we can get as far as armed merchant vessel, which everyone will assume means pirate, but that's about it. She'd need a new insystem drive, some decent shielding, and at least one—no, two—decent weapons systems. It'd cut our cargo capacity thirty percent, and it isn't that big already."

"You've already thought about it."

"Of course. I haven't been twiddling my thumbs. I've thought of several things. Running her as a cargo ship, under Vatta colors: likely to get us attacked and blown up entirely too soon. Running her as a cargo ship under other colors—my own, for one—and hoping nobody figures out she's really Vatta. That would require a new ship chip, of clandestine origin, and time to build up a clientele. The kinds of cargoes you can get in an uninsured, unknown ship are, as you know, minimal. Running her as an armed merchanter, trying to combine light cargo—probably clandestine—with covert attacks on the guilty parties, if we ever figure out who they are. That is dangerous and unlikely to make the kind of profits that will keep us going, unless we take on seriously bad cargo."

"Seriously bad cargo may lead us to our enemies..."

"Yes. It could. Either usefully or right into their trap. You surely know that Vatta corporate accounts are frozen, credit unobtainable right along with insurance for either ship or cargo..."

"I didn't realize accounts would all be frozen; I was able to access funds on Allray."

"They're frozen here, and other places I've heard of. I've sold off the cargo we came in with, and I have a few goodies that Aunt Gracie stuffed into a fruitcake for me, but not enough to buy a new ship or convert this one to armed merchanter."

"I'll add mine to the pile and see what it comes to," Stella said.

"What interests me," Ky said, "is that you and Rafe seem to have been doing the same thing for different employers. You really didn't know he was ISC?"

"No. I can't believe he never told me. And where he came up with that sob story from—"

"Doesn't matter," Ky said. "How reliable do you think he is, really? How much of that attitude is surface?"

"I would trust him to be who he is," Stella said, "but I'm not sure any longer who that is. Stick to the terms of a partnership, yes. Actually care about anyone? I'm not sure."

"We've got a tough task ahead, Stella. We can use all the allies we can find, but we need them to be allies. Or at least acting from enlightened self-interest."

"He's smart," Stella said. "I would say his self-interest is paramount, but intelligently adapted to circumstances. Reliable within limits. Within those limits, absolutely."

"What do you know about his expertise?"

"What you'd expect from someone involved in corporate espionage. There's not a lock—physical or electronic—that he can't open, few if any databases are secure if you turn him loose for an hour, and he has a remarkable collection of contacts in multiple systems. If he's telling the truth about being Dunbarger's son, then I suspect his actual illicit earnings are much lower than he's claimed. The opposite of crooks—he's hiding his legitimate income."

"Anything more I should know?"

"That personality," Stella said. "I'm sure you noticed—he's used to having women fall at his feet."

"I won't," Ky said.

"He hasn't really turned on the charm yet . . . don't believe it when he does."

"Did you?"

"Ouch. Yes, off and on. He still has an effect on me, and I've seen him with others."

"I wouldn't worry," Ky said. "Except that from everything you say, Jim and Lee both won't be able to keep him from snooping all over the ship. It will take Martin."

"Tell me about Martin. He scared me."

"Ex-military; he was at the legation on Belinta. And he's got supply experience, so he took on managing cargo in place of . . . of Gary."

"Impressive. You find him comfortable, I expect, because of your time in the Academy. Are you going to offer Rafe a partnership?"

"I'm thinking about it. Reservations?"

"No. Not if you're careful with the terms. Want advice?"

"I asked, didn't I?"

"Then let me review the terms before you offer. Or I can do a draft for you."

"Do that, Stella. Use my desk, if you'd like."

"And figure out how to get that implant in and functioning," Stella added as Ky was on her way out the door. "You're going to need it."

On the bridge, Lee had a dazed expression and Jim was scowling. Rafe, in Ky's seat, lounged as if he owned the ship.

"Excuse me," Ky said, with an edge to it. "That's my seat."

"Sorry," Rafe said. "Where do you want me?"

Under control, but that wasn't something she could say. "There's a fold-down seat over there." She pointed. "Lee, anybody offship?"

"No."

"Good. Nobody goes off until tradeshift tomorrow. Division reports?"

"At your station, Captain. Nothing much; we're down to the dregs for trade, though. MilMart's holding that advanced suite for us, but they'll require a deposit to hold it past the end of tradeshift tomorrow."

"By then I'll have an answer for them." Ky looked at the division reports. Quincy's had the most data. She had listed all the suitable ships for sale or lease, with costs including provisioning.

"Who's doing your dockside security?" Rafe asked, breaking her concentration.

"We are," Ky said. "Remotely."

"What system?" he asked. "I'm not just being nosy; I'm remembering that a Vatta ship in dock at Allray was blown."

"You know how it was done?"

"No. Outsiders, is what I heard, but I'm not entirely sure—it's one reason I wanted to leave. But remote systems can be . . . confused."

"Co-opted, you mean," Ky said. "We have mil-grade systems, installed by my own crew, as of two days ago. Does that satisfy you?"

"Almost," Rafe said. "Perimeter design?"

"Adequate," Ky said, "according to what I was taught. Do you have suggestions, Ser . . . Dunbarger?"

"Please don't use that name. Not even here. I'm sure your crew are all perfectly loyal—" Rafe shot a sidelong look at Lee, who looked studiously blank. "—but it would be a great embarrassment to me. Besides, it's not euphonious."

"*Vatta* is not exactly music of the spheres," Ky said.

"It has a certain earthy rhythmicity," Rafe said. "*Dunbarger,* on the other hand, sounds like something you'd remove during plastic surgery. Call me by the name Stella knows, or Murchison, which I used last. Or you could just call me Rafe."

"And you could," suggested Ky, "just answer my question. Have you suggestions for perimeter design?"

"Three independent systems, optical spider hooks set at one-meter intervals, each system capable of alarming the others, but not of damping an alarm. Broadband scanning, full chem and bio suites, a watch officer who knows how to interpret the output. Independent power sources, of course, and secure lines . . ."

"I think you would find my perimeter design adequate," Ky said. "That's pretty much what I've got. Anything else?"

"Anti-tamper?"

"Of course."

"I didn't see it when we came in," Rafe said.

"You weren't supposed to," Ky said. "But it's there. And we also have hull-based systems active. Our shields stink, but at least we'll know what hits us."

"I begin to hope you will offer me a partnership, Captain Vatta."

"I begin to think I might. But we have business to discuss. Perhaps you will return with me to the rec area?"

"Of course," he said.

"Jim, check with Sera Vatta in my cabin and see if she needs you for anything. Consider yourself at her disposal."

"Is that wise?" murmured Rafe, following Ky down the passage.

"Jim will do adequately," Ky said. "And Stella has better taste." She waited to see what he would answer, and when he didn't she added, "She found you, for instance."

His brows went up. "A compliment?"

"Recognition of reality. Don't preen."

"I never preen... well, I suppose I do, but only for cause. So, Captain, what shall we discuss?"

"Your potential contribution to my mission," Ky said.

"I would have to know what it is, to know what I might be able to contribute."

"To survive, first. To assist other Vatta ships and family members, like Toby, when found. To discover who our enemy is, and why they attacked us. And then to destroy them."

The brows went higher. "That's a substantial mission for one person and one—forgive me for being blunt—small, old, and apparently slow ship."

"Precisely why I'm seeking allies," Ky said. "I'm not crazy enough to think I can do it all alone. You claim to have expertise relative to ISC's current problems, which I cannot but think are related to ours."

"I think you're right on that," Rafe said, with perfect seriousness. "When do you think it started?"

"I know when I hope it didn't start," Ky said. "And that's when I got involved with that attack on the ansibles at Sabine. I think it possible that the organization, whatever it was, that planned that attack was sufficiently annoyed with my interference that it retaliated against my family."

"I can relieve your mind on that," Rafe said. "Your actions would be seen as typical of Vatta, and Vatta had already been perceived as entirely too close to the ruling cliques at ISC. Your high officers, for instance, were close to Lew Parmina..."

"Yes."

"Lew is my father's choice for a corporate heir. He has

many enemies inside the corporation, and outside as well. He's old-line ISC, very much in favor of the status quo. The innovators hate him."

"Innovators." Ky had no idea what he was talking about.

"Look, Captain, I'll be as honest with you as my other loyalties permit. More honest than I've been with Stella—you have my birth name, for instance. ISC has major internal problems. I can't tell you all about them. Some I don't know, and those I know I must not tell. But I've been warning my father for three years that something was going to blow loose. I guessed wrong about where—I thought it would be Allray, not Sabine, and that's why I set up there two years ago. I was trying to get some hard data on who, and how, and when. This secondary attack on the ansible network, knocking them all out—"

"Lastway's not out—did you know that?"

"I heard that from the crew as we came in. I really want a nice long chat with the local manager, because there's every chance he's one of them."

"Because the ansibles here work?"

"Precisely. They seem to work, but do they? Are all messages being sent and received correctly? I rather doubt it. The people I suspect of being responsible still need to communicate with each other and would need a network to use—but a network they control. How many systems do you know, of your own experience, are down?"

"My own experience? Slotter Key. A ship coming to Belinta System as we left told me Leonora was down, and reported stuffed message bins blocking an automated intermediate station."

"Full . . . that shouldn't happen. Can't happen without sabotage, but it's a very simple way to mess things up. Easy to fix, if the repair crews know what's wrong and are doing their job. But then easy to screw up again."

"Low cost?" Ky asked.

"If you're an ansible platform tech or administrator, yes. That's where I think the trouble's coming from anyway."

"So—you want to check out the local administrator."

"Very much. Actually, first I want to check out the ansibles themselves, the system software. I consider this my highest priority; partnering you would, at this point, be my second. I realize that no woman likes to come in second, but—"

"Don't be stupid," Ky said, more sharply than she intended. "I'm not a schoolgirl, even if I don't have gray hair. I understand—you have to consider ISC first. But why would you even want to partner with Vatta?"

"Mobility. More resources. Many of the same reasons you want allies. This is too big for me alone, and I can't—dare not—go straight to HQ. I can't claim a place on any ISC ship without revealing who I am, which would make it impossible to uncover the plots and counterplots. Our merged networks are bigger than either alone."

He looked honest, but then good liars did look honest. Ky was sure he was hiding things—he even admitted he was hiding things—but not sure if the things he was hiding were harmful to her mission. She was hiding things herself, for that matter. She caught herself wondering what he really looked like, with his own hair, with all disguises off, and dragged herself back to the issue at hand.

CHAPTER THIRTEEN

"So," Ky said. "You want to partner with Vatta Enterprises, Ltd., or with me personally, or with me and Stella and Toby, or what?"

"You're in command now, aren't you? I believe in going to the top. I'd like to partner with you."

"Stella's going to be my G-2," Ky said. She wondered if he knew the term.

"Good choice," Rafe said. "You'll want to have her vet the contract, I'm sure. Shall I write out what I'd like to see, since you don't have an implant?"

"Go ahead," Ky said. She called Stella, who arrived with a model contract already drafted. Rafe glanced at it. "This is fine," he said. When it was signed and recorded, he stood and stretched.

"I would rather not run my inquiries from here," Rafe said. "Your security may be as good as you paid for, but I don't want any back-traces."

"You have an idea who it is."

"An idea. No data. If the idea's right, then they have the same or better tech than I do."

"Better tech than ISC?"

"Better tech than I've been given. If you could direct me to a bathroom, so I can put my face back on—"

"Down that passage, second left," Ky said.

"Captain, there's a call for you on the bridge."

"Coming," Ky said. "All right, Rafe, go find out what you can. If ISC's whole local office is bent—"

"I didn't say that."

"No, but it could be. How long should I wait before rousing the troops?"

"The troops you don't have? Don't worry unless I'm not back in a full day cycle."

"All right. And where should we look for the body if you're not?"

"If I knew, I'd be safer. Just don't . . . get into trouble while I'm gone."

"I'll do my best. See you then. Call us from the perimeter—you can ping Stella, right?"

"Right."

On the bridge, Lee was holding an open contact with an odd expression on his face. "It's a Mackensee ship," he said. "Do you want to talk to them?"

"I wish I could afford to hire them," Ky said, wondering if the value of Stella's contribution would make that possible. Probably not. She sat in her command seat and flicked on her screen. "Captain Vatta here, go ahead."

"This is Captain Pensig, Mackensee Military Assistance ship *Gloucester*. I understand you are the same Captain Vatta who had a contract with Mackensee at Sabine?"

"That's right," Ky said. She hoped that contract wasn't under dispute somehow; they had seemed quite cordial when she left them.

"We're having a . . . a sort of situation has come up, Captain Vatta, and the officer commanding our mobile force would like to confer with you."

"With me?"

"Yes, Captain. I'm not sure if you're aware of Mackensee command structure: the ship crews and the mobile forces are, perforce, in different branches, as it were . . ."

"Are you here because there's a war on?" Ky asked. Enough fencing around; she wanted something solid.

"No, no, nothing like that. I mean, nothing other than whatever's attacking ISC installations. We're here on what should have been a routine mission, rotating personnel in and out of the local recruiting and consulting station. But something's come up . . . the ansible failure, among other things . . ."

"I see," Ky said, to fill in the long silence. "And your OIC wants to talk to me? What does he—she—think I can do?"

"I'm not sure. As I said, he's not in my chain of command, in fact he's . . . fairly junior . . . but he asked me to contact you, ship to ship. The . . . uh . . . officer who would normally be in charge developed a medical problem and is in cryosuspension. Would you be willing to meet with him?"

"Certainly," Ky said. "But I'm not leaving my ship at present. Where are you docked?"

"Five Alpha Blue. I'm sure you'd like to speak to him by com before meeting in person . . ."

"Yes, thank you," Ky said.

"Just a moment then. I'll have him paged."

Ky wondered why the other officer wasn't standing by, but the vidscreen of the Mackensee bridge made it clear he wasn't. His face, when he appeared, looked much younger than she expected.

"Captain Vatta, this is Lieutenant Mason of the Mackensee Military Assistance Corporation; he is the ranking combat forces officer presently in the system." The ship captain could have been Lieutenant Mason's father.

"Captain Pensig, I'll talk to Captain Vatta alone," the young man said. A slow flush mounted Captain Pensig's neck, visible on the scan.

"Of course, Lieutenant Mason," Pensig said with grave courtesy. "The com officer will seal the line." He stepped back out of vid pickup range, and the margins of the screen flickered then steadied as someone walked through the security curtain.

"You don't look like I expected," said Lieutenant Mason. He didn't, either; Ky had met only a few of the Mackensee officers before, but all of them had the kind of hard edge she expected from experienced military personnel. This young man did not; he belonged in a shipping office, someplace where everything fit into a routine.

"What did you expect?" she asked. *And why should you expect anything,* she wondered silently.

"Someone taller," he said. "Older, maybe." She looked at his face, and felt considerably older than he looked. "You had a contract with us—with Mackensee—after all . . ."

So the tales told, whatever they were, had not emphasized youth and inexperience. That had to be good for something.

"So what did you want, Lieutenant Mason?"

"I'd . . . uh . . . like to talk to you. I am the ranking Mackensee officer in this system." She could hear both surprise and pride in that. "I've heard of you—we all have. And I have a dilemma that you may be able to help with."

"I don't think we have a lot of extra resources, Lieutenant."

"I was thinking we might combine resources . . ."

"How?"

"Ma'am, I'd really like to talk to you in person, in a secure location. Could you come aboard our ship?"

"Er . . . no, thank you. I prefer to stay on my ship. You could come here." That would give her time to find out a bit more about Mackensee on this station.

"All right. I'll come right over."

"But watch for trouble on the docks."

A sound of throat clearing, followed by "Ma'am, I don't expect I'll have any trouble. I'll bring a squad . . ."

As soon as she was offline, Ky called Martin to the bridge and told him about the call.

"Mercs want to talk to us?" he said. "That's very interesting. I wonder what kind of problem they think we can help with."

"I have no idea," Ky said. "But they'll be here soon, and I'd like you to sit in."

"Of course, ma'am."

Less than an hour later, the external scans lived up to their reputation and programming by signaling the arrival of "multiple armed individuals in body armor." In the midst of ten Mackensee soldiers in nonpressure armor, faceplates closed, was their lieutenant, dwarfed by their imposing presence. Martin met them, gave the lieutenant a nod as crisp as a salute, and led him to the ship entrance.

Ky opened the lock and extended the access tube. "Lieutenent Mason, welcome to Dockside Vatta."

"My escort will remain here," the lieutenant said. He matched his appearance on the vidcom. "May I come aboard?"

"Yes, of course," Ky said. Inside the ship, she took him to the rec area and settled him at a table. Martin stood at ease by the hatch to the galley. The lieutenant refused refreshments, sitting bolt upright in his chair, lips pursed tightly.

"Well," Ky said, when he did nothing for several seconds. "Spit it out—what did you want to talk about?"

He glanced at Martin. "That man—"

"Is discreet and honest, Lieutenant Mason. That's all you need to know."

To her surprise, Mason flushed red, but he started in. "Here's the situation, ma'am. The local station director says that the ansibles here are up and running, but we aren't getting any messages. Any at all. We've sent them out, but we don't know if our people are receiving them. Maybe the ansibles are blocked where they are. I—we can't leave without orders; we don't know where to go. And... we're running out of credit."

"Wait a minute," Ky said. "What are you doing here in the first place? Did you have a contract to come here?"

"No, ma'am," he said. "Lastway's a good place to pick up contracts; that's why we have a recruiting station and consulting office here. Out on the edge of settled space, like this, things are... a bit looser, if you know what I mean. You have arms deals... there's MilMartExchange, you know about them... the largest purveyor of new and used military heavy weaponry and equipment... out here at the Fringe. When... someone... is thinking of fighting a war, they often come here to stock up on equipment. You must have gone by our recruiting station..."

"Yes."

"It's also the local consulting office. Whatever people say about mercs, ma'am, Mackensee is a quality outfit, platinum all the way. We don't sell war, we sell expertise to people who otherwise will get themselves in unnecessary wars and cause a lot of damage."

"Really . . ." That sounded like something he'd memorized from a brochure. Ky struggled not to glance at Martin and see what he thought of this spiel.

"Yes, ma'am. The Old Man says the only good war is the one that doesn't happen—that's why we like to take advisement contracts, not combat ones, if we can. And if the war has to come, better it be fought by people on payroll, because then the costs are calculable." More advertising language.

"How many actions have you been in, Lieutenant?" Something about the young man's glib delivery was making Ky wonder if he'd ever shot at anything but a target.

"Er . . . none yet, ma'am. But I've had two years of training, one at the Mackensee Combat Simulation and Practice Range."

"I see. What made you join Mackensee?"

He shrugged. "Oh, the usual. Got in trouble, the judge said jail or mail, and I picked mail. I was lucky; Mackensee made me finish school after I went through boot, and my scores qualified me for their officer training."

Ky thought they should have run him through a war first, but after all, she'd qualified for Slotter Key's supposedly elite Space Academy on test scores and school grades. And look how that had turned out.

"So . . . you're the ranking officer. Were you commanding here, on Lastway Station, or—"

"No, ma'am. I'm—I was the payroll escort officer, coming from our corporate headquarters out to Lastway . . . Major Delinn was the OIC here, and Captain Oscone was in charge of troops aboard the two ships. When the ansibles went out, we were at Teglin Junction. Captain Oscone diverted one of the ships back to HQ to get new orders and put me in charge of the troops as well. Then when I got here, about two days later, Major Delinn suffered an arterial blowout and had to be put in cryosuspension because there's no medical facility here that can handle that kind of thing. And that left . . . me."

He sounded both scared and excited. "How many do you have in your command?" Ky asked.

"Ninety-two, all told, not counting ship crews. It's more than a lieutenant usually has, of course. There's twenty in the recruiting station and consulting office, another twenty in the rotation that was coming in to relieve them, and then the ships' complements of troops. They're not even the same organization, you see . . ."

And a payroll escort officer shall lead them . . . maybe. "How many ships do you have here?"

"Two. There's a courier with the payroll, and a sheepdog to guard it. Not one of the big cruisers, of course, but well armed and capable of handling anything but major ships of the line. The other ship was much the same, the one the captain took back to HQ."

"So what do you think I can do to help you?" Ky asked.

"I was thinking you could hire us," he said. "I mean, we hear that someone's attacking Vatta ships and people and things. We could protect you. Then you—Vatta, I mean—would be guarantors for our support onstation."

Much as she'd wanted to hire Mackensee, this young man did not inspire confidence. She hedged. "Are you—forgive me for asking an awkward question—but are you entitled to make contractual agreements on Mackensee's behalf?"

"Master Sergeant Dolan says I am—I mean, it's in the regulations. The ranking officer may make binding contracts provided that such contracts are in the best interests of Mackensee."

"And how many personnel in ship crews?" Ky asked, thinking that probably explained why they were running short of cash even if they'd brought the payroll. She wondered how big it was. She had no idea what it cost to support a military unit in idleness, a topic not covered in the Slotter Key Space Academy.

"Fifteen in the courier, and probably a hundred in the other. Why? They aren't my problem."

They were his problem, and he was a very stupid junior officer if he couldn't see it.

"What sort of contract were you thinking of?" Ky asked.

"Like I said, we could protect you. You were attacked, right?"

"Yes, but as you can see I'm fine," Ky said.

"Yes, but if you had guards, it wouldn't have happened. And you were nearly killed, they said."

"Who?"

"The Garda." He reddened suddenly. "The... uh... Garda have an arrangement with Mackensee. Long-standing understanding."

"I see," Ky said. "So you know what they know?"

"Some, anyway. Master Sergeant Dolan does."

Ky felt a strong desire to talk to Master Sergeant Dolan instead of Lieutenant Mason, but she was sure Dolan couldn't negotiate contracts.

"So can we make a deal?" Mason asked.

"Patience, Lieutenant," Ky said. She felt years older than this young man. "I have to assess my needs, and you have to tell me what your rates are. Whatever you've heard, merchanters aren't made of money, and we don't have unlimited funds. Aren't you people usually hired by whole planets?"

"Yes, but you're not getting an entire expeditionary force... you're just getting us."

"Suppose you present a formal proposal, Lieutenant, with estimates of the cost to us, and I'll go over it with my financial officer and see if we can come to an agreement. I have no objection *in principle* to hiring Mackensee for a job of work, but I'm not going to give verbal agreement to an open-ended contract with no details specified. Surely you have a good clerk NCO who can draw up a sample..."

"Oh. Of course. Yes, ma'am, I do. Perhaps Master

Sergeant Roth... he'd know. Can he... uh... just ping your implant?"

"I don't have an implant," Ky said. "Why not have Roth work something up, get your approval on it, and bring it over to discuss?"

"Yes, ma'am, I can do that." He seemed much cheerier with a definite plan in mind, but then most people were. Ky would be much happier when she had a definite plan in mind. "Can we do this... uh... soon?" he went on.

Curiosity and amusement pushed her past tact. "Just how short of funds are you, Lieutenant?" Ky asked.

He reddened and for a moment she thought he was going to cry. "I—they—they just cut us off short, like that, and I know the ship captains have been after me to do something, but what could I do? I was trying to do the captain's work and the major's work and I didn't know where anything was, and Dolan and Roth kept looking at me like I was a five-year-old and finally Dolan said why not ask you—actually he said that two days ago, but I thought maybe if I just talked to the bank—we've always had a good credit rating, and maybe a message would come through from home..."

Twit, Ky thought. It surprised her that Mackensee had ever taken this one in, but maybe he had unexpected talents elsewhere... somewhere.

"I asked," Ky said again, this time with a little edge to it, "how short you are. Are your people going to have food for the next meal, for instance?"

"Uh... maybe."

Ky rolled mental eyes, and equally mental dice, and came to a decision she wasn't ready to share yet. "Send me your Master Sergeant Roth," she said, as if Lieutenant Mason were her subordinate. "Do it quickly."

"Yes, ma'am," he said. "And can I say anything to the troops?"

Idiot. "No," she said. "Not now. Get Roth over here."

"I'll call him from dockside," Lieutenant Mason said. She sent him away looking much happier, and looked at Martin.

"He must have got in trouble for stealing candy from babies," Martin said. "He doesn't have enough gumption for anything else."

"Is he really that bad?" Ky asked. "I kept wanting to smack him, but—"

"Not officer material," Martin said. "Not in my books. Mercs may have different standards."

"Slotter Key has no dim-witted officers?"

"Well, no . . . I mean, yes, they do, a few. I suppose he might have slipped by for some other reason."

"So, what do you think about his proposal?"

"If they're messed up enough that they're about to give the troops nail soup, they may not be any help."

"They were better at Sabine," Ky said.

"I'll keep that in mind," he said. "Maybe it's just the one young fool."

Ky called for Stella.

"You're looking lively," Stella said. "What's going on with those soldiers on the dock? Did the station finally come to its senses and give us official guard?"

"No. That's Mackensee Military Assistance Corporation. The people I contracted with at Sabine, after they invaded the system, and the people whose surgeons extracted my implant."

"The ones who nearly killed you."

"That was my own crewman," Ky said. "I don't blame Mackensee for that, though I wish I knew how much data they pulled from my implant. It was only the Vatta basic, not the full dataset, but still. Anyway. Through a series of mishaps, their local leadership is down to one very junior lieutenant, who was supposed to escort their payroll here . . . and is now in command. And overwhelmed and underfunded."

"He has the payroll—"

"But the banks have shut them down on credit, and the payroll intended for twenty doesn't last long when you're trying to support almost a hundred. He wants us to contract with them for protection, so that we can feed his hungry men and women."

"Protection..."

"Thing is, Stella, I thought about trying to work something with Mackensee before. They have the expertise, the weapons, the trained personnel. We could use them."

"Can we afford them?"

"Exactly what I need to know. Stella, I'm assigning you as financial officer, as well as G-2. You know what you brought into this. I'll tell you what we've got—" She called up the figures from the trading they'd done and the remains of Aunt Gracie's fruitcake diamonds. "We need to provision this ship, and decide what upgrades we can afford with and without hiring the Mackensee group. I'll be talking to one of their senior NCOs shortly, someone with more sense than that lieutenant. Give me some numbers."

"Right," Stella said. "I can do that. Fifteen minutes... you had the list of upgrades already loaded, right?"

"Right."

Rafe came back before Master Sergeant Roth arrived.

"Did you know the dockside area is full of big, noisy, obvious soldiers?" he asked Ky.

"Yes, of course," Ky said.

"I hope you don't think they're better protection," Rafe said. "They didn't notice me coming until I was close enough to lob any sort of weapon—"

"I wasn't counting on them for protection from sneaks," Ky said. "And I'd told them you were coming. What did you find out?"

"The local ISC rep is crooked as a corkscrew," Rafe said with relish. "The ansible is open all right—to him and whoever he's in contact with, but he's blocking all incoming and outgoing messages at will. He's got a probe into what are supposed to be unbreakable automatic systems. I can't tell yet if the next jump-point ansibles from here are really down, or if he's programmed this one to think they're down. That would take me several days. There are at least five in the deal on this end, though: the director, all three technical heads—one per shift—and a weasel in the records section.

That one tried to convince me faked records were real, and of course I believed him—to his face."

"Won't they suspect something if you're trying to bribe the records . . . er . . . weasel?"

"How'd you know—well, yes. They'll know I want information. From the look on his face, he's been taking bribes from everyone onstation who wants to know what's going on. The shoes he's wearing, the jewelry . . . he's rolling in more money than someone at his level ever makes. But with everyone asking, another one asking is just another source of money—he doesn't suspect who or what I am." He cocked his head. "Aren't you going to tell me about the soldiers?"

"There's nothing to tell yet." Ky sighed as he continued to look at her attentively. "No, I'm not going to tell you. When there is something to tell you, then I will."

"You are entirely too cautious, Captain Vatta. I must admire that caution, inconvenient as it is for me. Where is the fair Stella?"

"Busy," Ky said. "And your next project is?"

"Something I'm afraid you can't help with," he said. "I would give my left arm—or at least a couple of fingers—to get hold of a bit of technology no one is supposed to have yet. Ever hear of a pin ansible?"

"As a matter of fact, yes," Ky said. "But I don't have one."

His eyes had widened, now they narrowed. "Where did you hear of it?"

"Never mind that . . . what's it good for?"

"An ansible you can mount on a ship," he said. "And more important, an ansible that allows real-time communications while you're in FTL flight."

Ky stuffed her first thought, *That's impossible,* back in her mouth and said again, "That would be quite an improvement in communications . . . just having a shipboard ansible would be an advance."

"Yes. And those do exist. The full-capability ones, those you can use in FTL flight, were in development the last I heard. But I suspect they now exist."

"So why isn't ISC bragging about this and selling them for vastly inflated prices?" Ky asked.

"Come, Captain, you have more business sense than that. I hope. ISC derives its revenues from per-message charges through the current ansible system—we don't sell ansibles, ever."

"Yes, but this is something that would make a bundle—"

"Comparatively? We would have to price it very high indeed, and we would be subject to competition, I've no doubt."

"Yes . . ." Ky thought about it. "So you're saying that there is a strong motive for ISC to freeze technological development that would risk its monopoly?"

He smiled at her. "I would not ever say that, Captain, because that would be revealing company secrets. Should you come to that conclusion on your own, I can't stop you."

Ky grinned back. "I'm glad we're temporarily on the same side."

"The thing is, if I had a pin ansible now, I could easily find out whether the more distant transfer lines are really blocked, or software clogged. As it is, I have to risk tapping into the station director's control lines, and if he's at all suspicious, he'll realize someone's snooping."

Quincy called Ky on the ship com. "Can we find a time to talk?"

"Yes, of course."

"I'm concerned about something."

"Now, or a couple of hours? I'm expecting a visitor I really need to see."

"Couple of hours is fine."

Master Sergeant Roth fit Ky's model for Mackensee much better than the callow lieutenant. Ky noticed that he and Martin looked each other over and came to some apparently favorable mutual conclusion. Roth brought with him a variety of Mackensee contracts. "Captain, I'm glad to meet you. Heard from our people at Sabine you did a fine job coping with those pirates."

"Not much choice, Master Sergeant. Your lieutenant tells me you're in a real bind here."

The look on Roth's face was eloquent. Ky remembered it well from MacRobert. "The lieutenant is . . . not too experienced," he said.

"Your OIC had a medical emergency?"

"He told you that?" Roth scowled. "He doesn't—sorry, ma'am. But he shouldn't have."

"Well, let's see what you have," Ky said. "We both seem to have a situation that would benefit from cooperation."

"Thing is, we can't get through to our headquarters," Roth said. "We aren't sure that the local ansible manager is being straight with us."

"He's not," Ky said.

"You know that?" His eyebrows shot up.

"I have sources," Ky said.

"Your own G-2?"

"You could put it that way." She wasn't going to compromise Rafe's situation if possible. "We know he's not straight, but we haven't defined how bad it is."

"So . . . what are your mission parameters?"

"My mission priorities are what you'd expect," Ky said. "Survive, find other surviving Vattas and protect them, find out who's doing this and how, and intervene."

"Makes sense to me, Captain. You seem to have the intelligence; we have muscle. What would your strategy be if we were partners in this?"

"Unblock Lastway's ansibles first, then work out from there. Collect a surcharge from other users to bankroll the project that far. If we're out in space, we're harder to find; if we unblock communications, it'll be easier to figure out who's blocking them. Once the financial ansibles start coming online, trade should resume, including bank transfers, which will make everyone's life easier, including yours."

"So you'd like us to do what?"

"Be the muscle you are. This ship is old, slow, unshielded, unarmed. I'd rather spend money hiring you than trying to turn it into a warship. But I don't have much. As you may have heard, most accounts are frozen, not just yours. We have the money we made in trade, selling the cargo we had when we came."

"Ma'am, if you can provision us, I believe the Old Man would not be displeased at a contract that put us back in contact with our people."

"I believe I can do that, Master Sergeant. But what about your lieutenant? Will he sign off on this?"

"I certainly hope so. Our ship captains aren't directly in his chain of command, but they'll lean on him."

"Another thing," Ky said. "I've had a subcontract under Mackensee, but I've never been the contract holder. Who calls the shots in something like this? You? Your OIC? The ship captains?"

"Employer defines the mission, but has no direct command of Mackensee personnel. Ship captains command ship crew in space; troop commanders command troops but under the captains in space, and independently otherwise. In something like this, I'd advise stationing a Mackensee NCO as liaison aboard your ship, and your communications would be through him or her to our senior ship captain in space, or to the OIC otherwise. Would you anticipate any station or groundside actions?"

"Possibly station, not groundside. I would, however, like the option of direct consultation with your ship captains, captain to captain, should anything come up in space. If they're protecting my ship, they may need to give me data quickly—"

"Oh, that's fine. It's just that you can't tell them what to do, other than to carry out the mission you assigned in the first place."

"Then let's get it nailed down, get your lieutenant to sign off on it, and I'll contact the banks to release funds. I presume you'd rather provision yourself than have civ do it—"

"Yes, ma'am, that would be ideal. Our immediate need is for rations; if the captain will take my advice, release just enough for, say, three days' rations for a hundred troops, then your liaison can contact the ship captains and find out their needs. That would come to—" He looked blank a moment. "—just under five thousand credits."

"Fine," Ky said.

"There's just a couple of things," Roth said. "I'm sure it's not a problem; you had a contract with us before. I know your record. But it's something I have to say, since you're the primary contractor here; please don't take offense."

"All right," Ky said, wondering what was coming.

"Are you now or have you ever been engaged in slave trading?"

"No!" She could not keep the shock out of her voice.

"Sorry, ma'am, I'm sure these don't apply; it's just routine. I have to ask; it's regulations." He looked embarrassed but went on to the next. "Are you now or have you ever been engaged in transporting goods you knew to be stolen?"

"No." Now that she knew the kinds of questions coming, it was easier not to react to them.

"Are you now or have you ever been engaged in piracy?"

"No."

"Are you now or have you ever been in possession of a letter of marque issued to you by a planetary or system government?" Shock again. She paused, and Roth looked up. "Ma'am?"

"I . . . do have one. From Slotter Key. It was waiting when I got here, but—"

Roth looked worried. "You didn't have it at Sabine, did you?"

"No. I just said—"

"Because that would screw everything, ma'am. You're—you're a privateer?"

"No," Ky said firmly. "I'm not. I never—I didn't ask for it, it was here when I got here, and I'm not sure it's valid anyway, because the government—"

"Ma'am, I'm sorry, but this is a serious problem. I'm going to have to call Captain Pensig."

"Can you explain?"

"We don't do contracts with privateers. Legal problems; it's against regs. There've been a few cases, but—you say you haven't used it?"

"No, I haven't used it. It was here when I got here, and I've been sitting in dock—"

"That's something . . . ," he said, but he didn't sound convinced. "The thing is, ma'am, the term is *possession* of a letter of marque. Not proof that you've operated using it. Can you prove that you didn't have it before you arrived here?"

"I've got the delivery receipt somewhere," Ky said. Quincy would know, probably.

"I'll just go back to dockside and call Captain Pensig," Roth said. Ky started to ask why he wasn't calling Lt. Mason, but refrained . . . she didn't want to deal with Mason anyway. She hoped someone would straighten out the legal angles; it would be the worst sort of irony if a letter of marque that Slotter Key undoubtedly didn't want her to have kept her from getting the help she needed now.

In a very few minutes, Lee spoke up. "Captain, you've got another call from Captain Pensig."

Pensig looked grim. "So—Roth tells me you weren't a privateer at Sabine, but now you are. Was that some kind of reward from the Slotter Key government?"

"No," Ky said. "This is what happened." She went over it all again, finishing with "So I don't even know if the letter is valid now. There's no way to contact them; the ansibles are down."

"Hmph. The problem is, Captain Vatta, that under the law relating to privateering, possession of a valid letter is construed as sufficient proof that the holder is in fact a privateer."

Ky hadn't known that.

"And we don't contract with privateers, since that blurs the lines of responsibility should anyone question the legality of proceedings."

"I'm not following that," Ky said. Pensig sighed.

"I could explain it, but better if our legal staff did. Look here, Captain—we're both in a cleft stick. You need our protection; we need your money. I believe you when you say you have not committed any acts based on the authority of that letter. Under these circumstances, I think a limited contract might be possible, but you would have to agree not to use that letter of marque while we're in contract, and I must warn you that the contract will likely be rescinded as soon as we're back in contact with our headquarters. As you say the letter itself may be. Is that acceptable?"

Ky hadn't ever planned to use the letter of marque while with the mercenaries anyway. "Yes, that's acceptable," she said.

"For our own protection, I'll have to have that clause added to the contract," Pensig said. He sighed again. "I'll have our legal staff transmit the changes. Any other surprises?"

"Not that I know of, but I didn't know about this one," Ky said.

Shortly after that, Master Sergeant Roth reappeared with a revised contract; Ky signed it, and Roth transmitted the details of the contract to the Mackensee station and the ship captains. The lieutenant, predictably enough, thought the Mackensee contingent should get more money, but within the hour they had an agreement. Ky called the bank and had five thousand credits transferred to the Mackensee account.

"The men'll be pleased with this," Roth said. "They were not looking forward to survival rations or being put in cold storage."

Ky had not realized that last was a possibility—frozen soldiers? She repressed a shudder. "One favor," she said. "Could you find me someone other than the lieutenant for a liaison?"

Roth grinned. "Yes, ma'am, I think we can do that."

CHAPTER FOURTEEN

She was finally getting somewhere, Ky thought. Whoever was attacking Vatta, it wasn't her fault for having killed Paison at Sabine. Stella's contribution increased her resources considerably, and hiring the Mackensee local force at least ensured that they were on her side, and couldn't be hired against her. That had to help with her first priority, survival. Rafe... she wasn't sure of Rafe, but factions within ISC causing the breakdown in ansible communication made a certain sort of sense.

She stretched. It had already been a long, long day. Perhaps a nap... The exterior com line lit, and Lee answered. "Yes—yes, the captain's on the bridge. Just a moment." He turned to her. "It's Captain Pensig again."

No rest for the wicked was the ancient expression, but it seemed to apply to the virtuous just as well.

Ky sat up in her command chair and flicked on the screen.

"Now that you've hired us," Captain Pensig said without preamble, "what exactly do you want us to do? I assume not sit here like a target for your enemies and eat up all your credits..." The habit of command, well honed by conflicts, conveyed the impression that she should have an entire plan of action laid out already. Roth had only been gone a half hour.

"Er... no."

"We need a situation report as soon as possible," Pensig said. "Our intelligence considers the threat level to Vatta ships and personnel extremely high—"

"Too high to come aboard for a conference?" Ky asked, interrupting what looked to be a lengthy harangue.

"No," he said. "When?"

"At your earliest convenience," Ky said, hoping that would be at least enough time to eat something. And if not, what could she feed them? What courtesies did mercenary ship captains expect from employers?

"Half an hour, then," Pensig said. "Expect three of us: myself, Captain Garner's Exec—we can't both leave our ships—and Master Sergeant Dolan. Oh, and an escort, of course, but they'll remain in your docking area."

"Fine," Ky said. "I'll expect you then." Drat, drat, drat. She was hungry, she was tired, she was not in the mood for a strategy conference right now. But they were coming, and she was the host.

They'd been eating stationside food, as Ky had been saving space for shields or weaponry, so she called down and told Quincy to organize some refreshments for the coming conference. "Fresh nibbling stuff, nothing that needs cooking. At least two, wearing protection, one of them armed," she said. "And make it quick. They're coming in a half hour, and I want to get cleaned up. And don't let that miserable puppy get loose."

"Right, Captain," Quincy said, though she sounded as if she was laughing. "The pup's all right, in his way."

"He's in everyone's way," Ky said.

Stella, in Ky's cabin, was deep into computation; Ky hoped it was their financial status being brought up to date. "I'm showering; we have company coming," Ky said, on her way into the head.

"Who?" Stella asked.

"Our new employees. Strategy conference. You'll want to be there. Martin, too. Let him know." Then she was into the shower, twisting the knob for a hard pulsing spray. She toweled off quickly, pulled on her bathrobe, and went back into her cabin. Stella turned around from the desk.

"That was fast."

"Fast showers are a specialty at the Academy," Ky said, yanking underwear out of a drawer. Vatta dress blue, she decided, dressing in one swift flow of movement while Stella stared.

"Ky, it takes me that long to get my clothes off the hanger, even if I know what I'm going to wear."

Ky buttoned the jacket. "So?"

"I'm impressed, that's all. Why do you want me at this conference? I don't have any background in strategy."

"There are three of them and one of me," Ky said. "Yes, I'm the employer, but I still want better numbers."

"All right. Will these clothes do?"

"Yes. You're businesslike. You may not need to say much."

"In other words, shut up and let you handle it?"

"No. But I'm introducing you as a source of information and also as my financial officer. Vatta's financial officer. You can look grave when money is mentioned."

"Grave concern," Stella said. Her face settled into exactly such an expression, and Ky grinned.

"Excellent. Martin represents something they understand; he's so obviously ex-military. We have five minutes; let's go set up the space."

Quincy had sent Toby and Mehar up to straighten the rec area; Ky had them go into the galley and lay out some platters and plates in readiness.

"You invited them for dinner?" Stella asked.

"No. But I suspect employers are expected to offer refreshment, and since we're already feeding their troops, I might as well feed these officers. The food should be arriving shortly."

The officers arrived first, with their escort. Ky welcomed them aboard and led them to the rec area. Pensig she had seen onscreen; in person he was half a head taller than she was; she could feel her spine stretching in response. The Exec off the other ship was a stocky balding man about her own height with bright blue eyes; the enlisted man with hash-marks up his sleeve was, she assumed, Master Sergeant Dolan. He looked as if someone had hacked him roughly out of cast iron. He gave her an appraising look and then a slight, sharp nod.

"Please be seated," Ky said. "Refreshments are on the way." She hoped they were; she had expected them by now. The dock area's grocers weren't that far away.

"Thank you," Captain Pensig said. "This is Lieutenant Commander Johannson, Captain Garner's Exec, and Master Sergeant Dolan." He looked at Stella.

"And this is Stella Vatta," Ky said, ignoring Stella's married name. She wanted the implied heft of the Vatta name. "She is my senior intelligence officer as well as acting CFO for Vatta family interests off Slotter Key. And this is Gordon Martin, who's in charge of our security measures."

"Do you have other Vatta family members aboard?" Pensig asked.

"Yes, a survivor of the attack on a Vatta ship on Allray. But Toby's a little junior for this conference."

"I see. Master Sergeant Roth explained that you would prefer another liaison than Lieutenant Mason. That made it necessary for myself, as senior ship captain, to contact you. Would you care to explain your objection to Lieutenant Mason?"

She could not tell from his tone if he was displeased by it or not. "Lieutenant Mason told me he had no combat experience," she said. "While I have no doubt that the training he received was thorough, I would prefer to deal with individuals who have actually seen action."

"Ah . . . he told you?"

"Yes. How else would I have known?"

"I see. So, hiring mercenaries, you expect and demand experience . . . that makes sense." He smiled at her. "Do you perceive your need as including ships as well as ground troops?"

"Yes," Ky said, wondering what this was about.

"Very well. I realize that our command structure is unfamiliar to you, but if you define the mission you assign to us as including ships for more than mere transport, then I, as senior ship captain, become the ranking officer, and I may appoint anyone I choose as customer's liaison. You have not asked, but I will tell you that my combat experience is . . . extensive. You are welcome to peruse my file." He handed over a data cube.

"I'll take you at your word," Ky said, hoping that was the right response. His smile broadened; apparently it was.

"Well, then, I think Master Sergeant Dolan will do you very well for onstation or onplanet liaison, and once we're beyond the first stages of planning, Lieutenant Commander Johannson will be your fleet liaison. Will that suit?"

"Perfectly," Ky said. She had no doubt of Johannson's combat experience; he had the look.

"As I understand it, you have defined our mission in terms of protection of yourself and any family members, discovery of the source of the attacks, and counterattack against this organization. Is that correct?"

"That is my mission," Ky said. "My resources may not extend to obtaining your assistance in all of it."

"Understood. But first and foremost is your safety and security, and that of your family members whose locations we know—three, isn't it? I would advise you most strongly, Captain Vatta, to depart this station immediately. We are more able to protect you in space than here, where I understand you and your crew have already been subject to attack. We cannot move our docking slots to cover your flanks, for instance; there are other ships already docked there. However good your dockside security, there is no way to protect you against attack using the exterior of the station."

"I see," Ky said. "I had hoped the external monitors we have would be sufficient. You think not?"

"They were not at Allway," Stella said, "where Toby's ship was blown up in dock. I was told it was with mines placed on the ship from outside, probably by agents using the maintenance hoppers. And I know *Ellis Fabery* had external monitors; all that class did."

"Well, then, we'd better take advice. But I have a few questions. Captain Pensig, I had been waiting to complete resupply in anticipation of installing a defensive suite and possibly some weapons—they're on hold at MilMart. What is your advice there?"

"If you can afford better shielding, and have it delivered within a few hours and install it yourself, fine. Otherwise, my advice would be to load and go as quickly as possible. I can offer crew assistance in that, if it will speed you."

"Stella, contact MilMart for me and get a delivery estimate on the defensive suite. I know Quincy can install it en route. Then tell Alene to order in supplies. Leave just enough room for the defensive suite, if MilMart can deliver it dockside in two hours or less. And while you're at it, check on whoever Quincy sent out for supplies. They should be back by now."

Stella nodded and left the room.

"You have someone overdue?" Pensig asked.

"Yes," Ky said. "A pair of them. Damn it, they were only going as far as the grocer's down the way."

"With permission, sir, I'll check on that," Dolan said.

Pensig crooked an eyebrow at Ky, and she nodded. They had the resources and for the moment it was hers.

"Names?" Dolan asked.

"Just a moment," Ky said, and went to the comunit, flicking it on. "Quincy?"

"Yes, Captain?"

"Who'd you send out for food, and have you had any word?"

"They aren't back yet? Jim and Mehar—they weren't going far; I told 'em to get whatever was available at Farmboy's just down the way."

"Stella's going to ask you the same questions in a minute,"

Ky said. "Mackensee personnel are going to go looking for them."

Ky gave the names, descriptions, and destination to Dolan; she had a sick feeling in her stomach. Dolan nodded and left the room. Before Ky could say anything, Stella came back.

"MilMart says they can't deliver for at least six hours, but it's available now. Want me to find a delivery service?"

"We'll take care of that," Pensig said. "If you'll authorize our pickup. They do know us . . ." He smiled.

"Will do," Ky said.

"I notice you don't have an implant," he said. "You haven't replaced the one damaged at Sabine?"

"Your surgeon advised me to wait six months," Ky said. "Stabilization of neural repair or something like that."

"Had it checked?"

"Haven't stopped," Ky said. "Life became . . . interesting."

"I see. Would you like one of our surgeons to evaluate?"

"Not at the moment, if we're kicking out of here as fast as possible." Ky wasn't at all sure she wanted a Mackensee surgeon investigating her brain anyway.

"Any seizure activity? Sensory abnormalities?"

"No. I'm fine . . . I think. Why?"

"Only that it would be simpler if you also had an implant. But you're right, this can wait. Collecting your defensive suite shouldn't. If you'll contact MilMart with authorization, I'll get a squad over there right away."

"Excuse me," Ky said. "The secure lines are all on the bridge." She left them there, taking deep breaths on the way to the bridge. She had not anticipated that events would move with such speed, and yet why not? If you hired military, you expected action . . . or you should. She felt stupid and slow, and she hated that feeling.

On the bridge, she opened one of the secure lines to the bank and authorized a draft to MilMartExchange for the cost of the suite, and then spoke to MilMart authorizing Mackensee personnel to pick up the equipment.

"So—you've hired mercs. Well, you hired good ones," the accounting manager said. "When will they be picking it up?"

"Soon," Ky said. "Within the hour, I should think. By the way, your policy statement states that you maintain customer privacy and discretion—"

"Oh, sure. Nobody wants anyone to know what they're buying or who for. Don't worry, Captain Vatta. We've been doing this for years. Are you sure you don't want that weapons suite?"

"I'm sure," Ky said. She wasn't at all sure she trusted that casual assurance of discretion, but she had no choice, really. Lee cocked an eye at her as she shut down the line.

"Things moving, Captain?"

"Indeed, Lee. We'll be undocking today, soon as we can load up this defensive equipment and supplies. Start the ball rolling with the station about that." She shook her head. "And I thought, once I got back to Belinta with that load of tractors, that everything was going to be simple and boring again."

He chuckled. "Somehow I think you aren't cut out for boring, Captain."

Ky shook her head at him, and went back to the rec area. "You'll want the authorization number from MilMart," she said, handing it over. "They're ready for pickup any time; the bank's released funds. And they promise discretion, for what that's worth..."

Pensig pursed his lips. "MilMart's pretty good about it—they've made their reputation and their fortune by keeping their mouths shut—but they're big enough now that leaks could happen." He looked blankly into the distance for a few moments; Ky knew he was accessing his implant. "Well, that's taken care of. Now, how about a loading crew?"

"Good idea," Ky said. "I was just—"

"Captain—" That was Lee, poking his head in. "Rafe's on the line; he says he needs you."

Now what? Ky excused herself again and headed for the bridge. Rafe, looking a bit rumpled, looked out of the screen at her.

"We have a situation," he said. "Your crew are alive, but we're all . . . being detained."

"By whom?" Ky asked.

"The Garda. That idiot Jim got into some kind of row with someone, the beauteous Mehar backed him up, and there's a body in the produce department of Farmboy's, and another in the bakery. And a blood trail out the back, which is what I noticed when I was on my way back here from . . . another errand."

"And no one called me?"

"They say they've tried twice, and the line was busy. They're trying to take statements. I wanted to sit in; they wouldn't let me; I'm not listed as a ship officer. But they remember Jim from a previous encounter . . . what is that boy, some kind of explosive device in human form?"

Ky ignored that question. "So what is the situation now? Do you know?"

"I know they're being detained, and from the look on the desk sergeant's face, Jim won't be seeing anything but a lockup for a while. Mehar has those wide eyes; they think she was lured into trouble by a bad boy and is too young to have good judgment. But it would help if you could show up with some legal aid. At least they let me call you."

"I'll be there," Ky said. She met Captain Pensig in the passage; he looked grim.

"Master Sergeant Dolan just reported—"

"I heard," Ky said. "Some kind of dustup in the grocery, and my people are in custody. I have to get over there—"

"Not without an escort," he said. "And if you don't mind, I'd like to come along." His mouth twitched. "Getting my people out of trouble with local law enforcement is something I've done too often before. Do you have a local attorney?"

"Not really," Ky said. "I took advice on the disposal of

cargo originally consigned to Leonora, but that was purely commercial."

"Um. I'll have Joe send someone along." Again that blank look.

Ky ducked into her cabin for her formal captain's cape—no use trying for anonymity in this situation—and hurried down to the dock. She couldn't take Martin along; he needed to be dockside to receive and load the cargo coming in. He looked grim as she told him what she knew, but nodded when she said the Mackensee squad would go with her. Ky felt marginally safer surrounded by them, but still scared. She was sure that a gifted assassin could find some way to kill her anyway.

The section Garda station was some distance away. Outside it, two men in uniform stood guard, scowling as the group came toward them.

"You can't go in there like that," one of them said. "What are you up to?"

"Keeping Captain Vatta alive," Captain Pensig said. "Since the station refused to give her any protection, and she's already been attacked, she hired professionals."

Glares.

"Excuse me," Ky said, "but I believe my crew need me." She stepped forward. The guards said nothing as she led the way in.

Inside, Rafe lounged against the wall, straightening when he saw her; his expression remained ironic. Ky nodded at him without speaking and went to the desk.

"I'm Captain Vatta—I understand you have been trying to reach me?"

"Couldn't get through," the man said without looking up. When he did, his eyes widened. "You brought *them*—!"

"It seemed wise," Ky said. "Since my crew and I have been attacked onstation before and the Garda have refused to give us protection—"

"You have too many enemies," he said. "And so you hired mercs—"

"It's not illegal," Ky said. "I would like to see my crewmembers, please, and find out what the problem seems to be."

"Problem is, that murdering ruffian you have in your crew just killed another two people—"

Ky felt her brows go up. "I do not have murdering ruffians in my crew. If by *another,* you're referring to the man I shot, that has already been adjudicated as self-defense, and the dead man was part of the gang that attacked me—"

"Three of your people have killed someone on this station. I'd call that serious cause for concern. Most people make it through a lifetime without killing anyone."

"Most people aren't attacked repeatedly by someone trying to kill them. Self-defense isn't murder."

"There was no attack. He shot a poor old lady who has lived in the neighborhood for forty years, thereabouts, and—"

Ky's heart sank.

"I suppose you've done the forensic matching already," Captain Pensig said, peering at the ceiling as if he found it interesting.

"Well, no, but there's no need. Nobody but him and that girl had any weapons. And she only had that pistol bow."

"And the second body?" Ky asked.

"Dockworker. Only been here a month, but nothing against him."

"And the third?" Rafe asked from behind them. "Found the owner of the bloody footsteps yet?"

"I told you before, there was no blood trail when we looked. If you're one of this lot, I'm not surprised you lied about it."

"I think I'd better speak to your shift supervisor," Ky said.

"He's busy . . . busy with that crew of yours," the man said. "You can wait until he's free. You seem to think you're special . . ." His gaze went past Ky to the door. She turned to look; a lean man in Mackensee uniform with a lock case strode in; the escort moved smoothly aside and closed in after him.

"Captain Pensig," said the newcomer. "I got here as fast as I could."

"Thank you, Major," Pensig said. "Captain Vatta, this is Major Grawn, our legal affairs officer."

"What seems to be the problem here?" Grawn asked.

"The problem is, this Vatta crewman's been in trouble over and over since she docked—" The clerk nodded at Ky. "One thing after another—illegal biologicals and now he's killed at least two people—"

"Is *alleged* to have killed two people," Grawn said. "I believe this station operates under the General Code, does it not?"

"Well, yes, but things are a little different out here..."

Grawn cocked his head to the right. "Either you operate under the General Code, or you don't. Which is it?"

"The General Code... mostly..."

"And that means that accused persons have the right to legal representation, including during interrogation, isn't that right?"

"I'll have to check," the clerk said, reaching for a button on his desk.

"Go ahead," Grawn said. "I'm sure you'll find that's the case, and when your officer in charge confirms that, tell him that legal representation is here."

"But you're military and the murd—the accused—is civ. Her crewman."

"She's retained our assistance," Grawn said. "Her legal problems are our legal problems."

The clerk muttered into his equipment, then looked up. "All right. You can go back. She can't, nor any of the rest of you."

Grawn didn't move. "A ship captain is held legally responsible for crew behavior and damages to a station, under the General Code. Isn't that right?"

"Yes." Very grudgingly.

"Then Captain Vatta is also a party to the accusations, and has a legal right and duty, under the code, to ensure that her crew are being treated appropriately, and to have access to all pertinent information. She's coming with me."

"I—oh, all right. But nobody else." He got up to show the way.

"No one else," Grawn agreed. He nodded at Ky. "After you, Captain."

They passed a large office and two smaller ones. The corridor turned left, and she saw two doors, each with an armed guard outside. One opened as she approached, and a short, stout man in a business suit looked out.

"If it isn't Major Grawn," he said with no enthusiasm.

"Inspector Filgrim," Grawn said, mirroring the lack of glee. "How nice."

"The last time you were here," Filgrim said, "that was a mess."

"But not our mess," Grawn said. "So I am in hope it is not our mess this time."

"Only if you make it yours," Filgrim said. "Which I hear you have... frankly, were I you, I'd have been a little more wary of taking employment from a Vatta." That with a sour look at Ky.

"Oh? What do you have against Vattas?" Grawn said.

"They have enemies. People don't have enemies all over the galaxy for no reason. Probably been up to something for years and finally got found out."

"Until recently, have you had any complaints against Vatta ships or crews?"

"Well... no. But that's just because we didn't realize—"

"Or because Vatta's enemies have nothing to do with Vatta's wrongdoing, and are entirely self-motivated."

"Everyone's guilty of something," Filgrim muttered. "Never met a civ who wouldn't lie—"

"Or a law officer, either," Grawn said. "Enough. You're interrogating members of Captain Vatta's crew without legal representation present. I am now here; I will be present for one, and Captain Vatta for the other."

"That's—"

"By the code," Grawn said. "You have a male and a female

in custody, right? I'll sit in with the male, and Captain Vatta clearly should sit in with the female."

Filgrim looked as if he'd bitten into a sour fruit, but nodded, and opened the door wider. Ky got a glimpse of Jim, with a blackening eye and hunched shoulders, at a table inside. Then Filgrim nodded to the next door. "The girl's in there. I haven't gotten to her yet. You can go in."

Grawn nodded at Ky and she went into the next room. Mehar sat at another table, watched over by two guards.

"Are you all right, Mehar?" Ky asked.

"Yes, Captain. I'm sorry—"

"We have legal assistance now," Ky said, interrupting. "Major Grawn from the Mackensee Military Assistance Corporation. You will have a representative while you're interrogated."

"I don't know how it happened," Mehar said. "We had just picked up some fruit, and we came around the end of the radiated display—"

"You should wait until Major Grawn gets here," Ky said, hoping she was right. "I'm really more interested in how you are."

"I wasn't hurt. Jim fell down when the display was hit and fell on him."

"Display?"

"Yes... they had a tower of cans, and something hit it, probably a solid slug, and it fell. Jim was right beside it, and the cans landed on him. I was far enough back, so I ducked, and then I heard the shots."

"I'm surprised they missed Jim," Ky said. "If he was down and in plain sight."

"Whoever it was just shot at everything," Mehar said. "The lights above me shattered. I heard lots of people screaming, and things breaking and falling."

"And you—"

"I hit the deck, Captain. I didn't see anyone shooting at me, so I just lay there. Then the Garda arrived. They said we shot some people, but it wasn't us—"

"Did you see anyone?"

"There were people in the store when we got there. Just . . . people. I didn't really notice them, except for one of the quad humods. He—I think it was a he—didn't need a basket. I watched him pick up plums and apricots and apples all at the same time and use the fourth hand to twist the bag-ties. We were supposed to hurry, Quincy'd said, so we just picked out the fruit and went on—"

The door opened. "Ah," Major Grawn said. "Captain Vatta—this is Mehar Mehaar?"

"Right," Ky said. She glanced at Mehar. "This is Major Grawn, of Mackensee; he's their legal officer."

Major Grawn came in and sat down; Filgrim followed, looking even more sour than before.

"Mehar, have you given a statement?"

"I—I tried, sir."

"That's my job," Filgrim said.

"Well, then, get to it," Major Grawn said. "But try sticking to evidence this time."

"I—all right, Ms. Mehaar, what's your version of this."

Mehar, with nervous glances at Ky and Filgrim, told how she and Jim had been sent to buy refreshments and gone to the nearest grocer's, where the trouble landed on them.

"Why did you start shooting at everything?" Filgrim asked.

Grawn snorted. "Inspector—you're making rash assumptions." He turned to Mehar. "Did you fire your weapon? Did Jim?"

"No, sir! I tried to tell them that—"

"Did you see who was shooting?"

"No, sir. I never saw anyone with a weapon, but things were crashing down, the lights blinking, and people screaming—"

"You never shot anyone?" Filgrim was clearly dubious. "Which gun was yours?"

"Gun, sir? I didn't have one. I had the pistol bow, but no bolts loaded. They're in that belt they took off me when they brought us in. Jim had a gun, but he didn't have time to get it out before stuff fell on him." She looked at Ky. "I tried to tell them he hadn't fired, but they didn't listen to me."

"Two people are dead, Mehar," Ky said. "They had to consider that."

"I assume the store had a vidscan going," Grawn said. "Have you reviewed it? Or checked the weapons for discharge?"

"No," Filgrim said.

"Well, that seems to be a good first step... not that I'm trying to teach you your business, but Captain Vatta was on the point of departure and I believe had already signed on to the departure queue. If these people are not guilty, then here's a way to establish that quickly."

Filgrim scowled, but agreed to review the store's vidscan with them. There on the screen both vidscans played in synchrony: the left aisle and part of the middle; the right aisle and the rest of the middle. Jim and Mehar, heading down the left, pausing to pick up fruit from this bin and that, then turning, coming up the middle aisle as if to head toward the bakery... and then, as Mehar had said, shots, broken lights—

"You see," Grawn said, pointing. "They were on the far side of this set of display racks when it started and the old woman went down—"

"They could have—"

"There are muzzle flashes back there." Grawn pointed again. Filgrim boosted the IR sensitivity and the flashes shone bright, well away from Mehar and Jim. "They've got chameleon gear on—look at those blurry places..."

Ky spotted four, altogether, four shimmery blurs. All emitted bursts of heat and light. Filgrim ran the scan backward and forward several times. Now it was clear that four customers entering just after Jim and Mehar had suddenly blurred, the blurs moving swiftly past those two, to set up across the far end of the store.

"So it wasn't them at all," Ky said.

"I suppose not," Filgrim said. Clearly he wished it had been.

"They were waiting for your crewmembers, Captain

Vatta," Grawn said. "For anyone coming out of your ship. Whether to kill them or simply cause you trouble, I don't know. But the sooner you get offstation, the better."

"Not without my crew," Ky said.

"I can release them, if you're really going," Filgrim said. "This may not be your fault, exactly, but your presence certainly has caused trouble."

"We're going," Ky said. "Though I don't like being blamed for something I didn't start."

"We have an escort to take Captain Vatta and her crew back to the ship safely," Grawn said. "So we will not need to call on your forces."

"I don't have spare men anyway," Filgrim said. "Fine, then. Go." He waved his hand. "All you ever bring is trouble anyway, you traders."

Ky opened her mouth to say something, but Grawn shook his head at her, and she nodded instead. "I hope you have no more trouble," she said.

CHAPTER FIFTEEN

Nothing disturbed their passage to the dock; Ky arrived just as the defensive suite was being delivered by Mackensee personnel.

"Jim, go let the medbox check you out; Mehar, stand by for the moment." Jim, walking a little unsteadily, wandered up the access and into the ship, following the squad with the cartons and lifter.

"Any other supplies to come aboard?" asked Lt. Commander Johannson.

Ky looked at the status board just inside the docking tube. "No—we could squeeze on another five days' rations, but that's about it. We'll undock within the hour. Is that fast enough?"

"I hope so." He tapped the bulge in front of his ear. "Our people report unusual external activity—repair bugs, that kind of thing. Not right here, but enough of them that Traffic Control is expressing annoyance. I'd like you a solid ten kilometers offstation."

Ky tapped her handcom. "Quincy—how soon can we undock?"

"Without blowing seals? We've got a place in the queue in fifty-eight minutes, with the tug *Missy Mae*. Insystem's ready to warm up. Station seemed glad to have us going . . ."

"There's a concern," Ky said. "Ask Station if anyone else is in our way if we're a little quicker; I'm on my way to the bridge. Bring the insystem drive to standby." She turned to

Johannson. "I'll see what I can do—our slot is fifty-seven minutes."

"Right." He signaled to the Mackensee NCO in charge of the loading group. "We'll get out of your way, but watch the area." The squad that had delivered the packages came out the hatch on the double.

Ky looked at Martin, who was standing nearby. "Let's start buttoning up, then."

"Yes, Captain."

On her way to the bridge, Ky felt her skin tightening; she could imagine one or more of the little one-person repair scooters easing up to the hull, planting mines. Her ears registered the pressure fluctuation as the hatch sealed. She passed the medbox alcove; Jim sat hunched over the diagnostic module, holding something to his face that she hoped would take care of his black eyes. Stella, in the galley, turned; Ky shook her head and went on to the bridge. Lee was talking to the station.

"—We're small. We've undocked without a tug before."

The face in the display had a sour look. "And we've had ships undock without a tug that put us at risk with reaction—"

"You won't feel a thing," Lee said.

"That's what they all say," the duty officer said. "*Just a little squirt, that's all,* and we end up having to expend fuel to counter the rotational effects..."

"Well, if the tug can hurry it up—"

"They can't. There's a traffic jam up on Ring Five; some idiot kids decided to hold some kind of rally in repair scooters. Tug would have to risk collisions to come now. I don't see why you can't wait."

Icy tingles ran down Ky's spine. Someone wanted them delayed, still onstation when something went wrong.

"Captain Vatta here," she said, silencing Lee, who had his mouth open to reply. "We have received a credible threat, involving those same repair scooters. What's current traffic status on this ring?"

"Uh . . . there are a couple of nonscheduled scooters, probably just those kids—coming around Dock Four-B."

A sector away. What was the maximum acceleration on those scooters? The only external scans she had were focal scans of a few hull locations, not wide-area.

"Sorry," she said. "We're departing now; we believe that those scooters may intend to plant mines on our hull."

"But they're just kids—"

"Maybe," Ky said. To Lee, she said, "Shut down all external access, Lee." To the duty officer, "We're shutting off externals; we'll be pulling out as soon as the boards go green. Slowly, I promise."

"You Vatta . . . ," the man said. "If it weren't for you—"

"I didn't start this," Ky said.

"Air's clear. Water's clear. External com's clear—"

"Close curtain," Ky said. Unlike their emergency undock from Sabine Prime, she was not going to cause any more damage than she could help. The ship, external attachments retracted, lay in the docking bay with no more physical connection to the station.

"Confirm curtain sealed," the duty officer said. "Formal clearance . . ."

"Take us out, Lee," Ky said.

"Maneuvering," he said. The deck didn't so much as quiver, but the instruments showed their relative motion. Ky said nothing. Again unlike their earlier emergency undock, they weren't using the insystem drive, but the less powerful attitude controls. Ky switched on nearscan as soon as the nodes had cleared the station's blanketing structure . . .

"There they are," she said. Two tiny dots, just showing around the curve of the station. Their projected course took them directly to what had been *Gary Tobai*'s docking bay . . . as she watched, they angled outward.

"We're not clear yet, Captain," Lee said. His fingers twitched on the controls. One meter per second . . . and the acceleration was only 0.001 meter per.

"Insystem," Ky said.

"Insystem hot," Quincy said.

"We're too close—we could give 'em a wobble," Lee said.

"We'll give them worse than that if we blow up this close," Ky said. "I want the drive up . . . we'll engage as late as we can, but no later."

The tiny dots crawled nearer . . . they couldn't go far, but they were faster than the ship.

"Minimum coming up," Lee said.

"Rotate the ship parallel to the entire station axis," Ky said. "We'll do less damage that way . . ."

That took precious seconds, and the two tiny craft were within what Ky considered throwing distance when she said "Engage, one-quarter power."

Gary Tobai's rotation and the shove of the insystem drive sent them off at a solid ten-meters-per-second acceleration; in the scan, the two dots crossed paths and curled around, trying to chase them, but they'd already opened a distance. Repair scooters, Ky knew, couldn't top a ten-meters-per acceleration, and quickly used up fuel at that rate. One of them, though, closed distance. Not just your ordinary repair scooter, then.

"You're being pursued," the station duty officer said in a surprised tone.

"I noticed," Ky said. "Half power," she told Quincy. The ship opened the gap again. Something flashed in the scan behind them . . . the first dot vanished and the second boosted back toward the station. "You might want to intercept that one," she said to the duty officer. "You might learn something to your advantage."

"Uh . . . right."

"Where do you want to go?" Lee asked.

"Right now, I just want enough distance to be safe," Ky said. "Maybe ten kilometers—"

"Gloucester to *Gary Tobai."*

"Gary Tobai," Ky said. The screen flicked twice, then steadied on Captain Pensig's face.

"Our scans report an explosion near your position. Any damage?"

"No—we're fine."

"We recommend you continue on present course for six hours, Captain Vatta."

"But we—" Ky swallowed the rest of that. "Six hours, right."

His face relaxed. "We'll be in touch on a secured link, Captain. *Gloucester* will cover your retreat; *Scapa Flow* will remain onstation for the present."

On her nearscans, the Mackensee ship's trace edged out, carefully staying between them and the station.

"Station's not mad at us," Lee said. "Who do they think might take a potshot?"

"There's a lot of spare armament," Ky said. "Someone else could've made a critical purchase from MilMart, after all."

"Mmm. So we're not really safe until we clear the system, is that it?"

Ky thought about pointing out that they weren't going to be safe anywhere, and decided against it. "Well . . . the farther away we are, the safer. It takes a lot of power to run one of the big beam weapons. Missiles, though . . . we'd better get our defensive suite up and running." Ky turned to her com again and called Quincy. "How's the installation coming?"

"Installation! I just got the last carton unclipped!"

"Well, chances are we'll need it now or we won't need it at all," Ky said.

A silence on the other end, a mutter she couldn't quite hear, then, "I am definitely retiring after this trip, Ky—Captain. I am too old for this. I'm supposed to fit these things in one-meter intervals—do you have any idea how much climbing that involves?" Quincy didn't sound scared, just annoyed.

"Toby's young and agile; so is Jim. Martin probably knows how to install that kind of thing. And maybe Rafe can help."

"Rafe! You'd trust him with our defenses?"

"We need the suite installed and running, Quincy. Whatever it takes."

"Right."

Ky sat back, fingers drumming on the arm of her seat. They were alive, by the margin of a few seconds. They were back in space, where spacers belonged, and she had an ally now. Maybe more than one, if Rafe had been honest about his family name. She thought he was. But... alone, with two Mackensee ships, and a hole in the bottom of the budget... so they had provisions, but troops ate provisions as locusts ate grain fields. She would have to have money at the next place they stopped... she needed to spread the cost of all this... but how?

"Ky, have you eaten?" Stella, sandwich in hand, peered around the entrance to the bridge.

"Since when?" Ky asked.

"That's an answer of sorts. I've made sandwiches; here's one." She handed in a plate piled with neatly cut triangles.

"You cook?" Ky said. She had not suspected Stella of any domestic skills.

Stella grimaced. "Sandwiches aren't cooking, and I told you I could scramble eggs. I'll just send some down to the others."

"Good idea," Ky said. Now that they were—well, not safe, but definitely safer—she was hungry. That snack intended for the visiting officers had never been delivered. She put the plate between herself and Lee; both of them ate in silence for several minutes.

Then Lee looked at her. "Do you think we'll be attacked now?"

"I hope not," Ky said. She put down the sandwich she was eating. "It's all happened so fast... at least we have help this time. We can actually do something."

He picked up another triangle of sandwich. "You have a plan, then."

"I will soon," Ky said. "Actually I have a plan now, and

we're succeeding in the first objective, which is staying alive, with mobility unimpaired."

"And next?"

"Find and aid any family members we can, before they're all killed. Figure out who's doing this, and how to strike back. Same as I said in the first place."

"And you trust the mercs?"

"They hold to contracts, the same as we do," Ky said. "What happened last time wasn't their fault, and we were paid well for our trouble."

"Yes, but..." He chewed a moment in silence, then swallowed and went on. "Is there any chance we'll get back to regular trading?"

"I don't know," Ky said. "Nobody's going to be doing regular trading as long as the ansibles are down. If that's taken care of, and as long as our enemies aren't attacking us directly, we ought to be able to go back. It won't be the same, of course, with all the damage Vatta's sustained. We'll have to rebuild the business." Even as she said it, she wondered if it could be done at all. It had taken generations to build Vatta from that first ship to the shipping empire it had become. She cocked her head at Lee. "Why? Are you ready to go find another ship? Is adventure looking less attractive than a few days ago?"

He shook his head. "No, Captain. I'm just considering the ironies."

"The ironies?"

"Yes. Your father picked me as junior pilot to Riel, as you know, on the basis of my safety record. My reputation in the trade was as a solid, serious young pilot with no wild tendencies. He didn't know—because it would have done my application no good—that I had always wanted something more exciting than piloting a trader. But when my parents were killed, I needed to find a job quickly, and I was a year too young to qualify for military training. I thought it was a tragedy at the time and was prepared to be miserably bored for the next fifty or sixty years. I realized soon enough that even civilian piloting had some adventure in it, but it was still . . . missing something."

"You still crave adventure?" Ky asked.

"Even after seeing it close up. Yes, Captain. If you decide not to go back to ordinary trading . . . don't worry about me quitting, is what I mean. If you want me, that is."

"You're a good pilot, Lee; of course I want you on the ship. Let's just not have too *much* adventure, all right?"

"It's your call, Captain." He grinned and finished another sandwich.

Ky was still thinking about the next step and the five beyond that. She needed money. Traders got money by trading or by providing a service. They'd sold all they had to sell. What service could she provide, as the target of malicious attack? What resources did she have? What she had to sell, Ky realized suddenly, was protection. As long as she had Mackensee, she had something other traders might want.

"Captain Vatta, this is Lieutenant Commander Johannson."

"Captain Vatta here."

"Our sources confirm destruction of one stolen repair bug, and the other has been taken into custody. I understand you may have some information on the ansible problems?"

"Yes," she said. "We have an individual with considerable expertise in ISC internal affairs. At the moment he's helping install the defensive suite we just loaded."

"That takes precedence," Johannson said. "But we'd like to talk to him."

"I'll let him know," Ky said. "He's not actually part of my crew; we have a partnership agreement at the moment. He helped my cousins get off Allray in one piece."

"Ah."

"Another thing," Ky said. "If I'm reading our contract correctly, there's nothing to prevent your escorting a few more trading ships, is there?"

"In convoy, you mean? We'd usually have more ships for that, but . . . you're thinking of spreading the cost?"

"Yes, of course, but also establishing the legitimacy of

Vatta Transport again. Right now the other trader captains don't want to speak to me in case our problems are contagious. To get shipping contracts, we have to get some of that cleared off our reputation. If I can offer safe, or at least safer, transportation somewhere—anywhere—it should help."

"Good point. We'd want to vet potential participants, though, and we'd be limited."

"Make up a list of those you'd approve, and give me a target number," Ky said. "As word gets around Lastway about the attempt to blow us at the dock, captains should be getting nervous and anxious to leave. They may be more willing to listen to me now."

"Will do, Captain Vatta," he said.

When he signed off, Ky went down to see how the installation was coming along.

"We're working on it," Quincy said. She had the installation routine set up on the screen. All the telltales still read PENDING. "It's a good thing the holds aren't stuffed with ag machinery; we have to have these sensor units in every ship space, just about. I've got Jim on that job; he's got good manual dexterity, at least."

"Rafe?"

"With Jim, at the moment. I don't know how much help he is."

"Mmm. If he's not essential here, there's something else he can do. We need to deal with the ansible problems."

Quincy gave her a sharp look. "You trust him that much?"

Ky shrugged. "He's the only one who might know what we need to know." She considered telling Quincy all she knew—or thought she knew—about Rafe and decided against it. "He and Stella worked together in the past."

Quincy snorted. "That's a recommendation? I mean... Stella. Everyone knows about her."

"Not really," Ky said. "Everyone knows she screwed up years ago, just as everyone knows I was kicked out of the Academy—a different kind of screwup. Does that tell you all about me?"

"Well . . . no. But Stella—"

"Grew out of it, Quincy. And she's the family I've got left. Vattas stick together."

"I suppose." Quincy shook her head. "It's a new world, and I don't much like it."

"None of us does. So we'll make a better one, that we do like," Ky said with more confidence than she felt. "That's what great-grandfather did, and we can do it, too."

"I hope so," Quincy said. "So much lost, so many dead . . ."

"Quincy . . . are you getting enough sleep? This doesn't sound like you."

"I . . . can't sleep, Ky. Not enough. I keep seeing Gary's face . . . your father . . ."

Nothing Ky had ever read discussed what captains were supposed to do when elderly crew came apart. She found herself cradling Quincy, holding her gently, until the old woman stiffened.

"Role reversal," Ky said. "But it's reversible again . . ."

Quincy sniffed. "I'm sorry. I'm supposed to be comforting you."

"You'd known Gary longer than I had. Same with the other elders of the tribe. You've lost a lot of friends; I've lost a lot of acquaintances. Neither's easy." She watched Quincy's face relax gradually as she kept talking.

"I'm all right now," Quincy said finally, as she straightened up.

"Good," Ky said. "Let me know when Rafe's free, or if you need more help with this. I can use a socket wrench myself, you know."

"Oh, I know. But captains have other things to do."

"True enough. My next move is to spread the cost of our military assistance among the ships I hope will convoy with us to wherever we're going, when we figure that out."

"That's a good idea," Quincy said. "But do you think they'll come? What you said before—"

"Situation's changed," Ky said. "We were almost blown in dock; others have to be feeling anxious—that's what I told

Mackensee anyway. I'll bet some of the smaller independents will sign up."

Rafe ambled in from the far reaches of the #3 hold. "Quincy, Jim says he's ready for the next set of attachment pins..."

"Ah, Rafe," Ky said. "Can Jim get along with Toby's help, d'you think?"

"Easily," Rafe said. "Why? Do you have something else for me to do?" He put an edge on it that made Ky's teeth itch.

"Yes," she said crisply. "Quincy, let me know when the installation's complete, so I can let our escort know. Rafe, come on with me, please."

They settled in the rec area; Ky stepped into the galley, noting that Stella had left it spotless, and brought out a pitcher of water and two glasses. Rafe got up and came back with a lime and a small knife. Before Ky could say anything, Rafe spoke.

"You were much on Stella's mind, a few years past," Rafe said. He did not look at Ky directly, concentrating instead on taking the peel off a lime in one smooth, even curl. She had no idea why he wanted a peeled lime.

"Oh?" Ky waited.

"Yes. She spoke of you quite a bit. Apparently you were being held up as an example of a properly brought up young Vatta daughter. Courteous, cool—butter wouldn't melt in your mouth, is how she put it, not at noon in midsummer. Straight arrow, never makes mistakes." He glanced up; Ky said nothing. "You annoyed her quite a bit. Stuck-up young prig, I believe, is what she called you. Born to be a military martinet, all rules and rigidity. Is that how you remember it?"

"Not quite," Ky said. He would be getting at something, but she couldn't yet tell what; she wasn't going to let him drive a wedge between her and Stella. "I don't know who in the family was telling her that, but I was getting the lectures on how good girls didn't want to be spacers or soldiers, and what made me think I had the qualities necessary anyway, and why wouldn't I settle down with a nice boy from one of the other good families."

"And why didn't you?" Rafe asked. This time the look from those bright eyes pinned her, as neatly as ever her brothers had pinned the bugs they studied. "You're good looking enough, and Stella managed to find a boy she liked—"

"Who caused her a lot of grief," Ky said. "I heard about that. Besides, you ought to know about family ambitions—you went rogue, too."

Rafe winced dramatically. "Ah—a palpable hit. So you claim that you went rogue by going military? Or was it by being kicked out that you went rogue? What *did* happen?"

"Nothing that concerns you," Ky said. She didn't need to talk about that with this man, whom even Stella did not seem to trust completely.

"Oh, but it might," Rafe said. "Things like that last awhile, when you're young. It hasn't been even a year yet, has it? Seeing as you're the one in charge of this affair, I'd like to know how stable you are."

"Stable enough," Ky said. "Stable enough not to worry about what you think of my stability."

"Ouch." He mimed sucking a pricked finger. "Sharp as a tack, you are. Stella said that, too. Don't you ever wonder what else she said?"

"Not really." Ky gave him look for look. "Stella's probably said a lot of things, as I have, that she wouldn't say today. Makes no difference."

"Mmph. Maybe." The last of the lime peel came free. Rafe arranged it back into the shape of a lime. The lime itself, held in his left hand, he dropped into his water. "Do they grow these where you came from, on Slotter Key?"

"Limes? Yes, in the garden. We don't have a citrus orchard."

"Tik, as I recall, is your family's main cash crop. Valuable. Mild euphoric and stimulant, various fractions also useful in pharmaceutical manufacturing."

"Yes."

"Ever taken tik tea and added lime?"

"No," Ky said, wondering where this was leading.

"Don't. Not a good idea. Chemical reactions make it taste bad and give a headache like being slugged with a rock." He sipped his limewater, shook his head, and dropped in the peel. "The thing is, people are always mixing things they shouldn't mix. Limes and tik. Guns and butter. Morality and—"

"Not that lecture," Stella said, coming into the compartment. She had changed into a one-piece garment that looked like brown plush, and her gold hair shone against it. "Rafe, you ought to be ashamed of yourself."

"It's true," Rafe said.

"It's trite," Stella said. "You peeled that lime for her, didn't you?" She grinned at Ky. "It's leading up to why you and he should get into bed together, even if it doesn't work out, because mixing unlikes is inevitable or something. The lime peel trick is supposed to demonstrate his manual dexterity and fascinate you with inchoate possibilities."

"Worked with you," Rafe said in what was almost a growl.

"Not really," Stella said. "I already wanted to try it; you almost put me off with the professorial bit. I admit being impressed by the lime peeling."

Ky looked at Stella. "I thought you said—"

"We weren't *involved,*" Stella said. "I just slept with him and that was it."

Ky wondered if that was true. She could not imagine sleeping with someone and not being involved—though she had been *involved* without the *sleeping with*. Was the look Stella gave Rafe now really that cool? Rafe, meanwhile, had a stubborn expression that Ky did not want to see aimed at her.

"You still—" Rafe began.

"I thought we were going to be discussing strategy," Stella said. "Isn't that right, Ky?"

"Right," Ky said, switching tracks with some effort. "Now that we have some military assets, we can start doing something."

"Do we know enough?"

"We know enough to get started," Ky said. "If we wait until we know it all, we'll wait forever." On this she was confident; she saw surprise on Rafe's face, but Stella just nodded. "But I have a few questions for Rafe."

"And what are those?" Rafe asked.

"Does ISC know that some of its station managers are corrupted? Will there be . . . repercussions from them . . . if we remove one or two?"

"Remove, as in—"

"Kill," Ky said.

Rafe went still all over for a moment, then one hand twitched.

"There's not another quick way to get communications back up here," she went on. "The station polity has no interest in listening to me. They aren't suffering; they think they're better off as they are. Other shippers are suffering, but they're scared to do anything. Any legal approach will take weeks to months, and he'll get away while doing more damage. We need him gone, out of his position permanently and quickly. That will give us some legitimacy in the eyes of the others."

"Killing's a bit extreme," Rafe said, in a voice devoid of resonance. "Don't you think?"

"Not in this instance," Ky said.

"Ky—" Stella began, then stopped. She shook her head, then went on. "Ky, Vatta's not—not ever been—that way."

"Vatta's not ever been at war," Ky said. "We didn't start it; I want Vatta around at the end of it. So, Rafe, what do you think ISC's reaction will be?"

He was silent a moment, then folded his hands and gave her a steady look. "I think if there's sufficient evidence of his treachery, they will overlook a . . . an accidental death. At least in the sense of taking no reprisals against other Vatta. I think they will be upset, however. It sets a bad precedent. ISC has never allowed anyone—government, commercial entity, whatever—to judge its people."

"They didn't take care of it," Ky said. The edge in her voice surprised even her; she saw in their faces that they were both startled. "It cost lives—is costing lives. My position is that I am doing what they would do, and they had best accept it."

"You sound almost as if you're threatening ISC, Captain." She did not miss the shift to formality. "If that is so, then I must remind you where my primary loyalty lies."

"I hold your partnership agreement at present," Ky said. "If you forswear that—"

He winced. "I know that. But—but you are asking me—perhaps asking me—to breach an older trust."

"I don't think so," Ky said. "As an ISC agent—however covert—you are being asked to consider whether this ISC employee is guilty—"

"Oh, he's guilty, all right," Rafe said. "No doubt at all. Deep in the conspiracy. I have the evidence, too; I was on my way back to the ship with it when your people got in that trouble in the store."

"Well, then. What would ISC do, assuming they had the resources at hand?"

"He'd be . . . all right, he'd be dead. We do have an . . . an enforcement arm that is . . . not subject to any governmental restrictions. So, do you want me to take him?" He looked haggard now; Ky wondered at that.

"Would you?" she asked. He stared back, his expression grim, and did not answer at once. She went on. "I expect you'd wait for orders from home. I expect you've had to do it, and don't like it."

"Not much," Rafe said. His voice was breathy with the effort to keep it light.

"Then leave it to those who do," Ky said. Stella drew in a sharp breath; Ky did not look at her. "What I ask of you, as the ISC representative, is agreement that he is guilty, that there is sufficient evidence, and that a quick removal is in the best interests of . . ." Her voice failed for an instant, remembering too well *in the best interests of the Service*. "—of ISC and its customers."

Rafe nodded. "That—that I can do. I do not see a conflict between the partnership and my loyalty to ISC in making such a report."

"Good," Ky said. She smiled, but neither of them smiled back. Stella looked as if someone had hit her in the stomach; Rafe simply continued to look grim. "I'll tell our liaison. They want to talk to you about the evidence."

"It would be a good idea for me—for someone from ISC to have custody of it," Rafe said. "And to give them authorization."

"Do it," Ky said. "We might as well clean up the whole mess while we're about it. Lee can set up the secure line for you on the bridge."

"You surprise me," Rafe said, as he got up. He left without saying anything more.

Stella put out her hand as if to touch Ky's arm, then withdrew it. "Ky... I almost feel I don't know you. I mean, when you said leave it to those who do... you didn't mean yourself..." She let that trail away, then shook her head. "Of course not; you mean the mercs. I suppose they'd have to."

Ky's stomach tightened. On the one hand, Stella was her closest family member; she should tell Stella the truth. On the other... she could not face what she expected of Stella's reaction. Not right now, anyway. Later, maybe.

"I'll need a complete assessment of our financial situation," she said instead. "I'm going to try to get a few other ships to sign on with us as a convoy under Mackensee protection. We can spread the cost that way. But even so, we're going to have to be careful. That defensive suite wasn't cheap."

Stella nodded. "Right. And good idea about the convoy, Ky."

"Thanks. It'll depend on how scared the remaining traders are about attacks in dock."

CHAPTER SIXTEEN

Ky made it to the bridge before Rafe was through talking to their liaison. He looked grim; Lt. Commander Johannson looked satisfied.

"We'd like to have your . . . agent . . . aboard for this," Johannson said. "As he has ISC authorization."

"Rafe?" Ky said, looking at him.

Rafe grimaced. "My value, to you and ISC both, is at least partly in my being known only as a ne'er-do-well. If I'm part of the hit—"

"I didn't mean part of the team," Johannson said. "In fact we'd rather not have you; we have enough unknowns in the equation already. But aboard ship here, in direct communication, ensuring that our people got the right . . . mmm . . . evidence."

"Then only a shipload of your people would know who I am," Rafe said. "And how many is that?"

"Do you really think—" Johannson began, then stopped. "All right. I see your point. Even if they don't know your name, information could be stripped from them. Disguise?"

Rafe gave Ky a strange look. "Could I pass as Vatta, Captain?"

"The only Vattas declared aboard are me, Stella, and Toby," Ky said. "You'd have to have been . . . oh . . . hiding out on Allway, or something. Maybe a Vatta ne'er-do-well? Old Uncle Jonas, ditched from the family for . . . I don't know . . ."

"Being a ne'er-do-well," Rafe said. "It doesn't have to be

specific, whether I got the second upstairs maid pregnant with twins or embezzled to cover my gambling debts. Years ago and no one knew it; I'd been erased from the family tree. Of course that doesn't explain how I know what I know."

"Bad boys don't explain," Ky said.

Rafe shook his head. "You are entirely too knowing for a young sprig of Vatta virtue, Captain. I begin to think you've spent some time in the back alleys of the universe yourself."

"So . . . is that the story?" Johannson said, clearly impatient with their badinage.

"All right. I'll use the same cover name," Rafe said. "I was suddenly recalled to a sense of family duty when the Vatta ship blew up at Allway—or Stella seduced me, whichever is more believable—and Captain Vatta here put my nefarious skills to good use."

"Coming aboard may be a problem," Ky said. "You know—well, maybe you don't—but we don't have a standard passenger lock, only the emergency." At least the hatch would work smoothly now.

"We'll send a pod," Johannson said. "Do you need a suit as well?"

"I have a suit," Rafe said. "I might just mention how much I hate wearing it."

"You might get yourself into it and start checking it out," Ky said.

"Give some women command and they go . . . all right, I'm going."

Ky turned to the vidscreen. "Any progress on the convoy specs, Commander?"

"Yes: we can handle four ships, including yours. I'll transmit the list of those we think acceptable, ranked by our preference, which of course need not be yours. And there's a red list, of ships we would not accept."

"Fine. I'll start contacting captains at once."

* * *

Captain Solein Harper of *My Bess* looked just as forbidding as the first time Ky had talked to him, but at least he didn't cut off the contact the moment he saw her face.

"You've probably heard we've hired Mackensee for our next voyage," she said.

"I heard," he said. "Two warships to a trader is pretty hefty protection, I'd think."

"So it is," Ky said. "Would you be interested in convoy space?"

"Convoy?"

"Mackensee assures me that they can protect four ships in fairly close convoy."

"Where are you headed?" He wouldn't have asked that much if he hadn't wanted to come, she knew.

"Haven't decided yet," Ky said. "Where were you bound?"

"Nowhere until I can be sure of communications, but I'm eating up profit sitting here."

"Communications here will improve shortly," Ky said, hoping she was right. "If you're interested, a convoy share will be one-quarter the escort cost, minus the Vatta basic contract. Ten thousand."

"Ten thousand! What, you think I haul platinum or something? Eight."

"Nine," Ky said. "For you."

"Done," he said. He would have gone to ten, she knew, if she'd pushed. But nine was a big help, and his goodwill might be a bigger one. "In Vatta accounts here?"

"On safe arrival," Ky said.

"Ah." His face relaxed; now he looked tough but not vicious. "That's honorably done, Captain Vatta. You'll want another one or two, will you?"

"You have someone to recommend?"

"Polly Tendel—independent, fairly new, broke off from Dillon four years ago. Seems a decent sort, kind of rough around the edges."

Ky glanced at the Mackensee list. Tendel was there, though not in the first five. "All right. You want to contact her?"

"I can . . . same terms?"

"Yes."

A half hour later, Ky had the rest of the convoy lined up: Harper's *My Bess,* Tendel's *Lacewing,* and Sindarin Gold's *Beauty of Bel.* All the ships had passed muster with Mackensee, and—according to the transmissions from the station—all were in the process of clearing for departure. As the contract specified, Mackensee had control of the convoy, and thus the rendezvous point. Ky let them handle it. She spoke to Rafe before he transferred to the *Gloucester,* then tried not to hover over her engineering crew as they finished installing the new defensive suite. She could not resist loading the installation manual to her own workstation, where she could follow their progress without interfering.

She caught herself yawning, and remembered that many hours ago she had been wishing for time to take a nap before the Mackensee officers came aboard. Had she really been awake that long? Another jaw-cracking yawn, and she decided that *awake* might not be the right term. She called down to Engineering.

"What now?" Quincy asked.

"Sorry," Ky said. "Just letting you know I'll be in my cabin, hopefully asleep. You need a break, too."

"I had one, and it's about time you did. I'll put anything new on your board."

Stella, when Ky came into her cabin, said the same thing. "And someone will call you if they need you; you know that."

"Yes, Cousin," Ky said. She should shower . . . but she was on the bed, asleep, before that thought ended.

When the call came, she'd had almost five hours of sleep. It was Rafe, on the Mackensee ship.

"I'm going to have to go with them," he said. "I can't . . . explain how certain things work, and how to secure the evidence needed without compromising my other oaths." He grimaced. "Not as part of the . . . er . . . main team, but in a separate group. These people don't trust me, which I suppose is natural, so they won't let me go to the local office alone."

"If it's necessary," Ky said.

"Oh, it's necessary." Rafe glanced aside; though only his face appeared on the screen, Ky was sure he was conveying the presence of an auditor.

"Well, then . . ." Ky couldn't think what to say. *Be careful* seemed both unnecessary and insulting.

"I believe Lieutenant Commander Johannson wants to speak to you," Rafe said, turning away.

"Captain Vatta," Johannson said, coming into pickup range. "The other ships in the convoy are now beyond primary danger range, headed for rendezvous. Your representative has convinced us there is sufficient reason for the actions planned. I must now formally ask if your orders concerning ISC personnel remain?"

"Yes," Ky said.

"All right; just checking. We're scheduled to start the operation within the hour, with the transfer of your representative and certain other personnel."

"What's the plan?" Ky asked.

"You mean in detail?"

"Yes," Ky said.

Johannson frowned. "It's need-to-know, ma'am," he said. "I don't think you should be too concerned—"

"We studied this in the Academy," Ky said. "I'm just curious to know how you'd go about it."

He looked askance, eyebrows high. "You studied how to set up a takeout?"

"Yes. It was part of special ops, level two."

"Slotter Key must be an interesting place," he said. "Suppose you tell me how you'd set it up, and I'll tell you if you're right."

Ky thought back to Colonel Aspin's lecture. "You can do it with a minimal team, if you have to," she said. "Sniper and spotter. Better is a half squad, and better yet a squad. Squad leader commands the squad, but the spotter ranks the sniper. Ideally, you've got plenty of intel about the area. You have routes in and out planned. You are hot on com, half the squad spread, covering the routes, the other half in reserve."

"Hmmm. So... what do you know of the station manager's routine?"

"Not much. I know the ISC offices are on Hub Three, and I'd presume the manager's would be the most secure..." Rafe knew. They knew Rafe knew; they had Rafe aboard with them.

"Almost. Quite central, anyway. He lives on the same hub, two sectors away. Travels any of five routes, all distinct, and has staggered random times for arrival and departure. Once he's past the first intersection, he can be almost anywhere."

"Tagger? We were told to tag if possible."

"Tags are traceable. We prefer CAID—you know what that is?"

Ky did. It was considered the latest and best method of remote identification. "So you'd have a plan, and internal line of travel, from each of his known alternate routes, plus a way of detecting if he's off track and getting someone to him. Here, you'd probably use your people who were stationed here in the recruiting and consultancy positions. They know things about the station that aren't in the public specs, I'd bet."

"They do," Johannson said, without elaborating further.

"Now you need some kind of disturbance," Ky said. "Something to cover the moments around the hit, give the sniper time to break down the weapon and move out of the range of concern. Lots of ways to do that, but there's another place your local staff could help. Bet they've made friends with people onstation."

"You do have the main elements," he said. "But I still see no reason for you to know the specific details. One of the rules you haven't quoted at me yet is, there's no such thing as secure communications."

"You're right," Ky said. She didn't want him to be right. She wanted to see it all, learn it, but in this instance *learning* could be followed by *dying*. Though she was paying for them to take the risk, that didn't justify making it bigger. She left it there, not asking how big a team would go with Rafe to secure evidence and get the ansible working properly again.

Hours crawled by. She didn't know when to start worrying, when to stop worrying. They were still in close enough to pick up some near-com chatter, but Ky could make little out of it. Ship to ship, the convoy reported in as they cleared local traffic control. Ky, on her own bridge, waited for what she could not really anticipate . . . except trouble. Going back to sleep was not an option. Instead, she munched on food she barely tasted, and tried to concentrate on the operating manual for the defensive suite.

Finally the READY light on her Mackensee-installed secure com winked; Ky keyed in access. "Got 'im," was the terse response. "Clean, employee's agent reports ansible hookups restored, and backfiles accessed. Estimates less than fifteen minutes to open ansible contacts and file dumping."

"If anyone else has a working ansible," Ky said. "The backfiles should be interesting, though."

"We already have someone working on ours," Johannson said.

Lee turned to her. "Captain, the Lastway ansible reports eight blocks of stored messages for Vatta personnel . . . haul or wipe?"

"Haul 'em all," Ky said. "Somewhere in there might be a clue to what exactly is going on."

Ship chatter rose around them as the Lastway ISC operation opened the equivalent of vast ears and tongue and began responding to everyone. Evidently Vatta messages hadn't been the only ones sequestered.

"Hailing Vatta ship *Gary Tobai,*" came from Tendel on *Lacewing*. "What happened to the ansible? We've got a mass of backfile messages."

"Seems to be working better," Ky said. "That's all I know. We picked up eight blocks ourselves."

"Coincidence bothers me, Captain Vatta." Tendel's narrow scarred face tightened. "I prefer no coincidences."

"Seems a good one, to me," Ky said. "We leave, things get better. Might mean less trouble ahead."

"And maybe I don't need convoy protection."

"Maybe not. But you signed a contract."

"So I did. Well, people always said trading with a Vatta you had to watch your credit balance. I wonder if this is happening everywhere or just here?"

"Time will tell," Ky said.

Ten minutes. Twenty. Ky forced herself not to pace back and forth.

The secure line blinked again. She picked it up. "Yes?"

"Team's out safely, including your man. Genius with the com stuff, our fellas say. Everyone's on course; the squad'll be picked up by our courier."

Ky went to tell Stella that Rafe was safe. She took along the eight blocks of back messages; some were sure to be proprietary information, and she couldn't ask anyone else on the ship to go through them.

"How are they sorted?" Stella asked.

"By date, I think," Ky said. "I haven't really looked yet, but isn't that how backfiles are usually organized?"

"We can hope," Stella said. "Have a spare reader?"

"Use this one," Ky said, nodding to her desk. "We can isolate it from the rest of the ship."

"Oh. Of course." Stella loaded the first cube. "Mmm. I haven't done the dating conversions yet, but I think this is from before the trouble started, which would mean the ISC manager here was fiddling with Vatta data in preparation... let me see..." She pointed to the screen. "Just the kind of routine notice Vatta HQ sends—sent—every five days to all ports. Corporate news update: no hint of trouble."

Ky looked at the bulletin, its format familiar to her for years, the linked VT in blue and red, the summary of tons shipped, percent on-time deliveries, percent expedited-shipment bonuses earned, lists of retirements, promotions, new assignments. Her own name leapt out at her: the change in ship name from *Glynnis Jones* to *Gary Tobai* as the result of "uncontrolled conditions," the successful delivery to Belinta, and her promotion from contingent captain to list captain. Had it been her status as contingent captain that had convinced Furman he could order her around in the Sabine mess?

"Successful delivery at Belinta: it must've been posted just as I arrived, because trouble started shortly after that. I got a ping from my ship about trouble, and was on an ansible uplink to Vatta headquarters when I lost the connection. That's when things got really interesting, because a team of assassins came into the Captains' Guild—"

"You didn't tell me this before!" Stella said, wide-eyed.

"And we've had how much time to chat?" Ky said. "Anyway . . . it'll be in my log, the universal date. Let me check." She pulled out the notebook. "Here—"

"You keep a paper log?"

"Yeah. Anyway, it's . . . 13.34.75. What's the date on that message?"

"It's 13.32.75. Where would you have been then?"

Ky paged back. "Unloading cargo, Belinta Station. After that I went downplanet hunting cargo; we were headed for Leonora but had another several cubic meters of space. I was trying to come up with enough to finance a refit of the ship; she'd been destined for scrap, originally, but the hull is sound and I thought maybe I could save it."

"I don't have a paper log," Stella went on. "It's in my implant." She tapped her head. "Universal time, also 13.34. Odd, really. Even with ansible transmission, how did they set up almost simultaneous attacks light-years apart? Unless they used all local talent . . . ship schedules just aren't that precise."

"We had a course on interstellar terrorism," Ky said. "A large enough organization, with enough financial support, and enough lead time . . . and we don't know how many planned attacks didn't go off on schedule, because the ansibles went down."

"Did all ansible traffic at Belinta go down when you were cut off?"

"No. At least, no one said anything. The Slotter Key consul on Belinta told me the Slotter Key ansibles were down, but when we left, Belinta's seemed to be working fine. It was such a low-traffic system I'm not sure anyone would've noticed."

"Did you call out on it?"

"No, I didn't. I figured the bad guys knew exactly where we were, and we should get into space, go somewhere else, try to outflank them."

"I still can't figure out *why* anyone would want to do it," Stella said. "Okay, attack the monopoly, I can see that, but why disrupt all communications? Why not just display the ability and bargain from there?"

"If we knew that, we might know why Vatta was chosen as another target," Ky said. "Did those ISC couriers tell you that ISC ships were being hit?"

"No—but then they didn't tell me much. Not even the route we were taking."

"Which suggests to me they were worried about attack," Ky said. "I hope Rafe can pry more information out of the local ansible before we clear space. Something about all this just doesn't make sense. Why Vatta? We're—we were—important on Slotter Key, and we're a major shipper, but we're not the only major shipper, and Pavrati hasn't been hit that we know of."

"But we are, after the Sabine thing, known as a friend of ISC," Stella said. "Even before that, corporately, we've supported them in discussions with other shippers. And our unarmed ships travel on scheduled routes, making them easier to find than ISC couriers, which don't."

"Point." Ky rubbed her face. "So if I hadn't been so prominent at Sabine . . . if I hadn't been so obviously in tight with ISC . . . maybe none of this would have happened."

Stella touched her arm. "Ky, I don't think it's your fault. No one back home even hinted it was your fault."

"They didn't have time, did they?" Ky said.

"A few could have, but they didn't. You can't blame yourself . . ."

"Oh, yes, I can," Ky said. "I certainly can—and I do, in part. I know it's not all my fault, but I didn't make things better. Hindsight's no good if you don't use it."

"I just don't want you taking all the responsibility—"

"Not all. Just some. A mistake I don't intend to make again." Though how she was to avoid it, she had no idea. Wars are won by those who make the fewest mistakes, one of her instructors had insisted.

Stella looked at her with an odd expression. "Ky . . . is that coming out of your military training, or have you really changed that much?"

"Changed?"

"Well . . . I don't want to insult you or anything, but back when you were a kid—before you went off to the Academy—I thought of you as kind of a dreamy, impractical sort. You'd come out of it to do something hopelessly romantic, like champion some natural-born loser . . . we were always hearing about your lost pups."

Ky felt her neck getting hot. "Hard to lose a family identity even when it doesn't fit," she said. "You should know about that."

Stella's face hardened. "True enough. But you were different."

"Was I?" Ky turned away. "They even had me convinced that I was too softhearted and softheaded. If everyone tells you . . . what did they tell you, Stella, that led you to that first mess?"

Stella's eyes widened in shock, then she looked thoughtful. "I suppose . . . everyone always made a big thing out of how pretty I was. Jo was the smart one, Benji and Tak were the strong athletic ones, and I was . . . *Oh look at Stella, isn't she adorable* and *Good grief, Stefan, you'll have to use a cannon to keep the boys off her.* I couldn't outscore Jo—she's—she was—brilliant, and I never wanted to outsweat Benji and Tak." She paused. "So . . . are you telling me you aren't softhearted and an easy mark for stray pups? When we have a literal stray pup on this very ship?"

Ky snorted. "Puddles isn't *my* fault. Oh, I suppose I could've let the locals kill the beast, but they annoyed me."

"You saved the dog to spite the Garda?" Stella said, brows arched.

"More or less, yes. And it might prove useful yet. The vet's assistant said this breed makes good watchdogs."

"I suppose, if you have foot-tall assassins, it might be of some use," Stella said. "But otherwise?"

Was this the time to confess to a family member her self-discovery at the moment of killing Paison? No. Stella would be spooked, and she needed Stella's support . . . "I'm not just an idealistic nice girl," Ky said. Her voice sounded rough to her own ears. "Any more than you're just a sexy pushover for handsome men."

"Thank you for that," Stella said, in a voice that could have been expressing either anger or amusement. "So we're both renegades, are we? The surviving senior family members, barring Aunt Gracie, who is a renegade in her own way?"

"I suspect," Ky said, her good humor restored, "that Vattas have always harbored a fair number of renegades. Do we even know how our great-great-great-grandfather obtained his first ship?"

"I do," said Stella. "It's in my secured files. And I'm afraid you're right—he was not entirely respectable." She shrugged.

"Was he a privateer?" Ky asked.

"Privateer? Maybe. Definitely a raider of some kind, at least for a while. Why?"

"Remember that letter of marque? I was thinking maybe it runs in the family."

"But you didn't ask for it; you aren't using it."

"Yet," Ky said, as she got up to leave. Stella stared.

Down in Engineering, Ky found Quincy hunched over a screen, reading through the installation instructions again. Toby sat on the deck, with Puddles upside down in his lap; the pup looked ridiculous, kicking one stubby leg as the boy stroked his belly. Jim, across the compartment, leaned on an upright, scowling.

"How's it going?" Ky asked.

"It would be going fine if that idiot dog hadn't eaten a corner out of one of the cartons so we didn't have all the connectors . . . we spent hours hunting and we're still missing one. I think I can cobble something together. I hope." Quincy gave the pup a poisonous look; Toby hunched over it protectively.

"You aren't going to space it, are you, Captain?" Toby asked.

"No, of course not," Ky said. "But we probably need to confine it somehow out of the way."

"Not in a shipping carton," Quincy said. "It eats them. And then throws up."

"I told you—" Jim began, but Quincy silenced him with a gesture.

"Jim thinks if we give the pup the run of the ship, it will learn where everything is and be less trouble," she said. "I think it would be disastrous. As with that carton. I can just imagine us arriving someplace—wherever we're going—and finding that our salable cargo has been converted into dog messes."

"Dogs can be . . . er . . . trained, can't they?" Ky asked. Her family had never kept dogs. Cats, horses, birds, and some of the small arboreal creatures, mingas, but not dogs. She'd had friends with dogs, and those dogs didn't seem to be much trouble. They made their messes outside. Of course, here *outside* was a hostile environment. "Didn't we pick up some supplies from the vet?"

"And a book on training," Jim said, nodding. "They can be trained to use a box or something. But it takes time."

"You've trained a dog?" Ky asked.

"Not myself, but I've watched an uncle."

Ky was about to say *It's your dog; you found it* when she glanced again at Toby. The look he gave her said more than words. "Toby," she said instead. "You're caught up on your classwork, aren't you?"

"Yes, Captain."

"Quincy, how many hours a day do you need Toby's help?"

Quincy pursed her lips. "Right now? Not at all, really... systems are all green, and the rest of this setup is software alignment. Why?"

"Because I need him to do something else. Toby, that pup's your responsibility: I want you to keep it out of trouble, train it, take care of him. I know Jim found it—" She glanced at Jim. "—but, Toby, you've had a dog before, and Jim has other duties. If you need help, ask for it, but primarily I want this to be your job. Is that fair?"

His face lit from within for the first time since he'd come aboard. "Yes, Captain! I—I'll make sure he's not in the way."

"I'm sure you'll take care of him," Ky said. She felt a pang of guilt. The boy had been through horrendous stresses, and she'd spent how much time making sure he was doing all right? Next to none. "I hope he turns out to be a good little watchdog for our dock area, on stations where dogs are allowed. Be sure to keep me informed how he's coming along."

"Captain, could I change his name?"

"His name?"

"Puddles just isn't... a good name for him."

"What would you name him?"

Toby glanced at Quincy. "How about Rascal?"

"Sounds good to me," Ky said. "Now get Rascal out from under Quincy's feet so she can get on with her work."

"Yes, ma'am." The boy scrambled up, all ungainly legs it seemed, and headed for his cabin with Rascal—now awake and wiggling wildly—in his grip.

When he was out of sight, Quincy cocked her head at Ky. "That was well done, Captain. Annoying as I find that animal, he'll be good for Toby."

"And you won't be distracted while finishing the installation," Ky said.

"I certainly hope not," Quincy said.

CHAPTER SEVENTEEN

The convoy moved out on a slow arc. No incoming ships had been detected for days, but Mackensee had still advised a careful approach to the jump points. "If there's trouble, that's where it will be," Johannson said. "Ships going for a jump point are usually at max delta vee; they can't maneuver, and they offer an easy shot. What you want to do is go in slow, in formation, looking tough and preserving your ability to maneuver." Behind them, another ship left Lastway, but on a vector that gave no concern; it looked to be headed for a different jump point.

Stella, working through the accumulated messages, found that the Lastway ISC manager had been holding up Vatta messages there—or some Vatta messages at least—since the last scheduled Vatta departure, some eight standard months before.

"If any Vatta ship had come through, they'd have been told there was nothing pending," Stella told Ky. They were working in Ky's cabin, and the remnants of a hasty meal were stacked on the end of the worktable. "You should have had all this when you arrived. Most of it's not that important: updates on prices, margins, that kind of thing. The five-day bulletins I've put into the database for pattern analysis. Nothing's shown up yet. I can't figure out what good it would do to keep a Vatta ship at Lastway out of the Vatta loop, though. When were you originally supposed to arrive at Lastway? Did you have scheduled deliveries?"

"No, nothing with a late penalty, but we did have a tentative schedule. Let me see..." Ky called it up. "That's interesting—we were originally scheduled to reach Lastway a day or so before the attacks on Vatta started."

"So you'd have been there, incommunicado, rather than on a live ansible hookup to Slotter Key. Easy meat—no warning. I wonder if they specifically sucked off Vatta messages at the other stations where Vatta was hit?"

"Still doesn't tell us why Vatta was a target," Ky said.

"No, but it's clear the plot was laid before you even went to Sabine," Stella pointed out. "Then they had to rush assassins to Belinta, or find local talent, before you got back." She sat back. "What would you have done, Ky, if you'd come out in Belinta local space and been told of the attacks? Would you have docked at Belinta?"

"I don't know," Ky said. "I never thought of that...I might have docked at their station, to complete delivery, but I wouldn't have gone onplanet."

"They must have been frantic," Stella said. "Scrambling to adjust to your movements, knowing that you were the most dangerous Vatta to leave alive..."

"Me?" Ky had not considered she might be considered a special threat.

"You. Of course. Not just your military training, and your relationship to your father, but what you'd shown you could do at Sabine. Now...I would wager some of Aunt Grace's diamonds that you are well above their threat recognition level."

Ky felt a surge of satisfaction. "I hope so," she said. "Let them worry." It was ridiculous, in a way. She still had only the one small, slow, unarmed ship; Mackensee would desert her as soon as they had instructions from their headquarters; the other traders in the convoy were her putative allies only so long as they had Mackensee protection. Even so, imagining an enemy being afraid of her felt good.

"And now that you're officially a privateer, that's even more reason for them to worry."

Ky looked at Stella, startled. "I'm not really. You know that."

"Remember what the mercs told you?" Stella's perfect brows arched. "Possession of the letter, whether you use it or not, constitutes presumption of intent."

"But our enemies won't know about that," Ky said. "Will they? And I don't see that it makes much difference. For all the license the letter gives me to cause mayhem, there's not much mayhem I can cause with this ship. I'm sure they know about this ship." She pushed aside the existence of those mines in the cargo holds. "For now, I'm just a trader captain; I'm not ready to hunt anyone down."

"You're a trader with two hired warships," Stella pointed out. "That takes you out of the *just-a-trader* class right there. You had your mercs go in and kill some crooked ISC employees, and even though that was done with ISC authorization via Rafe, it was still done by your orders."

Put that way, the raid on the ISC office did sound like the sort of thing privateers were reputed to do.

"Legally, I'm not sure," Stella went on. "If you hold this commission from Slotter Key, does that mean that anyone contracting with you—for military services anyway—is actually working for Slotter Key?"

Ky stared at her. "That can't be right." Dim memories of military law classes cluttered her mind. But they had never studied the legal ramifications of letters of marque, she was sure. "It's not exactly a commission, anyway. They're not paying me anything, and they're not giving me specific orders. I can just trade if I want to . . ."

"But you don't want to," Stella said. "You want to protect and help family members, and you want to find out who attacked us, and you want to take them out. That's what you said."

"Yes . . ."

"I see conflicts of interest, Ky. Mind you, I'm completely in favor of rebuilding Vatta as a trading empire. Locating, helping, protecting our remaining family. Destruction to our enemies, all that. But when I consider this thing—" She nodded at the folder. "—I see problems you may not have considered. You have to decide whether you're fighting for Vatta or Slotter Key, for instance."

"Both," Ky said. "The ISC thing affects both, surely."

"It does now," Stella agreed. "In the long run, though, those are two different interests, and you need to know which has priority. So do I."

"You?"

"I am carrying your father's implant, remember? The Vatta command dataset. If you consider the recovery of Vatta your first priority, then you are the right person to take possession of it. But if you rank Slotter Key's interests above Vatta? Then I'm not sure."

"I suppose you're glad now that I haven't put it in," Ky said, astonishment and confusion putting an edge on her voice.

"Yes," Stella said calmly. She sat back, folding her arms. "Until I knew about the letter of marque, I had no doubts. Now I do. My interest is entirely family, I assure you. I still believe, like Aunt Gracie, that you are the one person who can help Vatta survive, if it can be done at all. It will take all your ability, though, Ky. If Vatta is not your top priority, we're doomed."

"I saw this letter as giving me a better chance to save Vatta," Ky said slowly. "Not a conflict of interest at all."

"A tool?"

"Yes. I've always thought the interests of Vatta and Slotter Key ran together. Whatever I needed to do to help Vatta would in some way help Slotter Key." Even as she said it, she realized how naïve it sounded. Certainly the government of Slotter Key had decided that its interests were separate from Vatta's.

"For now, that may work," Stella said. "Someday, though, those interests will be in conflict. You need to decide now which has priority, before you have to make that decision in a crisis."

Quincy's call to announce that the defensive suite installation was complete came as welcome interruption.

* * *

"You managed it without Toby's help," Ky said, half joking. Quincy didn't laugh.

"The boy's very smart," she said. "Good with his hands, too. He was helping—it was that dratted dog. But yes, we've got it in. Whether or not it works..."

"I'll tell our escort, and then we'll test it," Ky said. She called the bridge and had Lee contact Johannson.

"He says go ahead," Lee said a few minutes later. "They'll observe with their scans and let us know if it looks right from the outside."

"Do the honors, Quincy," Ky said. Quincy started the initiation sequence, and the defensive suite's control board lit up, segment after segment showing green telltales.

"This over here is the active shield function," Quincy said, pointing. "And this is the electronic countermeasures, here."

"They say the shields are up and look good," Lee reported from the bridge. "No gaps spotted, but they want me to roll her once to be sure they've scanned the entire hull."

"Go ahead," Ky said. "Can they tell anything about the ECM stuff?"

Another pause, then Lee said, "No, they say not without launching something at us, and they'd rather not."

"I feel the same way," Ky said. "We'll have to take that part on trust, then. How about power consumption, Quincy?"

"Right on target," Quincy said. "Our insystem has plenty of reserve power; it's speed we can't get out of her."

"Good job, Quincy," Ky said. "You and your crew should take a couple of shifts off, except for the usual."

"Thanks, Captain, we'll do that. This is a new one for me. Now, can I tell Martin to restow the cargo?"

"Yes—or rather, I'll speak to him. I think we should keep access open to as much of this as possible, for repair in case of damage."

"I thought the whole point of this was to prevent any damage," Quincy said. "You aren't planning to get into a space battle, are you?"

"Not if I can help it," Ky said. "But in dangerous times... it's just a precaution."

Martin and Alene had spent the time it took to install the defensive suite working out the most efficient way to restow the cargo. Ky looked at their figures, and agreed with Martin that the "odor barrier" crates should be readily accessible. She hoped they'd never need those mines, but if they did she wanted them easy to find and use.

Rafe returned to the ship shortly before the transition into FTL flight. Ky and Johannson had agreed that they should first check on an automated ansible in the next system over. The convoy captains accepted the course without comment, except to point out that there was no profit where there could be no trade. Mackensee personnel locked in the jump coordinates in the nav computers of all ships—someone could change it, but that would both break the contract and alert them that the ship was probably part of the conspiracy. Jump insertion went smoothly; they had planned a 13.2-hour jump to the neighborhood of the nearest automated ansible platform.

"I suppose you want me to check out the ansible itself?" Rafe asked. Ky nodded. "And how are you going to explain that one to the ship crews?"

"Your expertise in communications," Ky said. "They know about some of that already."

"Yes, but... last time it was just a simple file switch, or close enough they believed it was. This time, I have to get in there and muck with the hardware and the software. All of it proprietary, and how would even a renegade Vatta know that?"

"I'm sure you can come up with something," Ky said.

He gave her a dark look, then shook his head. "You really are a piece of work, Ky—Captain. You should have been born into a pirate family, not a nice staid bunch of law-abiding traders."

"As staid as the Dunbargers?" Ky asked.

"A hit, a palpable hit. All right, let's see. After being

booted out of the bosom of your family—our family—I managed to sucker ISC into hiring me for a time, then quit in disgust because they expected me to keep regular hours." His face settled into a sullen expression that went perfectly with not wanting to work regular hours. "How's that?"

"That works," Ky said.

Within hours, that ansible's message bins were unblocked, and contact restored with Lastway and other working ansibles.

"An easy fix," Rafe said when he came back aboard. "Just as I said before, it's a form of sabotage that's quick, requires no special equipment, and is easy to reverse. Unfortunately, it's difficult to make impossible, so if the raiders come back, they can undo my fix quickly."

"Would ISC reimburse you for fixing this, if they knew about it?" Ky asked.

"You want a bonus?"

"I'm thinking of the others in the convoy," Ky said. "If there's some profit in stopping to fix ansibles, they'll be more willing to do more of them."

"Ah. There might be, but I can't promise. And calling from here would reveal where we are, which I'd consider a danger."

"Raiders could follow us by the restoration of access, couldn't they?"

"Yes . . . but we might be an ordinary ISC repair crew, too."

Ky discussed their next destination with her Mackensee liaison. "We'd prefer to clear ansibles between Lastway and our home base," Johannson said. "Of course, that's subject to your priorities as long as we're working for you, but there are several automated ansibles along the way, and some excellent market worlds for the others."

"Let's talk to them all," Ky said. In conference, the other captains agreed.

In the next system, they found not only an automated and nonfunctional ansible, but also a civilian ship whose beacon carried the familiar Vatta tag, moving slowly along far from the ansible, as if transferring between jump points.

"She's a Vatta ship," Ky said. "We can't ignore a Vatta ship."

"Her beacon says she's a Vatta ship," Johannson said. "We could say we were, oh, Fitch's Rangers . . . would that make us Fitch's Rangers?"

"You have a database of ship registries," Ky said. "What does her beacon ID say?"

"It agrees with the call signal, but that's just common sense. That doesn't mean she's a Vatta ship, or commanded by a legitimate family member. What does your implant—oh, that's right, you don't have one." This time the disapproval in his voice was clear.

"I'll check with Stella," Ky said. "She probably has the complete list."

"She'd better. You hired us to protect you and the others in this convoy. All my instincts say that there's something wrong here . . . it's the classic pirate trick . . ."

"It's one ship and she doesn't scan armed," Ky said. "You have two armed vessels . . ."

"Captain Vatta, you may have *almost* graduated from a military academy, and I will grant that you performed well under pressure at Sabine, but you do not know diddly-squat about threat analysis in real life. What if that ship is mined? What if that ship is stuffed with biologicals that could kill us all? I do not have a full hazmat team aboard, and I do not want to die—or see my people die—because I walked into a trap."

Ky bit back the angry retort she wanted to make. "I appreciate your concern," she said instead. "I have no intention of asking your people to risk themselves. But as you recall, contacting and aiding other Vatta family members is high on my priority list. I'll go myself."

"Stopping at all is risking us. Doing anything but going back into jump is risking us." He wiped his forehead, though he wasn't sweating. "Look . . . you're making the classic mistake that bold youngsters make. You overvalue your own resources and you don't see all the problems. Did you ever read that old chestnut about the young officer trying to interdict a river crossing?"

"The Defense of Duffer's Drift," Ky said.

"Yes. The problem is, you don't get do-overs, in dreams or otherwise. Maybe the farm family really is loyal—but you can't take the chance. Maybe this ship really is your family's, and everyone on her is loyal and honest—but you can't take the chance."

"Actually I can," Ky said. "But I see that I can't ask you to. So you carry on to the next jump point, and I'll match courses and see what's what."

"You have lost your mind," Johannson said. "We can't let you do that; we've contracted to protect you."

Ky choked back the *You can't stop me* that came automatically and said instead, "Look. We want to unblock this ansible. We'll just put Rafe on it, get that job done, and give this other ship a call, see what she does, all right?"

"You're making a mistake."

"Maybe. But it was in my mission priorities."

"I know that, but—" A deep sigh. "All right, here's what we'll do. We'll support through the ansible repair. Then we'll escort the convoy just outside the system and stand by in case of trouble. With an open ansible and only a few hours' transit time, we should be close enough."

"Fine," Ky said.

When she called the crew together to tell them what was going on, Martin looked grave. "I have to say I agree with the mercs," he said. "If you'll take my advice—"

"Not if it means running away without finding out if a Vatta ship needs our help."

"That wasn't it. But have the defensive suite on, and keep the drives warm, even if you decide to match courses. Someone alert at the scans around the clock. And a plan for what to do if we're attacked. Boarded."

"A plan—"

"Who goes where and does what. That kind of thing."

"Is this something you—"

"Ma'am, my expertise is in security, not full-out combat. I can suggest some things, but whether they'd work, I don't know. And as for ship-to-ship combat, I can't help you."

"Get your suggestions in order, then," Ky said. She had thought of a sudden attack, the ship being blown, but... boarded? Maybe she should still take Johannson's advice and run for the jump point. But that left a Vatta ship here alone, a Vatta crew who might even, if they'd been in FTL space on a long jump, have no warning that they were in danger. "It's going to take us several days to get closer to her."

Martin nodded.

Fair Kaleen had the Vatta blue-and-red logo on the hull, but she looked battered by years of space debris. No weapons showed on the defensive suite's analysis screen. Her crew had given no sign that they were aware of other ships in the same system, which was sloppy at best. Ky pursed her lips. Ships of that class were brought in for cleaning and repair every two years, at which time the logo was freshly painted. Ordinary light shielding protected it for that interval.

"Stella?"

"Don't look at me. I'm not ship crew."

"Quincy, I'm going to transfer an external feed to your board," Ky said. "What do you think?"

"*Fair Kaleen*... haven't crossed paths with that one in decades," Quincy said. "She's one of ours, right enough, but I don't know what route she's on. Looks a bit battered; that logo should've been touched up before now."

"Well," Ky said, and sat motionless, trying to think things through. *Fair Kaleen* had been a Vatta ship, might be one now, should be one again, since Vatta needed every ship it could muster. If someone else had taken a Vatta ship—one of her ships, she caught herself thinking—she could take it back. "Let's give her a call," she said, and nodded to Lee.

Fair Kaleen answered the hail with commendable promptness, and in moments her captain was online. Osman Vatta, his broadcast ID stated; stocky and dark, his black hair liberally salted with gray, he looked at Ky with an expression she could not quite interpret. "Whose are you?" he asked.

"Whose?"

"Whose kid. I'm sorry, you're a captain, but to me, you're a kid. I was just wondering whose."

"Gerard's," Ky said. When he still looked blank, she added, "Gerard Avondetta Vatta..."

"Oh...old Moneybags Gerry." He gave a harsh snort of laughter. "Gods, girl, you don't look anything like Gerry. Luckily."

Very few people, most of them now dead, had called her father *Gerry*. And she didn't like his laugh.

"Don't look at me like that," he said, sobering. "I didn't mean to make fun of him, but...he always was a bit stuffy. So, he sent you out to straighten out this mess, eh?"

"Mess?" Ky said. Something was very wrong, but she couldn't figure out what.

"This whole thing with the banks," Osman said. "Credit and all. I mean, he is chief high financial muckety-muck, so it makes sense that you being his daughter—"

He didn't know. He didn't know or he was a far better faker than she thought he was. "That's the ansibles," Ky said. "When ISC gets them back up—"

"Not what my fella back on Harmon told me. Said someone was going after Vatta, and our credit was shot."

"Did your *fella* describe what *going after* meant?"

"Said someone had taken potshots at Vatta ships. Made me nervous, that did." *Nervous* was not the word Ky would have chosen to describe his expression. Tense. Alert. But nervous?

She should tell him, but she was reluctant and didn't understand why.

"Look, as you're old Gerry's kid—daughter, I mean—you can clear up the financial end, can't you? Talk to the bankers and such? I have a load of cargo, good stuff, too—"

"Where was it bound? What route are you on?"

His gaze wavered. "Um . . . well, you know, I'm kind of independent. Experience . . . family connections . . ."

"Been a while since you came in for refit, hasn't it?" Ky said, forcing sympathy into her tone.

"Oh, the ship's fine. No problems there. It's just . . . I can't draw on company funds, they tell me, on account of whatever this mess is."

Stranger and stranger. Not all Vatta captains were on fixed routes, but most of them were: profit lay in reliability. Senior captains vied for the most profitable routes, wanted the least variance in their schedules. And while this man looked like a Vatta, they weren't the only family in the known universe with those features, that coloring. He had shown some knowledge of her family, but only what an outsider could have picked up from public sources. He had cargo . . . he could sell the cargo, set up a ship account . . . she'd done that.

Ky touched the control requesting an emergency interruption. Almost immediately, a red light flashed on her board, winking urgently.

She looked down, then back up at the com screen. "Excuse me, I've got a problem here—I'll be right back." She cut the connection, and opened the internal com. "Anyone get anything on this one?"

Stella spoke up. "The ship's on a list from ten, fifteen years back as active, but on current lists as an adjunct."

"Which is?"

"I'm not sure. It might be undercover work or something. I was on an adjunct payroll for a year or so. Osman . . . I'm fairly sure he must be Lazlo Vatta's grandson, though there's another Osman . . . how old do you think he is? Apparent age, or was that a disguise?"

"Voice analysis suggests sixties," Rafe spoke up. "There's that little burr—of course, he could be a heavy drinker or addicted to something that's aged his voice."

"That'd be Lazlo's grandson. He's not on the current captain list, Ky," Stella said. "I can't get into the old personnel stuff—it's in the command dataset." *The one you didn't install* was unsaid but clearly communicated.

"A Vatta remittance man," Rafe said in smug tone that made Ky want to hit him. "Skeleton in the Vatta cupboard."

"So . . . why's he in a Vatta ship?" Ky asked.

"Adjunct," Rafe said. "They let him take a ship, but he's not authorized refit, and I'll bet he's not authorized access to company funds, except his remittance. He sounds like a con man to me. He's trying one on—he knows headquarters is down, he doesn't know we have a command dataset."

Martin said, "I don't like the whole setup. He sounds too glib, and I find it hard to believe his crew didn't pick us up on scan a long time ago. We haven't tested the defensive suite against concealed weaponry; the mercs weren't trying to hide theirs."

"Quincy," Ky said. The senior Engineering watch were all below, by Martin's plan. When the old woman answered, she said, "Did you ever hear of an Osman Vatta? Related to old Lazlo?"

Quincy's gasp was clearly audible. "That bastard? What's he done now?"

"Well, he claims to be captain of *Fair Kaleen,* which right now is matching courses about a hundred klicks away. I gather you know something about him?"

"Rotten little devil," Quincy said. "Smooth as an egg, and no morals at all. Fools you because he's not overtly mean, but he doesn't care for anything but himself and doesn't see why anyone would."

"Our defensive suite says he's unarmed," Ky said. "I don't see he can do us any great harm—"

"Don't bet on it," Quincy said. "If he's here and talking to you, then he sees a profit to himself in it. Figure that out and however slimy it seems . . . that's what he's up to."

"Here in the middle of nowhere," Ky mused. "What is he doing here anyway? Just randomly jumping from one unoccupied system to another? He's a long way from any regular Vatta route."

"Trouble," Quincy said. "He's trouble, through and through."

"Quince—what did he do? Any specifics?"

"Well. I was only aboard a ship with him once. He'd gotten in a fairly serious scrape his apprentice voyage—gambling debts he tried to cover with the ship's account. His father—Lazlo's son, Benalj that would have been—hauled him home and supposedly straightened him out. He was in his twenties when I ran into him again. I was engineering second that voyage, pulled off my regular ship because their first was injured. He was third in command; I heard scuttlebutt that he was under some suspicion of having done something earlier in the trip. But he was a Vatta; the idea was to straighten him out. Well... among other things he liked pretty faces, didn't matter what gender, and he was putting moves on an Engineering junior. I told him off for it, and he tried to bribe me."

"Bribe *you*!" Ky could not imagine that.

"Oh, yes," Quincy said. "I wasn't a gray-haired great-granny back then. He didn't fancy me, I don't think, but he was willing to try, if it would shut me up. It didn't. He tried to get me fired for insubordination; the captain wouldn't hear of it, and I watched my back very carefully the rest of the voyage. Good thing, too, as there were several accidents that could've been fatal. His father died young."

"So..." The knot in Ky's stomach tightened. "It may not be an accident that he's here, or that he wants to travel with us."

"I don't see how he could have figured out where we'd be," Quincy said. "That much could be accidental..." She didn't sound as if she believed it.

"Jump options from Lastway... how many were there?" Stella asked.

"It's not that." Ky's mind raced, throwing up an image of their route since leaving Lastway. "If they have those shipboard ansibles Rafe mentioned, and they've tracked us by the restored ansible functions, then *here* is the next logical place for us to go. Another node in the web, a mostly uninhabited system with multiple jump points."

"Couldn't we intercept their communications?"

"No more than with any ansible," Rafe said. "And thank you for sharing that little secret with everyone, Captain."

"You undoubtedly have others I don't even know," Ky said. "And that one, if it's operational, isn't going to be secret for long. Once others realize that the only way for certain things to happen is ship-mounted instant communications, they'll deduce its existence."

"I suppose. I still think—"

"Think it later. The question is, what do we do now? If I refuse to talk to him again, he'll know we know something's wrong."

"Wouldn't you? He'll expect you to have an implant. Surely that would tell you he's not on the main list."

"I guess he can't tell I don't..." A germ of an idea sprouted. She went back to the exterior com. "Sorry," she said to Osman. "We've got this pet someone brought aboard, and it keeps getting into trouble."

"A pet? You let your crew have pets?" The tone carried the implication that only young, inexperienced, sentimental captains allowed pets aboard.

"Special case," Ky said. She could feel her neck getting hot. "But back to your problem... what do you understand is going on?"

"I don't know," he said. "Frankly, I've been out on my own, pretty far out, not paying much attention to what's going on back home. But it sounded like trouble, so I came back to see what I could do..."

To help or scavenge? That was the question. Quincy's story was probably true, if this was the same man, but twenty years and more had tamed many a wild boy, her father always said. We don't blame people for who they were, if they act well now, her mother had insisted. She wondered what Rafe would be like in twenty years and pushed that thought away.

"It's pretty bad," Ky said. "Hard to tell with the ansibles down, but it looks like someone has it in for Vatta."

"Heard anything about your family?"

"They're dead," Ky said flatly.

A moment's shocked stillness, then his face creased into a scowl. "That's... that's monstrous," he said. "You poor kid—I mean, you're not a kid, I can see that, but still. Poor old Gerry dead... how'd they get him? He wasn't on a ship, was he?"

"No." Ky felt again that reluctance to reveal details, at least yet. "I wasn't there; I only heard they'd died. If the ansibles come back up—"

"I can't believe it," he said. His gaze was direct, his expression exactly what it should be. So why this reluctance? Just Quincy's belief? That wasn't fair. "Look," he said with sudden determination, "I can help. Let me help. Either of us alone, we're just a single ship, easy to ambush. But the two of us—I don't mind telling you, I've rambled around in some pretty rough places. This old ship isn't the worn-out hulk she looks like. We could help each other a lot. Family sticks together, eh? Blood thicker than water, all that."

Sincerity flowed out of him like water out of a spring. Ky could not believe he was anything but a rogue coming around... except for the bitter memory of another sincere, pleading voice, Mandy Rocher and his problem that had become her disgrace.

"I can't figure out why," Ky said, talking just to keep the talk going, trying to think behind the chatter. "Why would someone—anyone—take after Vatta Transport? We've got a better record of service than, say, Pavrati."

"Oh, lass. We're rich, that's why. The rich are always a target—"

"Not that rich," Ky said. "I can imagine an envious minor shipping firm resenting us, but it would hardly have the resources to attack us so widely."

"Well, no," he said. "But this attack on the ansibles... Vatta's always supported ISC's monopoly on ansible services. Could be it's our allies got us in trouble. Or it could be part of the humod base-stock controversy."

"What?" Was this just a distraction, thrown out to make her lose track of his argument?

"There's growing friction, you know, between the base-stock worlds that want to preserve what they call human nature, and the humods. From the base-stock point of view, we're all humods because we have implants. Makes us mech deviants. I don't suppose you've run into many base-stockers."

"Only the Miznarii," Ky said. "Back home."

"Good grief, are they still around?" He sounded genuinely surprised. "I'd have thought they'd died out long ago; went in for natural childbirth, I thought it was. I meant places like Allgreen and Purity—they're not on regular Vatta routes, but I've traded there. Took me for a criminal, they did, at first. No one has cranial implants, not even fertility mods. One of my old crew was a four-arm, genetic, and Immigration Control wouldn't even let him off the ship at the station. You'd have thought he'd been able to spit sperm straight into their precious daughters—sorry, did that shock you?"

She had to do better with her face. "I'm shocked that anyone would refuse entry to someone just because they had four arms," she said. Would he believe that?

"Oh, good," he said. "I remember Gerry was something of a prude and I should have thought before saying anything, but I'm glad you're old enough not to flinch at a little physical reality." His laugh grated. Ky smiled, but followed him into this side topic as if really interested.

"So, do the people on Purity avoid all medical care?"

"No, but they're strict about its limits. No genetic modifications, and no modifications that enhance normal human ability beyond a half sig above the mean. Of course that means their mean intelligence is well below that of most of us, but they get along reasonably well on their own world."

"Are they Miznarii?"

"No, no. They're evangelical Hurists, whatever that is. Doesn't help them any in business dealings, I can tell you that." He laughed again, with a wink that invited Ky into his scam, whatever it was. She wanted to wipe the screen, but knew better. "It's the weirdest combination of paranoia and gullibility you've ever seen. They're terrified of some outsider cheating them, but they make it so obvious what they're afraid of that it's easy to make whatever profit you want by just doing something else and pretending fear of their suspicion."

So the rogue hadn't reformed. "So you prefer humod planets?"

"Well, not the extremes. It's like some of them make themselves ugly on purpose, y'know? But a lot of 'em are just like real people, only with extra. Pretty much think like us." He peered at the screen. "You do have an implant, right?"

"Of course," Ky said, as if offended. "Got it at seven, like everyone else."

"So you have a current Vatta update? Because I haven't updated in a while, been out of touch y'see."

"Not really current," Ky said. "I was on my way back, actually." He couldn't know anything different, unless he was as bent as she suspected, and then it didn't matter. "As you probably guessed, this was my first trip, so I'm just a probationary captain, as it were. Only the most basic dataset. When I got home, I was going to get the full one, but—things happened."

"I see." He looked down a moment then suddenly back up, with a sharp glance that seemed intended to startle. Then his face softened again. "Well, we shall do well enough, I guess. Youth and enthusiasm, age and experience... we'll be partners, shall we?"

"But we are already family," Ky said, as if puzzled. She had been half expecting this offer, or demand. "Isn't it forbidden to make private contracts of partnership within Vatta?"

His brows went up. "What, you think I want to cheat you?"

"No, not that." Worse than that, but she had had four years—almost four years—in which to learn that earnest and tedious explanation of well-known rules had its uses. "But Dad said nobody should make private contracts because we should all be working for the benefit of Vatta as a whole. Private deals, he said, were like stealing from the company. And I want to save Vatta."

Now his expression shifted to benign amusement. "I forgot," he said. "You are Gerry's daughter; of course you would be a stickler for all the rules. But my dear, this is an extraordinary situation. We may be the only surviving Vattas—or do you know of others?"

Ky felt a chill roll down her back. She was not about to reveal the existence of Stella or Toby. "You're the first Vatta ship I've met since this happened," she said.

"And I suppose, for your first voyage, they stuffed the ship with faithful old retainers rather than family members, eh?" he asked.

"Pretty much," Ky said. "I hired a couple myself along the way."

"So, under the circumstances, we should cooperate and be partners—fine, if you don't want to enter a formal partnership, I understand that, given your father—but we can do better together than either of us alone."

That was true, if partners were true to their defined mutual goal. Otherwise, one could gut the other even more neatly than a stranger. Ky was tempted to refuse and depart, trusting her new defensive suite to handle anything he was likely to have aboard, but what if he knew more about the conspiracy and the attacks on Vatta than he'd yet revealed?

"Where are you going next?" Ky asked, deliberately furrowing her brow. "I don't know if we can—"

"Look," he said, exuding a fatherly concern that bordered on sickening. "I'll go with you, wherever you go; I can help keep you safe." He paused for her reaction; apparently she had not hidden it well enough. "I'm sure you're brave and resourceful; Vatta doesn't breed idiots or cowards. But you need someone to watch your back. I won't even pull seniority." Onscreen he shrugged, spreading his hands. "You're Gerry's daughter; he was our CFO. You can take over, if you want. I just don't want to see us die out because we couldn't work together for mutual profit."

He wanted her more than she wanted him. Why? And how had he known that her father was Vatta Ltd.'s CFO, if he'd been gone so many years? Unless he was legitimate in some covert way, as Rafe claimed to be with ISC.

"I suppose," Ky said. "Look—why don't you send me your cargo info, and I'll compare it with what we've got and decide where to go next."

"We share," he said. "You send me yours, too."

"Fine," Ky said. "I'll get my cargomaster to port it over for you." He would learn nothing from their cargo list except that they'd bought low and hoped to sell high. He would certainly not learn about the mines she had aboard, either kind.

CHAPTER EIGHTEEN

"He thinks I've got a probationary captain's implant, with incomplete data—nothing he needs to upload to his implant, for instance." Ky sipped a mug of nutrient-boosted tea while she waited for Osman to send her his cargo list.

"I'd be a lot happier if you had an implant at all," Martin said. "And the Vatta command set would give you everything you need."

"Certainly would make my head an attractive target, wouldn't it?" Ky said. "If he thinks I'm ignorant, inexperienced, idealistic, and rule-bound, I'm the perfect front person for him. A dupe he can enjoy duping for a long time before he finds it convenient to kill me."

"You do realize he'll try." It was not a question in tone, only in Martin's expression.

"Of course," Ky said. "I don't expect anything less. But he will find me tougher to kill once he's thoroughly convinced how simple it will be."

"You continue to surprise me," Rafe murmured.

"Good," Ky said. "Since you're the best model I have for how Osman Vatta thinks—he's supposedly got a history rather like yours."

He blinked at her. "You really think I'm that bad? I swear, I never put pressure on the unwilling to have sex."

Stella shifted in her seat. He looked sideways at her.

"I haven't forgotten that lime," Ky said. The others looked at her oddly; Rafe ducked his head.

"That was only . . . an invitation. Not pressure."

"Quite true," Ky said. "And if I thought you were that bad you would not be alive on this ship."

"I shall watch my step," he said, with a demureness that lay uneasily, like thin silk over a steel blade.

"Nonetheless," Ky said. "Rafe is my only current contact with the kind of life we think Osman's been leading. So when I try out ideas on him, his reaction may help me predict Osman's."

"As long as you don't get us confused," Rafe said.

"I assure you," Ky said, "I can keep you separate in my mind, even without an implant."

Suddenly Rafe's eyes opened wide. "Ky—Captain—call the mercs. Now."

"What? Why?"

"Just do it," he said. No longer languid, he sat upright, alert.

"Our whole plan is to let him think we're alone, harmless, helpless, in this system. If I call—"

"If you don't call," Rafe said, "you won't have the chance. He has an ansible on that ship. He's one of them."

"How do you know? And why now?"

"I know," Rafe said through clenched teeth. "Don't ask more—I know. He's not just Vatta's rotten egg; he's deeply involved, and he's using his shipboard ansible to call in your enemies."

"I think he wants to toy with me longer," Ky said. "And I still want to know how—"

"For the time it takes them to get here, maybe. Then he'll betray you, and there won't be time for talk. How far away are the mercs?"

"Next ansible over, I hope," Ky said. "But how do you know he's got one?"

"Captain . . . let's go to your cabin."

"What?"

"I need to speak to you privately," Rafe said. He was still tense, pale, his eyes locked on hers.

"If you must," Ky said. She looked at the others. "Call me if anything changes. Make sure everything's ready."

"Always," Quincy said.

Ky led the way to her cabin; Rafe followed her and shut the hatch without asking her.

"What is this about?" Ky asked. "You're—"

"Just listen," Rafe said. "I—there's another new tech I didn't tell you about."

"You have a shipboard ansible of your own?" she said. "Or some way to detect ansible activity?"

He tapped his head. "I have one here. Miniaturized, implantable. The power system's not adequate, so I need to hook into an exterior power source or link to an existing, working ansible."

Ky blinked. "You have an ansible in your *head*?"

"Yes. Small, underpowered, but nonetheless workable. Experimental tech, of course. So far as I know the only working model; I got it direct from the lab. You must not tell anyone . . ."

"I won't," Ky said. She was still fascinated. "So that's how you know he has a shipboard one? How do you know he doesn't have an implant like you?"

"They smell different," Rafe said. At her expression he sighed, shook his head. "They had to hook up a lot of weird connections to make it work at all. Humans have a lot of olfactory receptors we don't really use, apparently tied to the biochemistry of the planet we originated on; they tied the detector function to that. It's supposed to let me know when I'm in range and could tap power from an ansible, but my brain insists on giving me smells."

"I hope they're pleasant," Ky said. She could not help staring at his skull, every angle she could see. It could not be possible to fit an ansible in there; most of the ones she'd seen—the outsides anyway—were the size of a small ship.

"*Memorable* is the word I'd choose," Rafe said. "Whatever on our home planet smelled like that must not have been good for us. At any rate, I know he has a shipboard ansible and that he's just activated it. Now will you please call the mercs on the system ansible before he blows it or something?"

"You think he'd blow it?"

"He wouldn't want you calling for help, now would he?"

"I wonder why he doesn't just use the system ansible, now that we've got it unplugged."

"Because he knows we'd notice that, and he thinks his shipboard ansible can't be detected. That alone should tell you he's up to no good."

"Oh. Right."

On the bridge, Ky began the setup for an ansible connection and turned on the shipwide intercom. "We have a situation," she said. "Quincy, bring the defensive suite active. Our friend over there is contacting someone, we don't know who. Probably not someone we want to know." The ansible connection winked green, and she entered the Mackensee codes she'd been given. The lightlag to the system ansible seemed interminable; she watched the chronometer ticking off the seconds . . . outbound signal . . . inbound signal . . .

"Trouble, Captain Vatta?" Johannson must've been sitting beside the com shack. Ky had never appreciated instantaneous communication so much.

"Possibly," Ky said. "The ship was Vatta, and the captain . . . a Vatta troublemaker, apparently. It's not a threat, but he's just made an ansible call."

"Can your agent strip it?"

"No."

"Advise you go to max power and head for jump point," Johannson said.

"Right into whoever's coming in?" Ky asked. "And our in-system's slow, if you recall."

"The idea is that they blow by you while they're still having downjump turbulence fouling their scans. Shortens your vulnerability, though there is a risk. As I said before."

"And you?"

"We do have responsibilities to the rest of the convoy," Johannson said. "But I'll see what I can do."

Was he really going to leave them hanging out here alone? Or had that been a message designed to confuse an eavesdropper? Ky hoped it was the latter, but he certainly wasn't going to share his plans over an open ansible connection. That made sense, but it didn't make Ky happy. She looked at Lee, whose expression was more alert than anxious.

"You heard the man," she said. "Aim us at the jump point, and pour on the power. Not emergency max—we can't outrun much of anything, but we can open distance."

She called back to *Fair Kaleen*. "Ah . . . we're outbound, and I've decided on a destination,"

"Wait a minute . . . that's sudden. What happened?"

"It was what you said about the humod issue. It just occurred to me that the right market for a third of my cargo is one of the humod worlds. Look at the list. With the ansible here working again, I was able to get a little market data—we're off for Garth. Coming?"

"But wait—girl—I mean, Captain, sorry—you don't want to go to Garth—"

"I don't? Why?"

"Well, just slow down there and we'll talk about it. You don't just make decisions on the first bit of info you get off a public board. How do you know it's accurate?"

"Look," Ky said, finding it easy to simulate impatience. "We hung around in this system a lot longer than we meant to, waiting for you to match courses and then chatting. No disrespect to an elder Vatta, but if we're going to rebuild the company, we can't do it by sitting out here telling family stories. We need to be trading. I may be young and ignorant, but I know that much."

"Of course we need to be trading," Osman said. "But rushing into things can get you in worse trouble. How do you know the folks after Vatta won't be waiting for you in Garth?"

Because they're on the way here was on the tip of Ky's tongue, but she said instead, "I don't. But the only way to find out is to go there. I have some specialized electronics that will suit their humod market . . . just lying around, they were, and I got them at a good price."

"But—"

"So are you coming, or shall we meet later somewhere else?" She had half an eye on the ship's nearscan, which showed the range between them widening more slowly than she'd like.

"I'll . . . I'll have to get my insystem drive up. I'll follow you."

"Fine," Ky said, and flicked off the link.

He'd track her vector and report it, though if the allies he'd called were already in jump, it wouldn't help them. "Rafe," she said.

"Yes." He was close behind her.

"Is there any way at all that ships can communicate between each other while in FTL space?"

"No. Not that I know of, anyway. The advanced tech on the pin ansibles allows a ship in FTL to contact a fixed ansible platform, that's all."

"Good." She flicked on the shipwide com and explained the situation. "What we're doing is running for the jump point. As soon as we can jump safely, we will. We don't know where Osman's allies are, or how fast they can get here. We are fairly sure he has no weapons capable of damaging us, so we're not in immediate danger."

"What if they get here before we can jump?" Lee asked. "We're at least eighteen hours from the jump point. Are the mercs coming?"

"The mercs are not telling me or anyone else what they plan to do, but I'm hoping they're on their way. We'll deal with the other if it happens."

"Why did you even go talk to that old idiot?" Jim asked. He must have been near the Engineering com station. "Wouldn't it have been smarter to ignore him, like the mercs said?"

"Jim!" Quincy muttered.

"The only way to find out if he was legitimate or not was to talk to him," Ky said. They were all probably thinking the same thing, but lacked Jim's brashness.

"But Quincy told you shifts ago. And she told us about him—"

"Jim!" Ky could imagine Quincy trying to push Jim aside and shut him up.

"I just don't get it. We could've been halfway to somewhere else by now—"

Ky's temper boiled over. "You could be all the way to somewhere else in about two minutes... there's an air lock." Silence, complete, throughout the ship.

"'M sorry," Jim muttered finally.

"Good," Ky said. "Whether I made a mistake or not by talking to Osman will be clear in a day or so. In the meantime, we can increase our chances of survival by anticipating the bad guys and thinking of ways to make their task harder."

"We could put out a message on the ansible," Rafe said. "We've cleared several along our back route... it will go somewhere, even if it isn't picked up for a while. All stations, all recipients. Tell them about dear old Uncle Osman... or Cousin Osman, or whatever he is."

"Good idea," Ky said. "You draft the message, then let me see it before you send it."

"Do we have any ship weapons?" Rafe asked.

"Not offensive weapons. Or rather, we have the popgun equivalent that all the ships carry now. It wouldn't penetrate his ship."

"He may or may not know that."

"He's boosting," Lee said. "But he's not going to keep up with us."

"He wants a safe distance," Ky said, thinking aloud. "He's got the power to overtake us, but he won't. His scan trace will point to us but keep him out of trouble." Which meant he was expecting help, though she didn't say that.

"He thinks," Rafe said. Ky glanced at him. His expression was feral.

"Aren't you supposed to be drafting that letter?"

"I have; I've forwarded it to your desk."

Ky managed not to snarl. Of course, he had an implant. He could do that while she was limited to indirect input. If only she'd been near a real clinic where they could test and see if it was safe to put an implant in, she could have had the basic module. "Don't be smug," she said. "You and your implant." She opened the file on her desk. The letter looked perfectly straightforward; she hoped it was. She opened a query link to the system ansible . . . almost two minutes to contact.

"You're close to that six months you mentioned," Rafe said. "You could put one in now."

"No med tech," Ky said, watching the winking light that indicated the message was en route to the ansible. She wasn't about to wait for confirmation that the ansible was ready to receive.

"True, but it's possible to put them in without. I have. Changing implants is sometimes very useful."

"Risky."

"Not really. You can get a headache, and you can be disoriented for a few hours. I try to do it overnight—lie down, pull one, and insert the other. You do have to know sterile technique."

"Which I don't," Ky said. "So I'll wait, thank you."

"I do know sterile technique," Rafe said. "If it would improve our chances of survival, I'd be glad to help."

He would be glad to get his hands on the Vatta command database, however briefly. She could only deal with one trickster at a time, and Osman was the immediate threat. "I think not," Ky said. "It can't make this ship faster or add weaponry. For plain maneuver, the brain I have will work just fine." She hoped. A command implant would give her faster control of ship systems; it might even work with *Fair Kaleen*'s systems . . .

"Glad to hear it," Rafe said. "Is there any other assistance I can offer?"

"Don't know yet," Ky said. "I'll let you know if I think of something." She turned to Lee. "Do you know the nearest mapped jump point?"

"It's the one the mercs went to. There's another, a half point farther."

"So . . . the mercs should get here first. Maybe."

"If the bad ones didn't use an unmapped point. If they were just offscan, they could do a short jump in and be here in a few hours. We have enhanced scan, but the range is still well under system radius."

"Any idea what vector they might use?"

"No, why?"

"Diversions," Ky said. "The one thing that even defensive shields have trouble with is random mass."

Rafe snorted. "What, you're going to throw out some cargo?"

"You might call it that," Ky said. "If you consider mines cargo."

"Mines?"

"You're familiar with the concept?" She could not keep all the sarcasm out of her voice.

"Yes. I just didn't know you had any, and you said you didn't have weapons."

"Didn't have offensive weapons. I have some mines. Not many, and maybe not enough. We'll see."

"When will you drop them?"

"When I see the whites of their eyes," Ky said. At his expression, she had to laugh. "When I know what vector they're coming in on," she said. "Or if Cousin Osman gives us any trouble in the meantime. I hate to waste a Vatta hull—"

"You surely don't think you can get it back!"

"If I can, I intend to," Ky said. "Vatta Transport needs hulls. We've lost several that I know of, not to mention the capital investment in our headquarters. We make money by trade; it takes hulls to haul cargo. So—Cousin Osman's hull belongs, by rights, to Vatta. To me, if it comes to that."

Rafe stared. "You're either crazy or brilliant, I'm not sure which."

"Neither am I," Ky said. "Time will tell."

"You seem amazingly calm about this. Are you scared at all?"

Ky wondered if there was any way to explain, and decided it was a lost cause. "Not excessively," she said instead.

Fair Kaleen had increased her boost. On the ship-to-ship, a light blinked. Osman wanted to talk again. Ky didn't. Anyone with a shipboard ansible had to be part of the conspiracy.

"There they are," Lee and Rafe said together. On the enhanced longscan, two tiny dots. Ky reached over and flicked a button. Both turned red. She spared a moment of thankfulness that the defensive suite's designer had included a remote weapons detection function, and that she'd opted for the more expensive version.

"Weapons hot," Ky said. "They must be expecting trouble."

"Or a quick easy kill," Rafe said. "Do you want me to plot their course, so Lee can concentrate on piloting?"

"You know how?" It didn't surprise her. Interstellar navigation, in its simplest form, was a matter of looking up tables of figures and inserting them in the navigational computer. And having Rafe on navigation would be better than Sheryl—competent though she was, Sheryl was better off not on the bridge right now.

"Yes." Rafe grinned. "I can still surprise you, too, Captain. Anyway, if you have a way to use those mines, I want you to be free of all distraction while you do it."

The enemy ships—she presumed they were enemy, since they had not contacted her—had emerged from jump at high velocity, and were braking only slightly. Ky interpreted this to mean that they were getting data on her directly, and instantly, from Osman on *Fair Kaleen*. She looked at their own trace. The old ship could not accelerate any faster, and she had to conserve fuel for maneuvering.

"Lee, cut her back. We want to look like innocents heading for the jump point. I'm going to have a little chat with Osman and see what he tells me."

When she clicked the com back on, she started talking as soon as Osman's face appeared, with the wavery edge characteristic of diverging signal sources.

"Well, Cousin, are you coming?" Ky asked. "I have the feeling it's not healthy to stay in one place too long."

"Who would hang around in a deserted system like this?"

So he was going to try to keep her ignorant... surely he had noticed trouble on the scans. "Looks like a fine quiet place for raiders or pirates to me, Cousin," she said cheerily. "Surely they have rendezvous points far from heavily traveled routes."

"How would anyone know we were here?"

"Oh, I don't know. Blind luck maybe. Wait—" She pretended to look away. "Imagine that. I have two blips on my screen... what do you have?"

"Blips—oh... those. Those are... friends of mine, you might say. It's why I don't have to worry about raiders."

The slightest emphasis on *I,* the slightest smugness in the tone. "Don't worry, Kylara, honey, we'll take good care of you."

"Will you?" Ky asked, in the mildest tone she could manage. On the scan, the two ships closed distance steadily. It looked as if they had tracked and analyzed her course and were planning to intercept to killing distance. "You didn't mention your friends before, Cousin. Who are they?"

"My dear, you really do not need to know. It's better if you don't. In case—" He paused. She could fill in that blank easily: in case she escaped to tell the tale.

The ansible status light went from steady green to red. So they had blocked the ansible again.

"Told you," Rafe said softly, just out of pickup range.

"And now the ansible's not working," Ky said to Osman. He shrugged.

"These automated ansibles aren't as reliable, I've learned over the years. Were you trying to send a message?"

"Thinking of it," Ky said. "I guess I'll have to wait until we get to the next one."

A stupid exchange; surely he had detected her transmission to the ansible and surely he knew it had succeeded. But in following his misdirection, she might learn something useful.

"Your friends are coming in very fast," Ky said. "If you hadn't told me they were your friends, I'd worry about an attack." They were coming in spread formation, perfect for attacking a single ship and preventing its escape by any sudden maneuver. Not that her ship was capable of much evasive action.

"They'll take care of us both," Osman said. "In their way."

His smile no longer looked open and benign; it had a predatory edge to it. Ky considered the scan before answering. If those were military ships, with high-performance drives—and surely they were at least equivalent—they would be in range for beam weapons within six hours. Was it Osman's job to keep her calm and ignorant until then, loafing along on a course that made interception and attack easy? Had he done this before, setting up innocent traders for pirate attacks? Had he been involved in the Sabine thing, one of Paison's allies? And what would he do when he found that her shields held against them?

She smiled into the screen and saw Osman's expression stiffen before his mouth widened again. "I'm so glad you're here," Ky said. "It means a lot to me to have a senior Vatta captain's advice."

"My advice? I still say you shouldn't hurry off to Garth," he said. "Let us escort you, at least. A convoy would be safer."

"You won't have any trouble catching up with us. As you can tell, we have that old-fashioned slow insystem drive. I'm sure you have better."

"Well, yes, but... you young people are always in such a hurry. Take it from me, haste in dangerous situations can be fatal."

"So can sitting around waiting to be shot," Ky said. "Look here, Cousin, I'm glad to have your protection and your company, but I'm not going to take your orders."

"You are definitely Gerry's child," Osman said. "Too bad..."

"Too bad?" Ky's stomach lurched. Here it came, whatever it was.

"I might have found a use for you," Osman said in a tone of such fake geniality and regret that Ky wanted to gag. "After all, a daughter of the great Gerard Avondetta Vatta... niece to Stavros, the Vatta CEO... you might have been very useful. But—" His expression hardened. "—but you are just an arrogant spoiled bitch, fit child to the man who cost me my proper life, the life I should have had as a senior Vatta captain."

He couldn't resist boasting. She had read that about certain kinds of criminals, but she had never seen it.

"Your father and uncle, the pair of them: stuck-up arrogant prigs that they were, they used me—they ruined me—just to get a step up the corporate ladder. As if they never did anything wrong. As if a Vatta heir weren't worth twice what some sniveling Engineering apprentice was... stupid slut, I gave her a necklace." The veins bulged on his forehead, she noticed; the old rage still consumed him. "And now, princess Kylara, Gerry's precious daughter, I'm going to destroy *you*. I only wish Gerry were here to see it in the moments before I blew him away."

"I'm so sorry to disoblige you," Ky said. Her heart was racing; she hoped he would interpret it as fear. "But I prefer not to be blown away."

"Prissy-mouth! What you prefer doesn't matter... you have nothing on that ship to defend yourself with, nothing. Oh, I know you bought a defensive suite at Lastway—we got word of that, no fear. But it's not worth a minim on a credit, because we have a deal with MilMart: they sell only worthless junk to Vatta, and we don't destroy them."

Ky stiffened her face, but too late; he leered at her. "Ah—I see you hadn't discovered the flaw yet. You will, about the time your ship comes apart around you. Or... I have a better idea. If you're the honorable sort, like old Gerry, and want to save your crew—or some of them—you can always cut your drive and surrender. I'll wager they'd rather live than die, and while I won't promise to make *your* life pleasant, I have no quarrel with unrelated crew. Unless of course some of them were involved in my embarrassment." He chuckled. "Go ask them, why don't you? I can wait."

Ky cut the connection. Lee stared at her, wide-eyed but silent; Rafe showed no emotion but the pulse beating in his neck.

"That was interesting," Ky said. Her mouth was dry; her voice not as steady as she wished. "So he's got a grudge against Vatta because my father threw him out. And he's sure our defensive suite won't work. I wonder if that's even true. I can't imagine that MilMart's stayed in business if they're that easy to bribe."

"Captain—" That was Quincy, on the ship's intercom. "We have a problem."

"What's that?" Ky asked. Her voice sounded normal again.

"Well . . . I didn't spot this at first, but there's a problem in the defensive suite—not in the scan components, but in the shields."

"I wonder why the Mackensee scan didn't pick it up," Ky said. "They had us arm it and said it looked solid."

"Yes. I know. I thought that meant it was working, too. But Toby was bored having to watch that miserable pup, and I gave him a stack of instruction cubes to keep him occupied. He went looking for that missing component we replaced from stock, found it, and then thought there was something odd about it. He says it's not what the manual calls for, and the shields will go on all right but not actually protect against a strong hit."

"Can it be made to work?"

"Yes, if we have time. Hours. The hardware is mostly okay; the software could be, but the installation instructions we were given were wrong. We need to uninstall the software, replace the nonstandard components of the hardware, then reinstall. Seven hours, probably. I know it took longer last time, but then we were unfamiliar with the equipment."

A voice in the background. "Not now, Toby," Quincy said, half into the intercom.

"But—"

"Not *now,*" Quincy said. Then into the intercom. "I'm thinking at least seven hours."

They didn't have seven hours. Not now. Ky tried to think. Shieldless, they were easy prey, as easy as they looked.

"Quincy, where are the other crates from Mackensee, the ones labeled MODEL 87-TR-5003?"

"Number one hold. Why?"

"Because we need them, and we need them now. And the ones I called the odor barriers. Get 'em out, unpack 'em, and call me when you have them laid out on the deck."

"Let me tell her . . ." came faintly from the intercom. Toby, of course. Pity for the child who had lost all in his ship at Allway and was probably going to be dead in a few hours gave her patience.

"Let him talk, Quincy," Ky said. "Go on, Toby."

"It won't take that long," Toby said. "I was going to tell Quincy, but she called you right away. I located the places where the component needs changing and pre-positioned everything. I wouldn't do it without asking, Captain. I know that would be wrong, but I thought—I thought it would be all right to do that much."

"Good for you," Ky said. Would it shave the time enough? "Is Jim down there? And Rafe—he'll come down and help. You can show them where all the points are?" Martin, too, but she might need his help with the mines.

"Yes, Captain. Some of them are kind of hard to get to—"

"But you can wiggle in. Fine. Quincy—"

"Yes—" That from a different station, obviously.

"Toby's done part of the work already, he says. Located all the ones that need changing and put out the components needed. Time saved?"

"Maybe an hour, maybe more," Quincy said. "You're trusting a fourteen-year-old kid?"

"Quincy—it's that or nothing. We don't have seven hours; we might have five and a half. He found the problem; he went partway to solving it. I have to go with him."

"Right. I'm pulling your crates now—"

"And I'm sending Rafe down to do the software changes. Give Toby whoever's free and let him lead them to the locations."

Rafe had already left when she turned around. Lack of initiative wasn't his problem, either. "Lee, you have the bridge; I've got to go check out those mines myself. I bought the kind we studied in the Academy; if they're glitched I know how to fix them." She hoped. If it was something simple like an unattached connection. The other mines, the ones MacRobert had sent, were more specialized.

Stella was waiting between the bridge and the recreation area. "How bad is it, and what can I do?"

"Very bad, and if you've got the expertise with software, you can go down to Engineering and help Rafe."

"Osman—?"

"A grudge against our parents. I wonder if he's the real reason Vatta's under attack—though his grudge sounds very personal. He could have hit Vatta without involving ISC. But he wants our parents' children in particular. He doesn't know you're here, or Toby. And won't. Come on—I have to go check out something."

CHAPTER NINETEEN

The row of mines looked eerily like those laid out on the deck of her Academy class on defensive ordnance maintenance procedures. Then there had been only fifteen, one per study group of four, and those had been unarmed. Were these the same, only deadly? Or were they as useless as Osman said the defensive suite was? The bulbous forward end, with its navigational circuitry, and the plump cylinder holding the explosives behind—each, she was relieved to note, with the proper plastic guard inserted to prevent accidental detonation—the knurled section that could be unscrewed to allow a variety of propulsive and attitude adjustment components, depending on need. These came with the basics only: self-contained reaction engine and simplest of the attitude adjustment components. Ky had not been able to afford the extras. Still, a rock could destroy a spaceship if the product of mass and acceleration came to enough force; her instructors had been clear about that.

"Martin, how familiar are you with these things?"

He shook his head. "Sorry, ma'am, but it's been years since I armed or disarmed one. I know what they are, but ordnance wasn't ever my specialty."

That was a disappointment. "You'd better go help reinstall the defensive suite, then," she said. "I'll work on these."

Ky loaded the instruction tab into her hand display, and was reassured to find that what she thought she should do first was in fact what she should do first. She pulled out the bundle of safety cords that had come in the COMMAND

PACKET carton, freed one, and slipped its magnetic clip into a slot on the detonation control panel before removing the plastic guard that had served the same function. Now that mine couldn't detonate, no matter what mistakes she made during the examination and programming. She red-corded all of them first, then opened the navigational compartment of the first. Another glance at the instruction manual refreshed her memory; the mine's innards still looked familiar, and all the parts that should be there, were... A purple-coated wire caught her eye. It should have been attached... there. She clipped it in place, and opened the next control panel. The same purple-coated wire to reattach. Very simple sabotage, easy to fix if you were looking for something wrong. Did that mean she was missing something subtler? She hoped not. She didn't have time to disassemble each completely. Another look at the instruction manual. Attitude adjusters, main engine controls, each with one disabling wrong connection. She glanced at the chronometer. Ten minutes gone. Ten times twenty-one was two hundred ten minutes. Too long—she had to move faster. But carefully.

And how was she going to place them without Osman or his allies noticing? All very well to place what amounted to explosive rocks in the enemy's path, but that required accuracy. If their drives were on, they'd be detected, could be avoided. She didn't have enough to create a broad barrier behind the ship. She needed a way to get them away from her ship that Osman couldn't detect...

She had four of them done when Lee called down from the bridge. "He's hailing us again."

"He can wait," Ky said.

"He's offering the crew their lives if we overpower you, and a reward if we deliver you alive."

"So are you going to take it?" Ky asked.

Lee snorted. "Not me, Captain. I don't believe him."

"You don't have to tell him that," Ky said. "If he thinks he's got a taker, he might tell his friends to hold their fire."

"I thought of that, but I didn't want to do it without asking."

"Do it," Ky said. "Every minute helps." Even as she talked, her fingers raced over the tasks . . . open a hatch, find the loose connection, reattach, check that other components were normal, close and seal, open the next . . . "And if he closes in . . . maybe we get a new hull."

"Suits?"

Ky paused, hands still for a moment. Their suits might save them . . . or condemn them to a slow death outside the ship. They'd be clumsier in suits . . . "Not quite yet," she said. "But tell me if he closes, and be sure you don't let him know you're doing it."

"Right, Captain. Uh . . . I'll need another crewmember to act the part of mutineer. Who should I get? Rafe?"

"Not Rafe," Ky said instantly. Osman would see Rafe for what he was, and while he might believe that Rafe would turn on her, he would not trust anything Rafe said. Her mind flicked through the personnel files. Alene? Sherry? Mitt? Beeah? No, Osman might recognize any longtime Vatta employee. Not Martin: he was too obviously military. "Jim," she said. "You'll have to explain it to him; I don't have time."

"Will do," Lee said.

Ky went back to the mines, surprised to find that she was already on the sixth. Her mind wanted to wander off to the best deployment again, but she dragged it back. She must not make any mistakes here and now. Sixth, seventh, eighth . . .

Then Lee piped down to the nearest speaker the conversation he and Jim were having with Osman.

". . . just disable her," Osman said.

"You don't understand." Jim's voice sounded tense, whiny with the Belintan nasal accent. "She's *killed* mutineers before. She's dangerous."

"So am I," said Osman. "If you don't get control of that ship, I'll have to destroy it. And you. Look—she suspected trouble before. She thinks she's got a perfectly loyal crew now—"

"And most of 'em are, I'm sure," Lee said. "I mean . . . she's not bad, exactly . . ."

"Do they want to live or are they happy to die loyal?" Osman asked. "Ask them that. Not all of them. That old fool Quincy I'm sure would rather burn than betray a Vatta." His voice had acquired a sneer. "But that's the choice. Work with me, or die. And you don't have much time... No, leave the connection live."

He didn't trust Lee and Jim, and no wonder.

"I can't do that," Lee said. "If she comes back to the bridge, she'll notice... she told me not to answer."

"Where is she now?"

"All over the damn ship," Lee said. "She's checking on everything, but I know she'll come back in here—an' anyway, we have to get some others. Two of us, me and Jim, we're not enough. If that Quincy finds out—"

Ky was fascinated by Lee's glibness. Either he had some experience she didn't know about, or she had corrupted him in the past several months. She suspected both.

"How many do you think will join you?"

"Allie," Jim said, speaking up. "She's unhappy anyway; she doesn't like that new cargomaster, she told me."

"Mitt might join us," Lee said. "And he's good in a fight. Sheryl probably. Like you said, Cap'n, Quincy's no use to us and she's the one most likely to tell our captain."

"You can have twenty minutes," Osman said. "Then report back and tell me how it's going."

"What if she's on the bridge?"

"If you've got four people and you can't take down one, you're useless," Osman said.

"Right," Lee said.

Ky finished the ninth mine, her mind now racing on the larger problem. Or was it a problem? Maybe it was an opportunity. He wanted to close and board... if she had a crew trained in EVA, she could send someone over to his ship with a mine when they were close enough. She didn't have a crew trained in EVA. Besides, that would damage or destroy the hull she wanted, and would signal Osman's allies that the mutiny was faked. If she could knock out his ship's systems—she stopped moving, immobile for long seconds as her mind threw up yet another scenario. Pictures flickered through her mind, almost too fast to follow. Transfer tube. Air locks open. A blurred shape flying through the tube... not this mine, but one of the others, one of the EMP weapons MacRobert had sent her.

"Quincy. Martin."

"Yes, Captain?"

"Do we have any kind of... of machine or something that can throw a... say... seventy-kilogram mass about a hundred, two hundred meters?"

"You mean like a hydraulic piston sort of thing? No."

No. Not the answer she wanted, needed. Her mind threw up the picture of Mehar's pistol bow. Made it bigger. Back in the dawn of time, people had used big machines of that type to throw rocks or something... but they didn't have time to build one, and it would have to be wider than the escape passage anyway. Could some of the crew—all the crew—heave the thing down the passage fast enough? Almost certainly not. *Twang!* The sound of a packing cord coming loose made her jump. Then the plan appeared, bright and clear and complete in her mind.

"Quincy, how many packing cords would it take to accelerate that seventy-kilo mass?"

"Packing cords... *packing* cords!" Ky could see the engineering mind at work, as clearly as if Quincy's implant were printing the figures on her forehead. "That's the craziest—but—Alene! Sheryl! Get me all the packing cords you can grab—the priority on purple and green, three meters... you'll want some way to fasten them..."

"Yes." And some way to make sure the load was lined up with the internal and external hatches, and some way to be sure that Osman's air lock was open, and some way to take advantage of the confusion that would result if this worked and to recover from the mess if it didn't. But she felt a wave of confidence. It was a workable idea, the first she'd had, and from it flowed concatenated consequences—using Osman's ship as a shield against his allies, once she gained control.

"Ma'am, that's a very dangerous plan—" Martin began.

"We have a very dangerous situation," Ky said. "As several people, including you, pointed out earlier. Have you got a better plan? If this works it will prevent a boarding situation."

His plan if they were boarded had been complex, and she was not at all sure her crew could carry it out. Especially the last phase.

"I understand that, ma'am."

"Oh, and Quincy—with just the EMP pulse aimed into his ship, estimate the damage to grapples, transfer tube, and our control systems . . ." She ripped open one of the cartons.

"Right," Quincy said, sounding more cheerful. "And send Martin down here."

Risks. If this failed, they might actually be captured. That must not happen. Toby must not fall into enemy hands, nor Stella, nor Quincy . . . nor she herself. She thought it would work—it should work, it certainly could work—but what if it didn't? She called Toby, Stella, and Rafe to meet her in the rec area. They had a right to know the worst before the others. The final elements of Martin's plan, the ones she hadn't told them about before in case it never happened.

"The situation is . . . grave," Ky said. Toby paled, but didn't move. Stella, already paler by nature, sat as still.

"Hopeless?" Rafe asked.

"No. Not hopeless. Difficult, dangerous, tricky. Grave. But not ever hopeless."

Rafe pursed his lips. "Sometimes, Captain Vatta, it is necessary to recognize when there are no viable alternatives."

The formality alerted her. "You think there are not?"

"We're outnumbered by larger, faster ships, several of them armed with ample weaponry to blow us away if the defensive suite doesn't hold, and maybe even if it functions as advertised. Our enemies have proposed a plan that they claim will save some of the crew—do you believe that, by the way?"

"Of course not," Ky said. "They have no interest in the crew's lives. They assume I do."

"And this plan involves letting this ship be boarded. So . . . it might be time to eat the bullet."

"I think not," Ky said. "I think it's time to have our enemy eat the bullet. It's just that ensuring it goes down their gullet is not going to be easy."

"And the cost of error might not be a quick death," Rafe said, holding her gaze.

"That at least lies within our power," Ky said. She did not glance at Toby; she did not want to see that awareness enter his eyes. The pup moved suddenly, squirming out of Toby's grip with a grunt; his claws clicked on the deck.

"Rascal!" said Toby in a tense voice.

"It's all right," Ky said, almost relieved by the interruption. "Rascal's behavior is the least of our problems. I do feel it's imperative that every crewmember have the capability to ensure a quick death . . ."

"You mean . . . suicide?" Toby asked.

She had to look at him now. His brow furrowed with the effort to act calm; his jaw was clamped, mouth in a firm line.

"Yes," she said. "But only if it's necessary, if the rest of this doesn't work."

"My . . . my family didn't believe in suicide," he said, looking down.

"Neither did mine," Ky said. "For all the usual reasons. But Toby, if Osman captured you . . . it doesn't bear thinking on."

"I . . . don't want to die."

"Me, neither. I don't intend to die, in fact. I intend to kill Osman, and my parents also taught me that killing people was wrong. But you're signed to the contract as an adult, Toby. Adults sometimes have to do things they never thought they'd do. If you honestly can't . . . well . . . we'll take care of you."

From his face, he understood that, too. "Can we kill them?"

"I think so. Or I'd blow this ship myself."

"All right." His face stiffened. Ky glanced at Rafe and Stella. "Don't . . . I can do it myself, if I have to. Will it . . . hurt?"

"No," Ky said. Honesty, brutal to the end, forced her to add, "Or at least, not as long as Osman would." She handed out the packets.

Rascal was gnawing on her boot; she bent down and scooped him up. He wiggled furiously, managing to swipe his tongue over her chin before she was able to dump him back into Toby's grip. "Here you go, Toby," she said. She searched for something comforting to say and came up empty. What could you say, after telling a youngster he might have to kill himself? There was always the appeal to duty . . . and what teenager didn't have secret fantasies of being the hero? "You take care of him, and do whatever Quincy asks. You're clever—you may be the one who saves the ship."

"Yes, Captain," Toby said. He still looked scared, and no wonder, but his eyes also held a spark of interest beyond fear. "I'll—I'll try to help."

"Toby, you've helped already. You're going to make a fine captain someday." If he lived. If any of them lived. If she had ships for him to captain. But that was her job.

Her father had once said that the easiest person to cheat was the person who expected to be cheated. She'd heard that repeatedly from others, as well, most recently from Osman himself. He would certainly expect tricks, but what tricks would he expect? That the mutiny was faked, that her crew would really resist? That she would find out? What would he consider clues that this was happening?

Delay, probably. If her crew started equivocating, delaying, he'd think they were up to something. If, on the other hand, they urged him to get with it, from the beginning . . .

She called Lee on the private circuit. "Tell him it's got to be quick," she said. "Tell him you're worried that I'll find out, rally the loyalists or blow the ship, and it's got to be quick." Then another thought struck her. "Tell him you'll get my command implant."

"You don't have an implant."

"He doesn't know that. He asked what I had, if I could give him an update. I lied and said I had only the most basic, probationary one. But he won't believe that; he wants to think I have an advanced one."

"But you don't... do you?"

"Not in me. That's why he'll find a view of me unconscious with my head laid open proof that it exists. It's your safety lever, Lee. If he blows the ship, he loses a treasure—the information in a Vatta command implant. Bargain with him. Tell him you can deliver that, and the cargo, if he'll let you and the crew go with the ship."

"But—what about you?"

"It'll only be for a short time, while you put the vid pickup on me to prove I'm captive and helpless."

Stella shook her head. "It won't do," she said. "It's too dangerous. I'll be you—he doesn't know what you look like—"

"He would have vid images from Lastway," murmured Rafe. "If he suborned someone at MilMart, they could have taken plenty of shots."

"A wig, makeup," Stella said. "I'm good at impersonation; you know that. Likeliest thing, he'll want a constant vid pickup, not just that one glimpse."

"A bag over your head," Ky said. "That's even safer. But the close-up to show that the implant's out... that has to be my head. No matter what you do with makeup, your cheekbones don't look like mine."

"What about the implants? You have two extra now, the one your father sent to Sabine, with Furman, and the command dataset one from... from him."

"What's yours, Stella?"

"Currently? Admin Level Two. Lots of data, no command functions."

"The one Furman sent would give you command functions for this ship," Ky said.

"I don't want it," Stella said. "Remember, I was never trained for shipboard duties. Without time to assimilate what's in the database, I'd mess something up. Why don't you give that one to Toby? And you really need to have the command dataset yourself."

True, and she'd already thought of that. "There isn't time," she said. "If I can't make a quick adjustment, I'd be unable to act when they board."

"Rafe says it's possible," Stella said.

"And you believe him?" Ky said.

"It's his life, too," Stella said. "The best chance for us is for you to be augmented as much as possible, isn't that right?"

It was. Her earlier objections to putting in the implant now seemed foolish. If she had done it on Lastway, or in the safety of FTL flight... they would have had time to cope with whatever problems occurred. Even if it left her completely incapable, Stella could have asked the mercs for assistance. But she'd left it until the last minute, hoping to wait out the whole six months, and now—

"All right," she said, and turned to Rafe. "So... is it possible in the time we have left?"

"Possible to do, of course. Possible for you to regain full function... that's less certain. Probably; you're young, and the implant is presently set to a close genetic match. But it's going to be rough to push the adaptation. Things your brain normally does while you sleep, you'll have to do rapidly while awake. And you'd best do it now—you'll need every minute of time to adapt."

Time... time slipped away, the minutes disappearing far too fast. Ky prepared one of the mines MacRobert had sent her for its peculiar use and explained to Jim just what he should do when the time came. Martin would take command of the ship's defensive response if she could not. They would have just that one chance to disable Osman's ship, or part of it, one chance . . . she did not let herself dwell on the likelihood that they would all be dead in a few hours. They were not going to die; she was not going to let that happen.

The picture of Ky unconscious, with the implant out, they shot just before Rafe put the command implant in. "He's going to want continuous feed," Ky said. "He's going to want to know it's not a trick. So we give him continuous feed or what looks like continuous feed. Jiggly, a handheld remote brought in for the purpose. No vid pickups in the captain's cabin; he'll believe that. Show me with the implant out, with the implant in someone's gloved hand, then someone putting a pillowcase over my head and tying me up. Then wobbly, panning briefly, before it steadies again on someone else tied up on my bunk. That'll be Stella . . . are you sure, Stella?"

"I'm sure," Stella said. "I'm most expendable."

She wasn't. No Vatta was expendable. But neither were crew.

"Just be sure he doesn't get me alive," Stella said. "Me or my implant."

"He's not going to get you at all," Ky said with more confidence than she felt. A few minutes later, they had arranged the setup as well as they could. Ky lay on her bunk and let Rafe slide the needle into her vein; her last thought as darkness took her was a quick prayer that she had guessed right about him.

She woke after what seemed only a moment, on the dining table in the rec area, feeling sick and disoriented. Rafe's face and Quincy's were close above her. "Ky . . . ," Quincy was saying. "Do you know who I am now?"

"Quincy Robins," Ky said, struggling with her tongue, which felt clumsy. Her vision blurred, shimmered, and cleared again, this time with a foreground of text and icons: Quincy's entire confidential personnel file, retrievable by focusing on the icons that brought up additional text. "You were married four times?"

"That answers my next question," Quincy said. "Your implant's working, at least."

"Sorry," Ky said, putting a hand to her head. "It's . . . a little overwhelming. How long—?"

"Fifteen minutes," Rafe said. Somewhat to her surprise, data on him also popped up, referencing his association with Stella and filled with query marks. "It took a bit longer than I'd planned; that is one complicated implant, and the adjustment routines are . . . tricky. How's your vision?"

"Weird," Ky said. Everything she looked at brought up a screen of data; she should be able to suppress that, but so far the usual damping controls didn't seem to work. Had her father dealt with this visual complexity all the time? "How much time do we have?"

"Osman plans to grapple on in about three hours, he says."

At the name, Osman's data came up . . . even worse than Quincy had remembered. He had been sent for counseling, for mandatory psychiatric treatment, for mandatory control implantation . . . but he'd escaped then . . . he'd stolen, both by force and by embezzlement; he'd gambled, dishonestly; he'd tried to cheat shippers and his own ship alike. His approaches to sexual partners were abusive, threatening; his penchant for violence showed up early and never abated.

She'd been an idiot, just as Johannson said. She'd risked the remaining Vatta command structure, and only now did it occur to her that she might have sent Stella and Rafe aboard one of the escort ships, to safety, with the Vatta command implant, and risked only herself.

No time for self-recriminations, though. She felt around mentally, pushing every implant control she could find to see what happened. Dizziness . . . nausea . . . she was briefly aware of someone holding a bowl under her mouth . . . and then plunged again into the datastream. This was not how you were supposed to meld with a new implant, certainly not one of this complexity, but she had no time for that, either.

Finally her vision cleared. She looked at Quincy. No data screen blurred that worried old face. Rafe. Same there. Her head felt overstuffed; she wasn't sure of her balance, but she had to function.

"What do you take," she asked Rafe, "when you have to go on right away?"

"Coffee helps," he said. "Here's a mug. Unless you still want to spew."

"No, my stomach's fine now," Ky said. She tried to sit up and the room lurched, turned pale yellow, then settled back to normality.

"You don't look it," he said, steadying her with one arm and holding the mug with the other hand.

"I pushed all the buttons," Ky said. Upright again, she felt better but still strange. She held out her hands. The left one twitched in a slow rhythm. She willed it to be still, to no effect. Her right was steady. "Good thing I'm right-handed," she said, and took the coffee. A few sips later, her vision had sharpened to extreme clarity and she could feel her blood vessels vibrating. "Enough," she said to Rafe.

"The extra sensitivity wears off in about four hours," he said.

Four hours they didn't have. Ky opened her implant to the ship circuits and for the first time in months felt the direct connection to all functions that she thought she hadn't missed.

"How's Osman taking the video show?" she asked, then realized she didn't have to ask. Her implant linked to the ship's communications, and she had her own view of Osman's face on half a screen while also receiving the vid feed he was getting on the other half. She shrank both to an unobtrusive level, listening in to Lee on the bridge.

"They're still barricaded in the engine room," Lee was saying. "I can't get a feed down there; they've blocked the pickups."

"That would be Quincy," Osman said. "Well, we can handle her when we get aboard. Where's the implant?"

Lee looked stubborn. "I don't want to tell you, not yet," he said. "How do I know you won't just kill us all?"

"You don't," Osman said. "But I won't. I just want your captain, and Quincy, and the implant. I will take your cargo, since you offered it, but then you're free to go. Or join us, if you wish."

"Some do," Lee said. "I haven't decided, myself. I . . . it would be strange, not being Vatta . . ."

"You'd still be Vatta," Osman almost purred. "I am Vatta, after all. The Vatta heir, in fact."

"That's true, I suppose . . ." Lee looked thoughtful. Ky began to think he'd missed his calling; he was as good an actor as he was a pilot.

"So why don't you tell me where the implant is?"

"We put it in someone," Lee said. "But I won't tell you who. That way you won't want to kill any of us . . . for a while."

A shadow crossed Osman's face, but then he smiled again. "Ingenious. I admire ingenuity."

Ky grinned to herself. In that case, he should admire hers . . . about ten seconds before he died.

Her plan, such as it was, had too many failure points to satisfy her, but it was the only one she'd been able to devise and it was above all ingenious.

She pushed herself off the table and staggered; Rafe steadied her again. "Your coordination will return faster if you move around a lot," he said. "But you're going to fall into walls a few times."

"Great," Ky muttered. One leg felt longer than the other, then that reversed. Normally, a night's sleep allowed a brain and an implant to work out peacefully what individual differences mattered here, but she didn't have a night to sleep. She had a battle to fight. "Someone get me Mehar's target bow," she said. "If I can't walk straight I have to at least shoot straight. And I need my pressure suit." She took a couple of steps, feeling very unsteady, then sat in a chair and stood up again.

"Here, Captain." That was Mehar herself; Ky quickly damped the data screen that matched her face and voice, and took the target bow with its blunted bolts. Mehar had already placed a pillow on a chair across the compartment. Quincy now held her pressure suit, unfastened and ready.

Ky took the bow and aimed at the pillow; the bolt thwacked into it. "Well, that's something." She stepped sideways, and nearly fell into the table. "And that's something else . . ." Another shot, this one a foot wide.

"Dance it," Rafe suggested.

"Dance—?"

He did something, she couldn't see what, and music came from the speakers. "Come here," he said. "I'll show you."

Confused and still unsteady, Ky allowed herself to be held, and then he began to move to the music, dragging her along. "You do dance . . . ?" he asked in her ear.

"Er . . . yes." Like all the Vatta children, she'd been given dancing lessons in many styles; dance was, everyone agreed, a good preparation for spaceflight, teaching body awareness and control. But since . . . since the Academy junior ball, when she'd danced with Hal, she had not danced, or thought of dancing. Now the music and Rafe's movements brought it back. Her body's quarrel with the implant receded as melody and rhythm worked on older parts of her brain; she moved more and more smoothly with him. The tremor in her left hand ceased; she felt the warring components slide into harmony. More than that, she felt warm, alive, happy in a way she had not since . . .

"You dance well," Rafe said in her ear. "So you're not a cold fish after all . . ." Then, moving slightly away, "Is that better?"

"Yes," she said, surprised. "How did you know—" She hoped her cheeks weren't flushed with more than implant effects. This was not the time or the man.

"Bad experience," he said. "Switched implants in the men's room at an embassy ball, thought I could hide out pretending to be drunk for a few hours, but no such luck. Had to get up and dance—it would have started a war if I hadn't—

and just a few minutes later, I was fine. Mostly. Getting shut of that odious woman, though, that took a while."

Ky moved around the room again, this time smoothly, and five blunts went into the pillow from various angles. "Time to suit up," she said. In the suit's privacy no one would notice what she was feeling, surely very dangerous feelings on the eve of battle. Rafe looked at her, a very knowing look that seemed to go straight to her core, and she looked back steadily, willing herself not to blush, not to react.

"You'll be fine," he said. He turned to his own suit and began to clamber into it.

CHAPTER TWENTY

The last moments before the curtain goes up . . . the last moments before the music starts . . . Ky looked at the stage she'd designed, the music she would start, as *Fair Kaleen*'s grapples reached them, as they were drawn closer to the other ship, as the transfer tube bulged out and adhered to the hull around their emergency exit hatch. All the arguments over: Martin still thought he should be where she was, but she had final responsibility. It was her job.

Her stomach knotted, then unknotted. She and her father's implant were mostly in accord now, with no more balance problems, no sensory problems that she recognized. She hadn't had time to familiarize herself with all the faculties, the way he had chosen to organize the proprietary information, but the ship command functions all worked. She shouldn't, she hoped, need more than that. Foremost, already set up, were her links to her own ship's functions, and those of *Fair Kaleen*. Osman would have made some changes, in the years he'd commanded the old ship, but buried deep in its command layers, in kernels hardened from the attack she planned, should be responses to her Vatta command dataset that he could not anticipate and counteract. If she could get there.

In her earbug, she heard Lee describing—breathlessly—the chaos on the ship. "We've got her safe in the captain's cabin, you saw that, and it's secure, but Quincy's done something—"

"Never mind about that." Osman's voice sounded impatient. "We'll send a team over to take care of it, whatever it is. But you're sure the captain's secure?"

"You can see that," Lee said, sounding grumpy. "I just don't want Quincy to disable the ship and have us stranded out here—that old woman's crazy enough..."

Via the implant, Ky could tell that the other ship was broadside-on to its course, as were they: the safest close-maneuver configuration, since neither could fry the other with insystem drives if someone turned them on. This also meant that rotation about the long axis could impart angular momentum to objects shed from a hatch, right back down the course. She had a use for that, if she survived the next few minutes.

"Send someone down to open up," Osman ordered Lee. "Or I'll blow the hatch."

"I am, I am," Lee said hastily. "Jim, go unlock the door."

"Why is it always me?" Jim said in a sulky tone for the camera, but in moments he jogged down the central corridor, winking at Ky as he came past her, pulling up the hood of his pressure suit.

"Right side," Ky reminded him. He said nothing, but nodded. As he undogged the inner hatch, Lee spoke up suddenly. "Jim—look out—Quincy and that idiot Beeah are out of the cargo bay—"

"I'm on it," Jim grunted. "Don't worry—" He was now in the emergency air lock, working on the outer hatch. "Damn, this thing is stiff—" Ky assumed that Osman would have an optical link set to observe through the tiny safety window as well as monitoring transmissions.

"It's always been a problem," Lee said. "I told you—we had trouble with it at Sabine—but hurry up!"

"Send me some help," Jim said, making a dramatic lunge at the hatch's controls.

"Can't—have to hold the bridge—can't let them get to the—" Realistic sounds of gunfire cut him off.

"Damn it!" Jim snarled and lunged again as if frantic. This time he hit the controls, and the hatch opened halfway. He shoved, then flattened against the right side of the air lock as Ky cut the restraining line and the EMP mine, powered by every elastic lashdown cord on the ship, shot past his knees, through the twenty meters of transfer tube, and crashed into someone in a pressure suit, knocking him back into Osman's air lock. The man had been holding a fat disk that Ky recognized—in that instant's glimpse—as a limpet mine.

"Get that hatch closed!" she said to Jim, and raced to help him, mentally counting seconds. Damn, damn, damn, damn... outer hatch dogged... inner...

Whoomp. Ky opened her mouth to comment. *WHOOMP! Lights flickered, an alert signal buzzed. She peeked through the small emergency viewport in time to see a cloud of debris in her own ship's exterior lights, and the abrupt disintegration of the transfer tube. Grapple lines flailed. Something rattled against the viewport; she ducked, then looked again. Pieces of space armor... trailing clouds that glowed red in the spotlights. Her gorge rose; she swallowed against it. A second and third burst of debris from* Fair Kaleen*'s air lock, then a steady stream... and the intership distance increased; the other ship began a slow rotation about her longitudinal axis. Ky realized with horror that the ship's air was bleeding out, the automatic systems disabled by the dual explosion of two mines, not one—and one of them a hullbuster. If the air lock hadn't already been open,* Fair Kaleen *would have had a hull breach.*

She imagined the howling gale of decompression, terrifying in the darkness when their lights failed. Some compartments would be spared... those in pressure suits might survive for hours, even days... but depending on the damage done by the pair of mines, the ship might be helpless.

That wasn't what she'd meant to do. In her mind, a tiny voice explained to a nonexistent parent that it wasn't supposed to happen that way. It was just supposed to mess up the command systems... she closed the inner hatch of the air lock and shook her head at Jim's questions. She had to figure out what to do now. How long would *Fair Kaleen*'s systems be down before the automatic reset tried to restore functions? Would the loss of pressurization change that? How much damage had Osman's own mine done? How many of his crew were dead, and how much resistance would she face if she tried to board? And was he himself dead—had he been in the air lock—or was he still aboard, fighting to regain control of his ship and come after her?

"What was that?" she heard someone yell.

"Them," she said. Her implant displayed data on the debris still impacting their shields, a flowing mass of numbers—dimensions and presumed mass of particles, their velocities and vectors, hundreds, thousands of tiny impacts. She shut off that analysis as too confusing, checked on her own ship's integrity and systems function, relieved to find that no serious damage had resulted. On her way to the bridge, she stopped by her cabin to let Stella know they had won the first round.

"Get this thing off my head," Stella said; Ky helped her get out of the pillowcase, the bindings. She followed Ky to the bridge, where Lee had the controls.

"Can you snug us in against his ship?" Ky asked Lee. Stella, released from her role as a bound captive, leaned on the bulkhead.

"It's rotating," Lee said. "It'll be a tricky maneuver. What's the purpose?"

"For one thing, he'll be blind to where we are, even if he gets his main scans back online—we'll be too close. For another, even if he figures out where we are, attacking us will destroy his own ship. In the time it takes him to figure it out—if he does—we have the chance to get in and convert the ship's systems. Or we can just keep clobbering them with successive EMP attacks. And his allies, those two warships, will certainly attack us if we're separated from him, but possibly not if we're attached."

"You're assuming Osman's still alive and in control," Stella said.

"I hope not, but for now—yes. It's safer that way. At least

we're not still attached, and everyone in that transfer tube or air lock should be dead. Controls in all powered suits should be gone, too."

"Unless he has mechanical overrides," Martin said, arriving at that moment. "But you're probably right. And I imagine anyone aboard is too busy trying to survive to try to get to us." He grinned at Ky. "That was a brilliant idea after all, Captain. But how did you know they'd have a mine with them?"

"I didn't," Ky said. "I knew they'd try some trick to disable the crew here; I was actually thinking some kind of chemical weapon. Knock you all down alive, take all the implants—"

Stella shuddered. "That would have been horrible."

"I can match us to his ship," Lee said, "but it'll take a while. I have to get his current vectors, and then match rotation."

"Do we have enough power to stop the rotation if we're attached?"

"I don't know. We can slow it, probably. Why—oh. So we can hide from the other bad guys?"

"Yeah. If they shoot, I want that buffer between us."

"Right. We leave our defensive suite up, though?"

"Absolutely," Ky said. "Even if it's not working perfectly, it's all we have."

She called Quincy to ask about progress in the repair. "Toby did it," Quincy reported. "Better for him to be busy. Oh, and that dratted pup came up with the part he carried off before. Toby says it was defective to start with—it's mislabeled. It would've failed when we turned the system on."

"Toby is quite the little genius," Ky said.

"He's a good kid," Quincy said defensively. Ky felt her own eyebrows go up.

"I never said he wasn't—I think we're lucky to have him—" And not her own sulky teenaged self, though maybe she wouldn't have been as bad on another ship.

"Well . . . fine." Quincy cleared her throat. "Are we . . . still expecting boarders?"

"No. Let me put this on all-ship—" Ky switched channels.

"Status report, everyone. Osman tried to double-cross us, have someone carry a limpet mine aboard. We won the toss. Our mine detonated his, both of them in his air lock. His ship's disabled, losing air out the open air lock, and some of his crew are... gone. We're in pursuit now, trying to match courses and rotation; we still have his allies to worry about, but we have a couple of hours' grace. Stay in your pressure suits, but you can open up and have something to eat."

A moment's silence, then a cheer from somewhere back down the passage. "Does this mean I don't get to shoot anyone?" Rafe asked.

"Not at the moment."

"Too bad. What are your next plans, Captain?"

"I'm working on them," Ky said. "I didn't expect what did happen."

"Don't admit that," Rafe said. "I was admiring your prescience. I expected treachery, but not that he'd mine our ship before he got you and the implant."

"He wanted the mine in place," Ky said. "That was easy to figure. He could have set it off later. But I failed to consider that both mines might detonate together in his ship... and I should have."

"Ma'am, with your permission I'll go remove the booby traps I set up before someone bumps them."

"Of course, Martin," Ky said.

"I'd have thought the EMP from one would've turned off his," Stella said. "Don't all mines have electronic controls?"

"Yes," Ky said. "But the limpets like his are also pressure-sensitive—it's what keeps you from prying them off your ship if you find them before they go off. I got just a glimpse, but it looked like ours hit the limpet square on, with enough force to knock the man carrying it back into the air lock... and then it was just the usual few seconds' delay."

"Well, food sounds good to me," Stella said. "I'll be in the galley if you need me."

"We have a problem," Lee said. "Their ship's moving more irregularly... I can still match it, but until something smooths out their motion, our artificial gravity's going to be hard put to cope with the irregularities."

"Try it," Ky said. "I'll let everyone know to expect some problems."

Minutes crawled by. Ejecta from the other ship's air lock flashed against their defensive screen, but nothing penetrated. The scans showed the other ship's complex motion. The air lock was forward of the ship's center of mass, so its effect as a maneuvering reaction engine had created an erratic rotation rather than a smooth roll about the center axis. Lee edged *Gary Tobai* in slowly, using the nav computer to model and then match that eccentricity.

"If we aren't matched exactly, their greater mass could give us a fatal whap," he said. "The least relative motion's close to their center of mass . . . that's where we should grapple. Nearscan's accurate enough, but there's too much data with all that junk she's spewing."

"You think it's too dangerous?" Ky asked.

"Dangerous, yes. Too dangerous . . . compared to what, I'd have to say."

"I don't want to lose that ship," Ky said. "If it keeps losing atmosphere and tumbling, it could be ruined . . . or Osman might find a way to get it back in operation." If only she'd had a trained boarding team . . . the military could do it; if she'd had a squad of Slotter Key marines . . . but nobody on her ship—except her, and she could not leave the ship—could go out there, board a tumbling ship, and deal with whatever was inside. If the sturdy traditional Vatta systems reset themselves—and they might—Osman could regain control, and then . . . then things would be far worse.

And time was ticking away. The enemy warships would be in range in a few minutes.

She had the other mine. She had the skills herself . . . or she had had them, what was now a year and a half ago, standard. Her scores on EVA maneuvers had always been clears, no faults.

On maneuvers she had practiced repeatedly, in the zero-g gyms. Standard maneuvers, in standardized conditions. This was . . . this was nonstandard.

A dull clank reverberated up the main passage. From the hull? Something had made it through the screens?

"Helmets!" Ky said, before analysis had begun to catch up with instinct. She'd forgotten, she'd turned the exterior analysis module off. "The hatch—" She was moving now, down the passage, boosting the implant feeds, grabbing for pickups as she went.

Air lock in use, the implant told her. Outer hatch open, inner hatch shut . . . "Shut outer hatch," she said, to the implant. UNABLE TO COMPLY. PHYSICAL BLOCK OF OUTER HATCH, came up on her display.

Jim had closed it. She knew she had secured both hatches. But emergency hatches could be opened from either side—

A blinding flash of insight: not all those hurtling bodies out of Osman's air lock had been casualties. His crew *was* trained in boarding techniques, and she had not sent anyone outside to be sure their hull was clean . . . idiot that she was, with that misplaced sympathy for the crew she'd assumed was dead or dying. After a moment, her heart steadied again, and she felt an icy calm.

"Enemy aboard," she said. "Everyone get your suits sealed; section seals coming down." Her implant showed who was where . . . scattered, since she'd given them permission to relax from the first alert. Two in the head, one in the galley, some at duty stations, some in their bunks. The icons moved now, but not quickly enough . . . the section seals came down, securing them wherever they were, with whatever weapons they had in hand at the moment.

"Expect decompression," she said. It was the simplest way for the enemy to disable them; they were probably rigging a way to shut the ship up again quickly. She herself was now cut off from the bridge, from her cabin, from the other mines in cargo 3; the elegant little handgun she'd bought at Lastway, loaded now with frangibles, was the only weapon she had. Other than the one between her ears.

That one stopped her before she entered the last stretch of the passage to the air lock, still out of sight of the enemy. Her implant's display gave her a visual of the air lock . . . two figures in pressure suits. What blocked the outer hatch was a suit of space armor, apparently immobile. Through the implant controls, she zoomed the image. Inside the faceplate of the armor, a ghastly image—a face blue-gray, mouth open, eyes wide with horror, dulled with death. She changed the focus of the pickup, and saw that the two pressure-suited figures were indeed working on the inner hatch, attaching the ends of a hydraulic cylinder . . . they did not appear to be safety-lined in yet, though she saw coils of line around the shoulders of one of them. She didn't recognize the weapons they were carrying, but the tool set they were using on the hatch would certainly open any other hatch in the ship, in time.

If there was enough pressure—and she opened the inner hatch—then they could be blown out themselves . . . if that armor wasn't stuck too tightly. It probably was; they wouldn't have left themselves in that vulnerable position. The implant gave her a quick calculation of the amount of force needed to dislodge the armor . . . no, they'd wedged it in well. It would take another fifty kilograms of mass, and she didn't have that handy, not with the mines now sequestered behind a compartment lockdown, where they could do no good. She could manually open and shut each one, but she knew that would take too long.

Well . . . she did have fifty kilos of mass, but if she let go the safety grabons and used her own body to blow them out the lock, then she'd be out there, accelerating away from her own ship. Not where she wanted to be . . . not a good tactical choice.

She found another vid pickup just inboard of the air lock and aimed it up-passage. The packing cords that had launched her mine lay in a tangle. She could tie onto them as safety anchors; they'd pull her back. It wouldn't work. It couldn't work. But neither would letting Osman and his crew aboard. How many of them were there outside? She didn't have enough external pickups; the implant couldn't give her that information.

"There are two of them in the air lock," she said to her own ship intercom. "They have some space armor wedged in the outer hatch. Decompression alone won't blow them back out . . . it'll take more mass."

"How much?" Quincy asked, ever the engineer.

"Oh . . . fifty kilos would do it. Unfortunately, I don't have a spare fifty kilos." Quincy would have a fit if she knew what Ky was contemplating. Ky didn't like it much herself.

"Reopen the seals to the rec room and grab something?" Rafe asked. "I'm there; I could toss you a chair."

"Are you suited?" Ky asked.

"Yes. Upshift hatch is sealed; the galley hatch should hold for a brief decompression, and that would add additional volume—these chairs aren't that heavy, but they might be enough with the additional volume."

It was an idea, but she knew it wasn't going to work. The implant confirmed that when she queried it.

"Captain—" That was Martin. "Give me the codes for manual opening and closing—let me come help—"

"Where are you?" Ky asked.

"I'm right beside that carton of EMP mines."

"I'm closer," Rafe said. "Only one seal away."

"I have the skills," Martin said. "Hand-to-hand in vacuum and zero G—"

Just what she needed, two men squabbling over who was better equipped to help her. She would like to have had them both with her, but they weren't. "You'll both stay where you are," she said.

She rifled quickly through the emergency tool locker in the passage. Fire ax, zero-pressure sealant canister, long utility knife, prybar, boards, first-aid kit . . . she couldn't take it all, but the fire ax and knife went on her belt.

The implant noted that while she was 92 percent likely to

break the space armor loose from the outer hatch, she was 83 percent likely to break bones in the process, and 24.3 percent likely to suffer fatal injuries. But the alternative chances were worse: if Osman caught her, she'd be 100 percent dead after suffering she didn't want to contemplate. No choice, really . . .

Her suit—customized, top of the line from Deere Ltd.—was supposed to have superlative impact resistance, a combination of reinforced panels and impact-inflated cushions. She fed the suit data into her implant, and the probability of fatal injury dropped to 6.2 percent, broken bones to 21 percent . . . that was more like it, though a bone was either broken or not . . .

She moved on down the passage. The boarders could see—if they chose to look—through the window in the interior hatch. But if she was quick enough, all they'd see was a blur. The tangled cords lay in front of her now; she hooked them with the end of the fire ax and pulled them slowly to her.

Best not depend on the strength of her grip; she detached one of the packing cords—purple, breaking load twelve hundred kilograms—and looped it through the reinforced loop on her pressure suit designed for tethers, then around the other cords, and secured it. The implant display showed that the intruders were still intent on their work—no, one of them was looking up and around now.

No more time. Ky backed into the loop of the packing cords, pulling them as taut as she could, then told Lee, "I'm opening the inner hatch."

"But you're—"

Her implant took over. She had time to think *This was a really stupid idea*—and then the combination of elastic cords and escaping air flung her down the passage. She had thought she could hold herself rigid, like a spear, until the moment of impact, but the vortex of escaping air twisted her, threatened to slam her flailing body against the hatch opening. She pulled herself into a tight ball, fists locked on the cords, and struck the boarders with her right side, slamming them into the space-armored figure wedged in the hatch. With a shriek she could feel as much as hear, the space armor broke loose in that instant, and she and the others flew out the open hatch. She could see, in the external lights, someone else splayed flat against the hull. One of the boarders was loose, floating away; the other grabbed the tether, hands alongside hers, as it reached its full extension and began to retract.

Simultaneously Ky and the boarder each took a hand off the line and tried to shove the other off. The enemy managed to grab her wrist; his grip, possibly augmented by his suit, tightened painfully. She didn't need to hear what he was saying; she could imagine it. They rotated, struggling in the combination of forces, the lack of gravity, the pull of the retracting tether.

Ky let go the tether with her left hand, flipped it around her leg, and grabbed the clearing knife from her tool belt. Her enemy never saw it before she had slit his suit up under the right arm. Air puffed from his suit, pushing her away, yanking her arm. The suit's repair functions oozed foam, confining the loss to that limb, but immobilizing his arm. She stabbed again, this time ripping the left arm; his hand spasmed, releasing her; they rotated away from each other.

"Five seconds to impact," her implant warned her. Ky struggled, trying to see, to curl away from hitting the ship head-on. There—but something grabbed her leg, and pulled . . . she could feel the elastic cords stretching . . . she twisted. A hand clamped around her ankle; the suited figure trailed a thin stream that glittered in her headlamp. Powered suit. He had a powered suit—of course he did, that's how they crossed the interval in the first place—her mind gibbered wildly. The implant threw up a screen of information about powered suits, most of which Ky had no interest in. She was trying to curl up, avoid whatever that was streaming from the other's suit in case it was corrosive, and get that hand off her ankle. Her contortions made the other figure writhe, and their vector shifted irregularly, but he didn't let go.

She had been told zero-g fights were chaotic, impossible to predict even inside closed spaces. Outside a ship... Just don't get yourself in that situation, her instructors had said. Fine, but no help now. The suit resisted her attempts to bend over, get her hand and knife near the person clutching her; it had been possible in ship atmosphere, but not here. She tried another tactic, using alternating arm movements to impart a longitudinal spin... and that finally brought her arm close to the other. He had something that looked like a wrecker bar with a pointed tip in his hand, but she was inside his guard and almost behind him. She clutched him firmly to her with her right arm, and ran the knife blade up... in under the suit... up again.

The knife parted his suit from hip to shoulder; a mist clouded her faceplate briefly... he let go, and Ky managed to orient herself, finding her ship by its brilliant outside lights—its lights visibly nearing—as the elastic cords accelerated her back toward the open air lock.

If she stayed connected, she would smash into her own ship. If she didn't, she was hanging out here with no power, no way to get back... except she was already moving back. Was it fast enough? Ky cut the tether to the cords and watched them move away from her, writhing like the tentacles of the sea creatures she had watched on the reef at Corleigh. She queried her implant... she would hit the ship, but not hard enough to damage the ship—or herself.

She looked around as best she could. That dark moving blot across the starfield was Osman's ship, tumbling. The line of brilliant lights was her own, with its externals on, with its air lock still open, a larger area of light on the aft hull.

She cut her suit com back on. "Captain to bridge—"

"Where are you? What did you do?"

"I'm closing on the ship now," she said.

"On *Kaleen*?" Bewilderment and near panic were clear in Lee's tone.

"No. On us. I went out the hatch with the bad guys—two of them anyway." She bounced up the zoom on her helmet scan, looking for the one who had been starfished to the hull beside the hatch. He wasn't there. Where was he? "What's your internal scan say..."

"Somebody's inside, in the emergency passage. They won't answer; we thought it might be you with damage, maybe...we were just thinking of shutting the external hatch and airing up so we could open the compartments."

If she hadn't been in a suit, in free fall, she'd have pounded her head with her hand. Stupid, stupid, stupid. Captains should never leave the ship in dangerous situations. She'd had that pounded into her time and again at the Academy. Never. Whatever the temptation, the captain stays aboard to deal with the peril... and she had flung herself out the hatch, grandstanding, as MacRobert would have said. Correctly. And one of the scumsucking bastards had made it aboard her ship.

"Lock the hatch open, Lee," she said, even as she wondered why the boarder hadn't closed it already to keep her out if she escaped his allies. "Don't break compartmentalization. Scan for other powered suits between us and the *Kaleen*."

Abruptly, startlingly, *Fair Kaleen*'s running lights came on, the beacons defining bow and stern blinking and the others holding steady patterns that outlined her shape. Either the automatic reset had worked, or someone aboard was able to get the systems up. Reset wasn't a problem, but the other possibility...

Now that it was too late, she could think of other things that might have worked better...

"We lost vidscan in the emergency passage," Lee said. "We're still compartmented—"

"Good," Ky said.

"But we don't know where whoever that is has gone or what he or she is up to."

She knew. She knew with the absolute certainty that had not yet failed her. He was going to blow up the ship, and her family with it, and all he needed was the time he already had.

The time she had given him. A flicker of despair, the first touch of a black wave . . . but she had no time for that. “Patch me to Martin.”

“Right.” A pause, then Martin’s voice.

“Ky—Captain—what’s happening?”

“Martin, you’re in the same compartment with the mines, right?”

“Yes, but—”

“Take one with green markings, like the one I used before. Open the side—you saw me do it; you know where. There’s a manual control, a dial. Turn it to the left, all the way. Point the forward end so it will intersect the emergency passage. Set it to a five-second delay and get as far away from it as possible.” An EMP pulse could be focused to some degree. Her implant threw up a schematic showing what ship systems would be in the way of that destructive beam. Too bad . . . better that than complete destruction.

“But that will—”

“Do it now!” Then she tongued shipwide, and never mind if her enemy heard it. “Disaster stations! All hands, disaster stations and hold position.”

A second passed. Another. Another. Another.

As suddenly as *Fair Kaleen*’s lights had come on, *Gary Tobai*’s vanished. Her ship—her responsibility—now lay blind, all systems knocked out by a pulse of magnetics strong enough to injure the crew in some cases.

The hypercritical part of her mind screamed at her, *Really smart, Ky—now you’ve disabled your ship and you’re barreling toward it and can’t even see when to brace for impact, and that’s if Osman doesn’t blow it anyway*—Then she hit, hard, the suit’s protective mechanisms cushioning the blow—but the jar was still enough to take her breath for an instant. Her gloved hands scrabbled for something to hold on to, as rebound took her away, tumbling, and the loop of elastic in her hand caught a protruding stud . . . one of the eighty-two external mounts for the new defensive suite.

There was a control, if she could just get a boot onto the

hull...and the rotation from that one tenuous handhold brought her left heel down long enough to trigger it. She lost the handhold, but her foot was attached now, thanks to the emergency gripper attachment built into the boots. Now to get her other boot down...there. *So fine,* the nasty mental voice went on. *Now you're stuck to the side of your ship like an old-fashioned bowsprit ornament, and what good does that do?* Ignoring the voice, Ky leaned over slowly and gripped the nearest external mount. The faintly adhesive pads on the glove fingers gave her a good grip. The far more adhesive pads on her boot soles *grritch*ed loose, one at a time, as she lifted one foot carefully, obtained a second handhold, put that foot back down, and then lifted the other.

The whole trick in moving on a hull without safety lines, the instructor had said, is not to do it in the first place. But just in case you're blown out of your ship and onto an enemy ship, here's what you can try. Move slowly. Always have three points of contact. Be aware of gravity fluctuations.

That at least she didn't have to worry about, with her ship's systems down. Artificial gravity bleed-through faults in the external containment were the least of her problems. Finding the air lock, for instance, was likely to be a harder task. Figuring out what to do when she found it...could wait until she found it.

CHAPTER TWENTY-ONE

The flashing beacons of the other ship stung her eyes . . . and gave, as she moved, intermittent glimpses of her own ship. After months in space, *Gary Tobai*'s hull was no longer as immaculate as it had been, but it still gleamed dully when the light flashed on it.

Except where the dark hole of the air lock gaped, now under her feet, just over two meters away.

Her enemy was in there. Somewhere. Armed with a ship-destroying mine, she was sure, and personal weapons as well. He could blow the ship now, but he would want to be sure she was there to see it happen, and he also wanted her implant. He would wait—at least awhile—to see if she came for him.

Clearly he could handle himself in free fall and hard vacuum, but the change from a lighted passage at one standard g to a dark passage in free fall should have done something. He should be blind, disoriented, his suit com and any electronic suit functions dead. That left his ship-killer. Had he attached it yet? Had he armed it yet?

Her implant, protected from the pulse that disabled her ship, told her the minutes and seconds since she'd left the ship. Plenty of time, if he'd gone in immediately, to attach and arm a mine, to set the delay . . .

She felt around the hatch edge. As on all external hatches, geometric shapes defined the top and bottom, making it impossible to attach hatches, transfer tubes, or other equipment upside down. She was at what would be the deck side, if gravity were on. Carefully, she worked her way around, keeping the hatch itself between her and whoever was inside. He should have been on the deck when the ship had gravity. What happened when the systems went out would depend on what he was doing, but his mental orientation should still be that the deck was down and the overhead up... whereas in free fall it did not matter.

She eased cautiously into the air lock, as flat against the bulkhead as possible to occlude as little of the starfield... in case his vision had returned. Through her gloves, she felt some vibration, as something collided with the surfaces of the escape passage. She dialed down her own faceplate's transparency and turned up the implant's visual display to full bright. Working off the suit's external monitors, it gave her a ghostly pale sense of a tube with something lumpy moving erratically in it. She couldn't identify the mine she was sure the enemy had brought aboard, or how far away he was. She needed light.

Her suit light, up to full power, blazed, searing the passage with brilliant white light—she knew that, though her view was blocked by her mirrored visor, by her enemy's response. She had the one bit of luck she'd prayed for: he'd been facing aft, and the light hit him full in the face, half blinding him before his faceplate could adjust. The arm thrown up across his faceplate, the rotation that gave him, all gave her an instant in which to scan the passage for the... and there it was. At the moment, flat on what would be the deck... but whether already adhered and armed, or just there accidentally, she didn't have time to find out at the moment.

She pushed off the hinges of the outer hatch, turning her light off, aiming at the spot she wanted with the clean image her exterior vid had picked up and recorded. She bounced off the bulkhead just beyond the inner hatch, flicked the light on and off again quickly, to let the vids pick up enough to refine their image. Though it seemed agonizingly slow, this zigzag approach got her to him before he had controlled his own rotation. Then, her light blazing directly into his faceplate, she struck, the saw-bladed knife ripping into his suit fabric.

He was bigger, heavier, undoubtedly more experienced in space brawls onship and off. He clutched her arms, pushed off the bulkhead, moving them perilously back toward the outside—and worse, toward the mine on the deck. Another kick, off the overhead, and she knew they would hit it if she didn't change their vector. Twist, curl up to spin faster, stretch to slow... like a grotesque ballet, they rebounded again and again from bulkhead, overhead, deck, missing the mine by centimeters several times and only because Ky had marked it on her implant's view and instinct drove the maneuvers that avoided it.

She got one hand loose, briefly, and ripped her gun from its holster, remembering as she did the salesman's comments on zero-g and variable-g gunfights. No matter. Recoil would give her a vector she could not control, but she could not wait for something better.

The first shot shattered on impact, the many fragments each sharp enough to slice through a pressure suit. Her arm jerked back; she fought it into position and fired again, again, again. The helmet would be armored, as hers was; he might wear torso armor... but the legs, the arms...

Even in the created view her monitors gave her, where his blood was shown turquoise—the smaller droplets pale, the large blobs dark—it was grotesque. His grip on her other arm first clutched tighter, then loosened—the force of the impacts moved him away from her, and she was pushed back. Now she was no longer centimeters away, but a meter... another meter. Again. Again. She dialed her faceplate's protection down, slowly, letting her eyes adjust, seeing finally in true colors what she had done.

It was still shocking, how red the blood looked, how much blood hung in the passage in patches of red mist, blobs, strings. His suit leaked foam sealant from a hundred holes, too many... arms and legs motionless, imprisoned by the suit's attempt to save his life. The face inside the helmet looked gray now, the eyes wide. But still alive. He blinked. Beyond him was the black maw of the open air lock hatch. The way he was moving, he would rebound from the bulkhead before he floated away. Ky bumped gently into some surface and pushed off in pursuit.

She caught him as he hit the bulkhead; she had a leg locked on either side of the inner air lock hatch. When she pulled the head close, his eyes stared into hers. Osman. Rage greater than before rose in her like a tide of light. His eyes shifted, back to where the mine was positioned. Then he grinned at her, and stuck out his tongue.

"You killed my parents," Ky said conversationally. He could not hear, but he could no doubt figure out what she might be saying. "You killed my brothers, and my uncle, and far too many people I cared about, including the ones I didn't know." She had him braced against the bulkhead now, immobile. "Gerry's little girl," she went on, as her utility knife widened holes the frangible rounds had made. "Gerry's little spoiled bitch, I believe you said. You were going to have fun with me, you thought." And now the knife had opened the front of his suit, along the seam, and she ran it up under the helmet seal, up through his chin, through his tongue, through the roof of his mouth.

And his eyes went blank. And she was covered with a disgusting mess, and the mine was still there. The surge of exultation, this time mixed with righteous rage, did not diminish so much as she pushed it aside. Later. Later to savor that kill, but now—now for her ship.

She eased slowly back toward the mine, brushing the vacuum-frozen flakes of Osman's mortality off her suit, and examined the device. A standard, sturdy, inexpensive shaped-charge limpet, one of the several varieties they'd studied. Her EMP had fried its electronics, no doubt—the status telltales that should have indicated attachment and arming status were blank. If it hadn't been attached, then she could move it—slowly and carefully. If it had, trying to pull it off would trigger the pressure-sensitive override. One standard method of determining attachment involved a short blast of compressed gas, but she had none. Except—she did: the emergency buddy-breather built into all pressure suits to allow partners to share air if necessary.

In this model the auxiliary supply tube had a safety interlock, which took her long seconds to disable, but at last she could direct a stream of air at the base of the mine. It quivered . . . then slowly slid across the deck. Ky let out her breath. Not yet attached. *Not yet attached* usually meant *not yet armed*—to the military anyway. Who knew what Osman had done? She used the tip of a finger and the slight current of air to tip it up, letting her see the critical undersurface. There, the nonelectronic mechanical switch showed orange. Prearmed, not fully armed. Unless Osman had changed the settings . . . but she didn't think so. She could disarm it . . . but just in case, that would be better done somewhere else, with the charge aimed somewhere other than her ship.

Slowly, she nudged it down the escape passage, its deadly undersurface pointed away, past Osman's corpse, now bumping on the overhead. She was about to give it a final push when she realized that would take it toward *Fair Kaleen,* now lit up but still tumbling.

It would kill her or it wouldn't. Ky reached around and flicked the switch to disarm. Nothing happened. The mine was—or should be—inert now. She used the remnant of elastic cord at her waist to secure it to the exterior hatch, facing out, just in case, then pulled the hatch shut, dogged it, put Osman's body in the air lock, closed and dogged the inner hatch, and at last had a moment's leisure to consider what she might have done to her crew—her family—and her ship.

Somewhere along the passage—there—was a dataport connection. She attached a suit connector, keyed the implant, and asked for analysis.

AUTOMATIC SYSTEM RESET 92 SECONDS. OVERRIDE? Had the fight taken that long? She chose OVERRIDE. Weight landed on her shoulders and hips, then wavered, then returned. Pink snow fell to the deck. ARTIFICIAL GRAVITY FUNCTIONAL. Lights and life support should come back first. Gravity was nice, but the others were more important. She felt a vibration in her boot soles. LIFE SUPPORT FUNCTIONAL. THIS COMPARTMENT ZERO PRESSURE. REPRESSURIZE? "Pressurization reserves?" DATA UNAVAILABLE. That wasn't good. If life support was back up, she should have access to the life-support recharge capacity, including air reserves.

She made her way to the forward end of the emergency passage. That compartment division had a window into the passage beyond, with a partial view of the rec space. She doused her light and looked in. Red emergency lights only—and aiming her suit light through the multiple layers of transparent material only gave confusing reflections. A flicker of light, then another flicker. ONBOARD POWER 65%. DEFINE LIGHT PATTERNS. Ky looked at the ship's plan her display threw up. Bridge: light displays, one overhead light, controls. REMAINING POWER RESERVE 14.3 HOURS. So . . . the drive was down as well . . . that was a problem. Rec space: she needed to see something. One overhead light came on, showing two tables, someone slumped over a fallen chair . . . not good, not good. If they were all hurt . . . disabled—she would not think *dead,* though she already had—she needed to get where she could do some good.

"Air up emergency passage," Ky said. The passage filled with vapor; her faceplate fogged, then cleared as its automatic functions dispersed any surface contaminant. "Temperature?" SHIP AMBIENT TEMPERATURE 299 DEGREES STANDARD. Her implant thoughtfully provided a scale with normal shipboard range marked across the scale. Within reasonable limits.

Her suit eased its grip as the pressure rose, as the vapor slowly cleared . . . the pink snow now looked like what it was, smears of blood, rehydrated from the inflowing moister air. Finally—it seemed to take forever but was only minutes—PRESSURE EQUALIZED. COMPARTMENT LOCKDOWN? "Reverse," said Ky. In front of her, the thick compartment seal slid back into its recess; she could now hear the hiss and squeal and imagine as well the power being used.

She left her helmet fastened, her suit light on. The figure in the rec area was Rafe—helmet fastened, eyes closed, but she could see the movement of his breathing. Alive. She would worry about the rest later. Up the passage to the bridge... and as she passed her cabin, she heard the sharp imperative yips of the puppy. She opened the hatch there. Toby, on her bunk, with Stella's arms wrapped around him—both unconscious. The pup, tail wagging vigorously, yapped and scratched at them, trying to wake them up. He growled at Ky, making dashes for her boots, sniffing, backing away, his back hair raised in a miniature ruff.

She probably did smell like death, and not even warmed over. "It's just me," she said to the pup, who continued to wrinkle his lips at her. She backed out, closing the hatch behind her.

On the bridge, Lee was slumped in the pilot's seat, but stirring, groaning slightly. Ky looked at the boards. Drives: red, no response. Defensive suite: standby. Communications: red, no response. Environmental: yellow, emergency power level only. Personnel: red. Nothing picked up from sensors or implants. But she knew they weren't all dead...

Drives had to be the first priority—they needed internal power. She tried automatic restart first, without much hope, and wasn't surprised when nothing happened. Manual restart was a long tedious sequence that led to nothing but the discovery that there was no longer any electrical connection from the bridge engine controls to the drive.

"Power consumption analysis?"

40% ARTIFICIAL GRAVITY GENERATOR.

Of course. How had she forgotten that? "Cut to twenty-five percent, refigure reserve."

28.6 HOURS.

That was something. Not enough, but something.

"Uhhhh... ow!" That was Lee.

"Lee . . . talk to me; it's the captain."

"Don' wanna talk . . . my head . . ."

"Lee!" She went around in front of him and unsealed her own helmet. The stench from her suit almost made her gag. "Lee, what is it? What hit you?"

His eyes opened, the left one bloodshot, his gaze unfocused. "Captain . . . when ya ge' back? Where . . . we . . . are?"

She couldn't see any sign of head trauma but that bloodshot eye. "We're where we were, Lee. Did something hit you?"

"In . . . side. Spike in my head." His gaze wandered past her, then focused again. "Thought you were outside—"

"I was. I'm in, intruders are dead. Ship's got some problems."

"Others?"

"Unconscious, the ones I've seen. Haven't been everywhere yet. The drive's down; I can't get it started. But we have air and some gravity—don't try to get up, I had to cut it to conserve power."

He looked pale and slightly green now, and gulped visibly. His eyes sagged shut. "Feel . . . lousy. What's that stench?"

"Just stay there," Ky said. "I'll be back."

"Said that last time . . . ," he said; then his head lolled and he was out again.

But he was alive. She opened the door to her cabin again, and again Rascal rushed her ankles, bravely but uselessly. Toby was stirring uneasily; Stella didn't move.

"Toby," Ky said. "Toby, wake up."

His eyes opened slowly. "Ky—Captain?"

"Yes. Are you all right?"

"I'm—I'm—alive."

"Which is good. Hurt anywhere?"

"My head . . ."

Stella groaned and started to roll off the bunk; Ky steadied her. Her eyes opened. "This is the worst headache I have ever had . . . Ky. Is it over?"

"Not entirely," Ky said. "The ship has a few problems. Just stay where you are, for now."

Toby blinked several times. "I'm . . . I could get up." Then his gaze locked on to the front of her suit. "Captain—you're hurt—"

"Not my blood," Ky said. She had left smears on Stella's suit, she now realized, and a smudge on the edge of her bunk.

"I really could," Toby went on. "Help, I mean. I have a headache, but it's going away now."

"Let'm go," Stella said in a slurred voice. "I nee' slee . . ." and she, like Lee, went limp again.

"All right," Ky said to Toby. "But leave your helmet on and locked. Ship systems are coming online very slowly, and our power supply's limited."

"But yours—" He stopped himself. "Can I bring Rascal?"

"Sure," Ky said. "Just don't let him bite me. He doesn't like my smell."

But with Toby awake, the dog was more interested in licking her boots than biting her ankles . . . gruesome, Ky thought, suggesting that somewhere in the dog's ancestry was not a boy's best friend, but somebody's worst nightmare. Toby fairly bounced down the passage in low g with the resilience of youth.

"I could fix something to eat," he said, as they came into the rec area. Rafe was still sprawled over the fallen chair.

"We're conserving power," Ky reminded him. "Help me move Rafe." That was easy enough in the fractional gravity; they stretched him on the padded ledge along the far side of the compartment, on his side. His eyelids fluttered but didn't open.

They made their way then to Environmental. In the dim light, suit lights flashed. Mitt, Ted, and Mehar . . . Mitt and Mehar both with pistol bows aimed at Ky, until they recognized her face in their headlamps.

"What happened, Captain?"

"I made some mistakes, but we still have a whole hull and clearly you people have life support working."

"For now," Mitt said. "Did they set off an EMP mine? Is that why we lost power?"

"It was an EMP mine, but I set it off—one of the intruders

was setting up a limpet inside the ship. Only way I could think of to disable its programming before he could set it off."

"Well . . . we also lost a few circuits in life support. I gather the drive's down? And how are the others?"

"Some unconscious, Toby here's fine, I haven't checked everyone yet."

"Must've been quite a fight," Mehar said, nodding at Ky's suit.

"It was . . . strenuous," Ky said. Her back was beginning to tell her how many times she'd tried to tie it in a pretzel. She ignored it.

"How many of them were there?"

"I think three," Ky said. "But let me check everyone else first; we can tell the stories later, when the ship's back up."

"Want help?"

"Yes," Ky said. "Number two cargo and Engineering will be the worst, they were closest to it."

Mehar came with her; they found Engineering dark and silent. She looked around. On the far side of the compartment, a heap of bodies. As she watched, one of them rolled over, shook its head and looked up. Jim.

"What happened, Jim?"

He shook his head, pointed to his ears. Blast damage? Ky came closer, and spoke directly to his face. "Can you hear me at all?"

"A . . . little. Scared the—I didn't know what happened, Captain. Quincy ran over here, said get down, and then everything blew up."

"Not everything. We're still in one piece. The others?" She was already checking them for pulse, for any visible injuries.

"Dunno. I just woke up, kinda—" His voice sounded strange, uninflected. Quincy was underneath the pile. She, Alene, and Cele were all unconscious, but alive. Ky relaxed slightly.

"Let's get Quincy to the medbox," she said. Jim nodded, clambered up, staggered a moment, then steadied.

"Low grav . . ."

"Yes. We're saving power. Mehar, you help me." She didn't trust Jim's balance. In the light gravity, Quincy was easy to lift and carry. They were halfway to the alcove where the medbox was installed when Ky remembered that it wouldn't be functional now.

"On second thought, we'll just put her in her bunk," Ky said. "We've got to get the drives back up." They tucked Quincy into her bunk, and Ky hoped for the best, then checked on Sheryl. The navigator had been in her cubby when the mine went off; she was just rousing and claimed a mighty headache.

Now for the cargo spaces. Ky dreaded what she would find. Number two was as dark as Engineering had been. Again Ky ordered on the overhead lights . . . there was the weapon, chocked up to point at the emergency passage, and a large hole in the bulkhead beyond it. The stench of melted plastics made it through the suit filters. Martin lay sprawled a few feet away, alive but unresponsive.

"Number three wiring nexus," Ky said. "Damn. If we're lucky, that explains why the drives don't come on. Let's get Martin up near the medbox." If she could get the power back on, he and Quincy would have to take turns. She called Jim and Mehar to start working on the damage as soon as they were able.

When she had made the worst cases as comfortable as possible, she went back to the damage site, where Jim was poking at the melted mass of the hold 3 nexus. "Going to be a bitch to fix," he said. "Or we could just cut it all out and start over."

"And how long will that take?"

"On a ship this size, with the shop and equipment we have? Maybe a day. Maybe two."

She didn't have a day or two. None of them had a day or two.

"Can you patch controls onto the drive end of the mess? In a few hours?"

"Uh . . ." She could see the desire to show off warring with his awareness that soft soap and bragging wouldn't work this time. "Maybe. If I had help. I know—sorta know—most of it, but—"

"Toby, do you know how to patch in controls?"

"I know the main functions, but not the auxiliaries, Captain. But is there a reference manual in your implant?"

Was there? She still had not had time to access the special functions. "Get started on the main functions, the two of you. I want the insystem drive up enough to give us onboard power. Then we can worry about the rest. Use anything in stores you need."

In her mind the enemy warships moved ever closer, targeting her with weapons against which her defense might not hold even if it were up. With the crew all accounted for, she headed back upship. Rafe had managed to sit up and blinked as she checked him. "Did we win?" he asked.

"So far," Ky said. "How are you?"

"Headache. My implant tells me it was scrambled, but it's recovering functions."

"Good. Toby and Jim could use your help down in Engineering. Can you make it there?"

"Yeah. I think." He stood, wavered, then headed for the exit without another word. Ky watched him a moment, then went to her cabin.

Stella was up, too, slumped against the bulkhead. "Where's Toby?" she asked.

"Down in Engineering. You?"

"Do you have any idea how bad that smells?" Stella wrinkled her nose.

"Yes," Ky said. "But I can't clean up yet—there's other problems."

"Always other problems," Stella said. She sighed, pushed herself more upright. "So what can I do to help?"

"Feel better," Ky said. "I need some clear thinking from my staff. We have only reserve power—the insystem drive's down. Osman's dead, but his allies with the big guns are out there somewhere and we don't have scan."

"Where are the mercs?"

"I wish I knew," Ky said. "I hope they're coming to help, but I haven't heard from them in . . . a long time." When Stella said nothing, she turned away. "I have to get to the bridge," she said. "It'll be good news if the lights come on full."

"Fiat lux," Stella said. "But we have a hull, and air, right?"

"Right."

"And Osman's dead. So we won."

"A battle. Not the war."

"You're such an encouraging commander," Stella said.

"Thanks," Ky said. "I try."

On the bridge, Lee also was awake. His left eye looked more normal now, and he was working his way across the boards. "Drive's not responding at all," he said. "There's a disconnect somewhere."

"Number three nexus," Ky said. "Slagged. Engineering's working on it."

"Mmm. Can I have some power for scan?"

She had to know where other ships were. If nothing else, a large ship was wobbling around not that far from them. She also needed communications. "Yes. Just let me—" She plugged her suit interface into the dataport and instructed her implant to supply power to the communications and navigation boards. Their status lights went from red to yellow, and finally to green. Lee's screen lit with the current nearscan passive data. *Fair Kaleen* still rolled erratically in the near distance. Three other icons appeared, two whose position and courses were compatible with Osman's allies, and one—her heart lifted—whose icon already carried the Mackensee ID. Only one? But of course—they would not have left the rest of the convoy unprotected.

Ky flicked on the communications board to the prearranged frequency.

"—*Gary Tobai—Gary Tobai,* come in."

"Gary Tobai," Ky said. "Bogies insystem."

"Copy. Not a problem—they're boosting out. Your condition?"

She didn't want to let the enemy know that, not even if they *were* running. "Later," she said. "D'you have an experienced boarding team?"

"A boarding—what's going on?" Then another voice. "Rig secure contact. Give us a visual."

"Can't do that right now," Ky said. "We have a few problems."

"This is Captain Vatta?"

"Yes, this is Ky Vatta. We have disabled *Fair Kaleen* and I intend to claim it, but I do not have personnel experienced in boarding operations."

"You—your crew?"

"All alive. Can this wait until you've seen those raiders out of the system?"

"Oh, we'll see them out..."

A distant hum... and suddenly the lights came full on. The internal com crackled, then produced a loud drone, then went silent. Then Rafe's voice: "Calling the bridge—can you hear me?" He sounded normal.

"Yes," Ky answered.

"Good. Drive's up. We have it patched into the #2 nexus temporarily. All diagnostics show it nominal at this end, so I went on and turned on the lights. Jim and Toby are working on attaching the bridge-end connection."

"How's Quincy? And Martin?"

"Still out... Sheryl's keeping an eye on them."

"Mmm." Nothing she could do about that now, although since they had power again... "Can we draw normal power now?"

"If the connections to whatever aren't messed up. What do you want?"

"The medbox, for Quincy and Martin."

"Can do. Shall I send Alene up to help move her?"

"Yup. We'll be drawing bridge power for a secure comlink."

"Want to use . . . mine?"

"I . . . you'd let me?"

"You know about it already. Security matters. It's secure, and I've got a power source right here. Cuts the message lag."

"Yeah . . ." Ky thought a moment. "Can Jim and Toby handle the rest of that?"

"Yes. Jim's got a knack, and Toby's read and memorized every manual on this ship, I think. The boy's got potential. Between them, they could probably make a functional ship out of drink stirrers and rubber bands."

"Then yes, thank you, and come to the bridge."

"Right away, Captain, ma'am."

CHAPTER TWENTY-TWO

By the time Rafe reached the bridge, Ky had the scans on full power. The defensive suite had come back on its own when the system resets were complete. She now had exact vectors on the two raiders and the Mackensee ship; the raiders' icons showed them boosting, but they would still pass near enough to take a shot at her if they were minded to. *Fair Kaleen,* rolling drunkenly, continued to block them at unpredictable moments, but that was not protection she could count on. At least they were far enough away that they were not in danger of being struck.

"Lee, perhaps you'd go down and show Jim and Toby what controls you need first," Rafe suggested as he came onto the bridge. "If that's all right with you, Captain . . ."

"Yes—unplug your board, Lee, and take it down with you," Ky suggested. "They know wiring, but they don't know piloting."

"I'll need scan access," Lee said. "I can't pilot blind."

"I understand," Ky said. "But just give them some hints—make sure they don't power up the wrong component or something."

Lee shrugged, unplugged his board, and set off down the passage.

"Thanks," Rafe said. "Now—we'll need to set up the visual—"

"You can do visual?"

"Yeah." Rafe pushed back his helmet, unsealed his suit, and

reached inside, wrinkling his nose as he did so. "Bit of a whiff about that suit, Captain, if you don't mind my mentioning."

"I know," Ky said.

"You might want to clean up before the mercs see it."

"I'm sure they've seen worse," Ky said.

He stopped and looked at her. "Are you performing some religious ritual of self-punishment, or is there something else I don't know?"

Her patience snapped. "Like perhaps I have not had one second since I got back aboard without something critical for me to do? You, and the others, were all unconscious and all the ship systems were down."

"Everyone?" His brows went up, and he continued to dig about inside his pressure suit, finally coming up with a length of cord Ky recognized as a connector of some sort. He tucked it into his wristband, then took his helmet all the way off and set it in Lee's seat. He pushed back his hair, peeled back the flap over his implant access, retrieved the cord, and inserted one end of the connector into the implant orifice. "I didn't know that."

"Everyone," Ky said, fascinated.

Rafe glanced at the scans. "They're four light-minutes out; you'd have time to clean up now. I'll call if anything happens."

This time she felt a wave of exasperation. "Why do you care how I look?"

"First impressions are important in anything," he said. "Right now you look like a bloodthirsty, violent killer, not a nice sane tradeship captain of good family."

Ky grinned; she was aware again of those surges of pleasure she'd felt when killing. "I *am* a bloodthirsty, violent killer. I told you that before."

"It's not funny," Rafe said, shaking his head. "I'm serious. Your mercs weren't happy with you staying behind in this system anyway. You need them to see you as sane and sensible, which is what you really are."

It was not the time to make her point, but the words were out of her mouth before she could stop them. "I'm both," she said. "But your point is taken." She turned on her heel and headed for her cabin.

Stella was dabbing at blood marks on the carpet; she looked up when Ky came in. "Situation?"

"Improving," Ky said. "I'm actually going to clean up a bit."

"Thank you," Stella said, with feeling. "I'll go to the galley, then, and start heating some soup or something." Her nose wrinkled, and she was pale.

Ky started to get out of the pressure suit, then decided it would be easier to clean under the shower. A hard vacuum would have been easiest, but that wasn't available without going out past Osman's corpse. The shower sluiced off the worst of the mess on the suit; she cycled it twice, then peeled out of the suit and her shipsuit and ducked through the water. She could still smell Osman's death, but less. The drying cycle—into a clean shipsuit from her cabin—she looked at the pressure suit with distaste. It was damp from the shower on the outside, and sweaty on the inside. She hung it over her shoulder and made it back to the bridge in five minutes.

Rafe glanced at her and murmured, "Your hair."

Ky raked at it with her fingers; he winced dramatically but said nothing more about it. Instead, he pointed to the cables he'd attached to the bulkhead outlet, her deskcom's output, and his implant. "You can use your own com as usual; the video pickup's just the same. I've already entered the initiating codes for the ansible hookup, and the device itself is live right now. I can't move around much; I need to be attached to the power supply."

"Right." Ky sat in her chair, the pressure suit draped across her lap, and glanced at the scan screens. The two raiders were still boosting for jump; the mercenary ship had gained on them. She entered *Gloucester*'s ansible-access number. Instantly—so it worked!—her com screen lit with the INITIATING CALL icon. She glanced at Rafe; he looked blank and said nothing. She guessed he was monitoring the ansible function.

"Gloucester." No visual. They should have her visual.

"This is Captain Vatta of *Gary Tobai.* We have established a secure link now—"

"Captain Vatta." The screen now showed the *Gloucester*'s com officer and Lt. Commander Johannson. "What's your status?"

"We're repairing some damage," Ky said. "Ship's stable at this time, all personnel alive."

"Do you need immediate assistance?"

"Not immediate," Ky said. "*Fair Kaleen* is damaged; I don't know her crew status. Her captain's dead—"

"What happened?"

"He had boarded my ship and was setting a mine," Ky said. "I killed him." Again that surge of joy she must conceal, stronger now as she had time to reflect on it. "Anyway, *Fair Kaleen* appears to be tumbling, and if she's not to be lost, I need a boarding team to go aboard and get her back under control. We don't have any way to get over there. Then a prize crew—"

"Prize crew." He scowled at her.

"She was a Vatta ship. She was stolen. I'm taking possession in the name of Vatta Ltd."

"You do recall the details of our contract, do you not? You agreed not to act on that letter of marque."

She had forgotten that letter again. "I'm not doing this as a privateer; I'm doing this as Vatta. The ship belongs to Vatta; I'm taking her back."

"I see." He did not sound convinced. "Whatever you think, Captain Vatta, this is skirting very close indeed to breach of our agreement. Privateers take prizes. We do not. We will not jeopardize our status as legitimate mercenaries by taking a prize or putting a prize crew aboard. We will, however, board the ship and attempt to stabilize her, and take prisoner anyone on her. If you can then arrange a prize crew out of your own, we will transport them in a pinnace to the other ship.

The only reason I agree to that much is the Vatta ID of the ship's beacon. If a court decides she's stolen property belonging to your family, that's different. I reserve judgment. Is that clear?"

"Quite clear," Ky said. "Thank you."

"Meanwhile," he went on, "it seems important to chase these two all the way to jump, if they were involved."

"They were," Ky said.

"Ah—also part of the conspiracy against the ansibles, you think?"

"Definitely."

"Any objection to our taking them out?"

Ky thought of stating the obvious—the two-to-one odds—but refrained. "None at all," she said.

"We'll be back in a few hours," he said. Then the Mackensee ship vanished from scan, only to reappear in a tangled web of uncertainty brackets—VECTOR UNKNOWN, VELOCITY UNKNOWN—that dissolved to show it in the perfect position to fire up the sterns of the fleeing raiders. One blew almost instantly; the second produced a burst of acceleration that—less than a minute later—ended in another explosion.

Ky caught another whiff of her pressure suit. She would want it when she went aboard *Fair Kaleen,* and she'd prefer it dry and clean. It needed its internal powerpak recharged, as well. She was unlikely to need it immediately, with the raiders gone. She hung it back in its locker, hooked up the cable to the powerpak, and set the self-clean cycles to maximum.

The Mackensee ship stayed in the vicinity of the explosions for more than an hour—looking for survivors, Ky assumed—while her own crew continued to work on rewiring the drive control panels. She spent the time finally exploring her implant's data structure.

It was tempting to explore FAMILY FILES and see what her father had said about her, but she searched the files for more on Osman instead. And there it was: what she could have known ahead of time if she'd not been so reluctant to insert this implant. Her father suspected that Osman had killed his own father, though it could not be proved. Certainly he had lied, embezzled, and made sexual advances and threats to crew. He had inherited his father's shares of Vatta; he was going to be trouble no matter what they did. Her father and uncle, then the company troubleshooters when their father Arnulf was CEO, had been given the task of "taking care" of Osman. For a cash payment, Osman had been persuaded to give up his shares. He had decamped with a ship, and they had not prosecuted, on the grounds that they didn't want him that close ever again. Osman's section ended with her father's recommendation that any Vatta captain coming across Osman take extreme precautions and report anything learned to HQ. Ky scowled. Someone should have blown him away years ago; it would've prevented a lot of trouble. And she would like her father to have known that she was the one who ended that threat to the family.

Ky turned from that to the section headed POLITICAL. Osman might not be their only enemy.

INTERSTELLAR COMMUNICATIONS. Under that heading she found subheads: Contacts, Policies, Negotiations, Potential Conflicts. That looked promising.

Lee came back up the passage with his board, glanced at Rafe and the extra cables in the bridge, and slid into his own seat without commenting or touching any of them. He plugged his board back in. "All right to test functions?" he asked.

"Go ahead," Ky said. Her implant followed along the test patterns, offering her a choice of views. Then, as time passed, she checked on the medbox. Quincy, the medbox reported, was physically stable, but had suffered some blast damage, probably due to her age. Consultation with advanced medical care for long-term therapy was advised. Ky told Alene and the others to take Quincy out and put Martin in the box. She would have liked to check on them both herself, but she had to stay on the bridge.

With the drive now fully functional again, Ky warned her crew and instructed the ship to bring the artificial gravity back up slowly. As she settled deeper into her seat, she felt the aches from her exertion. At least she was sitting down.

Her screen came alive again, a call from the Mackensee ship. "We got both of them; we've picked up several prisoners. Your ISC rep will probably want them taken to ISC offices."

"I'm sure," Ky said, with a glance at Rafe, who still looked blank.

"We'll be back with you in another hour," her liaison said. "Out of communication for maneuvers until then."

"Understood," Ky said. She watched as the Mackensee ship disappeared from scan again, reappearing twice on its way back to her. Slotter Key Spaceforce had a few ships with that capability, but not many. She wondered what it felt like, those rapid transitions in and out of FTL flight, and how they navigated. She turned to Rafe. "Rafe—you might as well take a break."

He nodded without really looking at her, unplugged himself, and shook his head. "Makes my ears feel strange," he said. "That and the smells."

"Monitoring transmissions?" Lee asked.

"Something like that," Rafe said. He rotated his shoulders, stretched, and folded back up neatly, catlike.

Stella appeared at the bridge hatch with mugs of hot soup and a plate of ship biscuits. Ky sipped the thick broth, realizing as she felt alertness return just how much of her reserves she'd used. "I've already fed the others," Stella said. "Toby asked me to defrost one of Aunt Gracie's fruitcakes. He hasn't ever had one." She grinned.

"Some people like them," Ky said.

"Boys that age will eat anything," Stella said. "He's on his third slice."

"Stella carried that thing all the way from Slotter Key," Rafe said. "I asked her why, and she wouldn't tell me."

"I had two of them," Stella said. "The command implant was in one—"

"Is that where it was?" Rafe said, brows rising.

"And I have no idea what's in the other," Stella went on. "If anything. Aunt Gracie's sense of humor at work."

"We need to get the escape passage cleaned up," Ky said. "And the air lock, and Osman's body put somewhere."

"Why not just space it?" Rafe asked.

"There will be formalities," Ky said. "I'll need documentation. Anyway, I don't want to space it right now." She didn't want to move right now. What she wanted, suddenly, was a night's sleep.

"Heat soup, slice cake, clean corridor, move a body," Stella said in an odd tone of voice. "My, what my life has come to. Of course, I am still alive, and don't think I'm not grateful, Ky. I was very, very glad not to have to play the captive princess close up. And glad you foiled Osman's last ploy, however you did that." She paused. Ky thought of giving a blow-by-blow, but decided against it. "But," Stella resumed, when Ky said nothing, "when I thought of life as Vatta's secret agent, it didn't mean domestic chores. Though it has, as often as not, more's the pity."

"I'll get some of the others on it," Ky said. "I could use your advice on some of the things I'm finding in Dad's implant."

"Seriously?" Stella asked.

"Seriously. You've been home—well, in contact with home—the past four years and I haven't. Just a second . . ." Ky called Environmental and, after making sure everything was functioning normally there, told Mitt to take over cleaning up the corridor. "It's nasty—I'd suggest wearing suits. There's a body in the air lock; put it in a sealed bag and into one of the cargo holds. We'll move it over to the other ship if we can."

"Do we have to . . . touch it?"

"The corpse? Yes—why? As far as I know, it's not infected with anything. And you'll have gloves on."

"Well . . ." Mitt sounded less than eager.

"Why don't you let me take care of Osman's mortal coil," Rafe said. "If you happen to have body bags."

She didn't. She'd hoped very much never to have a corpse

on her ship again, but there he was, dead and in the way. "Not standard issue," she said. "Can you improvise?"

"Sure. I'll just go look for something... or we could wait for the mercs to show up. I'm sure they have body bags."

Rafe went out; Ky told Mitt that Rafe would deal with the body, but might need help finding the right container.

"Oh, we've got some supply sacks that might work," Mitt said, sounding more cheerful already.

Ky thought privately that getting the passage clean would be worse than stuffing Osman's corpse into a sack, but she wasn't going to argue that. "Fine," she said.

While the environmental techs worked on cleaning up the passage, she and Stella compared implant headings.

"I don't have ship functions," Stella said. "I told you that before. Mine's optimized for financial analysis and contact information."

"Who do you have at ISC?" Ky asked. "I've got about forty—everything from... uh... Mirellia Coston, executive assistant to the Slotter Key main rep—and her, too, of course—to Lew Parminer. I remember him; he came to Corleigh several times."

"Forty? I have both of those but only a few more. Do you have Rilendo Varise, in Outside Contracts?"

"Yes. I wonder why Dad kept Louise Sims-Delont in this list—she's just a file clerk." Even as she said that, the implant unpacked the reasons and displayed them. Louise Sims-Delont had been too willing to look something up for him five years before, a willingness he interpreted as a possible security leak for the relationship between Vatta Transport, Ltd., and ISC.

What relationship, Ky wondered, and the implant suddenly flooded her awareness with a cascade of numbers, names, dates, reasons.

"What's wrong, Ky?" Stella asked. Ky shook her head; she couldn't answer, not now. Stella reached out, shook her arm. "Ky! Answer me!"

Had Stella known? "Too much information too fast," Ky

said. She took a long breath. "Uh . . . how much do you know about the relationship between Vatta and ISC?"

"Relationship? We depend on ISC's communications, like all shippers. They've used us as general carriers—I don't know what their total tonnage is, but I'd say we have a reasonably healthy fraction of their business, perhaps a dominant share on our main routes. Vatta's always supported the monopoly—we didn't want to risk fragmentation of services and uncontrolled charges. Several other major long-line transport companies have done the same."

"Yes, and some have argued for open communications standards and competition. Pavrati, for instance."

"Oh, Pavrati." Stella wrinkled her nose.

"It's more complicated," Ky said. How much should she tell Stella? How much of their present problems related to the data on her implant, the implant that had been taken from her dying father? "This implant," she said finally. "It's . . . something we need to talk about at length, I think. In private. If we're what's left of Vatta—"

"There's Aunt Gracie, or was when I left home."

"Yes, well . . ." The compressed data under that heading was another problem. Ky had found it hard enough to reconcile her memory of the prickly, prudish Aunt-Gracie-of-the-Fruitcakes with what Stella had told her. The Gracie of the implant was several orders of magnitude less familiar. "You know she was almost tried for murder?"

"Gracie? Our Aunt Gracie?"

"Yes. They finally decided it was postcombat stress and hushed it up when the family put her in the spaghetti farm for a year."

Stella's eyes widened. "They thought about sending me to a clinic; Aunt Gracie said no, she'd take care of it—but if she . . . why did they listen to her?"

"Because she had more dirt on both our fathers than you could imagine," Ky said. The internal memos recorded on this implant had more detail on that than she wanted. She wished Aunt Gracie had been there; she could've argued for her own father's memory. He had always been so upright, so honest, so sensible; she could imagine he might have been a bit wild as a youngster, but not as . . . the word *conniving* slipped in and out of focus. Not her father. Not her father, dead after the attack on the Vattas. Or Stella's, though she'd always wondered if Stella's wildness came from her father rather than her socialite mother. "She was head of Vatta's internal security—you know that, that's the kind of work she had you doing. But she was also working with the Slotter Key government—well, part of it, anyway."

"You don't suppose *she* set it up—was working with Osman or something?"

"No," Ky said, even though the same dire suspicion had flashed through her mind a minute before. The implant made it clear how deep Gracie's dislike of Osman ran. "I'm sure she didn't. But the fact is that all three of us now have to work together, if Vatta's to come back . . . or just survive."

"We have to survive," Stella said. "There's Toby . . ."

"Yes. Well . . ." Was this the time to admit to Stella the real reason she had resisted using the implant? No . . . no more than she could confess her disgusting joy in the act of killing. "We'll need to spend considerable time, as I unlock various cubbies in this thing, figuring out what to do about what's inside." That sounded lame, but she did not want to get into the whole thing now. For one thing, she still felt limp. "And we don't want to involve Rafe—there's a lot of stuff about ISC."

"Oh, I agree," Stella said. "But he'll probably keep trying to worm it out of you. That peeling-a-lime thing—" She sounded annoyed.

Ky laughed. "I'm not susceptible to his type," she said. "Or any type, at present," she added, more soberly. She pushed away the memory of that brief, crazy dance with Rafe. That was postimplant befuddlement, nothing more.

"Dad told me you were involved with a very nice young man at the Academy," Stella said. "It's too bad—but maybe you can get together when this is over—"

"No!" Ky lowered her voice after that emphatic negative. "No. That's over and done with."

"Well... there will be others."

Not until this was over. Not until she understood more of herself. Not until she found a man who would not be horrified at what she really was... and would she want a man who would not be horrified? *She* was horrified.

"Besides," she said, hoping to distract Stella. "He's yours, isn't he?"

Stella flushed but shook her head. "Come on, Ky, he's not a commodity to be possessed. Besides... he wouldn't be mine, in that sense, even if he were."

"You said you were attracted..."

"Yes, attracted. But now, at this moment, we're busy with something else. I'm not controlled by my hormones, you know, whatever my reputation in the family."

"Sorry," Ky said. "I didn't mean it like that."

"Good. He's... interesting, yes. Skilled. But I don't know if he'll ever be... someone to partner with, long term. I was worried that you might fall for him and get hurt, when all he wanted was your trust."

"Never walk in on women discussing men," Rafe said, doing just that. "Stella, Stella... I don't know whether to be flattered by your interest—no one analyzes so minutely someone they care nothing for—or appalled at its erroneous conclusions."

"Stop that," Ky said, as Stella flushed again. "I don't give a flip what your relational strengths and weaknesses are; your timing is atrocious."

"My timing is impeccable, as always," Rafe said, settling against the bulkhead. "I come bringing peace to your soul, Captain: Osman's corpse is safely stowed for the moment, but retrievable when your mercs show up with proper body bags. Stella, did you know your baby cousin was a very thorough killer?"

"I'm sure she would do whatever was necessary in an emergency," Stella said.

"I'm sure that his other wounds would have killed him

without that stab through the throat to the brain," Rafe said. His gaze, deceptively mild, had settled on Ky; she felt the heat rise in her own cheeks. "That's not just a military cut direct, so to speak. That's more, isn't it, Captain?"

"Fatal, I'd say," Ky said, trying for an offhand tone. "After all, I thought he was dead the first time, when their ship security was breached. It seemed a good idea to make sure."

Rafe shrugged. "Whatever you say, Captain."

She was glad to have that conversation interrupted by a call from the Mackensee ship. It was close enough to use conventional communications. "I see what you mean about the *Kaleen* tumbling," her liaison said. "Do you think there are any live crew aboard?"

"I don't know," Ky said. "I haven't tried hailing her since the running lights came back on."

"Better tell me what happened," Johannson said.

Ky explained briefly, starting with Osman Vatta's relationship to the family and continuing through the full sequence that had ended with his death. Johannson's professional expression wavered several times, but he didn't interrupt. She was glad of that; she could imagine his comments on her idiocy in letting those boarders through the lock.

"So . . . you fired an EMP mine inside your own ship to scramble his mine's electronics?" was all he said at the end.

"Yes," Ky said, and clamped her teeth on justifications. She didn't need his approval anyway: it had worked.

"And his lock was disabled by the combination of your EMP mine and his limpet—"

"Yes."

"Interesting." She knew that *interesting* wasn't as mild as it sounded. "We'll be sending a pinnace with a boarding party to . . . uh . . . *Fair Kaleen*. You might want to back off another thousand klicks or so, just in case. Can you?"

"Oh, yes," Ky said. She glanced at her pilot. "Lee, back us out."

"Glad to," he said.

Ky followed that exploration by relay. The Mackensee

boarding party found that the main-entry air lock was too damaged to function, and the entry passage was still open to space. However, inner compartment seals had shut when the ship systems reset. They rigged a temporary air lock and convinced the ship to let them in. Inside, they found sixteen dead—seven in space armor, dead because their suit systems had gone down, the rest not even in pressure suits, victims of decompression. As they worked their way from compartment to compartment, they found a few survivors in those compartments that had been aired up. Some were injured, some not; all were taken prisoner, even the three in a storeroom off the galley, who claimed to be prisoners of the crew.

In the midst, Martin appeared on the bridge. "The medbox says I'm cured," he said. "Sorry I dropped like that, Captain."

"You weren't the only one," Ky said. "I'm glad it didn't scramble your brains permanently."

"Why didn't you just have Lee shut the ship system down?"

"Osman had a limpet mine inside the ship," Ky said. "This was the only way I could think of to knock out its systems."

"Oh." Martin gave her an odd look. "You take the big jumps, don't you, ma'am? And I suppose you killed Osman?"

"Yes," Ky said.

"Very thoroughly," Rafe put in.

"Martin, we're going to be taking over the other ship," Ky said, before Rafe could get started on that. "We need a prize crew—you'll be on that, of course, since that ship may have security issues the rest of us wouldn't recognize."

"Yes, ma'am," Martin said, looking more alert by the moment. "They'll have traps in her and such, same as I set here against boarders."

"Exactly. I can provide your implant with a layout of the ship as she was built and in use originally. We need a boarding plan as well, and if you have recommendations on crew."

"Yes, ma'am. I'll get right on it."

Johannson called Ky again when his personnel were sure they had cleared the ship to explain what he intended to do with those found. "We can sort 'em out later," Johannson said. "I'm not having strangers running around loose on this ship . . . they don't claim to be Vattas, anyway."

The engineers with the boarding party began to stabilize the ship's tumbling once they reached the bridge. Systems had reset correctly; it was simply a matter of giving the correct commands. In a few hours, Johannson informed Ky that the ship was ready to receive a prize crew.

"She's down on reserve air, as you'd expect. Cargo holds are still aired up; our engineers recommend pumping that air into the crew space once you've done something about that air lock. The ship inventory lists useful spares. Here—" A block of data came across; Ky's implant sorted it and displayed it for her.

"If we use your temporary air lock, we should be able to get to Section B-Four and put that replacement in," Ky said. "Are *Kaleen*'s repair bots functional?"

"Some of them appear to be. You want us to run systems checks on them?"

"Yes. No sense risking lives if the bots can do some of the vacuum work."

The Mackensee pinnace transported the survivors from *Fair Kaleen* to *Gloucester* while the repair bots started work on installation of a new air lock. Ky itched to get over there and see what her command implant could pull up from the ship's computers, but she had no way to transfer. Yet. She had to organize a prize crew, anyway. Johannson had made it clear that providing such a crew did not fall within their contractual obligations, and he was not minded to widen them. Minimally—if they did nothing but transport the ship to the next port—the ship would need a commander, pilot, navigator, someone in Environmental, someone in Engineering.

"We need a Vatta commanding both ships," Ky said finally, to Stella and Toby. "Toby, you know more about ships, but Stella's old enough that station managers might accept her, even though she has no papers."

"Captain, why don't you go aboard the *Kaleen*?" Toby

said. "This ship's simpler. If you left Stella here, and a few of the old hands, she wouldn't have any problems with her."

"It's . . . an idea," Ky said. "But think of the trouble I got into by leaving this ship even briefly."

"This is different," Toby said. "That ship—nobody here knows her; she needs more crew and more expertise. You should take her."

"I agree," Stella said. "If you'll let me load some of the ship systems stuff into my implant, I'm sure I'll be able to do what I must."

"I suppose." Already Ky knew this would work. She ran it all as a fast sim in the implant. Yes, it was the best solution. Now to choose who would stay and who would go. She needed Lee and Sheryl with her: they could set up a tape for *Gary Tobai*'s crew to follow. Martin, of course. That meant Alene had to stay on here; she would be responsible for cargo. Environmental, she had to have someone from there, and an engineer. Mitt and Mehar, she decided. Rafe, for his expertise with nonstandard ansibles.

By the time the pinnace came back toward *Gary Tobai,* she and her prize crew were suited up and ready to leave. On scan, the pinnace edged closer and closer.

Then came another call from Johannson. "My people say there's a limpet mine on your outer hatch."

"Oh . . . yes." She had forgotten about that. "That's the one Osman tried to blow up the ship with."

"Facing out . . . is it armed to repel boarders?"

"No," Ky said. "That just seemed a good place to store it."

"To store your enemy's mine . . . any particular reason why you didn't just give it a good shove out the hatch?"

"I didn't want to hit the *Kaleen* with it," Ky said. "Besides . . . a mine is a terrible thing to waste."

CHAPTER TWENTY-THREE

A long silence, during which Johannson turned dull red and appeared to be having trouble breathing. Then a harsh bark of laughter. "Captain Vatta, you—you are indeed—interesting. We'll send the pinnace to ferry you and your prize crew aboard."

Fair Kaleen, up close, looked even more battered than in the external vid pictures. The damage Osman's limpet had done to the air lock, for instance. That was going to be expensive to fix properly—the implant gave estimates. The repair bots had welded a replacement in, roughly, but it was not the kind of work Ky wanted on any ship she owned for the long haul. Once into the crew quarters, she found not the squalor she had expected from an outlaw's ship, but a tidy, workmanlike arrangement, marred only by stains from the recent conflict. The bridge, easily three times as large as *Gary Tobai*'s, resembled that of the ship she had apprenticed on, but with the addition of an extra row of boards.

"Weapons," her merc escort pointed out. "He's taken out part of two cargo holds to mount them. We haven't checked them all out, but I wouldn't hit those red buttons unless you want to kill something. We didn't inventory the munitions, either, but the hold hatches had warning labels on them. We've checked out the bridge for booby traps and have discussed the rest of the ship with your security command." He glanced at Martin, who nodded.

Ky looked at the control boards. Well, she had always wanted to command a warship. This thing could almost be a pocket cruiser, if the holds were full of missiles instead of cargo . . . no question at all that Osman had been a pirate. Which might help when a court adjudicated possession: whatever they thought of privateers, courts always thought poorly of pirates.

"Thank you," she said.

"Captain—environmental's salvageable. The cultures are fine; the higher taxons are badly shaken up, but I think we can boost production in the next few days."

"That's good to hear," Ky said. "Stores?"

"The ship's supplied for a much bigger crew, Captain, and none of the supply lockers I've seen so far was damaged. We won't have any problems for another three standard months at least; there are more lockers, but I'm not yet sure it's safe to get into them."

"Good," Ky said. "So we're good to go, then." Mehar and Toby hadn't said anything, but the drives boards were all green. Quincy, back on *Gary Tobai,* had said things about idiots who went off to strange ships with greenies for Engineering crew, but she was still recovering from her blast injuries, and Ky wasn't about to put additional strain on her. Quincy had finally subsided when Ky pointed out that Stella, as a completely inexperienced captain, needed the best engineer on *Gary Tobai*.

The Mackensee boarders had already tested the communications, ignoring the box they didn't recognize, which Ky knew was the ship-mounted ansible. Now she called up Johannson.

"We're ready to go as soon as your people are back aboard your ship," she said. "We'll be rejoining the convoy after jump, correct?"

"Correct. If your navigator is at the board, I'll transmit the coordinates—"

"Go ahead," Ky said, nodding at Sheryl.

"We're on our way," the merc escort said. "See you somewhere else, and good luck with this thing."

"We'll be fine," Ky said, with more confidence than she actually felt.

* * *

At last they were on the move. On Osman's excellent military-grade scans, *Gary Tobai* boosted for jump ahead of them, crawling along at less than half the acceleration *Fair Kaleen* could offer. Ky was not about to go off and leave her first command, though. Behind them, the Mackensee ship loafed along, keeping watch behind, weapons live. Ky kept *Kaleen*'s locked down. In those hours, Ky's implant explored the ship and her data banks, easily circumventing Osman's security routines: at root, the ship was Vatta, purpose-built for Vatta, and her deepest levels of programming gave anyone with the Vatta command dataset complete access to anything added later. Ky was able to tell Martin exactly where physical traps were located, and how to disarm them.

The cargo holds with the weapons held ample munitions for them, Ky found. In fact, the modifications Osman had made to the ship cut down her cargo capacity to just over half again as much as *Gary Tobai*'s... she would be uneconomical as a pure trader without ripping out all the changes. But as a privateer... she was perfect, except that the universe knew her as a pirate. She needed a new name, a new ship chip, an identity unsullied by Osman's years of criminal activity.

And what was in the other holds would easily pay for that new identity... the cream of a half dozen piracies, at least. Osman had kept all the compact, highly valuable prizes: luxury items such as jewelry, art, bioassays, implants—implants taken from "interesting" prisoners. Some had been downloaded into his own ship's computer, and some awaited that treatment. He had reloaded salable data onto data cubes; a good part of his profit for the past dozen standard years had been from the sale of proprietary information gained from such implants, she found when she looked at his records. Pirate he might be, but he kept financial records like any other businessman. He also had a store of ship-mounted ansibles for sale to potential allies in the war against ISC.

Ky mused on this as Rafe went to work on the shipboard

ansible console. Should she tell him about the others? No harm, probably.

"There's about a dozen of these things in the hold," she said conversationally. Rafe looked at her.

"Like this?"

"Yes. According to his internal records, he used to have more, but sold some. Do you need to know to whom?"

"I suppose I should," Rafe said. "But that cat's well out of the bag by now. I told them two years ago . . . but they wouldn't listen." He turned back to his work. "By the way, do you think Osman was the only reason Vatta was attacked? Was he just working out his grudge while helping his allies?"

"I'm not sure," Ky said. "If they were looking to make an example of a shipping firm to put pressure on the others—which is what some of the other captains at Lastway thought—then Vatta is reasonably conspicuous and has supported ISC's continuing monopoly in the past. Osman could have been a blessing to them, with his inside information and his personal interest in seeing Vatta suffer."

"There are other systems that don't like Slotter Key flags in general," Rafe said. "I don't suppose you know this, but Slotter Key runs privateers."

Her own letter of marque seemed to be burning a hole in her uniform—she was very glad Rafe was looking at the console's internal bits, and not at her. "I had heard something," she said. "I wasn't sure whether to believe it."

"Oh, it's true. Cheaper than enlarging their Spaceforce, I suppose. Privateers support themselves. From our end, we never knew Vatta to be involved in that, but this ship . . . your corporate headquarters disavowed it, but I did sometimes wonder."

"You . . . knew about Osman before I did?" *And you didn't warn me?* she wanted to add but didn't.

"Not for sure," Rafe said. "And if you were making rendezvous with the family privateer, I wanted to know more about it." Now he did look over his shoulder at her. "Don't look at me like that, Captain. It doesn't violate our partnership—check the terms—and I warned you as soon as I knew for certain something was bent."

Small comfort. She tried to think of something to say, but at that moment, Sheryl announced that they were entering countdown for endim transition.

"All stations, secure for FTL," Ky said, instead of any of the lame comments she'd thought of. "Section seals locked." Rafe got off the deck and strapped himself into one of the spare seats on the bridge, while the others acknowledged. Ky's stomach knotted. How would the *Kaleen* handle transition with that crudely repaired air lock? At least, if it blew, only the passage behind it would lose air.

Fair Kaleen slipped through the transition as easily as Ky herself would have walked through a doorway . . . of course, a pirate would keep his ship perfectly tuned. After a brief hour and twelve minutes of FTL flight, during which Ky thought of all the things that might have gone wrong with *Gary Tobai* and then what might go wrong if any of them reentered normal space at the wrong relative vee, the ship dropped out as smoothly as she'd gone in. Ahead of them, *Gary Tobai* appeared as their scan cleared, and behind them the Mackensee ship dropped out still at the same interval.

"Brilliant job, Lee and Sheryl," Ky said. She felt a wave of relief. There on longscan were the other Mackensee ship and the rest of the convoy. No unknown ships in the system. Here, the ansible wasn't working, but Rafe would fix that. She reversed the compartment lockdown.

"Ten hours to rendezvous with convoy," Johannson said.

Ten hours. She could not stay awake another ten hours. Who could?

"Toby, come to the bridge, please." Toby of the inexhaustible energy. On their present course, with no changes to be made, he could surely keep watch while the rest of them recovered.

"Commander, most of my crew's dead on their feet. I'm going to put us down, and leave one on watch."

"Good idea. Call if you need anything."

Toby, with Rascal bouncing at his heels, came onto the bridge. "Yes, Captain?"

"You have the bridge, Toby." No need to ask if he was alert enough; his eyes sparkled with delight. "See, I told you you'd make captain someday."

"Yes, Captain! I'll call right away if anything happens."

"You do that," Ky said, and clambered up, stiff in every muscle and joint. Martin had checked out enough of the crew quarters that they could each have a private cabin, though at the moment she was sure she could sleep on the deck in a pile with twenty others.

The captain's cabin was half again as large as hers on *Gary Tobai*. Osman favored black and gray with red accents; the cabin had an odd smell, which she supposed was essence of Osman. Ky kicked herself for not having thought to have the 'fresher cycle on during those hours on the bridge. She pulled everything off the bed—she was not going to sleep on his sheets. In a locker, she found another set—synthsilk, in black, shiny and slippery. At least they didn't smell like Osman. She threw the other bedclothes in the cleaning bin, turned the cabin ventilation to high, propped the hatch open, and was asleep before she thought to turn out the light.

She woke briefly once, as the light went off, then again when Toby's voice announced that it was time, the time she'd said, but if she wanted to sleep longer everything was fine.

"I'm up," she said. "I'll shower."

In Osman's private bath—which deserved the name, having a tub as well as shower—she found the kind of mess she'd expected from the first, though most of it was due to the tumbling in zero-G. Smears of green and yellow and pink goo streaked the black marble walls and floor. She took one look and dialed the cleaner bots into action. While waiting for them to get the broken glass off the deck, she rummaged again through the lockers in his cabin. Clothes . . . he certainly liked black. And silk. Silk shirts, blousy silk pants. Shore rig: Vatta uniforms, including an old one worn thin.

What must be costumes suitable for different worlds, various colors and styles. Underwear—it was a moment before she realized that the underwear could not all be his . . . it was a collection, male and female styles in various sizes, and all of it . . . she shuddered, and put the entire contents into the recycler. Maybe it would have been evidence, but she didn't want to share space with it, even behind a closed door. In one drawer, she found other evidence of his proclivities: restraints, masks, items she almost understood and didn't want to. She opened only one of the zippered leather cases; the array of tools horrified her, and she left the rest untouched.

She found clean towels, black but smelling of nothing but soap, just as the bots announced the bathroom was safe. Her implant informed her that the black marble wasn't really marble, but a tunable crystal; Ky changed it to frosted white. Now she could feel clean . . . maybe. The shower worked as well as her own back on *Gary Tobai,* and she took extra time to comb her hair in front of Osman's—her—mirror. That, too, was a tunable crystal; she changed the lower two-thirds to frosted white rather than reflective.

One by one her rested crew came back to the bridge or their stations.

"Could we redecorate the cabins?" Sheryl asked her.

"What, the gruesome murals bothered you?" Rafe asked.

"Rafe," Ky said. Then, to Sheryl, "Of course. It's our ship now. Osman's cabin was pretty grim—were the others bad, too?"

"Let's just say that Scovald's famous mural of the invasion of Bettany does nothing for my dream life," Sheryl said. "Not even when the previous occupant has added his own commentary and sketches to the original. And it smelled like that kind of person had been living in it."

"Not nice people at all," Rafe said. "I found what I thought was a simple one, plain walls with just a few pinups easy to ignore, but the instant I lay down on the bunk, the sound system came on. It left me in no doubt that whoever had that cabin was someone I do not want to know except over a weapon." At Ky's look he nodded. "Gone now. Flushed it. I figure you have enough on these people without that recording, and it was the only way to get it to shut up without dismantling the bunk. Which I was too tired to do."

"I put some things in the recycler myself," Ky said. "And I'm tempted to flush the bedding, too."

"Oh yes," Lee said. "In fact, I did. I'm not sure any cleaning cycle would take care of what was on those sheets."

"Well, on our next long cycle with nothing much to do, we'll get all that cleaned away. There's plenty of crew space; we won't be bored next transit."

"I suppose disgust is better than boredom," Sheryl said. "And it's better than excitement, too," she added. "I'll get on it; there's nothing for me to do before rendezvous. Unless you're hungry and want a meal."

Hands went up.

"I just hope I don't find Selenki worms or something in the galley," Sheryl said as she left the bridge.

Within the hour, she reappeared with trays; the smell of fresh-baked bread preceded her. "The galley's fine," she said. "And the supplies are . . . what I suppose pirates can afford. Prepacked from Escalion Catering, their gold-standard rations. I had to bake the bread, that was all. This is like that stuff the luxury liner had, remember?"

It seemed a lifetime ago that there'd been a fuss over goldeye raspberries. "Yes," Ky said, around a mouthful of warm fresh bread spread with something sweet and crunchy.

"I suppose we should share this with the others," Lee said, smearing his bread with a different spread, this one a rich purple.

"Already done," Sheryl said. "I called 'em. That silence you hear is people eating rather than talking." She started on her own meal, and silence covered the bridge, too, for a few minutes.

"Better than Aunt Gracie's fruitcake," Ky said, when she came up for air. She had not realized how hungry she was. "We can save it for another emergency."

"Which I hope doesn't come too soon," Lee said, stretching. "Ah . . . that's good."

As soon as they were close enough, *Gloucester* sent a pod to pick up Rafe so he could work on the system ansible. While he was gone, Johannson called Ky.

"We have another problem," he said. "It's your ISC agent, so called."

"Rafe? What now?"

"We've been running analyses of events since we left Lastway. It looks to us that Mister Whoever-he-really-is has to be the one who set up that trap. We're going to bring him back here when he's done with this ansible, and have a look at his implant."

"You can't think that," Ky said. "He's been fixing ansibles—he led us to the ISC conspirators at Lastway."

"It's not unknown for conspirators to sacrifice some of their people for long-term gain," Johannson said. "To gain your confidence, to gain ours—"

"And then he helped us survive the attack," Ky said.

"You say . . . I'm not sure you're competent to judge that, Captain Vatta. How else could Osman have known which system we'd be in? Nobody at Lastway knew that. How else could he have contacted his allies so easily? I believe Rafe is—or was—associated with ISC in some sensitive position, but the evidence is clear that he's using some kind of clandestine communications device."

"You can't just invade his implant," Ky said, all too aware that they could do just that. "He's my crew; he's under my protection."

"I'm afraid we must disagree on that, Captain Vatta. Your safety, and the safety of others in the convoy, is our primary mission. We believe he compromises that safety. I appreciate your sense of honor where your crew are concerned, but we can't risk it. We don't intend to harm him; we'll just check out his implant—"

Rafe would suicide first. Ky knew that, even though he'd never said it in so many words. He was not about to let anyone get access to his implant, or to that implant-mounted ansible. Yet she knew that telling Johannson that Rafe would suicide might convince him all the more that Rafe was one of the villains. After all, would an honest man commit suicide just to conceal the fact that he was honest?

"Rafe has told me things about his background," Ky said, trying to think what argument might work. "There is . . . sensitive material, things that I agree should not be widely known."

"We aren't planning to publish it, Captain Vatta. Just find out if he's part of the conspiracy. If you wish, I can promise to wipe the record, provided he's innocent."

What would he consider innocence? A bad boy, a remittance man, a rogue company spy masquerading as a petty criminal—a smuggler, a gambler, whatever else Rafe had used for cover? Hardly.

"Do you think I'm part of the conspiracy, Commander?"

"You?" That had clearly stopped his train of thought. "No, of course not. Young, inexperienced, foolhardy perhaps . . . but not a conspirator."

"Fine. Then perhaps you will let me examine Rafe's implant, rather than your people." If Rafe would let her.

Johannson looked flustered. "Captain Vatta . . . I don't mean to belittle your integrity, but . . . you're a young woman, and this Rafe is a good-looking man."

"Oh, for goodness' sake!" Ky said, falling back on one of Aunt Gracie's expressions. "I am not a silly teenager, Commander. Yes, Rafe is handsome. So is my pilot. So is one of my junior engineering techs. I'm not romantically involved with any of them."

"You have no . . . attraction to him at all?"

"Of course not," Ky said. "He's too old for me, and anyway he's not my type."

"Well . . . I'll talk to the captain."

Minutes went by. Lee glanced at her. "Handsome, am I?"

"You know you are," Ky said. "In a rugged, sturdy kind of way."

Lee grinned. "And which adventure vid are you quoting from?"

"None that I remember," Ky said. "Though I watched plenty of them in my school days. But I'm sorry, Lee, you just don't do anything for me otherwise."

"Nor expected to," Lee said. "I'm even older than Rafe." He sobered. "You know, though, some of us did worry. Stella was certainly smitten."

"I am not Stella," Ky said. "And Stella's over it, she told me."

"Maybe," Lee said. "But he is a charmer, when he's not being an arrogant, sarcastic—"

"He likes to tease," Ky said. "Get a rise out of people, if he can."

"You're defending him?"

"Against what Mackensee suspects, yes. You were there; you know how he was in the crisis. If he'd wanted us to lose to Osman, he could have done us a lot of damage."

"Captain Vatta—" Johannson was back onscreen. "Are you willing to come aboard the *Gloucester* when we bring your man in for questioning?"

"Absolutely," Ky said.

"No promises, but the captain's willing to hear your argument."

"Thank you," Ky said. "You'll send a pod?"

"For you, we send the pinnace," Johannson said, smiling. It seemed to have no edge to it, but Ky wondered.

Rafe was under guard in sick bay, strapped into a recliner, when Ky, Johannson, and Captain Pensig came in. He looked pale and stubborn.

"Your captain argues for you," Pensig said. "I'm not persuaded that a young female, even one with her background and experience, isn't liable to influence from someone like you." Someone like a mess to be scraped off one's shoe, said his tone.

"I have no romantic interest in her," Rafe said, not meeting

Ky's eyes. "She's too young, too naïve, and entirely too priggish. And—no insult intended—she does not meet my standards of beauty."

"You were aware of his opinion, Captain?" Pensig asked Ky.

Ky shrugged. "I told you already. Rafe's not my type; I'm not his type. I respect his ability, which is considerable, and I'm convinced he's been honest with me and true to our partnership agreement. But romance? No."

"Our information from the Sabine incident suggests that you are susceptible to young men."

Ky flushed. "He's not a *young man* to me, Captain Pensig. And I would respectfully suggest that your report from Sabine was in error. The idiot that caused such trouble there was a new addition to my ship, a refugee of sorts."

"He was in your cabin—"

Ky realized that this was being played out for Rafe's benefit, as well, and that only increased her irritation. "He ran into my cabin without my knowledge," she said. "Against my orders to stay in the rec area with the others. He'd never been in it before." She let more of her anger show. "Whatever you think, Captain Pensig, I am not a hormonally dominated brainless twit who falls for every pretty face that comes along."

"I didn't suppose that," he said. "But before I trust my ships and my responsibility to your interpretation of this man's implant data, I want to be sure you will report it without bias."

"If he is in fact collaborating with the people who killed my parents and my brothers and the rest of my family," Ky said, "I will be glad to tell you."

"Very well. Rafe Whoever-you-are, will you consent to having Captain Vatta connect implant to implant to determine if you are the traitor I suspect?"

"Yes," Rafe said through set teeth. "On condition that she swear in front of you all not to reveal anything she finds in there that is not relevant to that one point."

Captain Pensig glowered, but finally muttered. "All right with me."

"I swear," Ky said. She sat on the matching recliner and lay back.

One of the military medical techs pulled out a cable with identical plugs on both ends. "This won't hurt," said one of them, lifting her scalp flap and plugging the cable in. At first she felt nothing but a weird hum on that side of her head. Then the other technician made the connection with Rafe's implant.

The sensory analogs of connection flooded her: smells, tastes, textures here and there on her body. Then she had control, a sense of some kind of pipeline . . . and she was in Rafe's implant, faced with the hierarchal structure in his organization of his implant's data. She could ask him for keys, but keys he gave her could be contaminated. She searched on keywords, values, and finally reached the area containing ISC-related information. Some subgroups were secured even against direct connection. Ky pushed harder.

At her touch, Rafe opened secured subgroups; Ky raced through them trying not to remember anything she saw that wasn't relevant. She needed message logs, to prove he hadn't been in secret contact with Osman and others. There . . . she reached into that area of the implant . . .

And time–space exploded around her. In her implant, the self-repairing modules scrambled to rearrange data, make new connections, build what was required.

Ky stiffened. Was it a brainworm? Was Rafe taking her over? Her vision clouded, and suddenly a strong, unpleasant stench seemed to rush up her nose and make her sneeze.

No . . . desecrations! Don't do that! That was Rafe, but not the Rafe in the recliner. This Rafe was in her head, in the implant. Direct contact through the cable?

No. Function transfer. Don't tell.

Don't tell what? She managed not to say that aloud, opened her eyes (when had she shut them?), and said the first thing that occurred to her. "He has some fairly disgusting porn tucked away in there."

"Oh . . . not unexpected," said Pensig. "What about ISC?"

Ky took a deep breath. "Well, he is one of their agents. No, he's not a traitor. I got into his message logs for all forms of communication; he drafted everything in his implant. There's no record at all of any communication with Osman, or to anyone we didn't already know about, between my meeting him on Lastway and our meeting with Osman. He's innocent—of that, anyway."

"You're quite sure?"

"Yes. What we think is that Osman and his allies have shipboard ansibles—"

"You think that's more than a rumor?"

"I'm sure of it," Ky said. "Now if you can have him returned to my ship, there's something I'd like to discuss in private..."

"You still don't trust him, then?"

"This is something that doesn't concern him. Something between us—Vatta and Mackensee."

"I can take a walk," Rafe said, "If someone will release me."

When he was released, Rafe asked directions to the bathroom, and left Ky alone with Pensig and Johannson.

"Rafe does not know about the letter of marque," Ky said. "And I don't intend to tell him anytime soon."

"Ah," Pensig said. "The letter of marque... you're right, we do need to discuss that. This matter of the prize—or return of stolen property. You'll take it to court, of course."

"If I do," Ky said. "it will be seized and sold for payment of debts—defaults on delivery and the like. Vatta needs that ship."

"You're planning to seize it without due process?"

"Not exactly," Ky said. "I'm just planning to keep it out of the hands of the breakers."

Pensig looked at her a long time before speaking, his lips folded tightly. "I'm trying to be fair," he said finally. "You are young; you have been through a very difficult time. Nonetheless, I have stretched our regulations to their elastic limit and beyond. If you do not submit that ship and its title to proper adjudication, I will have to consider your acquiring it as an act of privateering, which with possession of a letter of marque clearly makes you a privateer. Someone we cannot have a contract with. I can take the rest of the convoy to the next system with a market, but my contract with you is null and void at this point."

"You mean we can't come along?"

"Oh, I suppose...I'm in enough trouble already...but we're not bound to protect you."

"Sorry," Ky said.

"Oh, and you might want to change your ship's name, so we don't just blow you away on spec someday."

Ky smiled and said, "So, you will transport us back to my ship, right?"

"As soon as possible," Pensig said. "Immediately, in fact."

Back on *Fair Kaleen,* Ky took Rafe to her cabin, past the appraising eyes of her bridge crew. "We have to talk," she said. "What *was* that?"

"That, dear Captain, was my cranial ansible."

"So how did it produce that bad smell in my nose?"

"A theoretical problem with the tech," Rafe said. "The reason there was only ever one. With an implant-to-implant link, if the implant is advanced enough, the possibility existed that the ansible would replicate itself in the linked implant. We now know that's possible."

"You mean I—"

"Now have one, too. Yes." He sighed. "I should have just blown my head off. I didn't think the theory would hold in real life."

"I wish you'd warned me," Ky said.

"Thank you for not telling them," Rafe said, not responding to her comment. "And by the way, I don't really think you're ugly, immature, and priggish. Nor do I think you have absolutely no feelings for me."

"Trying it on, Rafe?"

He moved closer. "I think you're a very accomplished liar, Captain Vatta."

Her heart beat faster, but she kept her voice cool. "That's for me to know and you to find out, Rafe."

"And I intend to," Rafe said, closing the distance.

Without thinking, Ky hooked a foot behind his leg, blocked his intended embrace, and shoved; he hit the floor hard and looked up at her, eyes wide, shocked out of his usual pose of amused superiority.

"Not like that, you won't," Ky said.

Read on for an excerpt
from the next novel
in Elizabeth Moon's thrilling
Vatta's War series

ENGAGING THE ENEMY

Available from Del Rey Books in April 2006

In the afternoon sky, the sound of the approaching aircraft rose above the sea breeze, a steady drone. Nothing to see . . . no, there it was, too small to make that much noise . . . and then the sudden flood of data from the implant: not an aircraft, no one aboard, a weapon homing on the airfield's navigational beacon. Visual data blanked, overloaded by heat and light, auditory data an inchoate mass of noise, swiftly parsed into channels again, stored, analyzed: primary explosion, structural damage, secondary explosion, quick flicker of building plans, primary visual restored . . .

Ky Vatta jerked awake, heart pounding, breath coming in great gasps. She wasn't there, she was here, in the captain's cabin of *Fair Kaleen,* darkness pricked with the steady green telltales of major ship functions. All she could hear beyond her own pulse beating in her ears were the normal sounds of a ship in FTL flight. No explosions. No fires. No crashing bricks or shattering glass. No reverberative boom echoing off the hills minutes later.

"Bedlight," she said to the room, and a soft glow rose behind her, illuminating tangled sheets and her shaking hands. She glared at her hands, willing them to stop. A deep breath. Another.

The chronometer informed her that it was mid-third shift. She had been asleep two hours and fourteen minutes this time. She went into the bathroom and looked into the mirror. She looked every bit as bad as she felt. A shower might help. She had showered already; she had taken shower after shower, just as she had worked out hour after hour in the ship's gym, hoping to exhaust or relax herself into a full night's sleep.

She was the captain. She had to get over this.

This time she dialled the shower cold, and then, chilled, dressed quickly and headed out into the ship. She could always call it a mid-shift inspection. Her eyes burned. Her stomach cramped, and she headed first for the galley. Maybe hot soup . . .

In the galley, Rafe was ripping open one of the ration packs. "Our dutiful captain," he said, without looking up. "Mid-shift rounds again? Don't you trust us?" His light ironic tone carried an acidic bite.

She did not need this. "It's not that I don't trust the crew. I'm still not sure of this ship."

"Ah. As I'm sure you recall, I'm on third-shift duty right now, and this is my mid-shift meal. Do you want something?"

She wanted sleep. Real sleep, uninterrupted by dreams or visions or whatever . . . "The first snack you pick up," she said.

He reached into the cabinet without looking and pulled something out. "Traditional Waskie Custard," he said, reading the label. "The picture is an odd shade of yellow—sure that's what you want?"

"I'll try it," Ky said. He had put his own meal in the microwave, now he handed her a small sealed container and a spoon. She looked at the garish label; it did look . . . unappetizing. Inside the seal was what looked like a plain egg custard. Ky dug the spoon into it. It should be soothing.

"Excuse my mentioning it to the captain," Rafe said, sitting across from her at the table. "But you look like someone slugged you in both eyes about ten minutes ago. I promise to perform all my duties impeccably if you'll go back to bed and look human in the morning."

Ky started to say something about duty, but she couldn't get the words out. "I can't sleep," she said instead.

"Ah. Reliving the fight? It must've been bad—"

That attempt at pop psych therapy almost made her laugh. Almost. "No," she said. "I had my post-manslaughter nightmare the second night. This is something else."

"You could tell me," he said, his voice softening to a purr. When she didn't respond, he sat up and said "With the matter of the internal ansibles, you have enough on me that I wouldn't dare reveal any secrets of yours."

"It's not . . . it's . . . I'm not sure what it is." Ky tented her hands above the custard, which was not as soothing as she'd hoped. Something in the texture almost sickened her. "I think . . . somehow . . . I'm seeing what happened back home."

"What . . . the attack?"

"Yes. I know it's impossible; I don't even know if Dad's implant recorded any of it, and I haven't tried to access those dates anyway. But I keep dreaming it, or . . . or something."

"A high-level implant could record it all," Rafe said. "If your father wanted a record, something for a court. Are you sure it's not bleeding over? I mean, if he put an urgent-to-transmit command on it—"

"It couldn't override my priorities, could it? Everything's user-defined. . . ."

"True, but this implant's had two users. It may not know you aren't your father."

"That's . . ." Ridiculous, she had been going to say, but maybe it wasn't. She'd had the implant inserted in an emergency; she hadn't had time then for proper conditioning, for adjustment of implant and brain. She'd gone directly into combat, essentially, and she hadn't had time since then to investigate all the functions and capacity of the implant. Then the direct connection to Rafe's implant had made changes in hers, changes that essentially reconfigured it into some kind of cranial ansible. That might have damaged or changed control functions. And she'd never had someone else's implant before. Why, she wondered now, hadn't Aunt Grace downloaded the data into a new one? Unless it couldn't be done. "I hadn't thought of that," she said instead. "What do you know about transferred implants?"

"Not much," Rafe said. "I know it's possible to use one; I don't know how much residual control might be involved. That one was your father's command implant, right? I'd expect it to have special features."

"It probably does," Ky said. "It certainly does now, after linking with yours." She looked at the cup of custard and pushed it away. "I suppose I'd better look into that."

"If you don't want to go insane from lack of sleep and nightmares, that would be a yes," Rafe said, pulling his own meal pack from the microwave. "Real food wouldn't hurt either. How about some noodles and chicken? I can make myself another."

It smelled good. Ky nodded; Rafe pushed the tray across to her, picked up her container of uneaten custard and sniffed at it, then wrinkled his nose and dropped it in the recycler. He pulled out another meal pack and put that in the microwave before sitting down again. Ky took a bite of noodle and sauce; it went down easily.

"See if the implant has a sleep cycle enabler," Rafe said. "They don't put those in kids' implants, but the high-end adult ones often have them, along with a timer. It should be in the personal adjustment menu somewhere."

Ky queried her implant and found it: sleep enhancement mode, maximum duration eight hours, monitored and "regulated" brain-wave activity and damped sensory input. Users were instructed not to use this function more than five sleep cycles in a row without medical advice . . .

An Urgent tag came up: "Authorized user request: review sealed files." The dates fit, in Slotter Key's calendar. Ky scrolled mentally to check the priorities of sleep enhancement vs. Urgent Message, dropped the priority of the message to allow sleep enhancement to override the other, and set a condition for waking. Then she finished her noodles and chicken.

"I'm going back to bed," she said. "Tell first shift I may be late."

Initiating sleep enhancement mode was like walking off a cliff into oblivion. She woke feeling rested for the first time since before she'd put the implant in . . . languid, comfortable. After a shower and a change, she went up to the bridge.

"Good rest, Captain?" Lee asked.

"Very good," Ky said. "But I'm going to need to spend a lot of time today exploring data stored in this implant. I suspect it's going to be very intense. So if there's anything you know you need for this shift, tell me now."

"We're doing fine," Lee said. "All systems green—this is a lovely ship, despite the way she's been used. Whatever else Osman was up to, he maintained the ship systems perfectly."

"Call if you need me," Ky said. "I'll be in my cabin."

She puttered around briefly, stripping the bed and sending the linens through the 'fresher cycle, reluctant to face what was coming. When she realized that, she sat down at her desk, and activated the secured files.

In the afternoon sky, the sound of the approaching aircraft rose above the sea breeze, a steady drone . . . but this time she was awake, and viewed the audiovisual data as an outsider, not a participant. Her father's emotions did not flood her awareness; she recognized the silhouettes of the two crafts before the implant matched them.

Still, the violence of the explosions was shocking. Her breath came fast. Deliberately, Ky slowed the replay, returning again and again to the same image: were they aircrafts with missiles or bombs, or were they the weapons? That hardware could be either. They had come in low and fast; the implant did not record—her father had not thought to look for the telltale evidence that might tell her which they were.

Ky put a tagger on the best of the early images, and told the implant to find any similar images after the explosions, but apparently her father had not looked for the aircraft again, nor had he tapped into the airfield's scan data after that first moment.

Back to the beginning. The implant didn't tell her what her father was thinking that afternoon, but it held his planned itinerary—a flight from Corleigh back to the mainland—and his planned schedule—a meeting with senior management at Vatta Headquarters—the agenda including the quarterly financial reports—dinner with his brother and his brother's wife, and the next two days a series of meetings with the Slotter Key Tik Growers' Association, the Slotter Key Agricultural Commission, and the Slotter Key Shipping Advisory Commission. An address to the graduating class of Nandinia School of Business (the text of which was stored in the implant; Ky ignored that for the moment). He normally spent at least six days out of ten on the mainland; her mother preferred Corleigh's gentler climate except during the main social season.

His flight plan had been properly filed well in advance; anyone could have known when he would be at the little private airfield, and yet no explosion occurred there.

She had started a commentary file; she noted that oddity and went back to the visual record itself.

The local offices exploded; debris rained from the sky. Another explosion; the visual output darkened. Along the margins, a row of red numbers appeared, giving her father's vital signs. She tried to steady her breathing—was this when he died?

No. The visual record returned, as someone pulled debris off him. She recognized the faces: old George, their pilot Gaspard, someone she had seen around the office . . . Marin Sanlin, the implant told her. Her father looked toward the house, now a tower of flame and smoke . . .

Even seeing it, she could not quite believe it. Surely the comfortable sprawling house with its tall windows to catch the sea breeze, its cool tile floors, had not really gone so fast, so completely. Some walls still stood, as fire raged inside, still consuming everything from her past: the long, polished dining room table, the library with its shelves of data cubes and old books, the paintings, the family rooms . . . the pool, its surface crusted with debris, shards of wood and ash, and then the horror on her mother's face . . .

Ky terminated the playback, squeezed her eyes shut, and opened them again to the bland blank screen of the desk display. Her mother. Beautiful, intelligent, graceful, infuriating to a daughter who had never felt as beautiful, as intelligent, as graceful. . . . she had been annoyed so often, rebellious so often, resistant so often to her mother's advice, and now . . . now she could never hope to say how much she admired and loved the woman who had given her life.

Ky pushed away from the desk. She'd had as much as she could take for the moment. It was real; it had really happened; her mother was really dead . . . no mistaking that . . . and she would have to find a way to cope, but not right this moment.

She headed for the ship's gym. Osman had not run a slack ship, and the *Fair Kaleen* had a superb facility for keeping a crew of pirates battle-ready, from the usual run of exercise machines to an onboard firing range. She would work off some of this and counter the effect of all those premium grade rations at the same time.

Gordon Martin was there before her. She paused a moment, watching him do a gymnastics sequence, rolls and flips. He came upright facing the hatch and nodded to her. "Morning, Captain."

"Do you feel like sparring with me?" Ky asked.

His brows raised. "Of course, Captain, but . . . you seem upset."

She didn't want to explain; she just wanted to hit something. Somebody. "Exercise will help," she said.

"You need to stretch first," he said. Ky nodded, and went through preliminary stretches as fast as she thought she could get away with. Then they squared off on the gymnastics mats. Ky forced herself to start slowly, with the basics; Gordon matched her. They had trained in the same system and they had sparred enough before to have a feel for each other's styles. She was sweaty and sore when they quit, but she felt somewhat better for it.